Lily went cold turkey. There was no shirking the pain, loss and fear. She was paralysed with her tragedy. Her life had been derailed. She had never dreamed of a future alone. Now she could think of nothing else. How would she function? How would she live? Could she afford to stay in the house? Would she be safe? Would there ever be anyone else? Who would she go on holiday with? Was there a future? Would she ever get dressed again?

May Roper has worked in publishing for many years.
She lives in London.

Cutting the Rocks

May Roper

ORION

An Orion paperback
First published in Great Britain by Orion in 1998
This paperback edition published in 1999 by Orion Books Ltd,
Orion House, 5 Upper St Martin's Lane, London WC2H 9EA

A CIP catalogue record for this book is available
from the British Library.

ISBN 0 75282 676 X

Typeset at The Spartan Press Ltd,
Lymington, Hants
Printed and bound in Great Britain by
The Guernsey Press Co. Ltd., Guernsey, Channel Islands

To Arthur and Else

Acknowledgements

Many individuals contributed to this novel. I thank them all.

Some deserve special mention. I'm grateful to Gillon Aitken and Rosie Cheetham for their professionalism and belief. Rosemary Russell's assistance was fundamental. Alison Burns and Sian Miles offered infinite support and wisdom. Biffo insisted on warmth and companionship. Lee Hemphill was and is a superlative pal and partner.

RIP Buster.

Chapter 1

If she had known it was their last fuck, she'd have – well, what exactly?

1) Baked a cake?
2) Waxed her legs?
3) Wept?

This is not a trick question. If Lily had known it was the end, she would have behaved just as she did when she eventually found out – take to her bed, lose six pounds and despair of the future.

But she did not know.

It was Sunday morning. It was spring. Frank had woken with his morning erection. They had not made love for at least six weeks. They were sleeping in the same bed for once. While still asleep, his hand strayed to her right breast. And all of a sudden there they were again, travelling down the same old road.

It was like an old, familiar dance routine. It *was* an old, familiar dance routine. Ninety seconds on the right breast, fifty seconds on the left breast, fingers first, lips and tongue second. She stroked his chest, he stroked her stomach. He opened her labia, she rubbed his stiffie. He moved on top, she widened her legs. Once he was inside, there was nothing else for her to do. She wasn't going to come. He was. It was only a question of patience. Soon he would make that unpleasant throaty cry and stop thrusting, to slump on her chest and pass into unconsciousness for a couple of minutes. Then the cooling, the disengaging, the snail trail on her side of the sheets, and the silence.

So why did she submit to it? So that she could tick off

another fuck in her diary, of course. As long as they kept making love, it was still a proper relationship, wasn't it? If there was still sex, then they had not descended into the platonic, brotherly/sisterly companionability that was beckoning from the sidelines. Lily could still tell herself that they had a future, that she and Frank would find a way through.

That was the last time. Sunday, 14 April. Her diary gave her an absolute record of the three last acts of intimacy they had shared that year, not to mention the eight in the preceding one. But it was only today, Sunday 30 June, that Lily, alone, in bed, swollen-eyed with tears, could comprehend. Because Frank had gone. After ten years of shared lives, home, cats and (decreasingly) bodily fluids, it was all over.

She had had to go away for the weekend. It was work – a fancy-goods convention in Glasgow. She had flown up on the Friday evening, and while sipping a gin and tonic at 20,000 feet, felt not especially confident of her future with Frank, but not expecting anything sudden either.

The previous weekend they had gone for a walk in Surrey – didn't they always? – and tried to talk their way out of the increasingly narrow funnel that their relationship had become.

'What if we had a baby?' Lily asked.

'What?'

'A baby. Would that be a good idea?'

Neither of them wanted children. Never had. Frank loathed his parents and his own childhood. He had no desire to inflict his depression on an offspring. And Lily had never come across a maternal note in her make-up. Yet all of a sudden, it didn't seem such a bad idea. Baby, sharing, cement to the relationship. Why not? She could even convince herself that she might enjoy it. She crashed through some waist-high bracken, lost in a fantasy of a cuddly, kitten-type bundle with a longer life-expectancy.

'Get real.' Frank was gruff, then softened and reached for her hand. 'No, Lily, that's not the answer. God knows what is.'

Not God, Lily thought. Surely Frank himself knew. Couldn't he think of a mechanism that would reignite his desire for her? That was all they needed, a proper love life. If they had that, then Frank wouldn't sleep with other women, he wouldn't keep badgering her for an 'open' relationship. There was no other reason to separate. He had told her how much he wanted to stay living together, how he wanted to hold on to everything else.

Lily couldn't understand why it was so difficult. After all, she didn't much desire Frank but it didn't stop her receiving his penis on the rare occasions he pushed it at her. Why did it matter so much? Their sexual voltage had never been incandescent. Admittedly, at the beginning they had fucked often and reasonably inventively. They had touched too, even kissed. But over the years it had all withered away. She had discovered, memorably, two years earlier that he had been serially promiscuous throughout their relationship. That was when the conversations about 'the future' had begun. A depressing cycle of 'trying' – which meant forcing themselves to have sex – and talking through a limited range of other options. This conversation was just the latest in a very long line.

'What about make or break?'

Frank's question startled Lily. But as she absorbed it, she quite liked it. After all, he would never leave her. She had never felt the need to take that threat seriously. Despite everything, she knew she made him happy. What was more, they had fallen in love with Italy together, and art deco junk. She had changed his sartorial style and educated his palate. He would never throw all that away just for better sex.

'What do you mean, exactly?' she asked.

'Well, I'm thinking aloud here, but say we tried, just for a fortnight, to find a way. Focused on nothing else. Really gave it our best shot.'

It sounded quite convincing. She had agreed. And for the entire previous week they had really put their backs into it. Best behaviour at all times. She had not watched soap operas immediately on returning from work, but had forced herself to talk to Frank, to go down to the corner shop and sit with him in the kitchen afterwards while he cooked his chops or pasta. He had resisted the urge to sleep in the spare bedroom and had stayed with her, in the big bed. He had come home straight from work every evening. They had been a perfect couple. She regretted having to go to Scotland for the weekend, but the fair was unmissable, and things seemed to be going just fine.

She was booked into surely the most unpleasant hotel Glasgow had to offer. One arm of its curious L-shape formed a wall of the main railway station and Lily's room looked out on to an artificially lit concourse seething with people and humming with travellers' babble and train announcements. In her narrow, grubby room, a strange metallic device attached to the wall was presented as a hotplate and she had visions of impoverished secretaries warming the contents of individual-portion baked bean tins in battered saucepans while darning their underwear. She rang reception and insisted on being moved to the best room in the hotel. A terse debate ensued, centred around a reminder to Lily that there was a jewellery fair taking place and all the rooms were full. Lily knew this. Once resettled in a longer room, no cleaner or brighter but facing on to the main road, she bathed, watched a little TV and fell into a dreamless sleep.

Saturday dawned grey yet oddly warm. After a quirky, perhaps typical local breakfast of muesli and bagels, Lily was ready for work. Down in the ballroom, the massed stalls of the jewellery trade awaited her. She put on her weekend work uniform, a tweed jacket over Lycra T-shirt, jeans and loafers, and wandered down the thinly carpeted stairs to the basement.

There before her stretched stand after stand, cubby-hole after hen coop of jewellery displays, ranging from the flimsiest Far Eastern gold chains to the most colossally vulgar gemstones, from comfortingly old-fashioned cultured pearls to the wackiest hand-crafted torques and nose ornaments, from the elegance of fine style to the sleaze of mildly suggestive body adornment. This was one of the British jewellery world's three annual selling fairs, when everyone from the tackiest fancy-goods manufacturers to the 'by appointment' crafts firms displayed their wares to buyers from all over the UK. It was an ethnic melting pot, with Asians, Jews, Europeans and South Americans all drawn into the same space. The dingy basement twinkled with rack upon rack of gold, silver, crystal and stones, fashioned into every kind of ornament and graded through every extreme of taste and appetite. Aladdin's cave, kitsch cornucopia, tat palace; there was something here for everyone.

This was Lily's world. The child of a Midlands jeweller, she had been introduced to gleaming metals and minerals earlier than she could remember and had never entertained another career preference. Her childhood had been indelibly marked by annual out-of-season trips to Blackpool for the winter jewellery fair. Each freezing February, she would drive with her parents to the grey seaside, and spend the morning trailing her father from one tiny stand to another, where curiously accented men offered him trays of rings, lucky charms, watchstraps and cufflinks, while she spun fantasies round strings of beads, marcasite brooches and silver candelabra. It was a world which linked magic and beauty to the haggle of the market-place. She adored it, and would leave reluctantly with her mother for a trip along the front in a tram and then tea in the Tower Ballroom, where slender mannequins walked between the tables dressed in fashion gowns and hats, trailing their jackets behind them as they glided across the floor. Lily was distracted by their elegance and the cream cakes, but she would rather have been back at the fair, where each corner dazzled with waterfalls of flashing light.

The strangely accented men – middle-European refugees she now knew – had long gone from the jewellery business, and their sons had inherited, voices thick with Birmingham or East London accents. But the glamour and the tackiness were the same, and Lily's job, as buyer for Girl's Best Friend, a small, eclectic chain of fashion jewellery stores, gave her the chance to submerge herself in its nostalgia and barter.

She strolled the aisles, chatting to acquaintances, seeking out the unpredictable and the amusing, the unusual imports and the retro stock among the more conventional suppliers. Steering a careful course, relying as much on instinct as geography, she neatly sidestepped those merchants who specialized in the less-than-conventional. There were places where jewellery and fancy goods shaded off into more peculiar territories of taste and application. GBF was not interested in the wilder shores of body piercing or clips that could be applied anywhere other than ear lobes and hair tresses. Lily knew her market and stayed within the charted world.

She was buying for Christmas, and rounded off an uneventful morning's work with the discovery of a range of powder compacts and matching lipstick cases, reproductions of old 1950s styles which lifted her heart and the corners of her lips, and made the whole trip worth while. At that point, she decided to pause while she was ahead and step outside the hotel for a bite of lunch.

It was as she descended the hotel steps into the fresh air that the thought struck her like a headache: Frank was at it again. Call it intuition, but she had known before and she was convinced once more. He was not at home, working on the make or break; he'd got a new lover and he was with her.

Transfixed as she was by this fear, Lily lost appetite and impetus and returned to her room. She rang home. The answerphone spoke to her in her own voice.

'Frank and Lily can't take your call right now. If you want to leave a message, you can speak for as long as you like, after the tone.'

Lily's first message was short. The next one, recorded half an hour later, ran a little longer and the third made all of three sentences. After that she hung up each time the message clicked in. By midnight, after innumerable calls sandwiching a few desultory hours back at the fair, she forced herself to stop dialling. Frank was not there. He had betrayed her. He had abandoned the cats. What the hell was she supposed to do now?

Her mind seethed. This was how she had first discovered his infidelities two years earlier. Away for the weekend visiting her parents, she had repeatedly rung home to no reply, and had rushed back early, fearing Frank was lying dead on the kitchen floor. But no, he was just lying, some nonsense about a crisis at work, although finally he had confessed to the truth – a lover, the latest in a long line. Then, Lily's heart had sunk at the mountain she knew she would have to climb, to get back to the safe placidity of her previous life with Frank. Now, on the first Sunday-morning flight out of Glasgow, she was once more overwhelmed with mental fatigue at the labour ahead. The talks, the promises, the effort. But then this was what a relationship was all about, wasn't it?

The plane circled Heathrow, and as it did she thought she could glimpse her street, near the Common, possibly even their house. Perhaps Frank was home by now (and the cats fed). Perhaps they could sort it all out today. After all, they still had a week of make or break to go.

Sod the tube, she took a taxi. Its chuntering engine soothed her a little as they cruised through Sunday London – car-washing and Sunday papers, parking spaces and amateur football teams. Finally they were home. Lily paid the driver, grabbed her bags and put her Yale in the lock. But the mortise was on too. Frank wasn't at home. As she walked into the hall, she could smell the emptiness of the house. The cats were sunning themselves in the garden, their plates still half-filled with cat food which had developed that slight crust at the edges from having been left out overnight. On the kitchen table was a note:

Dear Lily
I have been unfaithful to you again. Rather than put you through all that pain once more, I have left. The cats have been fed. I have put some of your favourite ice cream in the freezer.

These last weeks have been very difficult. You may not believe me when I say I do not want to go. Sometimes I can even glimpse a future for us.

But I will never be the monogamist you need, so this is the best way. I will carry on paying money into the joint account so don't worry about the house.

In spite of what you think, I do love you.
Frank.

8

The combination of synthetic solicitousness and covering of his back, as if he were writing for an audience, made Lily heave. She crumpled the letter up in a ball, threw it in the wastebin, retrieved it, smoothed it out, laid her head on the kitchen table and howled.

Chapter 2

Denial, despair, anger, bargaining, acceptance. She had read in some novel about the stages of a trauma. But for her it was all academic. This was not something she had ever experienced before. There had been no bereavements, no splits of real heartbreak. Yes, the previous cat, dear Minnie, had met a sticky end and Frank had insisted they go and see the body, at the vet's, in order to let go and grieve properly. But on the life disasters scale, this was a first.

Lily was sick with pain. She was bedridden with it, insomniac with it, appetiteless with it. All of these were novelties, but so distracted was she that she could not even enjoy entering the realms of slimmed-down, hollow-eyed adulthood.

For her, the five steps seemed to arrive out of sequence. Despair first, with acceptance tucked inside like a kangeroo's baby in its pouch. Denial came next, along with bargaining. And anger, well, give her time.

Alone in the house, she did not quite know what to do with herself. The cats knew when to keep a distance and remained in the garden, watchful but not offering themselves for therapy. A foggy blanket had descended on her brain. What was she to do? Where had Frank gone? What was she going to tell people? Humiliated almost to the point of annihilation, Lily realized that in order simply to relieve herself of the need to go to work the following morning, she had better phone her boss.

Margot Pink was a wordly-wise woman whose widowed state and blocked Fallopian tubes had freed her up to exercise her entrepreneurial spirit in the era before feminism had touched down in the UK. What she lacked in aesthetics she made up for in dynamism and business acumen. The Girl's Best Friend costume jeweller's chain which she had invented, developed and now ran offered a range of sophisticated ornaments Margot herself would never wear, or necessarily even admire on other women, but she had identified and exploited a niche and was an unparalleled spotter of talent in others. Lily was only the latest in a series of buyers who had ridden the fashion wave for Margot, whose cleverly placed shops, razor-sharp pricing and alluring window displays had beckoned the clued-up woman of any age since the late 1960s.

Margot's office wall was decorated with photos of window displays through the life of her business, a kind of museum of the groovy bauble. The first shop had majored in daisy earrings, op art plastic and self-adhesive jewels for navel and eyelid, all displayed against Biba shades of plum velvet. Moving through Indian filigree and Perspex, rough-cut amber and diamanté, the photos evoked the decades in all their ephemeral glamour and transitory moods. Lily's own jewellery box contained a number of Girl's Best Friend classics, including a glass-bead-encrusted choker and a fake ivory shark's tooth, two of the many bestsellers which had paid for Margot Pink's caramel Mercedes and her hand-made shoes.

On the Sunday evening, Lily rang Margot's flat in Swiss Cottage. She knew her boss spent the weekends in splendid isolation, surrounded by tabloid newspapers, face-packs, Belgian chocolates and her Persian cats. Margot's motto was 'It's only business', which meant many things including a prohibition on any discussion in the office of significant others. Mr Pink had died in the first year of their marriage, and his legacy had enabled his widow to embark on the career she had always craved. Had there been lovers since? Was there one now? Lily didn't know. Margot's peachy skin, generous frame and erect posture gave no clues. Margot knew of Frank's existence, but had not enquired beyond that. Lily was not expecting much sympathy, but the way she was feeling, she didn't really care. All she wanted was permission to stay under the duvet for the foreseeable future.

The phone was picked up after a single ring.

'Hello.' The familiar, nasal, nicotine-roughened tone.

'It's Lily.'

'Are you in Scotland?'

'No. I'm at home.' This was the first time Lily had spoken since returning to the house. To her own ears, her voice sounded as dry as kindling, all moisture having been leached out through her tear-ducts. She could hardly manage to swallow. 'Frank's left me. I don't think I'll be able to come to work tomorrow.'

There was a silence. Lily listened to the echo of her words while her eyes filled, miraculously, with yet more tears.

'I'm very sorry.' Margot's voice was cool but had dropped several semi-tones. Her sympathy sounded genuine. 'You must take as long as you need. Hold on to the details of what you bought in Glasgow. They will keep. Call me again when you want to come back.'

Lily had nothing to say. The gratitude would have to wait until she could resume control of her vocal cords. They both put down the phone to the sound of her strangled croak before the wail blared out of her mouth again.

Two hours later, after a bath and a slug of Italian fruit brandy – a souvenir of their last holiday in the Veneto – Lily knew it was time for the second most important call, to her parents. This would be the real crusher, and yet she wanted them to know, her mother and father who had never liked Frank but had always treated him with civility, even after the discovery of his infidelities. She dialled their number without thinking, listening to the ringing tone and imagining the phone in the cool vestibule of her childhood home.

'Hello?' It always fell to Lily's mother to answer the phone, and her tone was always anxious, sensing the blow about to fall.

'Hello, Mum. It's me.'

'Lily? How are you, dear? Everything alright?'

Again, the sympathy tapped straight into Lily's fathomless reserve of self-pity. 'Oh, Mum,' she sobbed. 'It's Frank. He's gone.'

'Gone where?'

'I don't know. He's taken his stuff. He's left me.'

'Oh, Lily. My poor dear. Just a minute, I'll get your father.'

'No – ' Lily's first impulse was not to involve him, although she knew this was ridiculous. But her mother had gone anyway. There was no division between them. They operated as a seamless unit, and sure enough Lily now heard the sound of the phone extension being lifted so that they could speak to her together.

'Lily, it's Daddy.'

Yes, I know, she hummed irritably to herself.

'Is it true? Has he gone for good?'

Interesting phrase, she thought. 'Yes, he's taken his stuff – clothes, records.'

'And are you alright? Do you want us to come down?'

Despite the tears wet on her cheeks, Lily had been well trained and rose to the challenge. 'No. I'm alright. There's no need for you to come. I'll manage. I'm a bit upset just now, the shock I suppose. But I'll be okay.'

'Would you like to come home? We could take care of you for a bit.'

God, that really would do for her, being cooed over and sympathized with by her quietly vindicated parents. 'No, I can't. There's work. And the cats.'

'Well, if you're sure . . .' This was her mother, straining to jump on the next train.

'No, really.' Message delivered, she was now desperate to close the call, not to cry more but just to stop externalizing the pain, to stop opening her mouth and shaping sounds, especially reassuring ones. Numbness was within reach, if she could just shut down.

'Well, we'll call you again soon, and don't forget, we're here if you need us. For anything at all.'

'Thanks, both of you. It's reassuring to know that. Speak to you tomorrow.'

There, she had done it. The handset was back on the cradle. She had cleared the decks. She could climb into the huge double bed they had had specially made to accommodate Frank's six-foot frame and really become acquainted with her misery.

During the next three days, Lily went cold turkey. There was no shirking the pain, loss and fear. She was paralysed with her tragedy. Her life had been derailed. She had never dreamed of a future alone. Now she could think of nothing else. How would she function? Where would she live? Could she afford to stay in the house? Would she be safe? Would there ever be anyone else? Who would she go on holiday with? Was there a future? Would she ever get dressed again?

These thoughts spun through her mind on a continuous loop, in parallel with the raging, disbelieving, shattered and raw bursts of emotion which were to do with Frank.

She was astounded that he had left no number or address. What if she had tried to injure herself? How could he be such a bastard? Her feelings reeled through every shade of passion, pride and utter self-abnegation. On the Monday morning, after an interminable night with a couple of hours of light sleep, two more brandies, a dose of

Night Nurse and much grave companionship from the World Service, she assumed he would be at his desk in the Social Services office, but was not ready to speak to him.

She wanted to be in control of the conversation. She wanted to know beforehand what she was going to say. At the moment, she did not know – assuming she could articulate at all – whether she would screech fury at him like a banshee or beg him to come back. Did she want him back? Well, of course. The alternative was desolation. But he was incorrigibly promiscuous and their only future would be effectively as brother and sister. Well, that would be better than loneliness, wouldn't it?

The day-time passed in a haze. The radio was her constant companion but the honeyed flow of Radio Four passed over her without registering. She fed the cats. She walked from room to room, drawn to windows where she stood unseeing, gazing at the garden or the road. She saw no one, which was just fine. She avoided mirrors, knowing her swollen eyelids and bloodshot eyes would only exercise her tear-ducts once more.

In the kitchen, she contemplated the fridge, the store cupboard, the freezer, but lacked the energy to boil the kettle. Food? Now why would she have any interest in that?

Back in the lounge, sprawled on the sofa in a kimono and a pair of Frank's tennis socks, taken unwashed from the dirty-linen basket, she had an urge to call Dorothy. But much as she craved her friend's unquestioning support, she shrank from yet another account of her humiliation. Before she trotted out the story again, she had better get it right in her head. Maybe if she said, 'We've split up,' instead of, 'He's left me,' that would lend a shred of dignity to her bare loss. She was, after all, going to have to get used to this. In her soul, Lily knew that Frank was not coming back.

At various points, she felt the want of him. Sounds,

smells, patterns of behaviour, good and bad habits came to her memory as she haunted their shared home like the ghost of relationships past. This was the bath where he lay for hours in grey water reading second-hand science fiction novels. This was the cupboard where he kept said science fiction novels, a teetering pile of yellowed and stained pages with a rancid odour all their own. (These had not yet been removed.) Here were his frozen lamb chops in the freezer, over there the pint tea mug he emptied twice at breakfast.

His clothes were gone, the music centre and his records and CDs and the box file in which he kept his personal papers, documents and memorabilia. But everything else in the house was intact. He could have just walked down to the Asian grocer's for a pint of milk, as he so often had. His absence was palpable, it shimmered in the air. It mocked her from the corner of her eye. And the silence was appalling. If she turned off the radio, there were none of the familiar sounds – Bob Marley records, tuneless hummings, croonings to the cats. No key turning in the lock. No demented sewing-machine sounds of his 2CV drawing up outside. Never more, quoth the raven.

All the nevers were a cue for more weeping. All the unrepeatables, the last times. No more bedtime hugs. No one to bring her hot Ribena if she caught laryngitis again. No one to teach her European history as they drove across France on holiday. No one to cook Sunday roasts for, or scour junk shops with. No partner, pal, helpmate. Oh, the pity she had for herself.

Then night-time came round again. She was neither tired nor alert. She went to bed and circled the same mental loops. She could scarcely distinguish between dream and wakefulness. It was all a nightmare. The clock ticked, the hours slouched past. At some point the birds sang and she knew she had survived another night.

By Wednesday evening she noted that her lips felt

cracked and she forced herself to make a cup of herb tea, Blackcurrant Bracer, just the job. In front of the television, she found herself disorientated by the colours and noises. She could not focus. Was she going mad? She looked at the clock. It was after midnight and she was the only person alone and awake in the whole world. And now, having avoided any phone calls, having not left the house or glimpsed a soul, suddenly she was desperate to talk to someone. She would lose her mind if she did not connect with a human being. But who could she wake up at this hour? The depth of Lily's isolation cleared a little space in her tired turmoil of a brain and she reached for the telephone directory. There was one number she could call, she remembered vaguely, one ear that never slept, one resource she had never imagined she would be desperate enough to contact.

It took three rings before the receiver was lifted. Then a remarkably wakeful voice said, 'Samaritans. Can I help you?'

The words piled up on Lily's tongue, but the speaking mechanism seemed to be atrophied.

Again, the calm female voice. 'Are you having trouble talking? Don't worry, take your time.'

More kindness. Lily's eyes prickled, but yes, she could communicate. 'Hello.' Good start.

'Hello. My name's Lorna. How can I help you?'

Reasonable question. And what were the formalities of this anonymous intimacy? An exchange of identification? Should she give a false name? Was this in confidence? Oh, sod it. 'I'm Lily. I just felt desperate to talk. I've been alone for a few days, haven't spoken to anyone. Well, I couldn't. But now I needed to. Is that okay? Just to talk.'

'Yes, of course, Lily. That's what we're here for . . . You say you've been alone – is that unusual for you?'

Lorna's voice was concerned but not too intrusive. Lily

17

opened up to her like a sun-starved mesembryanthemum. It all tumbled out, Frank, the other women, her abandonment, her terror of a Frankless future. It took fifteen minutes and left Lily breathless and smeared with tears and snot. She stopped to calm herself and mop off the secretions. Her last phrase – 'I feel so desperately alone' – rang in her ear and presumably in Lorna's too, who took a moment to come up with her response.

'Lily, would you say you were feeling suicidal about what has happened?'

Now there's a thought, she felt like quipping, but realized that Lorna had expressed an idea she recognized, even though she had not previously admitted it. She fell silent, awed at the idea of rubbing herself out. Could she? Probably. But how? Slashed wrists in the bath, she supposed. She had no pills and couldn't hurl herself off or in front of anything. Yes, warm and wet and slowly fading out, but with clothes on. She could manage that.

But would she? Well, it would answer everything. Do away with all that awful uphill stuff which lay before her and which exhausted her merely in the act of contemplation. Imagine having to narrate her whole life story to a new man. And listen to his. The thought was appalling.

But what about her parents? And the cats, Huntley and Palmer, curled around each other on the rug like a pair of quotation marks? At some sensible, non-hysterical level she knew that she could not do such a thing to her mother, who had miscarried twice before giving birth at last. Nor could she disappoint her father, the orphan-made-good who had clawed his way to middle-class security through a combination of innate dexterity, opportunism and a Darwinistic belief in the philosophy he had picked up in the orphanage: 'Remember, Lily, there are only two kinds of people in this life – those who kick and those who are kicked. Which one are you going to be?'

She who idolized him would always rise to the challenge, deny her weakness, fight on.

'Lily, are you still there?'

'Yes, Lorna, I was just thinking about your question. The answer is no, I'm not suicidal.'

They talked on for a while. Lorna continued warm, gently inquisitive, non-judgemental, in fact she refused to give any advice at all – policy, Lily was told. After a while, she began to tire of the impersonal sponginess of Lorna's responses, kindly meant though they were. She struggled to end the conversation.

'Do you think you might get some sleep now, Lily?'

'Yes, I think I might.' Actually, she did think she might.

'Well, you know we're always here, don't you?'

Yes, that's why I rang. 'I do, and it's good to know.'

'So you will call again if you need us.'

Yes, sure, promise. 'Yes, thank you, Lorna. You've really helped. Goodnight now.'

'Goodnight, Lily.'

Peace at last. But of course Lorna had helped. Not in the way she perhaps thought, although Lily was not denying the value of being able to connect with someone intelligent, awake and happy to enter into conversation at this hour. No, it was the suicide bit that had really been of value. The first thing Lily had learned as a result of her new situation was that she was not going to fade out of the picture. She was going to have to find a way to carry on.

Now she had better try to sleep, because tomorrow she had things to do.

Chapter 3

It was Thursday morning, the surprisingly normal hour of seven o'clock and Lily awoke to birdsong and the sound of Huntley dragging his claws down the stripped pine of the bedroom door, an invention of his which combined a luxuriant S-bend of a stretch to his spine, a little gentle claw-sharpening and an act of mild vandalism which often awoke dozing sleepers and could lead to an early breakfast.

Lily felt oddly refreshed and even a little hungry. Was she ready to resume the orderly pace of life? Well, she could make a start. She fed the cats, ran a bath and found some clean underwear. She washed her hair and drank a glass of orange juice. She rinsed her eyes with Optrex. She looked in the mirror and applied moisturizer to her dry skin, then some eye pencil, and felt capable of presenting herself to the newsagent at the bottom of the road where she bought a newspaper and some fresh bread. After a slice of toast and a desultory sweep through the broadsheet pages, she felt ready to communicate with the world.

First she called Margot, by now undoubtedly at her desk in the office, near Holborn Circus.

'Hi. It's Lily.'

'Well, hello. How are you doing?'

'Let's say I'm functioning. I've got a couple of things I need to do, but will it be alright if I come in around lunchtime?'

'No problem.'

'Can Monica check my diary – I think there's a rep coming in this morning. Perhaps he could call next week?'

'She's already done it. It's the Stargazy man. And we've

also rescheduled one from yestereday – Aziz, the chap with the gold chains?'

Yes, she'd forgotten. But Margot, fiercely efficient, had not. 'Good. Okay, then I'll see you later.'

'Lily, are you sure you're ready? We can manage awhile yet.'

She knew Margot meant this and was touched. But she also knew the business was too small for one key person to be out of action, unplanned, for long. Everyone at GBF (inevitably known as GBH to its 200-strong nationwide staff) worked at full stretch. Margot conformed to an old-fashioned sense of business propriety – firm, fair and fully expectant that in exchange for decent wages her workers would not stint themselves in her service. Lily felt an immense loyalty towards her. But more importantly, she felt that she wanted to return to the distractions of work.

'I'm sure. See you in a bit.'

'Good, and don't forget your Glasgow orders.'

Call two was to Dorothy. Lily's best friend was a freelance book editor who worked from home. They had met at a mutual friend's birthday party, something like twelve years ago, and an instant rapport had blossomed into a life-sustaining mutual support system communicated as much by phone as anything else.

Without looking at the numbers, Lily keyed in the digits.

'Yes,' Dorothy barked after the first ring. She had been freelance for under a year, having been downsized from a publishing conglomerate, and seemed to be making a point of not mastering the user-friendly telephone manner supposedly befitting her more obsequious station.

'Hello. It's me.'

'Well, hello you. What happened, did you fall in love with some brawny, black-eyed Scot and stay on in Glasgow? I thought you were going to call me on Monday.'

'Not quite. Frank and I have split up.' Now that seemed to slip out without too much forethought. 'I haven't spoken to anyone until today.'

'God, Lily. What happened?'

'Well, seeing as it's you, the truth is that he's left me. Even though we were supposed to be giving it everything for two weeks. There's obviously yet another woman, and I suppose he's gone to wherever she is. He's taken his stuff. It's the real thing this time.' There, she could manage it with no more than a single teardrop sliding down her cheek.

'So how do you feel?'

'Mad, really. I mean crazed and in a sealed-off bubble. Angry too, but mainly scared. And very tired.'

'Do you want me to come over?'

'No, but thanks. I'm going to go to work today. Margot's been great but I can't just abandon all that. Could you maybe come to supper later in the week, say Saturday?'

'Yes, sure. But I'll call you before then. What a shit, Lily. You know I never liked him, but to run out on you while you were away . . . He's such a coward.'

'Maybe. But it would have been worse if I had been there and watched him go.' Christ, she hadn't thought about that. But now that she had, she realized it was a mistake. A big lump seemed suddenly to have filled her throat.

'Perhaps you're right. So what happens now?'

'Well, I have to call the mortgage people today and my lawyer, but I hope I can afford to buy him out. I don't feel ready to move, on top of everything else.' She had thought about this as much as anything. Before buying the house with Frank, Lily had had her own flat, complete with noisy neighbours and unreliable leaseholders. But more than that, she had had a problem with feeling safe. Years of patient reassurance by Frank had helped her to feel less anxious about marauders storming through the window at four o'clock in the morning, but her sense of security was deeply rooted in the little house they had made their nest, situated safely in the middle of a terrace, unassailable from the back and carefully locked at the front. 'In fact I had better get on. Lots of calls to make and I said I'd be in the office by the middle of the day.'

Dorothy and Lily said goodbye. After a moment to draw breath and check that her resolve was firmly in place, she phoned the building society and her solicitor, leaving them to make contact with each other and get back to her on the question of whether she could take on the full mortgage.

Having done all that, she picked up the phone one last time. Another familiar shape to be traced on the telephone keypad, and within seconds she had a connection.

'Hello, Social Services. Frank speaking.' So he was at work, and not only that but sounding like nothing of significance had changed in his life.

'You bastard,' she hissed.

'Oh.'

She had planned the opening remark, but in spite of efforts had not been able to imagine much beyond it. The point was really to establish that he hadn't left the country. Despite the rupture, Lily still needed to know where Frank was. This was something she knew she was going to have to wean herself off.

'How are you?' he asked finally.

A range of replies flitted across her mind, but she settled for, 'How did you think I would be?'

'I've been worrying about you.'

This didn't seem worth acknowledging.

'We are going to need to talk.'

'Yes. Of course,' he agreed. 'Do you want me to come round?'

A strange, surreal feeling washed over Lily. He was going to visit her in their house? 'Well, yes, I suppose so.'

'How about tomorrow?' He was being so accommodating, as if politeness and amenability would absolve him. Lily thought it was pathetic.

'Okay. Eight o'clock.'

They rang off. Lily's heart was thumping, but she was dry-eyed. One blessing with Frank was that there would be no fighting about money or possessions. Whatever else he was, he was not grabby about the material things in life. And he was using a version of his Eeyore voice, which meant that he was feeling defeated and self-pitying as well as apologetic. Lily felt more than a match for him, provided she could stave off her own martyrdom. Well, she had twenty-four hours to get on top of that.

Pleased with herself but emotionally drained, she got up from the sofa to find her briefcase and coat. The phone rang.

'Lily dear, it's your mother. I just wanted to see how you were.'

Lily felt guilty. She had not acknowledged either of the phone messages her parents had left.

'I'm coping. Not doing too badly, I think. I've started sorting out the house.'

'Have you seen Frank?'

'No. But we've spoken.'

'Is he coming back?'

The question shocked Lily. She had moved beyond this. It wasn't a consideration. Was it?

'He's left me. I hadn't even thought about it.'

'Well, it's between you two. But if you want him, dear, then do what you must to get him.'

Was this her mother talking? Diligent wife and mother, long-suffering parent and partner whose commitment to the conventional could not be faulted?

'That's quite a surprise, coming from you.'

'Lily, only you know what is in your heart. You know

how your father and I feel about him, but if he's what you want, then have him back.'

Modernity in a mother was not just surprising, it seemed faintly improper. 'I'm assuming Dad isn't with you.'

'No, your father's gone out. And you're right, he wouldn't agree with me. But what do men know about these things?'

The ordered world had shifted a few degrees on its axis. Lily glimpsed an element of calculation in her mother that had been concealed for over thirty years. What was more, she had long held the view that, if all relationships contain one doting partner and one doted upon, it was her father who was the latter.

'Are you telling me that you've been in my position, with Dad?'

'No. Your father has never been unfaithful to me, nor left for someone else. But there was a moment, early on, well, I don't need to go into it now. The point is that there's a time for sentiment and a time for being clear-headed. You never know what has been agreed between a couple. There's an infinite variety of marriages in the world. And if you want Frank back and can agree the terms, well, no one will ever know.'

More confusion. As well as having no idea what her mother was alluding to – had she had an affair herself? No, inconceivable, wasn't it? – Lily was now going to have to think about doing a deal with Frank. She knew he wasn't bluffing. He really had gone. But was there a way back? She had twenty-four hours to get that one sorted out too.

Chapter 4

Public transport, office, word processor, conversations, telephone calls, more commuting, bath, bed. Lily's afternoon was a whirlwind of pretence. She looked like the other wage slaves; she picked up the threads of her job – examining samples, placing orders, discussing stock with individual branch managers, checking payment rates with Clive who ran Accounts – she conversed normally with her colleagues; she didn't drop anything fragile or forget anything important. But she was an android with Lily's face. No one could tell that she had been gutted, her innards removed and replicant organs inserted instead. The stomach wasn't functioning normally but no one had noticed yet. The salivary glands needed adjusting – her mouth was dry – and she noticed her fingers trembling. But she did it. Went there, did her stuff and got home. Now, exhausted, lying on the duvet, bracketed by cats and sipping a brandy, she tried to draw a line under her mental gymnastics.

To ask him back or not to ask him back? Well, just how low was she prepared to stoop? On reflection, she thought the question had already answered itself. For two years she had effectively thrown her scruples away, living with Frank, knowing his foibles and not doing what she had always promised herself in such a situation – quitting immediately. And what about earlier? Those nights when he came in smelling of perfume. That time he gave her pubic lice, and when confronted said he must have caught them trying on a pair of jeans in the cut-price shop. She had long learned to suppress her instincts, swallow her pride and principles. Why not submit the final inch and allow

Frank the open arrangement he craved, which would offer him domestic security and as much pistol-packing as he could achieve?

Lily was torn. The blessed stream of continuity offered dullness but safety, frustration yet stasis. If she was honest, she had lain awake on a number of nights these last few years, listening to Frank's snores and asking herself the sisterhood's favourite question: Is this all there is? But at thirty-six, with statistics against her, what likelihood was there of starting over, by which she meant another relationship? Because of course Lily did want another relationship.

Drifting into sleep, skewered on the horns of her dilemma, Lily recalled the first time she had suspected Frank, way back in the first year of their relationship. Those were the days when he played badminton two evenings a week with a colleague named Helen. Appropriately enough, he returned regularly at about nine, still in shorts, smelling of sweat and the one beer he claimed he drank before leaving. When she had asked him, all innocently, whether Helen was a friend or a lover, he had been outraged. Trying to present herself as a rationalist, Lily had explained how his ritual might easily be exactly what it seemed, or an elaborate subterfuge.

'Do you see?' she had said. 'The only thing I have to hold on to is my trust in you.' This was, of course, a *very* early stage in their life together and Lily, an inexperienced twenty-six-year-old, was still basing her sense of how relationships were constructed on the propaganda disseminated by women's magazines.

'That has to be our guiding light – that we trust each other to be honest.'

Frank had said nothing.

'We will always tell each other the truth, won't we?' she had badgered.

There had been a pause of some length, then Frank had

answered, 'Look, Lily, I love you and I want to be with you. But I can't promise always to tell you the truth. If being honest would hurt you, then the sensible thing would be to lie.'

Lily remembered feeling as if she'd entered Looking-Glass land. Honesty, bad. Lying, good. Well, there was a novelty. But Frank was older than her, more experienced in long-term involvement. Maybe his cynicism was more truthful than her cracker-barrel philosophizing. Lily had felt a chump then. And she felt a chump now. She slept anyway.

Friday dawned grey and so did Lily. The busyness had fallen away. She had stepped back into her role at GBF, the signs on the house – according to her lawyer – were good, she had established the vestiges of a Frankless order of life (no more cleaning woman, no more subs to the *New Statesman* and *Viz*, no more meat in the freezer. Huntley and Palmer had stuffed themselves to bursting) and she had joined the annals of failed relationships.

The adrenalin had faded. Now she just had to carry on living.

She could neither be bothered to weigh herself nor sit down for breakfast. A cup of coffee and a high-fibre rusk, consumed while she stood looking out on the garden – more work in prospect – sufficed, before she left for the office and another day of 'putting a brave face on it'. Margot Pink had said nothing to her at all so far, and her colleagues had either noticed nothing in her gaunt, un-frivolous mood or tactfully held their peace.

Friday at GBF was generally a hectic time, with supplies to the shops for best-day-of-the-week Saturday needing to be sorted and delivered as a priority. None of this directly involved Lily, but she generally picked up the pace anyway and used the day to clarify product ranges and chase up supply.

Monica, office factotum and general administrator, was already printing off a batch of overnight orders when Lily arrived. Her cubicle, like everyone else's, was awash with paperwork, its walls stuck with old GBF posters. Although housed in a redeveloped corner of Hatton Garden, the company's premises looked as if they dated from the pre-computerized era. Pink priorities ranked office technology rather low. Monica's old laser printer was, as usual, rattling away like a cotton loom. It broke down frequently, but no one expected it to be replaced. Monica herself was deaf to its racket and already two tasks further down the day's order of priorities. Lily, calling hello, headed for the kitchen where she picked up a mug and a glass, for the herb tea and mineral water she would sip through the day, then went to her own tiny, doorless office. At her desk, jacket off, handbag stowed, VDU logged on, she ground to a halt, lost in a sea of misery, unable to summon a shred of mental energy. Her in-tray looked about as inviting as the cats' litter box.

It was not that she wanted to cry any more. She simply wanted to sleep, and not out of fatigue but merely for oblivion's sake. Blackness, anonymity, these to her were currently a girl's best friend. As she sat, glazed, in her swivel chair, a rap at the partition wall dragged her back to consciousness. Framed in the doorway stood Margot Pink, eyeball-searing in hot fuchsia with gold accessories.

'Well, I can't say you're looking good, but you've looked worse,' she opened, with what was probably meant to be a caring expression.

Lily could think of no response to this.

'Are you coping?' Margot continued, taking a pull on her cigarette.

'I've followed up on all the Glasgow orders, cancelled those pearl droppers that were faulty, taken ten dozen assorted single- and double-row crystal beads from Mitchell's on appro – '

'I meant personally.'

'Oh. Well, yes, I think so. I'm trying to keep the house. And Frank's coming round tonight, for a so-called chat.'

'Are you eating?'

Margot Pink as Jewish mother? Lily smiled. 'Not much.'

'Then come to lunch on Sunday. Twelve thirty. You know the address, don't you? Flat 21A.'

Now here was a novelty. Margot's heavy footfalls were already drumming down the corridor before Lily had time to thank her or ask what to bring.

Monica, bat-eared, appeared like Margot's after-image in the door-frame. 'Everything alright?' she enquired.

Lily decided to come clean to Monica and short-circuit the jungle drums.

'Could be better. I've just split up with my bloke,' she said flatly.

Monica was forty going on ninety-nine. She was the office mother, her desk drawers a perennial source of boiled sweets, Elastoplast and spare tampons. Married to a plasterer and desperate to conceive, she looked genuinely sorry. 'Poor you. You must be feeling dreadful. Is Margot giving you a hard time?'

'Surprisingly unhard, in fact. She's asked me to Sunday lunch.'

'Bloody hell,' said Monica. 'Maybe she's not solid mineral after all.'

At the end of a wearying day, in which she had achieved little, Lily picked up her bags and joined the weekend commute. In the office, she had sensed her colleagues looking at her in a different light now, standing further back as if to leave her floating in her pool of sad solitariness. If that were true, she knew it was only kindly meant. And yet she felt more isolated.

Now, among the gladsome-hearted Friday night workers, many reading the overexcited *Evening Standard* week-end supplement and presumably planning two days of febrile socializing, Lily felt even more like Le Petit Prince, consigned to a planet of one. Was everyone going clubbing, dining, partying or to the country? Logically she knew it could not be so, but emotionally she felt she had stepped off the turning world, back into a solo land of single portions, single supplements, single beds and single tickets.

She dragged herself from tube station to front door and collapsed gratefully inside, where at least the cats came to greet her, waiting silently for crunchy treats on the kitchen step, which was the price they exacted for an evening how-do-you-do. While two black forms munched noisily on pilchard-flavoured biscuits, Lily sat at the table, fingering the uninteresting mail. Then she remembered her imminent visitor.

Somehow, while never having forgotten for a moment that Frank had gone, she had let slip from her memory that he was calling tonight. Instantly, she headed upstairs, to wash her hair, apply more make-up, change into a silk T-shirt and white jeans. If nothing else, she would receive him looking as together as she could manage.

For once Frank was punctual. At eight sharp she heard the car draw up, as did Huntley, curled up on her lap, who lifted his head and waited for the sound of Frank's key in the lock. Lily did too and wondered how Frank must be feeling, knocking at his own (well, half anyway) front door.

When she opened it, he was standing halfway down the path, wearing his favourite Irish linen shirt (an impulse purchase of hers at the sales three years ago, because the faded blue matched his eyes) and black Levis, and smiling his daft smile, the one he adopted at times of acute embarrassment. Lily thought again that his jaw was just a fraction too long for him to be thought truly handsome, but the floppy black hair and tall frame still appealed to her.

'You'd better come in.' She stepped aside awkwardly to admit him into the hall. 'I'm in the living room,' she said, as he stalled by the coat-rack. Clearly politeness was to be the order of the evening.

He went into the room, thankfully took a seat without asking permission, and took out his cigarettes.

'A drink,' Lily offered, feeling mad.

'No, thank you,' he answered, rather prissily, she thought.

They sat in silence for a moment, while the cats registered Frank's presence in a satisfied fashion.

'Well,' said Lily, not knowing what was going to come out of her mouth. 'Who is she?'

'No one you know. Her name's Anna. She's a therapist at the Centre – lives in Bromley.'

'And you're living there too?'

'Yes. With her and the children. Two teenage girls.'

This silenced Lily. She had never imagined losing Frank to an older woman with a family.

'And how long had you been planning this?' she said after a moment.

'I don't know, Lily,' he said tiredly. 'No time, all the time, what does it matter?'

'It matters a helluva lot to me, if I've been the one hand clapping in our relationship. It makes me feel a bloody fool.' She wouldn't let herself cry.

Frank looked irritated. 'Shall we try and be practical? Talk about money and things?' He was smoking heavily, but looked quite composed. Hardly surprising, with a pipe, slippers and all home comforts to go back to. Bromley, for God's sake.

'Well, let's just be clear about this, shall we? You're

saying that this is definitely the end?' She gulped down the lump in her throat. 'So, if I were to agree –'

'No, Lily. Don't. There's no going back. It wouldn't be right.'

He sounded very firm. She felt an utter, absolute and total fool. Her house of cards had now collapsed completely. She had no bargaining strategies. He didn't want to come back, not at any price. Frank was somewhere else. She looked at him and no longer knew this man.

Another bad night. Lily tried her various decoy tactics – camomile tea, herbal sleeping tablets, a half-remembered yoga routine involving naming of body-parts – but none was effective. She lay, gloomily wakeful, sometimes spooked by the house's creaks and groans, for most of the hours of darkness. Glad of the short summer nights, she greeted the first reassuring notes of the dawn chorus like an old friend.

She still burned with humiliation at the memory of Frank's poise the night before, the ease with which he had discussed dividing up the material proof of their life together. At some point he had transferred his allegiance – when? when? – and now she, who had been the privileged one, shielded and excused by his love and commitment, was just one of the others. Special no more. Somehow this loss of protected species entitlement wounded her more than anything else. No one was looking out exclusively for her now. No one knew her whereabouts from moment to moment. Who would know if she disappeared? Friends, family, eventually, sure. But what were they compared to the curved enfoldment of a guardian angel's wing? (On reflection, she thought this comparison might be just a little over the top.)

Lily was on her own. No one sought her compromise any longer. She had no choice but to move forward. This phase of her life – ten years of playing house and assuming the happy-ever-after – had run its course.

Chapter 5

Supper with Dorothy was not a great success. Lily wanted company but also silence. Dorothy hadn't been able to identify which role to take: commiserating sister, blithe single, philosophical thirtysomething. She had tried them all, and Lily had tried in turn to acknowledge the gestures of friendship, but conversation kept petering out. By nine thirty they were marooned amongst the dirty plates and glasses, defeated and silent.

'I know,' Dorothy said. 'Why don't we catch a late movie somewhere?' She delved into her bag and produced *Time Out*.

Lily shook her head. 'No, not tonight. I couldn't face people, even in the dark.'

This was true, but there was more. Lily couldn't bear the thought of coming back to the empty house at night. After work was okay, she was used to that. But late, with no lights shining? How would she be able to enter the house without checking and rechecking every room for lurking shadows? She did not dare tell Dorothy about this, knowing she would only insist they depart immediately, for that very reason.

'Okay. What about TV then? Some music? Or does the silence suit you?'

'To be honest, yes it does. Do you mind?'

Dorothy, being a trooper, did not. She stayed while they finished the Chianti she had brought, and at midnight she went home. Lily felt certain enough in their friendship not to need to apologize. She hugged Dorothy hard before closing the door, turning the deadlock and fixing the chain.

She slept till five and felt as if she had achieved something major.

What to wear to lunch with Margot? Smart casuals? Informal formals? After much wardrobe scouring, Lily settled on a pair of linen Oxford bags with a matching waistcoat. She allowed herself generous time to cross London and bought a newspaper to read on the tube and a bunch of exquisite pale peonies to give.

Margot's flat, high in a modern block facing Regent's Park, was exactly as Lily would have fantasized. She had walked past a shop near Sloane Square once whose whole room-settings might have been airlifted in. The floors were various shades of marble tile, scattered with long-haired rugs. A large number of low coffee tables with glass tops and complicated yellow-metal legs stood close to various sofas upholstered in cream leather. Ivory, ebony, crystal and gilded objects stood in corners and sat self-consciously on shelves. Everything seemed too large, too shiny, too cluttered. Lily stepped warily through the hall and lounge, frightened of skidding and crashing into one of the sharp ornaments. She followed Margot and a Persian cat into the dining room. Her opinion on the decor was not solicited.

The long, polished dining table was laid for two, but first Margot insisted Lily sit with her on the balcony, for a cigarette and a glass of Liebfraumilch.

'I love this flat,' she said as Lily admired the view. 'I always wanted a place like this. I know what some people would say about my taste, but I've never worried too much about the subjective things in life. We can all have a say about them. The objective things, now they're a different matter. Cheers.'

Lily raised her glass mechanically. She had always sensed that Margot was a woman of strong moral codes, but she was bewildered now by the absence of small talk, compounded by the effect of more alcohol on her not quite sober system.

'So, Lily. We're not in the office now. Tell me how you're getting on.'

Margot's brown eyes gazed at her across the wrought-iron table and Lily was shocked to read concern in them. This was not a soft face, not the blurred countenance of her mother. Here the lines were marks of character, the generous lips and white, expensively set hair the distinctive features of a handsome if fleshy late middle age. She was a little moved at the idea of sympathy being offered to her from this quarter, and confused too by the change of roles.

'I'm not sure how to measure. Well? Badly? Compared to what, or whom? I'm still functioning, but I feel as if I'm sealed in a bubble, breathing different air.' A pause. 'Forgive me, Margot, I'm finding this all very disorienting too.'

Margot smiled. 'I can understand that. Why don't we eat? Perhaps that will help.'

They lunched on the finest prepared foods Selfridges could offer. (Lily had glimpsed carrier bags in the kitchen. Not that Margot was in the slightest coy about not cooking the meal herself.) Her host had bought widely, a magpie selection from various nations – tabbouleh, marinated Italian vegetables, wild mushroom quiche, salmon steaks in aspic, bhajis and samosas, with salad, and English, French and Jewish bread. There was an endless supply of chilled white wine, slightly sweeter than Lily liked, and soon she was following Margot's lead, picking slowly but lengthily at the glistening, loaded platters.

Once the edge had been taken off their appetites, Margot said, 'You mustn't be too shocked that I am breaking one of my own taboos. This isn't the first time I've entertained

36

colleagues here. But, yes, it's rare, and I do think a clear demarcation between work and private is important.'

'So why me?' Lily asked.

'Fair question,' Margot answered. 'We haven't talked much, previously, have we? Although I hope you know that I am more than satisfied with your work. Buying is an instinct. I have it, so I know. GBF has a very special image. You've always been able to tap straight into it. Just like me. Look at us. Our styles couldn't be more different.'

Lily had to smile wryly at this.

'But show us a range – bangles, earrings, whatever,' Margot continued, 'and we would go straight for the same first choice. And be right. But that's not the point. And nor am I treating you like a substitute daughter. I've never felt the need for one of those. No, I've been watching you going through your ups and downs, and now that matters have finally come to a head, just wanted to make my own contribution to the range of advice you're likely to be offered.'

Margot was right, Lily acknowledged to herself. Advice was coming from all quarters. Everyone had an opinion, Dorothy, her parents, Frank himself. Why not hear Margot's tuppence-worth?

'But tell me first, if I'm not being presumptuous, why your relationship has come to an end.'

That was an easy one. 'Frank's incorrigible promiscuity,' she answered without hesitation.

'So that was his contribution. And what about yours?'

'How do you mean?'

Margot reached for another slice of sunflower bread and cut a wedge of goat's cheese. 'You know what I mean. It takes two to tango. So Frank couldn't keep it zipped. And what did you do, or not do?'

Lily began to feel uncomfortable. 'I suppose I took it,' she said eventually.

'You were a mouse.' Margot's words did not end with a question mark.

Lily put down her fork and lowered her eyes. She thought her tear-ducts were under control, but now, to her horror, embarrassment and possibly fury, she could feel her eyes filling up. She reached into her handbag for a tissue.

Margot's voice softened marginally. 'I'm sorry. I don't want to make you cry. But I do want to see you get a grip.'

Lily had covered her face with one hand, while the tears flowed freely. Margot went to fetch a box of Kleenex, left them at Lily's elbow and sat down again.

'Look,' she resumed. 'What I want you to see is that this is one of life's turning points. You might even, eventually, come to see it as an opportunity. I know I sound like an agony aunt, but the truth in the cliché is that you have a chance, just at the moment, and I want you to realize that, and to take advantage if you can. But to do that, you have to be truthful to yourself about what has happened. You chose Frank, and at some point you must have known the real choice you were making. I've seen you at work. You're a tough negotiator and you're not easily intimidated. I'm like that. And I was like you in my marriage. A pushover. Hard to imagine, I know, but I was younger then.'

Lily had stopped weeping and was blowing her nose. 'You're saying I was responsible for Frank being unfaithful.'

'I'm saying you're responsible for choosing him, and in choosing him, opting to agree to his behaviour. Because you're not the one who threw him out, or did I get that wrong?'

Lily shook her head.

'Did you think it would work?'

Lily was puzzled at this question. 'When? At the beginning? Of course.' But she neither felt nor sounded sure of herself. 'It was Frank who was the certain one. He said he wanted to grow old with me, that we would always be together. I suppose I was flattered. I wanted him. I wanted a relationship. I thought I could make it work.'

'Did you love him?'

That old question. 'No. But then I've never understood what that word means. He said he loved me. That seemed like a good start. We got along. I didn't want anyone else. I thought that was as good as I was likely to get.'

'And now?'

'Now?'

'Any regrets?'

Lily took a sip of wine. 'If you're asking me whether I would have done better not to have known Frank, not to have lived with him for nearly a third of my life, the answer is no. I wouldn't have missed it. It's failed, but I don't wish it hadn't happened.'

'Now we're getting somewhere,' Margot commented. 'Let's have coffee in the lounge.' She disappeared, leaving Lily to ponder herself as mouse.

Is that me? she wondered. My God. She was awestruck at the collision between self-image and external appearance. Lily thought she was tough. Her father had raised her to be. At school they had called her Bossyboots. At work she knew herself to be assertive and direct. Margot had just confirmed it. But what about at home?

Had she been the Laurel to Frank's Hardy? A flush crept over her. Had she been a dishrag when all the time she had thought she was compromising, like grown-up people were supposed to do?

In her heart, Lily knew that Margot was right. She had settled down with Frank and simultaneously shut down her critical faculties. She had been the sleeping partner. And now she had had her rude awakening. It was time she accepted her share of the blame.

She got up slowly, dropped her napkin on the table and went into the next room, where light seemed to dazzle her from a thousand polished surfaces. The walls were hung with mirrors in intricate frames composed of mosaic and cut glass. In the corners stood plinths bearing metallic sculptures. Lily squeezed past what looked like a mammoth tusk tipped with gold and made for a sofa next to which one of the coffee tables was set with cups, saucers, plates and cutlery. Margot could be seen approaching with a gold cafetière in one hand and a cakestand in the other.

'My advice in these circumstances is very simple,' she said, seating herself. 'Eat some chocolate. What would you like – an éclair, a slice of Sachertorte or a florentine?'

Lily was too busy digesting the revised version of history to answer, so Margot dropped an éclair on a plate and passed it over along with a cup of coffee. For herself she selected a slice of the cake and demolished it with a fast-moving cake fork. Then she leaned towards a strange gilded metal cylinder which, at the touch of a button, offered a sunburst of cigarettes. Margot took one, lit it with an onyx lighter and sat back, exhaling noisily.

'It's a curious phenomenon,' she speculated, half to herself, 'the woman who feels free to make decisions at work but assumes submissiveness at home. Lionel, my husband, never let me work, so I didn't have to become such a schizophrenic, but I knew that out in the world I would be strong too. In the house, we conform. Maybe you didn't iron his shirts, wash his dishes, I don't know. But I could tell that you'd let him take the lead. It's easy for us to put ourselves second. Next time, make sure you get what *you* want.'

'Is that what you did?' Lily asked, genuinely curious.

'Ah, me, that's a long story. Who knows what would have happened if Lionel had lived. It wasn't my fate.

Instead, I got the chance to make my dream come true, start my business. After that, men seemed less important. And freedom became very precious. Maybe too much so. But such choices as I've made – ' a pause here while Margot's inner eye seemed to flick through a card index ' – they've not been so bad.' And the corners of her mouth curled up.

'I can't imagine you as a wimp, Margot.'

'We didn't have that word when I was a girl. But I could droop and simper with the best of them. I'd seen my mother do it for long enough. It almost seemed natural. If something real came up, something that made the men stubborn or angry, then you were too accustomed to maidenliness to be angry back.'

Both women contemplated this for a moment. Lily tried to remember being angry with Frank, really angry, something comparable with the radio he had smashed when she had asked him to do more cleaning, the bottle of HP sauce he had hurled at the kitchen wall when she had said she didn't want to go camping. Rage was not her style. Even when she had discovered his infidelities, she had only wept; sorrow not anger.

How could she be two people? She could think of innumerable instances at work when she'd used aggression, assertiveness, power plays of various conscious kinds, to get goods at the best price and fastest delivery. She followed up on orders, she argued with suppliers, she cancelled for late delivery or poor quality. She had heard Monica call her a Rottweiler.

But the domestic Lily had a different, gentler tactical armoury. Tears, silence, withdrawal. At home she was a martyr. And who did that remind her of? Not by any chance her mother? Oh my God.

Lily's reverie was interrupted by Margot, who had finished her cigarette and was topping up their coffee cups.

'Enough of the search for self,' she announced. 'I have something else I want to talk to you about.'

'Oh yes?' said Lily, reaching at last for her cake plate.

'Yes.' Margot's expression had changed to something Lily couldn't quite read. 'I've decided to sell the business.'

Chapter 6

'Never,' said Monica. 'She'll go on till she drops. She'd never sell.'

'That's what I thought. But I heard it from the horse's mouth. She said she had other plans. Wouldn't be drawn.'

'Do you think she's ill?'

'She doesn't look it,' Lily said thoughtfully. 'She didn't even look unhappy when she told me.'

'Maybe it's a man.'

'Maybe. But he'd have to be quite a catch. She said GBF was her dream come true.'

Monica took off her spectacles and polished the lenses. 'I'm going to ask Tom,' she announced after a moment. Tom was Margot's most faithful retainer, the chief of Dispatch, the man who kept the globe on its axis by ensuring the constant and correct flow of goods and paper. He had been with the firm since the beginning and like Methuselah contained much age and wisdom. 'Maybe he'll know something,' Monica said, clopping off in her sandals. It was a reasonable assumption.

Lily sat back in her chair. At least Margot's announcement had served to push the Frank business off her mental front page. And she had also refused so far to face up to the horrible revelation that she had already turned into her mother.

But the last thing she needed just now was job insecurity, and despite Margot's most reassuring noises – not so very reassuring in her case – the future was murky.

All that seemed definite was that the business was on the block, which meant that Margot was already in negotiation

43

with two individuals who had been expressing interest in Girl's Best Friend for years. No details were forthcoming on their identities, only that one was a large organization and the other a private businessman. A conclusion might be expected within the next couple of weeks. No, it was not a secret, although Lily was the first to hear about it. Yes, Margot would do her best to guarantee that everyone would keep their jobs, but obviously the new owner must be free, etc., etc.

Lily could sense gloom flickering in her peripheral vision. To keep the house she was going to have to double her mortgage *and* pay it all, instead of half, as previously, as well as all the other domestic bills. The last thing she wanted at the moment was a lodger, although she acknowledged she might have to make a concession on that one. All her sums suggested that, with a modest lifestyle and no unexpected financial disasters, she could scrape through. This would not be a good time for unpredictability of income. Thanks, Margot, she thought darkly. Perhaps you should have served a few antacid tablets with the chocolate.

The phone rang – a charm-bracelet supplier in Manchester, querying the breakdown between silver and gold in her order. She was dragged into the present, into the working week. She rolled up the sleeves of her Paul Smith shirt – no more of those for the foreseeable future – and got on with it.

By midweek, the office was incandescent with rumour. All along the floor of the office-block which GBF occupied, at the coffee machine, in the unofficial smoking corner (outside Tom's loading and dispatch bay), in the surrounding sandwich shops, wherever colleagues gathered together, the air buzzed with controversy. Margot was watched on all sides. Her visitors were scrutinized, her conversations unpicked. One day the word was that GBF was being swallowed up by the Next group; the following morning Alice, one of the two junior accountants, claimed to have seen Gerald Ratner in the lift. For the first time in his working life Tom was besieged with visitors. He knew no more than anyone else and clearly didn't want to be quizzed about change, franking the mail noisily to convey his distress. Lily tried not to get sucked on to this roller-coaster of gossip. She knew her nerves were already stretched to twanging tautness. She was just about holding it together. She did not want to risk being reduced to a blancmange all over again. She kept her head down.

At the end of the second Frankless week, she had a surprise visitor, an ex-colleague, Andy Hillman, who had been GBF's accountant when she had first joined. He had since moved on, to work for a chain of fashionable off-licences, but they had stayed in contact, meeting for the occasional drink. Lily had always found Andy's relaxed, loose-limbed style mildly attractive, but, being monogamous, had never explored the feeling. In any event, there had seemed to be no corresponding interest from his side. But they had laughed a lot together.

He had never before visited her at home, so it was quite a shock to find him on the doorstep early in the afternoon. How had he got her address, she wondered, at the sight of him, but in the rush of conversation forgot to ask.

'Hello, Lily. Is this a convenient moment? I heard about your break-up. I was passing and thought you might want some company.'

Lily had been sitting in the garden, contemplating Frank's herbaceous border and wondering what to do with it. When they bought the house it soon became apparent that while Lily's ideas of gardening might be modelled on Sissinghurst, Frank's aspired to something closer to Eden after the fall. So radically opposed were their tastes that the only solution was to divide the number of flowerbeds between them. This explained the garden's split personality. On the right-hand side could be found some semblance of order and colour harmony. Pinks and cornflowers were backed with roses and then hollyhocks and delphiniums. On the left was luxuriant disorder, a tangle of indigenous perennials left to seed themselves indiscriminately. Lily had always hated the thicket on Frank's side. Now she felt overwhelmed by the thought of taking responsibility for the jungle he had left behind.

She invited Andy to join her on the rug she had spread on the lawn and went in search of something to drink. When she returned with a carton of fruit juice, he was stretched out, stroking the cats. He looked at her hard as she dropped down opposite him, and she suddenly felt a little uncomfortable in her pony-tail, smudged cotton vest and shorts.

'So how is it going?' he asked.

'Everyone asks that,' she answered. 'I think it comes with a matching answer – either bloody awful, and then we do a lot of commiserating, or not too bad, and then we look on the bright side. I'm pretty bored with both.'

'I'm sorry. Unimaginative of me. Clive just mentioned your news in passing and I wanted to get in touch.' Clive had replaced Andy as GBF's chief accountant. 'Have you had lots of people telling you they've been there too, and survived?'

'Thousands.'

'Then I've absolutely nothing to contribute whatsoever.'

'Well, you could give me your account of getting dumped,' Lily said.

Andy took a deep breath. 'Most recently? Two years ago. The end of an eighteen-month affair. I was desolate. She wanted more fun – not my strong suit, apparently. I still dream about our sex life.'

'Did you find someone else?' Lily was not wholly disinterested.

'No. But I don't mind too much. I've gotten rather to like the single life. Except for when I get overwhelmingly horny.'

'I won't enquire what you do then.' Lily had a feeling Andy was indirectly sending her a message of platonic friendship.

'You'll find out for yourself, I dare say,' he replied.

Now she was sure. She turned over and started picking at the rug's fringe. 'So did Clive tell you the hot news at GBF?'

'That Margot's selling? Yup. But then I knew her birthday had come up in May so I wasn't surprised.'

Lily sat up and looked at him. 'What do you mean?'

'The Plan. Didn't you know about it? Well, no reason why you should really.'

'What plan?'

'Margot's grand strategy. She told me about it once, a Christmas party I think it was. Maybe she was a bit pissed. She said that GBF was the apple of her eye, but only ultimately stage one of The Plan, stage two being to sell it when she was sixty and move to New Mexico.'

'*What?*' Lily gaped at him.

'Albuquerque, apparently. She has this dream to live in an adobe, maybe dabble in a little Native Indian silver and turquoise jewellery as a sideline, but basically live in the desert, breathe dry air, no more winters.'

'She's a woman of infinite mystery,' Lily said, awed at the wildness of Margot's ambition as well as the chess strategy of her progress to achieve it. 'But I've seen nothing less like an adobe than her flat.'

Andy laughed. 'I went there too. Hideous or what? But that's just her chrysalis stage, apparently. In the desert she will emerge in her pared-down state – all polished stone and sculpted cactuses against the skyline. That's what she told me. I can actually see her with leathery brown skin and strange woven garments, can't you?'

On reflection, Lily could. Scarlet fingernails and gold sandals. Yes, she could see it all.

'But do you know anything about the prospective purchasers?'

'Not a thing myself, but I asked Clive the same riveting question. He was appropriately cagey but did drop a couple of veiled hints . . .'

'Yes? Come on, Andy, don't be such a bloody tease.'

'Well, have you heard of a man named Hugo Padmore?'

The name meant nothing to Lily and she said so.

'No reason why you should have, especially. He's not in your business. He's not in anybody's. Made a bit of money in computer software and has kept moving it around since. Touch of property development here, rag trade there. Hugo's one of those opportunists who'll invest anywhere he can see the prospect of a swift or fat return. Preferably both. He's a bit of a wide boy, really. I only know him because we were at LSE together. He's not a big player or anything. But he's always said he wanted GBF and never passed up an opportunity to sweet-talk Margot.'

'She has to be the last woman on earth susceptible to that treatment.'

'Ordinarily, yes, but Hugo might be just what she wants right now – he's cash rich and can move quickly. If she's talking to other players, they may not be so liquid or so impulsive. Of course, Hugo's price would reflect the advantages he offers, but even so . . .'

'So what's he like?'

'Hugo? Not my cup of tea, but he has his fans. He's the kind who likes to have fun and doesn't worry too much about the consequences.'

'He sounds a charmer.'

'Well, lots of your gender have found him so. Although I've never quite seen why. And that isn't sour grapes.'

'You mean he's pug ugly?'

'Not quite. But not Cary Grant either. You want a description? Owlish springs to mind – round face, curly hair. Body gone to seed a bit. Scruffy dresser. Every mother's roguish son. But each to their own. Anyway, if he does get GBF, hold on to your chair. One thing about Hugo, he cuts costs like a butcher slices bacon.'

Lily absorbed Andy's potted profile in silence. This Padmore sounded mildly dangerous, not at a personal level – she felt immune – but where she could really get hurt, in the pay-packet. Still, if he didn't know jewellery, surely he wouldn't want to be rid of his buyer? She decided not to worry for the moment; plenty of time for that later.

'What about the other possibility?'

'A chain, forgive the pun, and a mid-market one at that. They fancy adding a touch of class. They'd pay more, I imagine, but the wheels would grind slower.'

Lily considered GBF's absorption into an organization already well staffed with buyers. Seemed like a choice between frying pan and fire.

'So what are your plans for the evening?' Andy interrupted her thoughts.

'Plans?'

'Yeah, you know, the weekend starts here and all that. Are you going up-town, top-ranking?' His attempts at modernspeak dropped clumsily from his tongue.

'Grow up, Andy. I'm thirty-six.'

'So what. You're single and solvent. Where shall we go?'

Andy was deaf to Lily's increasingly clearly stated preference for an afternoon in the garden and an evening of couch-potato-ship. Being a stubborn man, convinced of the rightness of his mission, there could be no peace until Lily confessed her fears of returning to the empty house at night. And after she had, he was obdurate. They were to leave immediately, and not return until late. Lily took some mild comfort from being taken in hand in this way. She felt

49

she could trust Andy to help her over this hurdle. After all, someone was going to have to, or else she would turn into a kind of Looking-Glass Dracula, never to be seen out after sunset. So she went and changed into clean jeans and a cropped T-shirt, and dragged a brush through her hair. Then they went round the house together, checking rooms and leaving random lights on, even though the summer sunlight was still at full strength. Andy urged her not to worry too much about the electricity bill just at the moment.

He watched Lily lock all the doors and then frogmarched her to his car. 'How about some culture?' he suggested, as she snapped her seatbelt in place.

'High or low?'

'You choose.' They settled on a film at the cinema across the Common, an action movie of infantile though state-of-the-art pyrotechnics. It contained much celluloid violence but was utterly unbelievable, with no real consequences, and gave them something to tear to pieces together over a pizza afterwards. Then Andy drove Lily home.

'Would you like me to come in with you?'

Lily knew this was not a euphemism. But she decided to decline. This was one of those 'firsts' and her instincts told her that she would progress further faster if she faced up to it.

She kissed Andy on the cheek. 'I'll be fine.' Here she was, rising to her father's challenge again. She wasn't sure she meant it, although she knew it was what she was supposed to say. 'But could you sit out here for a minute, just to check I don't appear screaming at an upstairs window?'

'Of course.'

'And thanks for being a bully. I did need to be hauled out of the house by my hair, I'm sure of it.'

He smiled. 'You take care of yourself. Ring me if you need me. And let me know if you come across Hugo.'

She got out of the car, braced herself and made a big display of opening the front door noisily. Palmer was sitting like a sphinx in the hall, the model of feline reassurance. Clearly there were no marauders at home, but Lily checked round carefully anyway. She ended in the bedroom, and waved to Andy who waved back and drove away. This left her feeling abandoned again. Don't think about any of it, she instructed herself, but couldn't resist a mental genuflection in Andy's direction for pulling her back into the world, including the quagmire of heterosexuality. Here she was, at the start of a new phase of an old life: socializing, chatting up, fancying and not, being rejected – and not. Under the smothering duvet of relationship fatigue, generalized anxiety and post-Frank depression, she could feel a whisper of a flicker of excitement. The Kraken wakes.

Chapter 7

Lily had not seen her parents since May. She dreaded the thought of them coming on a rescue-mission visit, still able to remember the withering embarrassment of the food parcels they had delivered to her at college. But she was committed to seeing them soon, and, waking not too late on Sunday, decided to take the plunge and go to them. She phoned to see if the house was empty of visitors, then agreed to be met off the one o'clock train. This would allow just enough time for a late lunch but not too much for the inevitable ensuing family conference. She would catch the six thirty back.

At the station, a burst of indulgence led her to upgrade to the first-class weekend saver carriage. An extra £6 seemed a bargain for a plush, wide seat and the filtered air of superior travel. As the train wound its way north, through suburbs, new towns and finally the sun-baked fields, she began to ponder her mother and the secret personality she had encountered on the phone, encouraging her to unheard-of pragmatism. Wasn't that exactly what Margot had been talking about – the split self? A doormat with attitude. Do as I say, not as I do.

Lily still felt shocked at glimpsing the hidden, other side of her mother. She had spent her childhood in the company of the domestic Edna Braithwaite, helpmate to Alec, mother to Lily, martyr and provincial Cassandra, not an iconoclast or radical. Of course, according to Margot, Edna would never have been those things at home, but as she had no other life, no job, she had no outlet for her stronger, more forthright self either. Yet if the split were there – as the phone call proved – was that the source of Lily's own recently exposed double standard?

Lily knew, as every woman knows, that her adult life was an imperceptible progress down the path to physical replication of her mother. She knew her own smell was subtly shifting into her mother's, the fruity tones subsuming into something earthier, darker. She noticed moles appearing on her back like her mother had. The way the skin around her eyes and on her neck was loosening was similar. Perhaps, if she were lucky, she would develop the deeper eye-sockets, but avoid the arthritic fingers. Certainly her own sprinkling of white hairs looked as glossy yet springy as her mother's still mercifully dense cap of curls.

However, that was the body, the flesh extension. Why shouldn't it revert after some years? Domesticated plants often did. An entirely natural process. But what about behaviour? Did that slowly slide and merge too, perhaps while you slept or your consciousness was looking the other way? No, not acceptable, she knew. After all, she had a brain and free will, didn't she?

As a teenager, Lily had been as condescending towards her parents as any of her school friends. None of their mothers had serious jobs, although plenty worked part-time in shops and building societies. To Lily and her peers, these were not role models. They set their sights on the metropolis, media jobs, boardrooms and company cars. Their mothers' husband-bound horizons were mocked, along with their chainstore clothes and limited sexual experience. These girls pitied women who were strangers to the notion of equality, who were wearing engagement rings before the sexual revolution had been invented.

Not for Lily's generation the resignation and consciously inferior status of their mothers. They would have an equal say, share the decisions with their men, be as direct and free. Lily had aspired to all of that, and had achieved the job and the wardrobe. At one level she even thought she had the relationship. At another she knew she had made a different choice. So what did that make her?

Hypocrite was not a comfortable label. She bought a cup of sham coffee from the passing trolley – it seemed appropriate. Right colour, right temperature, wrong flavour. Was that true of her life with Frank? Well, yes and no. She had not entered into the relationship on a fraudulent basis. She had not two-timed herself or Frank for all those years, or lived a lie. But all the same, she had always known that at the centre, in that dark eye of truth within her common-law marriage, there was a gap in her scrupulousness towards herself and her partner.

Pretending she liked country walking when she did not was not an awful sin; all part of the seduction process, she still reckoned. But pretending to herself that she fought Frank for the relationship she wanted was patently untrue. And pretending to herself that they cared enough for each other to validate the whole exercise was another whopper, if she would but admit it.

At some point – early? late? – she had exchanged honest scrutiny for what she imagined would be comfortable permanence. She had opted for a kind of relationship pension, but had taken out her emotional life insurance with Lloyd's.

Why had she closed down? Why had the certain knowledge of coupledom asphyxiated, like algae, all the living, breathing bits of a modern partnership, like good sex, real communication and a truthful conscience?

She drank the cool coffee, eyed the disturbing black grit in the last mouthful and reached for the Sunday paper in her bag. She was faintly nauseated by the feelings of guilt and disgust she now seemed to have about everyone – Frank, her mother, but principally herself. Some time in the last ten years, she had transmuted from the woman she had wanted to be into one of the silent internalizers, the mole wives.

She turned to the style pages, eyes alert as ever for GBF accessories, and decided to draw a line under her dark musings. Nobody's fault, she kept telling herself. But she was not convinced.

Her father was waiting in the car, engine idling, as Lily emerged from the station. Semi-retired now, he had become one of those aliens visible daily in supermarkets throughout the land – early sixties man in leisurewear with not enough to do. Alec Braithwaite had not quite descended to Marks & Spencer tracksuits and Velcro-fastened trainers, but his two-tone pastel windbreak and pale grey loafers worried Lily, as did his expanding waistline.

'Hello, love.' He leaned over to kiss her as she settled in the front seat. 'Good to see you.'

Whatever was to be mistrusted in the turning world, Lily knew she could fall back on the unswerving adoration of her father. Like St Peter's rock, his love was gritty and immovable. Never interested in boy children, or more than a single offspring, he had been completely satisfied with his long-awaited daughter. More than that, she had lived up to his aesthetic and intellectual heights, such as they were: she had long shining hair, which he loved; she shared his passion for jewellery, as well (in teenage years, at least) as for Beethoven and Dennis Wheatley novels. Edna, wife and partner though she was, took no interest in these last three, and as a result Lily's opinion was often consulted first and ranked higher.

It was not suprising then that mother/daughter tension was a feature of the household, although in the late years, before Lily left home for her business studies course, a female camaraderie had sprung up, perhaps because Edna knew the end was in sight. Their late-flowering sisterliness had slightly rocked the matched pedestals on which Alec and Lily had set one another, but once Lily had left and become an adult, the triangle had somehow reverted. Lily swooped in for her brief visits, her father gave her his undivided attention and her mother took the back seat – literally, if the three were ever in the car together.

None of her boyfriends had been good enough for him and Lily was used to his silent disapproval in this one area, whereas her mother, unsurprisingly, had tried valiantly to befriend them all. Even when Frank had invented the unsubtly malicious practice of presenting Lily's parents with large, spiny cacti for Christmas presents, Edna had tried to make a display out of them on the bathroom windowsill.

But how would Alec deal with his quiet satisfaction now? Lily wondered. Tactfully, as it turned out. As he drove her through the impoverished streets of the town, towards the middle-class housing estate where Lily had grown up, he asked only about work and her state of health.

'I'm fine, Dad, honestly.'

'You've never looked skinnier.'

'Yes I have – remember that tummy bug we all caught in Tunisia?'

He smiled. 'I'll never forget it. Three of us under a palm tree and not one with the strength to swipe a mosquito.' He negotiated a roundabout. 'Now you're not to worry about the job. I'm sure everything will settle down – like you said, any new owner would be mad to get rid of the person who brings in top-selling products. But anyway, you know that if you ever have any money worries, you've only to ask.'

'Yes, Dad,' she replied, knowing that this was the last thing she would ever do.

He pulled into the drive and Lily glimpsed through the kitchen window her mother standing by the cooker, poking into a pot with a fork. She felt an eddy of irritation run through her as she got out of the car and opened the back door. But hot air caught her in the face, and the combined scents of roast meat and boiling vegetables flung her back into childhood. Was that *Two-Way Family Favourites* on the radio? No, it was *The World at One* burbling in the background, but the Sheffield plate cutlery, the willow pattern plates, the food itself were unchanged. She could shut her eyes and be eight again.

She opened her eyes wide. Today of all days, infantilism was to be rejected. She bent to kiss her mother's flushed cheek. Edna was short while Lily had inherited a taller, rangier frame from her father.

'It'll be ready in five minutes. Would you like to wash your hands, Lily?' Edna asked, formally.

The good daughter trudged obligingly upstairs to the bathroom. All was irksomely familiar, the Imperial Leather soap, her father's flannel drying on the bath taps. On a shelf over the basin sat her mother's engagement and eternity rings, the former a recent replacement for the modest diamond chip Alec had bought her in the early 1950s. Edna wore them to go out or when entertaining. Otherwise she preferred the simplicity of her plain, worn gold band. Lily was pondering the symbolism of this when called by her mother to table.

In honour of the prodigal's return, they were eating in the dining room. Lily sat down next to her mother and contemplated a plate heaped with lamb, new potatoes, peas, cauliflower and gravy. Her mother passed her a small china dish.

'Mint sauce, dear?'

'Thanks.' She put a spoonful on the lip of her plate, then passed it on to her father. Mother came last.

There was a silence. No one seemed to know their way into the conversation. Lily ate a forkful of meat, then complimented her mother on its flavour.

'Good old Cheadle's,' Edna answered, happier to pass the compliment on to the butcher.

'Garden's looking good, Dad,' Lily continued gamely, after another silence.

'Yes. It's been quite a summer for the roses. How's your garden looking?' he pursued, as politely as a stranger.

'Pretty parched,' answered Lily. 'I've not been watering like I should and now there's twice as much to do anyway . . .' At last the phantom of Frank had crept into the room.

'Would you like me to come down one weekend and give you a hand?' Alec had never stopped, for the last ten years, offering himself as a substitute handyman. It was an area in which Frank had displayed neither expertise nor enthusiasm, yet he had guarded it jealously, fearing his masculinity was in question.

'That's kind, Dad. Maybe later, when things need pruning, you could bring the big secateurs?'

Her father's eyes lit up at the prospect.

Lily's mother laid down her cutlery. 'Do you think you'll be able to manage that big house on your own? All that cleaning, as well as the garden.'

'I'll have to.' Lily was not, in fact, too worried about the cleaning.

'Well, if you ever want to do a spring-clean, you know, give the place a real bottoming, I could always come down with your father.' Lily shuddered at the thought, her mother looking into every cupboard, rearranging her books, CDs, pots and pans, taking mental notes on her private life.

'Thanks, Mum,' she replied vaguely.

They finished their meat and vegetables, and Lily stacked the plates while her mother went to fetch pudding. She reappeared with a tray bearing a gooseberry pie and a jug of custard. Having served everyone, she passed Lily the jug and a spoon. In the Braithwaite household custard came thick, the way Alec liked it. It had been the still point around which Sunday pudding revolved for as long as Lily could remember. She spooned some out – it was as solid as jelly – and noticed that the quivering lemon-coloured mousse was peppered with brown flecks.

'Burnt custard, Mum? That's not like you,' she observed with a smile.

Edna pursed her lips.

'Is that what all the effing and blinding was about?' Lily's father asked, quite gently.

'Stop it, both of you,' Edna snapped, angrily brushing away their fond mockery. 'The phone rang just as it came to the boil. Anyway, it's not so bad. And you can leave the bits if they really bother you.'

Her exasperation was a common enough phenomenon, but Lily, with her transformed vision, wondered now at her mother's short fuse. Had she always been irritable, or had it grown to match her father's domineering placidity – chicken or egg? It was obviously one of her safety valves, along with the self-pity which cropped up periodically. Now Lily saw these behavioural tics as subversions for Edna's stifled nature. She both pitied and was annoyed by them. But then she realized she must have such a repertoire too. What were hers? Tears, certainly. Frank had nicknamed her the Gusher. But in the early years her weeping had softened Frank, led him to console her, allowed her to give voice, softly and sobbing admittedly, to whatever was amiss. Latterly he had just left her to cry.

What else? Well, unlike her mother, she favoured the silent option. Lily's withdrawals at times of stress were a kind of adult come-and-get-me. Frank was shrewd enough to see through them, and to avoid a reliable response.

59

Sometimes he had come, others not. But Lily still felt there was greater dignity in eloquent, wide-eyed silence than in her mother's ragged snarls.

There was silence over the pudding. Melting and juicily tart though the pie was, Lily and her father knew better than to comment. Edna, when in this kind of abraded state, was best left.

Lily wondered petulantly at the timing of her mother's mood. She was the wounded one, wasn't she? But there was something else; she felt something new and more lofty towards her mother. Edna was a sad woman, whose flashes of revelation were rare and possibly self-deceiving. She had lived too much of her adult life in the shadow of her marriage. Her feistier self had probably all but atrophied by now.

Even if Lily were forced to acknowledge that she had taken on board some of her mother's ways, she could see the overlap was not total. Some of the mistakes were her very own. And, to the extent that she had put up and shut up, like Edna, well at least, blessedly or not, she had both woken up to that behaviour and been released from it. Edna's was a lifetime's servitude.

The dishes were left for later. All three moved outside to the patio with its reclining chairs and sunshade. The garden was a picture of English suburbia in high summer: the hedges shaved to geometric precision, the borders buzzing with lethargic bees binging on marguerites, nicotiana and the many roses. The lawn, mown in hypnotic stripes, gleamed a near-cosmetic green. Birds visited the rustic bird table. From surrounding gardens could be heard the play of hoses, the hum of distant strimmers.

This was the moment Lily had been dreading. The reckoning. Her father cleared his throat.

'Now, Lily, if it won't upset you too much, we thought we should just take stock. See how the land lies. We've not

60

told anyone about your . . . well, you know . . . about Frank.'

'It's not a secret, Dad.'

'No, but we wanted to talk to you first. After all, it might be a temporary thing. A trial separation, is it called? Plenty of couples have divorced and then got married again.'

Edna looked at Lily but said nothing.

'No, Dad, that isn't going to happen. Frank's gone and I'm buying out his share in the house.'

'Can you afford it?' Lily had always been irritated by her mother's crude interest in her income and as a result remained secretive about it.

'It'll be a squeeze, but I think so. And worst-case scenario is letting a room, although I'd rather not.'

'What about splitting up the furniture?' her father enquired.

Lily glimpsed him taking his axe to the dining table. 'I don't think that's going to be a terrible problem. Frank was never difficult about money or material things. And he doesn't seem to be in any hurry.' Presumably Anna of Bromley came with all fixtures and fittings.

In fact Lily had heard nothing from Frank since his visit. They had clarified then how to proceed on the house and she had dissolved their joint account, sending a cheque for his half of the balance to his office, with no accompanying note. Presumably there would need to be another meeting to agree custody of the vegetable steamer and other domestic items. Lily was in no rush for this. She both ached to see Frank and would be happy if he'd been vaporized.

'Well, you make sure you stand firm. Don't let him get away with anything.' This was her father, reverting to his standpoint on Frank – a villain as slippery as a Vaselined eel. Her mother was nodding vigorously.

'It's not like that,' Lily protested.

'It is from where we're sitting. You've always let him get away with too much. Well, hold on to the goods and chattels.'

'What do you mean?' Lily was stung. What was this conspiracy of silence, now lifted, about her being Frank's pushover partner?

'I remember when you came here one Christmas,' her father harked back. 'He let you carry the cases out to the car. I've never forgotten it.'

Lily smiled. This venial sin encapsulated all her father's disgust for Frank. They were on familiar terrain after all. Her parents' strict adherence to a gender-based division of labour was a well-worn source of friction. She knew what was coming next.

'You should have made him behave like a gentleman. If you'd been more like a proper wife, done more at home –' This was her mother, waspishly.

'Don't, Mum. I really don't want to hear you tell me again that I should have washed Frank's shirts and cooked his supper.'

'I know you don't think my opinions count for anything, but I could see this coming. No man likes to come home to a bare table.'

'This isn't the time to lay blame on Lily,' her father reproved Edna. Lily sat in the warm glow of his protection. 'She has her faults' – he smiled indulgently at her – 'but Frank's carrying-on can't be laid at her door.'

There was silence all round.

'Shall I do the dishes?' Lily offered, wanting to move away from the question of fault, wanting the inquisition to come to an end.

'I'll wash, you can wipe.' Edna liked to retain command of the hot tap and pan-scrub.

Alec felt no pressure to join the women and reached for the *Mail on Sunday*.

Lily and her mother transferred the plates and glasses from the dining room to the kitchen in silence, making many short trips during which they passed and repassed each other but did not speak. Lily returned the Sunday-best silver cruet set to its place on the oak Welsh dresser and took the tablecloth out to the patio, to shake off crumbs, before folding it. Her father was asleep in his chair, the paper slipping on to the stone flags. She picked it up, folded it and tucked it next to him.

Back in the kitchen, her mother stood at the sink, her back expressive of resignation and some residual anger. Lily was not inclined to apologize but the opportunity to ask her mother about their phone conversation was irresistible.

'Mum, when you rang me last week, what was it you were referring to – the thing that happened early on, that you made a decision about?'

'What?' Edna asked with a frown. It was as if it had never happened.

'You know, something in your marriage – when you had to be clear-headed.'

'I don't know what you're talking about.' Wrong moment, Lily saw. Her mother was too reflexively angered by the usual split – Alec and Lily in one corner, she in the other – to want to reach out to her daughter as an equal. 'Anyway, it sounds like you've made all your decisions about Frank without consulting me. I only get my head bitten off if I say anything.'

With this, Joan of Arc turned her face back to the flames – or in Edna's case the custard pan, with its heavy overlay of brown crust – and set to with her Brillo pad.

The rest of the afternoon passed quickly. There was just time for a tour of the greenhouse and a cup of tea, and then Alec backed the car out of the drive while Lily kissed her mother's slightly averted cheek. She felt the familiar mix of guilt, hurt and detachment in the face of her mother's equally familiar discomfort. Most of all Lily wished that the obstacles might have been cleared away on this day at least, and that family squabbles had not got in the way of the wounded daughter's return to the family bosom. An instant's fear flashed through her as she imagined what kind of reckoning there would be between herself and her mother if her father were no longer there both to protect her and simultaneously deepen the rift. But he was hooting the car horn and she had better grab her jacket and bag.

'Lily,' her mother called.

She paused at the back door.

'Look after yourself,' Edna said with a watery smile.

Lily felt a little tearful. She turned back and hugged her mother. It had always been like this. An uncomfortable love, caring in so many tangible ways, but full of conflict too. But now, when there was a softening and a chance to make contact, there was no more time. Lily smiled ruefully at Edna and ran out to the car.

Chapter 8

There followed a couple of weeks of relative calm, in which the alterations in Lily's routine began to seem less obvious. Work lent a thread of continuity. Nothing in the office had changed as a result of her return to single status and no one made reference to it. Margot, when seen, which was rarely, confined herself to business matters only.

At home, Lily decreasingly noticed that Frank's donkey jacket no longer hung in the hall, or that shopping consisted more of vegetables and brown bread than haunches of meat and packets of fig biscuits. She was free to watch all the soaps and none of the sport. She could go to bed as early as she liked, although there was little delight here since sleep was still a recalcitrant visitor. The cats' basket had been moved from the landing to the bedroom; when the summer nights were too hot for them to sleep on the bed with her, she was comforted to hear the wicker creaking as they blindly wound round each other.

These were reluctant and minor pleasures, but she forced herself to acknowledge them in an attempt to look for the silver lining. The cloud of her depression was still stationary overhead, and although she felt she was moving – or being moved – on, Lily was in truth very miserable.

'Do you think I should put an ad in the lonely hearts column?' she asked Dorothy who had come round for a mid-week drink.

'Are you ready for a new man?'

'Do you think that's what I'd get, someone into knitting and aromatherapy?'

Dot snorted. 'I met him. Russell I think his name was. He brought his embroidery along to our first meet.'

Dorothy was a long-term dabbler in the black arts of lonely hearts copy, being permanently in search of a full-time relationship to replace the part-time affair she had been engaged in for three years with an ex-colleague, a married editor named Peter. Peter, delighted to have his cake and eat it too, took up just enough of Dorothy's life to spoil her appetite for something bigger and more whole. So, reflexively, she would advertise for a single man, but when the letters arrived and the vetting process began, she was never quite hungry enough to take the plunge with an untried substitute. Lily had counselled her often enough about not wasting the best years of her sex life, and encouraged her to join couples' world full-time. 'Look how happy Frank and I are . . .' But privately she thought her friend didn't want to share all her space any more, and was happy for the messy, relationship bit to be neatly confined to two evenings a week. Sometimes now Lily even wondered if such a solution would suit her too.

'Or maybe I should go to one of those dating agencies. You know, one of the executive ones.'

'For old lags with fat wallets, you mean.'

'Is that how you think of me?'

Dorothy protested but in fact a gap had grown between the friends' incomes since she had lost her job, and their shopping trips and social outings reflected her need to be watchful where once she had spent freely.

'They're bloody expensive, you know,' she commented.

Lily did not know, had never previously needed to enquire.

'Yeah, I called one once – the one for arty types – after there was a piece in the paper. Clutching at the Stars or something. Lots of hundreds of pounds it cost, and of course they had plenty more women than men on their

66

books. Wanted to interview me and take my photo before they'd decide whether to accept me. Sounded too much like Miss World for my liking. And clearly they hoovered up *any* man, no matter how scrofulous, to make up the numbers.'

This was slightly more than idle conversation on Lily's part. Bruised and exhausted though she was, she also wondered how and where she would ever meet another prospective mate. Her job generated limited social contact and on the whole reps for jewellery wholesalers did not live up to her ideals of brains and beauty. Meeting men had not been a piece of cake ten years ago. She had regarded herself as blessed for falling into conversation with Frank at her local arts centre, which turned out to double as canteen for the Social Services office across the road. More recently, she could count the numbers of interesting new men she had met on the fingers of one fist.

It was the morning after this conversation with Dorothy, with fantasies of her ad – Abandoned paragon seeks replacement cad – running through her brain, that she arrived in the office to find a xeroxed note on her desk: 'GBF meeting, boardroom, 12.00.'

Monica was huddled in a group with David from Marketing, Alice, the blonde accountant, and her opposite number, Sanjay. Even Tom was there, in his overalls, like a stoker up from the engine room. Lily went to joint them. They were all holding their xeroxed notes.

'This is it, then?' Lily asked.

'Well, I don't think it's one of her quarterly updates. Wrong month for a start,' said Monica. Margot normally gave addresses to her staff on a three-monthly basis, part of the information cascade as she referred to it, in other words a one-way flow.

'No, it's the big one,' Sanjay observed in his quiet accountant's voice. 'Clive's been with her practically nonstop since Monday. He's been the soul of discretion, as usual, but they've had at least three meetings outside the building and he's taken all kinds of files with him.'

'How did he seem?' asked David.

Alice, who was economical with her words, replied, 'Calm. Like someone who knows it's useless to struggle.'

There was a half-hearted pretence at work for the next few hours, but knots of employees formed and dissolved around the place like blood clots responding to a sluggish heartbeat. Lily felt jittery, for which the best treatment seemed to be a thorough spring-clean of her desk drawers followed by a few hands of Solitaire on her computer.

At 11.55 the staff, nearly a hundred of them, were fully assembled in the large, scuffed room looking on to the lobster brickwork of the Prudential Building. There was an unnatural hush among the men and women perched on windowsills, sharing the formal chairs, leaning against the walls. Lily sat next to Alice whose freckles appeared all the darker against the paleness of her serious face. On the dot of twelve, Margot opened the double doors which gave direct access from her own office and approached the top of the table. She was wearing a distracting emerald, yellow and navy patterned silk dress and for once was without a lit cigarette, although pack and lighter were in her hand.

Behind her followed a man in his early forties with a broad frame and a barrel chest. Lily thought he looked as if he had been pulled through a hedge backwards. His tie was loosely knotted, his shirt seemed unironed, his suit jacket hung askew. He had brown curly hair and a letter-box mouth. It had to be Hugo Padmore.

Margot was her usual cast-iron self. 'I won't procrastinate. I know you have heard about my decision to sell Girl's Best Friend. This has not been an easy step to take, even though it was entirely of my own volition, planning, as I am, to move abroad. I'm very pleased to tell you that I have successfully concluded a deal with Hugo Padmore' – here she glanced at her companion, who had been examining his fingernails but now looked round the room and smiled wolfishly – 'who will be taking over GBF from the 1st of September.'

She paused. Were they expected to applaud? No one moved a muscle.

'Hugo is going to say a few words, but before he does, let me explain that he will start work here from next Monday, so that we can overlap for a few weeks. I will quit formally at the end of August.

'Hugo will speak for himself, but I have his assurance that he has only positive plans for the business and therefore the people who comprise its success. I would not have been able to entrust my life's work to anyone who would not nourish it and help it grow.

'I have loved every minute of my work here, with you.' Margot paused. Was that a drop of excess moisture gleaming in her eye? No, just the way the sun was reflecting on it from a nearby window, Lily decided with enormous relief. 'You have been an ideal team and I want to thank each and every one of you for your contribution. There will be plenty of time in the coming weeks for more thanks and maudlin reflection, but that's it for now. Over to you, Hugo.'

Classic Margot, not a wasted word. Now the new owner stepped forward. Still the room was one indrawn breath.

'You must all be feeling apprehensive,' he said in a surprisingly deep voice. 'I would be if I were you. Well, there's no need. I bought this business because I respect it, and you as the professionals who make it happen.

'I'm the new boy here. I know nothing about jewellery except what I've learned from Margot in recent weeks. I want to understand the whole process, which will give me a great opportunity to get to know you all individually.

'Changes may come over time, I'm not ruling that out. But if they do, they'll only be for the better, for all of us. You'll find me a fairly relaxed kind of boss, but I have three guiding principles: I believe in hard work, I believe in making money, but above all I believe that work should be fun. Let's hope we achieve all three. Thank you.'

How would they ever escape from this room? It was like a *tableau vivant*, Margot and Hugo standing facing their audience, the people around frozen in attitudes of doubt, puzzlement, sadness, indifference, cynicism.

Thankfully, Mark, the sales manager, finally opened a side door and the staff drifted out. Margot and Hugo both lit cigarettes and returned to the inner sanctum. Conversation began as a low buzz, but rose to a crescendo as more people filled the corridor. Lily, disinclined to chat, heard snatches of phrases as she threaded her way through her colleagues. Opinions veered from hope to instant dislike. She had kept Andy's description of their new MD to herself and there seemed little point in sharing it now. She would wait and see. She had no choice.

Hugo Padmore breezed into GBF the following Monday as if he had worked there all his life. Not a shred of self-doubt was visible under his bluff *bonhomie*. He arrived in the company without a single ally or imported cohort, and so stood alone in a sea of sceptical new employees. But it was as if he welcomed the task of winning them over, individually and *en masse*. Margot did not walk him round the offices: he chose to do that on his own, appearing in people's doorways, peering at papers on their desks, fingering items of stock. He seemed unafraid of asking basic questions, but underneath the naïvety, a brain of some vivacity could be detected.

Monica had already encountered him in the kitchen, making himself a drink. She reported this sighting to Lily, commenting favourably on an owner who would deign to spoon out his own Nescafé. Lily privately wondered how far Hugo would go to ingratiate himself in such small yet significant ways, but then criticized herself for her suspicious nature.

She was on the phone to one of her regular suppliers, Jimmy Khan, with whom she had a boisterously irreverent relationship, when Hugo materialized in her office. Together, Lily and Jimmy had been riding the wave of New Age jewellery for some time, and were currently trading a combination of rings, thong necklaces and pendants featuring crystals and runic symbols in stones and metal.

'You'll love these rings,' he was telling her. 'They're Indian, solid silver shanks with big faceted stones, deep set, no claws.'

'And they drop out at the slightest tap, I suppose.'

'Rock solid, ha ha. No, I promise you. I'll take any back if you get complaints. Let me send over a sample range. The aquamarines will knock your eyes out.'

'Enough with the patter, Jimmy. I'll see for myself. Send the blues and pinks. Not the greens.'

'They're on their way. Call me when you've got your powers of speech back.'

She grunted, put the phone down and looked up to see Hugo leaning against the doorjamb, smoking. Well, at least he had something in common with Margot, she thought, waiting for him to open the conversation.

'You must be Lily Braithwaite,' he said, without reference to notes.

'Yes, that's right. Hello.' She stood up and extended her hand which, after an instant, he shook firmly. 'Do sit down.'

He pulled up a chair rather close to her desk and lolled in it.

'So you're the one person with taste in this organization, as I've been told.'

Lily smiled, a little embarrassed. 'Do you like the GBF range?' she countered.

'I love it,' he said, so quickly that she had no idea if he meant a single word. 'I must have bought my wife at least half of it.'

Ah, Lily noted.

'Anything recently?' she enquired. 'Or, I mean, since I've been buying.'

'Don't worry, I didn't think you were asking how often I bought my wife presents.' He was watching her steadily. 'But I did get some earrings at Christmas. Dark red with lots of gold twiddly bits. Was that you?'

'Oh yes. One of my favourites.' This was a white lie. Lily had not personally liked the range, too obvious for her preference, but now was not the time to say so. They had sold quite well. 'The Baroque, they were called. Spanish, I think. The manufacturer went bust, unfortunately.'

'Why no greens?'

'Sorry?'

'Your phone conversation – blues and pinks but no greens.'

'Oh. Basic customer superstition. People don't buy green jewellery.'

'Really?' A beat. 'And when will I be able to have a look at your purchasing records?'

She noted his switch of speed, from genial chat to no-messing demands. 'As soon as you like. I can print out whatever you want – scheduled deliveries, goods against budget, whole-year commitment, breakdowns of any of those.'

'Let's start with commitments for this year and next,' he replied. 'I'm going to be based in the office next door but

72

one until Margot leaves, so why don't you leave them on my desk?'

'Of course.' So she was going to have the sharklike Hugo cruising in her vicinity for a few weeks. Well, that would keep her on her mettle.

Hugo's unpredictability became a recognized pattern over the following days – his ability to disconcert by shifts of conversational gear, his informal manner scarcely concealing his hungry application to the learning curve. The general opinion was cautious optimism. One or two senior people seemed to be being favoured with a greater frequency of drop-in visits: Mark in Sales and Clive in Accounts could often be seen in his company, and on a couple of occasions were spotted drinking with him in the Jupiter after work. Not something Margot would ever have done, Monica reported darkly.

Lily had left Hugo the paperwork as requested, and when he came back with queries, she patiently talked him through her systems. He picked things up quickly and was not shy to suggest improvements: altered payment structures to improve cash flow; more aggressive discounting. It was clear that his strengths were financial. When it came to the goods, he had the selectivity of a locust. He sat in on a couple of Lily's meetings with reps presenting new ranges, and although he had the grace to keep quiet while she examined the samples, afterwards was heartily enthusiastic about items which Lily had rejected from the outset.

'What about those bracelets?'

'Bangles.'

'Yes, those, the carved bone ones.'

'Plastic.'

'It looked like bone. And tortoiseshell.'

'Hugo, they were horrible. Cheap isn't always bad, but those were simply tacky. Our customers want goods that

73

either look like a million dollars or revel in their irony. Or are just too fashionable to miss. Anything else is a mistake.'

He was not offended by her rebuke. Perhaps it was a test. Instead he grinned like a schoolboy and stretched in his chair. 'Okay, you win. This time, anyway. But when we go to one of these fairs, you're going to have to indulge me in one small bit of buying. Boss's perks.' He yawned. 'End of a long day. So what will you be doing this evening?'

Lily considered the question. Retiring to the sofa with the TV guide and a bowl of frozen yoghurt was the truth. 'Having a meal with a friend,' she fibbed. 'And you?'

Hugo looked at his watch. 'I'll probably get the seven thirty train, home by nine, a good bottle of wine, feet up, nothing too strenuous.'

'Serious commuting must be pretty exhausting,' Lily commiserated. Hugo, it had emerged, lived in rural Essex with his wife and three daughters.

'Oh, it's not so bad in first class, with a taxi at this end and the car at the other. I don't believe in short-changing myself on life's little luxuries.' He ran his fingers through his already-rumpled hair and got up. 'Okay, see you tomorrow.' And he ambled away, shirt-tails hanging out.

But Lily's evening was not quite as uneventful as she expected. When she got home, her key would not open the front door. Confused, she tried again and again, simultaneously checking that the mortise was open. Peculiarly, it seemed as if the catch were down, locking the Yale in place, but how could that be?

Lily's stomach dived to her boots. The explanation was obvious. Someone had been – maybe still was? – in the house. Trembling, she went next door and asked her neighbour, an inoffensive pensioner named Ron, if she could gain access to the back of her house via his garden. Clambering over the fence, she could think only of the cats.

Were they safe? Would anyone harm them? For her property she cared not a fig.

Ron passed her a hammer and stood watching while she peered through the kitchen window. Sure enough, there were signs of disturbance. A pretty tin box in which she kept odd recipes was upturned on the table. Cupboard doors hung ajar. Worst of all, the cat flap had been kicked in two. Too panicked to think of trying the back door, she swung the hammer hard against the plate glass of the kitchen window. To her astonishment, it bounced straight off. Averting her face, she swung harder, and on the third try broke through. Forgetting to wrap her fingers in anything, she tried to clear away the glass, to reach the window-catch, and succeeded in slicing open her knuckle. Heedless of pain and danger, she unlatched the window and climbed in.

There was no one inside, thank the Lord, but her home now resembled a set from *The Bill*. A trail of disarray had been laid from room to room. At a cursory glance, Lily noticed the absence of ornaments, bottles of wine, a picture, electrical goods. The Indian bedspread from the spare room had gone, presumably to carry away the swag. But her one thought was for Huntley and Palmer. Frantically, she called them, running from room to room, then up the stairs. In her bedroom, from which a Venetian mirror and her jewellery box were now absent, she knelt down and peered under the bed. Thank God. There, among the balls of fluff and dusty suitcases, huddled two black shadows. She knew, from when she tried to catch them for trips to the vet, that cats could magically reduce themselves to half their body sizes and fit into minuscule corners. For once she was glad of the talent. Either the intruders had looked into this space before Huntley and Palmer took refuge, or had not seen them curled in the darkest spots, behind the bed-legs.

But Lily could see her own fear mirrored in their yellow eyes. Gently she reached out a hand to them and eventually they sniffed it and acknowledged her. She did not try to extract them. They would emerge when they were ready. She was also too overwhelmed with relief to do anything now but sit on the bedroom floor and let the hot tears course down her face.

The hours of the evening flew by at an incomprehensible speed. By the time the police had been, and Dorothy, and a list of missing items drawn up, the house fingerprinted, an emergency glazier summoned to replace the missing pane, Lily's hand bandaged and stiff drinks drunk, it was after one o'clock.

Lily was once more in shock. It was not so much the thought of intruders riffling through her possessions. That had happened at college once and, distasteful though it was, could be endured. No, it was that her safe haven, her impenetrable stronghold had been violated. The police informed her that hers was the second house to have been burgled in the terrace that day. The thieves had slipped the lock at number 32, walked through the house and out of the back door, climbed over the garden fences to reach hers, gained access by reaching up via the cat flap to unlock the door, come in, locked the front door to protect themselves, robbed her, dragged their plunder back to 32, stripped that house too and then probably driven away. No one had seen anything. The likelihood was that her house had been picked at random, but there was no way of being sure.

So all her assumptions about the safety of the enclosed gardens were shattered. She was encouraged to invite the crime prevention officer over as soon as possible, who would advise on securing windows and fitting a burglar alarm. Meanwhile she should change the locks, since a number of keys seemed to have gone missing.

Lily was reeling. What to do first? Could she even stay here? Dorothy offered to spend the night with her and wait till the locksmith had been in the morning. Lily, already enormously in her friend's debt, could only sob out her gratitude. Sleep, however, had fled, along with peace of mind, and Lily tossed miserably till dawn, when, leaving Dorothy unconscious in the spare room, she crept downstairs to make tea. The cats joined her, calm now and hungry. She cuddled them far beyond their tolerance limits, but they were patient with her and did not twist out of her grasp until the very last bearable moment. She gave them their favourite tuna flakes and watched, weeping again, while they ate.

As the sky lightened and colour began to seep into the gardens, she realized she had an overwhelming impulse to ring Frank. She had not thought to call him before – a notable fact in its own right. Had such a distance already opened up between them in – what was it? – little more than a month? Incredible. But several missing items – the electric drill, the camera, a couple of art deco statuettes – belonged to him. Anyway, he should bloody well be told. She wanted him to feel guilty for abandoning her to violence and danger. That would serve him right. She phoned just after seven.

A sleepy woman answered, her voice unremarkable.

'Can I speak to Frank, please? It's Lily.'

No real pause to speak of. 'Yes, of course.' Lily, trying to spot things to hate or mock, was out of luck.

Then Frank was there. 'What's up?' Neither warm nor cool.

'I've been burgled. They took some of your things.'

'Are you okay? Were you there?' He sounded concerned, but then he did that for a living.

'No. It was during the day. I'm alright. So are the cats. It's more the shock, and the fact that they got in.'

'I'm sorry.' He probably meant it, knowing better than anyone how badly Lily feared invasion. 'Do you want me to come over?'

'Yes.' She did, desperately. By now, Dorothy had joined her, standing yawning in a borrowed T-shirt, her dark hair falling in her eyes. She saw the expression on her friend's face and silently came and held Lily, who had put down the phone and was howling her loneliness.

It was after ten when a pasty-faced Lily reached her desk. Hugo was sitting on it.

She was still wearing her sunglasses, not wanting the whole office to see her distress and feast on her latest upset. But even with their protection, she could not look him in the eye.

'Hey, are you alright?' He got up and came towards her. 'What happened?'

She sat down heavily, bumped her cut hand and swore. After a minute she said, 'They broke into my house. It's not the stuff. I don't care about that. It's feeling unsafe . . .'

'You live alone?'

'I do now. We split up, at the end of June.'

He absorbed this, then offered to get her a coffee. When he came back with it, he asked if she needed some time off.

'Thanks. I will, to get alarms and things arranged. But not today. Thanks for offering though.'

'You just do whatever you need to do,' he said. His concern seemed convincing. Lily, caught off-guard, was touched.

Chapter 9

Hugo was turning out to be an amusing boss. He continued to treat Lily kindly, unexploitatively, and they both seemed to enjoy working together. It was a relationship of mutual respect and pleasure, she acknowledged to herself. They were colleagues doing exactly what Hugo had said, having fun.

This tipping of the balance at work, a rounding out of her nine-to-five role from mere worker into someone invited to be playful and jocular, helped draw her mind away from the fears engendered by the robbery. The first night after the break-in she had told herself to make a thorough and complete check of each room as soon as she came home, and then accept the fact that her sealed environment was safe, and forget about it. She had obeyed her rules, gone to bed at the usual time, even willed herself to sleep for several hours. The pattern now set, it became a little easier, each evening, to follow it mechanically and not think about what might have been, what might still be.

She looked like someone who had lost the power to relax her eye muscles. Every time she glimpsed her reflection in window or mirror, she saw a fixed, wide expression, which matched the rigidity in her neck and shoulders. She was waking up with an aching jaw, the result of holding her mouth set in a grim line. But despite these physical expressions of her tension, she had taken the first step, reclaimed a little territory, and each calm night was another graph square crossed in the curve of her passage back to confidence.

If home was a mental assault course, with Dot her

cheerleader, standing encouragingly on the sidelines, then the office had become a place of relative relaxation, where, as well as the simplicity of performing a role, there were jokes, new informalities, unexpected little treats. One evening, a few days after the theft, she heard sounds of jollity coming from Hugo's office. Approaching his door on her way home, she saw Mark, Monica, Colin from Design and the entire accounts department lounging around his desk, drinking wine and talking at some volume.

'Come and join us, Lily,' called Hugo, bottle and paper cup in hand.

'What's the occasion?' she asked, always glad, at the moment, to stall the challenging moment of returning to her fragile house.

'My fortieth birthday,' he answered and a ragged chorus of 'Happy Birthday, Hugo' went round the room, probably not for the first time.

The others beckoned her in and before she knew what she was doing, Lily had pulled up a chair and joined the party. No one was talking about work. On one side there was a conversation about cricket and on the other, comparative criticism of a new science fiction blockbuster. Hugo was leading the sports debate, arousing Sanjay to uncharacteristic animation on the subject of ball tampering. Lily turned to the cineastes, and was arguing spiritedly for *Alien* as all-time best SF movie when voices suddenly dropped. Turning, she saw Margot standing in the doorway.

Hugo was not in the slightest abashed, even though Margot's expression said everything about her views on office-hours drinking and socializing. 'Margot, come in, come in,' he invited. Alice shunted her chair to one side, to make space. But Hugo's words bounced off Margot's force field. She did not speak, there was no need. Her first rule of business had been broken on her very premises. She turned her jaw away and walked on.

Everyone grinned at each other like conspirators.

'If looks could kill,' said Mark, his bald head shining from the alcohol.

Hugo shrugged.

Behind her specs, Monica looked forlorn. But soon they were all sipping wine and being rowdy again.

'We'll see how blotto we can get her at the party,' Hugo said. 'If she doesn't soften up then, she never will.'

'Party?' Colin asked.

'At the end of the month. Haven't the tom-toms been beating today?' Hugo, topping up cups and mugs, was the picture of mine host. 'Well, you're all invited. I thought we should make an event of Margot's leaving, the change of ownership and all that, and have a do. Not just for us, though. I want to ask the suppliers, the trade press, everyone. Celebrate GBF's second coming and cosy up to all the useful people at the same time. I thought we could take over that wine bar up the road, you know, the one with spit and sawdust and candles in bottles.'

Everyone approved, or said they did, even Lily, although she knew such an evening would be more like work for her, since so many of the external contacts were hers. But it was a good idea. On her way home she reflected further on the very great shifts in style that were clearly going to be characteristic of Hugo's management. The contrast between Margot's puritanism and Hugo's flamboyance had an oddly spiritual dimension. Lily could not help but feel a little like a character in *The Pilgrim's Progress*, that in falling in with the new order she was somehow taking her first steps down the primrose path to a sulphur-scented future.

So it continued at work. Hugo's wattage increased and around him circled satellites whom he quizzed and charmed while stripping them clean of their knowledge and opinion. Lily's heavy heart lifted at the sight or sound of him, and these were frequent. A coffee break, a question, a request for data, something would come up most days, and she would feel herself flattered, softened somehow at his approach.

One night she was even invited to the sanctum sanctorum, for a drink at the Jupiter, along with Mark and Clive. 'It's where I run my informal management sessions,' Hugo explained. 'Tonight we need buying expertise.'

When Lily got to the pub, the three men were already settled at a table with a bottle of wine. Hugo poured her a glass. They seemed to be discussing a reduction in staffing.

'It's only a hypothetical scenario,' Hugo was telling Mark, genially.

'Hypothetical or not,' the salesman answered, 'there's no way I could envisage cutting my team by ten per cent. It would be wholly counterproductive.'

'Wholly?' queried Hugo. 'Or partially?'

Lily realized she had joined a senior management forum on cost-cutting. Andy's warning came back to her – Hugo the butcher, with his finely graded bacon slicer. She awaited her turn.

'We're looking at trimming next year's running costs,' Clive explained to her. He turned to Hugo. 'Although you'll find no flab on Lily – so to speak. She runs the tightest ship of all.'

'Not difficult, with a department of one,' she answered with a half-smile. It was a Pink tradition that buying was a solo department, without benefit even of a secretary.

'Even so,' continued Hugo, 'there's no harm in a speculative exercise. I'm curious as to whether, if we had to tighten our belts, we'd be better off spreading the pain across the board, or just targeting the fattest areas. Nothing personal,' he added, with a nod at Mark, whose physique tended to blur at the edges.

Was Lily right to sense sheathed claws behind Hugo's game of 'What If?'? She couldn't shake off Andy's thumb-nail sketch.

'So you *are* including my budget when looking for general shrinkage, are you?' she asked.

'Why would you be exempt?' Hugo countered.

'Simple. With less to spend, you'd have fewer goods to sell.'

'And less stock sitting about as frozen assets.'

Lily thought Hugo's tactics were pretty transparent. By suggesting overly harsh reductions, he was trying to propel her and the other managers into volunteering midway solutions, thereby achieving the measures he had sought all along.

'If you wanted me to order less, more frequently, I could. But you'd sacrifice discount,' she told him.

'So what would be the solution?' he asked.

'Have we established that supply is the problem?'

He smiled at her. 'Nice try. I'll admit your stock-turn is good. Mark's said as much too.' He turned to him. 'You can see why any axe would need to fall more heavily elsewhere.'

'Actually, I don't see why any axe would have to fall at all,' commented Clive, settling his long frame back in his chair. 'We're not in bad shape.'

'We're fabulous, but no one ever got rich from looking at themselves in the mirror and deciding they couldn't be improved. We have to keep moving, changing, innovating.'

'I didn't have you down for a management guru,' Mark said with a chuckle.

'Oh, this didn't come out of books. It's all instinctive with me,' Hugo said, standing up. 'Who's for another bottle?'

Lily watched him grope for his wallet. She was still basking in his approval.

*

At some adjacent point, and Lily could never isolate the precise instant, she realized that she had begun to find Hugo attractive. Never before had she been interested in his physical type. If asked, she would have said her ideal was a non-smoking ectomorph with good dress sense. Yet here she was responding to a slightly run-down bruiser who wore tan shoes. She began to notice that her temperature rose in his presence, that she became conscious of the movements of his hands, which were never still, fiddling with cigarettes, pieces of paper, ruffling his hair. Their conversations often seemed to her to take on a secondary, unexpressed quality of meaning, to hang in the air while he watched her and she watched back. She began to dress for work a little more carefully, a little less neutrally, to apply her cosmetics with slightly more art.

Undecided whether to share any of this with Dorothy, who always went through a bad patch in high summer, when Peter was away on the family holiday, she suddenly thought of Andy. She had not entirely forgotten his words of warning, but at the same time felt they did not seem to apply to the Hugo she knew. Hungry for a chance to talk about her hero, she called him anyway. He seemed pleased to hear from her.

'I've been wondering how you were getting on.'

'Do you mean at work? That's all fine, not at all like you said. But I've had a disaster at home.'

'What do you mean?'

She explained about the burglary.

'Oh, God,' Andy said, 'your nightmare scenario. I'm so sorry. What did you do?'

She made a humphing noise, to convey her embarrassment. 'I called Frank. Well, at least I waited until the next day. But I still felt it was his business too, although I don't think he did. And the police came and gave me lots of advice. I've had an alarm fitted, and locks on all the windows. There's a "trembler" on the back door' – she tried to inject some humour into her voice – 'and something called a London Bar at the front. Apparently I'm safer now than I've ever been.'

'You don't sound convinced.'

'Well, I try not to think about it. Oh, did I mention the panic buttons? I've got one by the bed. That's probably the best thing. At the touch of a button I can set bells ringing and lights flashing. Whoops.' She stopped, realizing the *double entendre*, hoping that he didn't think she was making a play. But he only laughed.

'Did they take anything that really mattered?'

'Not really. Some pieces of antique jewellery from my father, but the rest is replaceable and the insurance will cover it.'

'And do you feel okay on your own there? You *sound* as if you're coping.'

'Ha. Thanks for the compliment. It's not how it feels. But yeah, I suppose I'm managing. And thank heavens work is going quite well. In fact, your friend Mr Padmore isn't turning out anything like the ogre you described.'

'Really?' Andy's voice had cooled.

'Well, I can see how he falls short of some of Margot's standards of comportment. It's a much more casual style, to put it mildly – sort of management by wandering about. But it's lively. I like it.'

'Sounds like Hugo's lost none of his charisma,' Andy commented drily. 'People were always drawn to him like flypaper.'

'You really don't like him, do you?'

She wasn't surprised. Apples and oranges. The two men had dropped off different trees.

The day of the party was hot and humid, as it had been now for more than a week. London had transformed itself into a

European capital. The air never seemed to cool, just lost its heaviness as the sun set and people relaxed, keen to stay up and eat late. Compared to the irritability of the day, the evening had become a time of gregariousness, of friendliness between strangers.

Lily had had some difficulty deciding what to wear to Hugo's do. She had never greatly favoured skirts and dresses after an early boyfriend had commented casually on her shapeless legs. But it was hot and she wanted to be comfortable while standing around all evening. She tried on some favourite silk trousers, but somehow their charms felt jaded. Then she remembered a crêpe de Chine dress, not an antique but something she had bought a couple of years earlier for the delicacy of its flower print. It had a scooped neck, cap sleeves and fell from a fitted waist in a gentle flare to her ankles. She tried it on. Somewhat thinner now than when she had acquired it, she felt happy with its loose, light fit. A pair of leather ballet pumps seemed to work with the dress, as did a string of milky glass beads like moonstones that had once belonged to her mother. She decided it was too hot for a jacket and went to work feeling as light as thistledown in her airy clothes, her hair skimming her shoulders.

The day turned out to be a busy one and she did not see Hugo until a few minutes before the party was due to begin. He had made no sartorial efforts at all, but was standing near the entrance to the wine bar, a glass in one hand, a cigarette in the other, looking less like the host than someone who had dropped in for a quick one. He did not speak to Lily as she walked in with Alice, just smiled, but she knew that he had noticed the pretty dress which left exposed her arms, throat and her collar-bones.

Before she had time even to get a drink, the room began to fill up with staff and guests. Lily had deputed some of her colleagues to help mind the wholesalers she knew were coming. Hugo had asked to be introduced to the more senior ones, and those working for firms with whom they did the most business, so periodically she would seek him out and present him with her companion, whose hand he would shake and whose name he would repeat.

As the evening wore on and the effects of the wine they were all drinking were not absorbed quickly enough by the canapés, everyone's social skills mellowed and Lily's introductions became less formal.

'Come on, Sammy. I want you to meet the big enchilada. Hugo, this is Sammy Morris, the king of paste.' Hugo looked blankly at her. 'You remember paste, Hugo,' she said in a stage whisper. 'The sparkly stuff that isn't diamonds.'

Sammy shook Hugo's hand in a hearty way. 'You know you've got one of the brightest buyers in London working for you, don't you?' he declared. 'I hope you're taking care of her.'

Lily blushed and grinned.

'Not another one,' Hugo said to her. 'This is beginning to feel like a put-up job.'

She left them to it, pleasantly intoxicated and free in a room where she knew many people and could move from group to group without ever, magically, getting trapped in a corner. The wine vault was warm and full of noise, but nothing seemed overpowering and she realized that for once in what seemed an age she was enjoying herself. She went to the toilet, and in the mirror over the washbasin noticed approvingly the slight flush the wine had brought to her pale cheeks.

When she emerged, Hugo was standing on some steps near the door, with Margot nearby, and calling for hush. She had not realized he was going to make a speech.

'Ladies and gentlemen,' he began, his voice comfortably audible, 'it's a great pleasure to welcome you here tonight.

This is one of those hail and farewell occasions, and it only seemed fitting to ask all our friends as well as the whole family.

'You'll notice I'm already speaking proprietorially about Girl's Best Friend, and that's because my adoption by the company has been one of the swiftest and pleasantest I've ever experienced. So to all my staff, I would like to say thank you, and stay as sweet as you are.' A ripple of amusement at this.

'To our guests, I would like to extend a very warm thank you too, for your support to date. This operation could not survive and flourish without each and every one of you. We have great plans for the future and hope you will be a part of them.

'But there is one person here to whom we should all turn this evening. Without Margot Pink, we would have no reason to congregate or celebrate, and no prospects for a magnificent future. Whatever GBF becomes under my ownership, it will always stand on the rock-solid foundations you built for it, Margot. So thank you. To mix my metaphors, you've handed your baby over to me in the pink' – a polite guffaw went round the room – 'and I'm going to make sure she carries on growing up strong and healthy. So, everyone, let's raise our glasses to Margot, and wish her all joy of her exciting new future.'

'To Margot,' rang out the toast, and there was no doubting the unanimous warmth in the assembled voices. Some of the staff looked sad and weepy and Lily too felt a jolt as she acknowledged the end of an era.

Now Colin was approaching Margot with two elaborately wrapped parcels, which she refused to accept until she had said her own piece.

'I'll keep this brief,' she said, resplendent in an iridescent green waterfall of a dress. 'Why change the habits of a lifetime?' The laughter this time was genuine. 'The only way I'll be able to cope with missing you and the business as much as I know I shall will be to put an ocean between us. I'm going forward to a new life, in a new place, but if any of you ever find yourself in New Mexico, there will be a welcome for you there.

'This is the end of a chapter in my life. The next page is clean and I'm looking forward to making my mark on it.' Here she seemed to catch Lily's eye, and Lily remembered with clarity Margot's encouragement over lunch – 'Next time, make sure you get what *you* want.' Easily done, Lily thought, if your life plan were as clear as Margot's. 'My very best wishes and thanks to you all,' she concluded, and then turned regally to accept the gifts.

'You've got to admire her,' Clive acknowledged, behind Lily, as they stood around in an awkward silence while she unwrapped first a large book on cactus cultivation and then a very expensive piece of engraved crystal that resembled, at this distance, an exploding cauliflower.

Finally, Hugo, who had hung back, encouraged everyone to applaud, and the clapping turned into a kind of thunderous cheer which went on for moments. Eventually it died away and people began to turn to each other and pick up their conversations. Lily, still near the back of the room, moved forward, wanting to have a moment on her own with Margot, to express personal thanks, best wishes, somehow say her own goodbye to her surrogate mother. But even as she moved forward she could see Margot slipping away, alone, towards the entrance and out into the heavy night air. By the time Lily reached the doorway, she had disappeared. Lily felt a sudden sense of profound loss and stood outside for a moment, full of panic and uncertainty, before turning to resume her duties.

Although the invitations had defined the party's hours as

six thirty to eight thirty, it was after ten before the final revellers decided to call it a night. A small group of GBF staff were left in the wine-scented room and Lily found Hugo standing beside her as she said goodbye to the guys from Stargazy.

'Whew.' She mimed mopping her brow. 'Quite an evening. Are you pleased?'

'I think so. A good turnout, a good mood too. But I'm absolutely knackered now. Do you fancy some fish and chips?'

Of all the invitations Lily might have fantasized receiving from Hugo, this was about the least alluring, but she was hungry and maybe fish and chips were a euphemism for finer fare.

'Yes,' she said, and before she knew it had agreed to meet him outside the GBF office, where he had left his briefcase. So it was that they left the wine bar separately, Hugo unnoticed, Lily turning down an offer to join a bunch of others who were heading off to a Mexican restaurant in Covent Garden.

By the time she reached the darkened office block, Hugo was standing outside, briefcase in hand. 'Where do you fancy eating?' he asked, and then suggested one of the trendy brasseries that had sprouted near Smithfields. It was only a few moments' walk away, and as they arrived, a table came vacant outside, on the pavement. They sat down, Lily grateful to be off her feet at last. Menus appeared, and fizzy water and a bottle of Beaune, ordered by Hugo when Lily confessed she preferred red wine.

Wondering what to eat, whether indeed she had any appetite at all, she felt herself shiver. It was getting on for eleven o'clock and the air temperature was finally cooling. Hugo noticed. 'Would you like my jacket?' Before she could answer he had taken it off and draped it round her shoulders.

How odd, she thought, in her gently alcohol-befuzzed state, to see him sitting in glowing white, almost phosphorescent shirtsleeves. And she now had this strange weight hanging from her, warm admittedly, but lumpy too with wallets and so on, and smelling of cigarettes and Hugo. Somewhere in her groin she detected the soft thump of sexual arousal.

'What do you want to eat?' he asked.

'Er, not very much. Maybe just a starter and a salad.'

'What about some smoked salmon?'

'Perfect.' It was true, just what she fancied.

Once the food was ordered, Hugo lit a cigarette and gestured to a plane passing overhead. 'Do you think Margot can see us?'

'Is she leaving tonight?' Lily asked, amazed.

'Straight from the party to the airport. I've never met anyone so utterly purposeful.'

Lily tried to imagine walking out of one life and into another in the space of an evening. She was awed.

'So, Ms Braithwaite, here we are, alone at last.' That got her attention, even though she knew it was a parody. 'Now, tell me something about yourself.'

'What would you like to know?' she answered bluntly.

'Well, why your relationship split up, for a start.'

She had no need to hesitate. 'Sexual incompatibility.'

'Oh,' Hugo said, possibly a little stunned. But he soon got his breath back, and while they ate he quizzed her more, though not especially hard, on life with Frank, its length and depth, their habits and hobbies.

'And what about you, Mr Padmore?' she asked, at the end of the inquisition. 'Tell me about your marriage, your foibles, your little weaknesses.'

'I've been married for twenty years,' he answered openly. 'Jay was pregnant, so I married her. We've been through a lot together, not all of it pleasant, but like old married people say, we have an understanding. She lets me go my own way.'

'And you let her go hers?'

'Oh, no.' He was not joking. 'No, I'd hate it if she went astray. But she doesn't mind me doing it.'

Lily wondered whether Mrs Padmore would agree. 'And do you stray often?' She felt herself becoming disengaged, hearing such unromantic frankness.

'Not often. But they can be long attachments. There's a woman in Paris.'

'You mustn't be able to see her very often.'

'No,' he admitted, 'but I have suits there. I'm like a father to her boy.'

'You live parallel lives?'

He seemed unable to understand. 'It doesn't harm Jay. Everyone understands the score.'

'But each gets less,' she observed.

'No one gets everything,' was his answer.

The meal puttered to its close. Lily felt unable to gauge Hugo's mood. There was nothing overtly flirtatious about it, although their talk was of sex and infidelity. Finally he yawned, and she realized he needed to catch a train.

'No,' he explained. 'I knew I'd be late, so I've arranged to stay with some old friends.'

She was getting up from the table by now, handing him back his jacket. 'Well,' she commented, reaching for her bag, 'I'm going to take a taxi. I could drop you off somewhere.'

'You could,' he said, standing so close that she could feel his breath on her ear, 'or I could come home with you.'

The words reverberated inside her head, and for a moment Lily had a flash of terrible premonition. But there was no doubt about her answer.

'That would be lovely,' she said, very politely.

Chapter 10

So it was, after a brief yet slightly awkward taxi ride, that they were both to be found on Lily's doorstep, while she fumbled for her keys. Then she had to tap her code into the newly installed alarm keypad, and finally, there Hugo was, in her hallway, and she was in his arms. She had to stand on tiptoe to kiss him, and that, and the pure, exhilarating physical joy of the moment, made her tremble.

'Mm,' he said, 'delicious.'

'Er, would you like a drink?' she offered, showing him into the sitting room and drawing the curtains.

'Is there any brandy?'

The Italian bottle still had enough in it for a glass each, so they sat on the sofa and he looked around the room. 'Where's the music?' he asked.

'There isn't any. Frank took the sound system with him.'

'Then let's go to bed.'

She led the way upstairs, closed the curtains, switched on lamps and drew back the bedspread. While he went to the loo, she removed her beads and decided to clean her teeth, wondering at the quotidian feel of it all. Wasn't she supposed to have been swept off her feet, literally, never mind all this washing and flushing? But just as she was finishing, Hugo appeared behind her. He was naked. 'I can't wait any longer,' he said, and took her by the hand.

Before he even touched her, she was thrilled by his body. Frank was tall and slender. In his wellington boots, when they went walking, he looked like an overgrown Christopher Robin. Hugo seemed an entirely different species, Dionysian in form, with his convex stomach and broad shoulders. She could see him in the mirror as he unzipped her dress, nuzzling her neck and ears, running his fingers over her shoulders. The crêpe fell silently to the floor. Then he undid her bra and pushed down her pants. His kisses were different, tasting of tobacco and alcohol; his tongue was a different shape and he pushed it into her mouth without hesitation.

She wanted the comparisons to go away, and yet they were part of the pleasure, the glorious, reassuring return of her full sexual excitement. Yes, she remembered, I've felt like this before. She both had and had not. She had enjoyed sex rather more before Frank, but she could never remember being so utterly enraptured as she was now, with Hugo's hands on her breasts and his erection pressed against her stomach. She moved it, pushed it between her legs and felt the unspeakable glory of the triangulation between nipples and clitoris. He gasped and bit her on the shoulder.

She could have stood like that, transfixed, liquefying, but he was making all the moves, was leading her to the bed where, luckily, she had laid fresh sheets only a couple of nights ago. He threw back the duvet, picked her up and set her gently on the bare expanse. There seemed to be no question of turning off the lights, but to her surprise Lily felt no sense of exposure.

Now he was beside her, reaching for her, crushing her to him. And having passively accepted his lead until now, she awoke to an all-consuming hunger for his skin, his lips, his touch. Their kisses were long and wet and seemed to range like dialogue. They sucked at each other's tongue and lips; nipped with their teeth. His hands were lost in her long hair, holding her head, while she was gripping his forearms, astounded that flesh could be so unyielding, such an essence of strength.

What about safe sex, she wondered, but she knew there

94

were no condoms in the house. Hugo didn't seem worried. And anyway, sweet heavens, she could already feel the tip of his penis inside her. The thought seemed prosaic. The sensation was rhapsodic. Frank's cock was lean like his body. Hugo's was thicker, its girth leaving her no space. He was going to fill her and she was going to receive him. She could think of nothing more splendid.

But he was in no rush. His head bent to her nipples, to lick and suck them too. His hands moved to her buttocks, so that he could control the rate at which he penetrated her. Eyes closed, Lily was drowning in sensation, her own hands picking up the warmth of his smooth skin as she stroked him, pushed and pulled at his shoulders, back, hairless chest. There was electricity in her fingertips and a buzzing in her ears. She thought she was making sounds. Hugo was silent and she sensed his utter concentration on the infinitesimal progression of his entry into her. Wet, drenched though she was, she too could feel the minute process. Her embrace of his penis seemed tailor-made, the entry of measured flesh into a bespoke silk glove.

Side by side they lay. His hands had returned to her breasts while his cock reached its full depth. She had lost the power of movement. They were joined, she felt, in some elemental fashion, as perfectly as an acorn and its cup. Made for each other. Had they invented this? Were they laying down a paradigm? This was to be the gold standard of fucking for ever more. Hugo and Lily had created the mould.

He began to move now and she joined him in an easy rhythm, inventing a swing of her hips at the top of his stroke that made him breathe harshly. Her pubic bone was jammed against his abdomen and the root of his cock pressed against her clitoris, setting up heat that travelled to her breasts and cheek-bones. Yet he still seemed in no hurry, following a blind route of his own, feeding her own

95

desire with touches to her nipples, her lips and ear lobes, but always gathering his own momentum. She could feel his cock engorging further. She seemed preternaturally sensitive, but equally her focus on Hugo was fading as she acknowledged the onset of sensations which heralded an orgasm.

My God, was she going to come like this? She never had before, had always needed a helping hand, which Frank, over time, had lost the willingness to lend. But there was no doubting it now, the pull like gravity in her belly, the gratifying ripples that seemed to be an answer to her call. A pulsing seemed to be gathering, and before she could speak, it had swept in, leaving her contracting around Hugo's penis and jolting from the shock waves.

He paused to hold her while the tremors moved through, while she dissolved into the *petite mort* and then awoke to his tight, reassuring embrace. His own orgasm he seemed to be able to hold in abeyance, another novelty compared to Frank's tunnel vision.

While she became calmer, he kissed her face and eyelids lightly, making only slight moves with his pelvis. After the spasm, her vagina seemed almost bonded to his penis and she flexed her internal muscles too, loving the totality of their union.

On top of her now, Hugo moved his hands to her knees, flexing them and opening her legs wider. His hips settled lower, nearer to the bed's surface.

'Don't move,' he said and she obeyed, happy to luxuriate in surrender while he set up a strong, slightly rough stroke. He raised himself over her, propped on his arms, and the cords in his neck stood out.

'Oh, God,' he breathed and she reached out to put her hands on his clenched shoulders. His muscles felt locked. His excitement was still mustering. He was thrusting harder now, lost, she could tell, in his own pleasure until, with a violent surge, he shouted, 'Christ, Lily,' and came with convulsive spasms that seemed to travel up to her womb.

'Bloody hell.' His breathing was still ragged, his hips still quietly circling.

She kissed his damp brow, stroked his neck, marvelled at the clean, sharp smell of his sweat. She held him, rocked him a little, until finally he said, 'I need a cigarette.'

With enormous reluctance, she allowed his softening penis to leave her and went to fetch his jacket and a saucer for an ashtray. Returning she found him splayed on the bed, hands behind his head, sated and shameless.

'You witch,' he said and stretched out an arm, to hold her snugly against him while he smoked.

The cats, ignored and uninterested observers in their basket, now lifted their noses at the acrid smell and decided to adjourn to the garden.

Lily was smiling in every particle of her skin and psyche. What delight, what utter, brilliant pleasure. She was lying beside her dream lover, more sexually satisfied than she had ever been in her life. And if she was any judge, Hugo seemed to have quite enjoyed himself too. Something blissful had begun.

He turned to stub out his cigarette and noticed the alarm clock on the bedside table. 'Hell, it's three o'clock. I've got a meeting with the bank at nine. I suppose we should try and get some sleep.'

'I don't want to,' she told him. 'Or are your powers exhausted already?' She pulled a face like a temptress and ran her hand languidly up the inside of his thigh.

'You want more, do you? Beautiful Lily. Sexy and insatiable,' and his hand dawdled at her breast, sending arrowheads of stimulation to the nerve-ends in her groin. 'I may need just a little rest, after such a spine-tingling fuck. But you have my permission to wake me up well before breakfast and perhaps I can have another shot at meeting your gargantuan appetite. Now be a good girl and put out the light.'

She did as she was told, a little sad that he did not simply want to stay awake with her, but settling down in the dark, his arm across her shoulder, he whispered, 'We're going to have so much fun in the weeks ahead,' and she was reconciled, bribed by pleasures in store.

Wide awake though she believed herself to be, possibly even glowing in the dark, in fact she fell into sleep like slipping underwater, and the next moment it was light and the clock face said seven. Hugo had his back to her and, well, there was no romantic term for it, was snoring. She put her hand on his waist, slid it oh so gently towards his groin, ran her fingers through his pubic hair and cupped his genitals. 'Hugo,' she whispered breathily in his ear.

He awoke slowly, turning to allow her a better grip, and she fitted herself alongside his body. 'What time is it?' he asked, eyes still closed.

'After seven,' she confessed.

'Bugger.' He disengaged her hand and made to get up. Romance had fled. One hand rumpling his hair, he swung his legs out of bed and padded off to the loo. Lily acknowledged to herself that time was perhaps a little short, but could they not have shared just a few more moments? Seemingly not. He was back now and reaching for his clothes. 'Can I have a shower?' was all he said, and then disappeared into the bathroom, leaving her to contemplate her swollen lips and bird's-nest hair in the mirror.

Sod work. She wanted to stay in bed, savour the creased sheets, relive the arching passion. But there was no question that Hugo was heading for the office, so she had better be hospitable, offer breakfast, feed the cats and tidy herself up a bit.

She loaded the kitchen table with fruit juice, toast, cereal, coffee, and took her own turn in the bathroom after he had emerged. When she came downstairs again, in linen trousers and a green sea-island cotton sweater that was reputed to match her eyes, he had touched nothing except the liquids, was standing barefoot in his shirt-tails reading the label on the cat food tin.

'This stuff is full of crap, you know. Ash and "derivatives" – imagine what they are. There's even sugar in it.'

'They like it,' she said defensively. 'Are you not eating anything?' She sat down and poured out some muesli.

'In the morning? Never do.' And he roamed the kitchen like a caged beast, picking up packets and jars, infecting her with his restlessness.

She wanted to talk about the night just past. She wanted to make plans for the next time. She wanted words of tenderness and admiration. He just wanted to get on.

'When will we do this again?' she asked finally, unable to resist, although for God's sake, why hadn't he asked first?

'Soon, I promise. Life's just so bloody hectic at the moment,' and he went to find his trousers and the all-important briefcase.

Within minutes they were ready to leave, and he stood humming impatiently on the pavement while she set the alarm and turned keys in all three locks which now sealed her front door. At the bottom of the street he went into the newsagent for a *Financial Times* and a packet of cigarettes. At least he had the grace to buy her a paper too, but that only meant that on the tube he felt free to abandon her to her own stack of newsprint while he scanned his.

Lily did not want to read. If Hugo was not going to talk to her or explain how they were to organize their affair, then she would just sit and picture, in as much detail as her mind's eye could record, the scenes of their first night of passion. Would anyone notice that she had become a little flushed as faint sonar pulses of sensation echoed in her sexual extremities? Who cared? She wanted to hold on to, to evoke every degree of texture and pressure for as long as she could.

While remembering the perfect skin-on-skin motion of penetration, she suddenly came awake to a significant omission. She was no longer on the pill. She had stopped taking it the day after Frank's visit. She turned to Hugo, but he was lost in his broadsheet. Should she say anything? What was the point? No, the die was cast anyway. Assuming she had a period soon, she would certainly go back on the pill again, and in the meantime, *que será será*. Lily allowed herself an instant's fantasy of being pregnant by Hugo. Rosy-hued as every prospect was that morning, she found the idea rather appealing.

As they changed trains at Leicester Square, Hugo suddenly said, 'I think I'll walk to the bank from here. It'll save time. See you later,' and before she could react, he had gone. No touch, no kiss, no terms of endearment. What was going on? Lily felt herself gasping like a guppy, but forced herself to board the next train, to finish the journey and get to her office.

Everyone she bumped into within GBF was discussing the party, and those who had gone on to the meal in Covent Garden wanted to give lengthy accounts of a variety of indiscretions. Lily, shielding her precious secret, listened patiently to Monica and Pat, fearsome guardian of the switchboard, who had already perfected a double act to report the tired and emotional state of a group of GBF shop staff. All of these had been invited up from the branches, although this part of the team, especially the nonmetropolitan set, had long been regarded as a lesser life form. Their behaviour had only confirmed the London office's expectations.

Having smiled and tutted at appropriate intervals, Lily was finally permitted to move on. At her desk, with a cup of peppermint tea, she sat and brooded. Surely Hugo wasn't rebuffing her. No, he had promised pleasures in the weeks to come. Perhaps he felt he needed to make it clear to her that it was *only* an affair, strictly behind-closed-doors stuff. Well, she knew that, for heaven's sake. She did not want to marry him. (Lily pictured Dorothy's raised eyebrow here.) She just wanted the sex. The amazing sex. Oh, and the touching. Yes, the physical contact after the parched desert of life with Frank.

She could reassure him that she would be the discreetest of partners. Although she had never been involved with a married man before, she felt utterly confident of playing the role of mistress in an adult fashion. If he would just agree with her the pattern of their liaison, then she would be happy.

She felt like Sleeping Beauty, awake at last after years of sexual slumber. She couldn't wait to tell Dorothy. Hugo would probably visit her later in the day and they could plot their next stolen moments then. After sex that good, he would have to come back for more.

Chapter 11

Lily saw practically nothing of Hugo that day. She heard his voice, glimpsed him in corners of the offices, but he did not call in on her and she could think of no formal reason to consult him. Tired and hungover as she was, she did not linger late at her desk, but went home for a long bath and an early night.

In the house, she found Hugo's juice glass and coffee mug stacked among the washing-up. Upstairs, she pressed her face into his pillow, to inhale that distinctive masculine scent, the same one that pervaded the crumpled sheets. The only other trace of his presence was a faint odour of cigarette smoke. He had covered his tracks like a professional.

In her bathrobe, hair washed, face scrubbed, she settled on the sofa to call Dorothy, but was met with the answerphone. Of course, Peter was back from the Algarve. Well, she was going over for supper on Saturday. Her story would have to wait for forty-eight hours.

Friday dawned, and the usual manic mood swept over GBF, heightened by the knowledge that the weekend included a bank holiday and the shops would be busier than ever. Lily could scarcely contain her impatience to see Hugo, and after her monthly sales and stock update meeting with Mark, decided to go on the offensive. But Hugo's office showed no signs of life. Where were his briefcase and brimming ashtray? She went to Pat's screened-off cubicle and asked the fount of all knowledge.

'Taking a long weekend, apparently,' Pat answered, putting aside a true-crime volume on serial killers. 'He gave me an emergency number, somewhere in Norfolk he said, but I'm on pain of death not to disturb him. Is it urgent?'

'No,' said Lily, managing to swallow the sigh of dejection accumulating in her nostrils. 'It'll keep.'

'So I shan't see him until at least Tuesday,' she concluded to Dot, sitting in the kitchen of her friend's flat in south-east London, which looked out on to a small park. Typically, the hot weather had broken that morning and grey clouds hung heavy over the wind-stirred trees, forcing Dorothy to turn on the light while she blended the gazpacho and whipped the egg whites for the spinach soufflé. She was a good cook and had become very clever, in her reduced circumstances, at conjuring up gourmet meals from marked-down supermarket stock.

'Maybe,' said Dot, her real energy, at that instant, going into the labour of manipulating the egg whisk. Small, but stocky and strong, she soon had the whites thrashed into peaks.

'What do you mean, maybe?' Lily had delivered a blow-by-blow account of her relationship with Hugo, mistaking her friend for an oracle on the subject of extra-marital affairs.

'Well, maybe you will see him, or maybe he will keep on avoiding you.'

'Is that what you think he's doing?' asked Lily, wanting to have the rules of the game explained to her by a pro.

'I've no idea. I've never met him,' Dot answered, finishing folding in the eggs and preparing the soufflé dish for the oven. 'But he doesn't sound in any hurry to make another date. Maybe he doesn't feel he has to, knowing how keen you are. Sounds like he can have you whenever the opportunity arises.'

Lily flushed at the truth of this. But then what was so wrong with being open? She had never been much of a games player when it came to relationships. Where was the self-respect in being dishonest or playing hard to get?

'So what should I do? How did you set it up with Peter, so that you knew where you stood?'

'That was different,' her friend answered, sitting down at last, with a corkscrew and glasses, and reaching for the bottle Lily had brought.

'How?'

'Well, to be frank, he was a lot keener. No, don't misunderstand me, I'm sure, from what you say, that Hugo had a great time with you. But you've only just met him. You don't really know what his track record is with other women. With Peter, I was – am – the first, and it took him ages to persuade me. I really didn't fancy him at the beginning, don't you remember? We were just colleagues, went for the occasional drink, and so on, and he kept on asking if he could come here. And when I finally said yes, he was so grateful that I could lay down my own terms.'

'I know Hugo's had at least one affair. He admitted as much.'

'Then all I'd say is watch yourself. You're not in great shape, Lily. I'm really glad that you've been reminded how much fun sex can be, and Hugo sounds like a great lay. But if you're just another notch on his belt, the worst you can do to yourself is make yourself too available. After all, he may already have had what he wanted. Why make a fool of yourself?'

Wise words, Lily knew, as they sat down to their meal. But her appetite had deserted her. Was Hugo just a noisier, bulkier version of Frank? What was it with her and promiscuous men? Was she perversely attracted to the faithless? Or did it work the other way round? Did she have 'victim' tattooed on her forehead? Thank heavens Margot was halfway round the world. If she had seen Lily repeat her mistake practically within minutes of her warning, she would have given up on her completely. Because she had repeated the mistake, hadn't she? She had let Hugo set the agenda. She had let him into her life absolutely on his own terms, and here she was, quite impotent in the face of whatever it was he was going to dictate to her.

The problem was that she wanted him terribly. If she could just put it down to experience and move on, that wouldn't be so bad. But as the weekend wore on and her mind went obsessively over the events of the previous week, she realized she was hopelessly in thrall to this man. In spite of his withdrawal, she felt they had something special. No, he wasn't her soul mate, but there was a rapport, both sexual and emotional. She loved his company, his gossipy irreverence, his tough insouciance. He would make a wonderful part-time lover – light-hearted but utterly satisfying. Why wouldn't he agree to something as delightful as that?

It was the most boring long weekend Lily had ever endured. She cleaned the house to a standard even her mother would have approved; she groomed the garden, picking up individual leaves and petals. The cats had never been offered so many opportunities to play. Their already low boredom threshold was quickly reached. She was unable to settle to a book or a television programme, and even bedtime was spoilt, now that the ghost of Hugo could be glimpsed in the mirror or imagined in the empty left-hand half of the bed.

Finally Tuesday dawned, but now she felt nervous about seeing her hero, unsure of what to expect and half-afraid of pain. Yet there was excitement too. She could see it in her eyes as she applied an extra coat of mascara.

She had resolved that if nothing happened, then she would approach Hugo herself, but not until later in the day, when he was more relaxed and happier to think of social matters. And in fact her morning passed in a flash, after a crisis blew up over the nondelivery of an urgent order of silver hoops, earrings that were core stock and essential to the bread-and-butter turnover of nearly all the shops.

When she looked at her watch it was four o'clock. It would be perfectly reasonable to go and make a cup of tea and wander past Hugo's room in an entirely casual fashion. So, with mug in hand, she sauntered by, and there indeed he was, cigarette hanging from his lip, reading through an untidy file. Perfect. She drifted in.

'Hello, Lily,' he said blandly. 'What can I do for you?'

'Nothing special,' she said, in as relaxed a fashion as she could manage. 'You heard about the hoops presumably.'

'Mm, but it's all sorted, isn't it?'

'Yep,' she said, taking a sip of tea. 'So how was your bank holiday?'

He leaned back, expansively. 'Not bad. Family stuff, by the seaside. Although the weather was a bastard.'

She noticed that he did not enquire about hers.

'Hugo,' she began, deciding she would invoke the spirit of Margot and try to get what she wanted, 'I was just wondering. Do you think you'll have any free time this week?' A pause. 'You know, you mentioned something about the weeks to come. I thought it would be nice to pencil something in.'

'What a lovely idea,' he answered, 'but I can't make any plans just at the moment. You do understand, don't you? We will arrange something, though, I promise you.' He stopped. It was clear the audience was over and Lily was dismissed. She had thrown her cards and he had trumped them. What was there left for her to do, but wait?

Life revealed itself to be very empty in the weeks that followed. Although, around her, the seasons were subtly shifting, Lily felt a leaden immobility descend. Work followed its predictable pattern. The graph of her social life showed a regular shape – films, meals, drinks with Dorothy or one of the smattering of couples who still kept in touch. One weekend she went to Leamington Spa to visit Vanessa, an old college friend who was now a part-time lecturer, married to a solicitor. She spoke to her parents, she began a programme of redecorating the kitchen, she cared for her cats. And she waited for Hugo to beckon.

The realization that he had lied to her dawned slowly and sullenly. But when she admitted it, she felt enraged. He had no need to lie. He had already got into her bed. There was nothing to be gained by sketching in a future, of however casual a nature, for the two of them. So why do something so cruel?

Perhaps he was not aware just how raw she was. Perhaps it all meant nothing to him. Perhaps one taste was enough. Yet he knew about Frank. A little sensitivity might surely have been possible.

She felt as if Hugo had struck her on exactly the site of the wound inflicted by Frank. The same emotions swirled about her – impotence and rejection; the same overwhelming humiliation engulfed her, enhanced by the fact that it followed her to the workplace, the location where previously she had been able to bury her feelings under professional obligation. Work was now torture, because Hugo was there, and not just there, but as fun-loving and playful as ever. In meetings he was just as flirtatious, just as ambiguous as before. She still felt that he was interested in her, in spite of his blanking on the future. It was horrible to endure, the pleasure, the pain and the unextinguished hope.

Lily had stopped trying to engineer opportunities to see him. She had found a shred of pride and that helped her keep a little distance. It did not stop her desiring Hugo, though, with an all-consuming lust that filled her dreams and waking fantasies. Why had it been so good? She could not be sure, although there was something about his strong arms and large body that, even as she remembered them, filled her with heat.

It was one evening in mid-September that Dorothy dropped her bombshell. Lily had returned home feeling chilled, aware that it was that time of year when summer clothes were no longer adequate, yet the light was too bright for winter tones and fabrics. She decided to have a bath to warm herself up. Pink-fleshed again, and comfortable in a tracksuit and thick socks, she was just wandering downstairs in search of a snack when the phone rang.

'Hello, it's me,' said Dot, sounding a little out of breath.

'Hello, you. How's it going?'

'Well, pretty amazing, actually. Are you sitting down?'

Lily wasn't, but did, and said so.

'It's Peter,' Dorothy began. 'He's going to leave his wife. He wants to move in.'

'Crumbs,' was Lily's initial response. Her first impulse was a rush of jealousy, there was no denying it, but she swallowed it and tried to sound as delighted as she could. 'That's wonderful.' It didn't sound too hollow.

'Well, yes, it is, isn't it?' Dorothy seemed somewhat dazed. 'It came absolutely out of the blue. I'd long given up dreaming about it, or asking. It's always been horrible to see him get up and leave, but that was the deal. He hadn't even been going on about how bad things were at home. Then last week, he asked me how I'd feel if things changed to something more permanent. I didn't understand at first, but apparently there's been a big deterioration in the marriage – no sex, lots of rows, everyone very unhappy, including the children. Carol doesn't know about me so, thank God, I'm not dragged into it. And Peter has decided to tell her tonight that he's moving out – a trial separation. He's arriving tomorrow.'

108

Lily wanted to ask her friend many questions, but her head was spinning with parallels – her and Frank, her and Hugo. How was Carol feeling? Was this what she really wanted? What was it like for Dot, for her years of patient mistresshood to have paid off?

'I assume you're pleased?' she asked, just to make sure.

'I think so,' Dorothy answered. 'I'm frightened of the change, that it won't last, that we'll feel differently, that he'll blame me. And I'm amazed to be becoming a couple, with the one person who had always been off-limits. And then what will it be like when he sees me when I'm not making an effort? But yes, I'm over the moon, really.'

Lily could not help, in spite of her own disappointments, experiencing some joy for her friend. Murky though such situations were, at the centre was happiness, two people making a new unit out of love and sharing. It was what everyone craved. At her and Dot's age, coming newly forged to a relationship, like Romeo and Juliet, was pretty much impossible. This was perhaps as good as it could get for thirtysomethings. Lily wanted to cheer Dorothy on.

'Then I'm really happy for you. It's wonderful. I wish you all the happiness in the world. Do you want to come over and celebrate? We could have a mini-hen party. Your last night as a single woman.'

'It's a great idea, but I can't. I've got a rush job to finish, and I've also got to try and clear some junk out of the spare room, so that Peter can keep his clothes and stuff somewhere. But don't worry. We'll do it soon. And I'm not going to stop being an independent person with a life, even after he moves in.'

Lily *was* worried. Dot's friendship was a mainstay. But she would have to trust her friend on this one. Tonight was not the time to express her fears.

'Soon then. I'll get in something fizzy – you just name the day.'

'Okay, ducks. Speak to you soon.'

'Mm. Best of luck for tomorrow.'

Lily put the phone down and made a mental note to send her pal a good-luck card in the morning. It was a pleasure that somebody's life was going through an upturn. She mused on the way, if friends' lives were conducted in a kind of permanent, parallel race, suddenly one would leap ahead of another. Well, Dot had had her share of bad fortune, what with downsizing at work and long-term other-woman status. Now she was out in the lead. Good for her.

Lily got up and headed for the kitchen. It was getting dark and she turned on the light, which seemed to act as a beacon to Huntley and Palmer. They followed each other through the cat flap like a double act, then sat and blinked on the mat. She spooned out some yoghurt for herself and chopped some plums and an apple into it, then sprinkled some nuts on top and a swirl of honey. She decided to have a glass of wine too, in honour of Dorothy's ascension to the summit of emotional attainment. Glass in one hand, bowl in the other, she went back to the sitting room and was just sitting down again when the phone rang once more.

'Hello,' she answered distractedly, trying to get comfortable in competition with the cats, both of whom had designs on her lap.

'Lily, it's your mother.'

Lily's brain came into focus. A mid-week family call. Must be something serious.

'Oh, Lily. How do I . . . ? I don't know how to tell you . . .'

Lily's stomach lurched. 'Tell me what?'

'It's your father. He's had a heart attack.'

Chapter 12

'No.'

Unthinking, Lily's answer to her mother's statement was an absolute rejection. She would have no truck with her father's frailty.

'No. Not Dad. Tell me what happened.'

Her mother described a trip they had taken to a nearby garden centre, a huge acreage visited from afar by people in charabancs. Alec and Edna had made a day of it, spending hours walking round the various indoor and outdoor sites, exhausting themselves and only stopping for a cup of coffee. On the way home, the car full of winter pansies and shrubs for autumn planting, they had decided to have a meal at a country pub. Alec had eaten heartily, ordering favourite and substantial dishes, steak and kidney pudding, jam roly-poly and, inevitably, custard. Tired but full, they had risen from the table and decided on a brief final stroll down to the river, to help settle their stomachs. It was on this walk that Alec had complained of chest pains and then collapsed.

The ambulancemen had arrived quickly, whisking both of them to the local hospital, from which Edna was now phoning. Alec had been rushed into 'crash' in the accident and emergency unit.

'They're working on him now,' her mother sobbed.

'I'll come,' said Lily, then realized the impracticality of it. Late trains were a thing of the past. What about work? And the cats?

But her mother was being surprisingly sensible. 'No. Wait a bit. Let's see what the doctors say yet. I'll ring as soon as I've heard more.'

'But you're alone, Mum. Don't you want someone with you?'

'I'll ring Mary. She'll come. Sidney can drive her over.' Mary was an old friend, the wife of a bookie whose shop had been adjacent to her father's. Neither woman could drive.

'You promise you'll do that now, and then ring me the minute there's any more news?'

'I promise.'

Lily sat on her sofa, staring unseeing at the bowl of food. She found herself mechanically sipping her wine, and stroking Palmer's head in an automatic, repetitive movement which began to make him cross. A fog had descended. She could not think clearly at all. Her father, mortally ill? But lots of people survived heart attacks. True, he was overweight and unfit, but he could exercise, take up a sensible diet. There were all kinds of surgery they could perform, drugs they could offer. He had never been ill before. It would be okay.

She wished she had visited more often, more recently. Well, she would in future. Her parents were not in their dotage, but neither was the time infinite. She should make an effort, see them on a more regular basis.

She looked at the clock. Half an hour had passed. What was happening? She was desperate to know, but there was no alternative but to sit and wait. Should she pray? She had never been a believer of any kind, but where was the harm in trying? Oh God, be with Dad. Help him pull through. Don't let him die.

Her glass was empty. Her left leg was stiff from the weight of two cats. She tumbled the warm furry bodies on to the floor and stood up, at a loss to know what to do with herself. The thought of television and radio was unendurable. She would have liked to talk to someone but who?

(Frank? Hugo? Dorothy?) Everyone, for whatever reason, was out of bounds and anyway, she could not block the phone line. She prowled the flat, topping up her glass *en route*.

Three-quarters of an hour now. Surely there was some news. How long would they 'work' on someone? Was longer better than shorter? This was agony.

As the phone rang again, Lily knew it was her mother. At the sound of her indrawn breath, Lily knew the news was bad.

'No,' she said again, without a thought. 'Oh, no.'

'He's dead, Lily. They couldn't save him.' Edna was not crying now. She sounded entirely calm.

'Oh, Mum.' Lily could not think of a single word more to say.

'They won't let me see him yet. So I'll stay until then. And then Sidney will take me home.'

'Don't you want to stay with them tonight?'

'No. I'd rather go home.'

'I'll come first thing in the morning,' Lily promised.

'Yes. You come, Lily.' Her mother sounded exhausted.

'The very first train.'

By the time she put the phone down, it was ten o'clock. Fatigue had crept into her bones, but the rational part of Lily's brain was thinking about the morning. She had better get a message to the office, she had better pack a bag, she had better book a taxi to take her first to the vet's – on the assumption that there was space in their cattery – and then on to the station.

She did not know who to ring at work. She had no one's number. Then she thought of Andy. Andy knew Clive. She had better call him now.

Thankfully he answered on the first ring. 'Lily. This is a surprise. Is anything wrong?'

Now the dam in her throat broke and tears coursed down her cheeks. 'My father's died.' It was true. It was out there. The man who loved her best of all was gone.

'Oh, Lily. I'm so sorry. What can I do? Shall I come over?'

'No. No. But thanks. I just wanted Clive's number. I need to go home and I have to tell the office.'

'Hold on, I'll get it.' Sensible and straightforward as ever. Andy the rock. 'Here. Have you got a pen?'

She noted the number, then fended off again his offer of assistance. She was better off without help just now. Forcing herself forward would be a good way of getting through the next hours.

She rang Clive. His wife answered, jovial to start with but more sober when she heard more of Lily's tone. Soon Clive was there, brisk but sympathetic too. 'Of course I'll tell Hugo. Don't worry. I've got his number, though. Would you like to call him yourself?'

More than anything. 'No, thanks, Clive. If you don't mind. I've got other things to get on with so that I can get away first thing in the morning.'

'No problem. Just let us know if you won't be in on Monday.'

Lily paused for an instant, to indulge a fantasy of having Hugo with her now, to hold and comfort her. How safe she would feel, held in his arms. Tears were trickling steadily down her face. This was not helpful. She stood up and began to gather necessities together for her suitcase. Slowly she became conscious of an ache. Was it real or psychic? She could scarcely distinguish. But somewhere in her torso, pain was growing, not a throbbing or a stabbing, but a hard, cold pressure. This was loss.

She had dreamed once, as a teenager, of her father's death. Awake, she had still felt able to retain the sense of utter bereavement, the steel door closed between them, the absolute finality of all communication. She had been able to glimpse then the grief of the experience. And yet now, it was different. It was not that they would no longer have regular discourse, more that the river of his presence, his unquestioning encouragement and approbation was dammed up, dried up, gone underground. Who would ever love, care for her as much? Who else would subordinate his own life, go to such extremes to tend and protect her? If she had thought she was alone before, that was as nothing to this new isolation. For ever into the future, Lily would perforce be standing on her own two feet. No more the good daughter. No more the fledgling adult, with the shadow of vigilance still hovering over her. Hello grown-ups.

About time too, the less histrionic Lily might have said, but now, on this dark, autumnal evening, she would have given much to dwell a little longer in her well-over-extended adolescence.

Her bag was packed. The cat basket had surreptitiously, under cover of Radio Four, been brought down from the loft and hidden in the bathroom. She locked up, set the alarm, switched off lights, automatically climbed the stairs to the bedroom, took off her clothes and lay down, pulling the duvet up over her nose. Pictures of her father flashed through her mind – swimming on holiday, driving the car, glancing up from the television to give her a dazzling smile, bringing her breakfast in bed, eating egg on toast, holding her hand. Tears now ran from the corners of her eyes to the pillow, and the cold push was there again, under her ribs. Sleep was impossible. And when she next looked at the clock it was six a.m.

The morning went without a hitch. Punctual taxi, helpful cattery, ungridlocked central London. She bought her train ticket and joined the business travellers with their laptops and *FT*s, alighting a couple of hours later at the station where, for once, there was no one to meet her. Dry-eyed but set-faced, she took a taxi home.

All the curtains were drawn, in the old-fashioned signal of mourning. Lily was almost inclined to knock at the front door, but decided to try the back first, which was indeed open. Her mother was sitting at the kitchen table, cup in hand. She looked quite normal, except that her cardigan was buttoned up in the wrong holes. She kept fiddling with the collar, bewildered that it would not lie flat. She did not get up, just smiled at Lily in a tired way. Lily dropped her bags, went over and held her mother awkwardly. Edna's white head was nestled against the place in her abdomen where the pain lived. Somehow it seemed fitting.

After a few silent moments, she released her mother, fetched a cup and joined her at the table. Then she waited.

The silence extended a while, and Edna's eyes seemed fixed on a point in the middle distance. She looked as if she might be listening to music. 'I saw him,' she began eventually. 'They'd wrapped him up, all but his face. I don't know what they did to his body, but his face was quite calm. There were lots of people about, though, in the background. I didn't get a chance to say goodbye properly.' Her eyes filled at this thought.

'Can we go and see him today?' Lily asked. She was trying to meet her mother's need, but realized that she wanted to see her father too.

'Yes. At the funeral parlour. He's at Jones's. Sidney arranged it. We can go this afternoon. We have to sort things out anyway, for the funeral and all that.'

'When is the funeral?' Lily had not thought about any of this, had never before had to engage with the vocabulary of parlours and coffins.

'I thought Monday. That should give us enough time to

tell people. Can you stay that long?' Edna was looking at her properly now.

'Of course.'

'He wanted to be cremated. But that's all I know. You'll have to sort out the music. There's an awful lot to do. All his clothes. And what are we going to do with the ashes?' Her mother looked lost, swamped by responsibility and detail.

'Let's make a list,' said Lily, keen to be helpful and practical, even keener to avoid the kind of conversation she dreaded but which would be unavoidable at some moment, reminiscences of Alec as refracted through her mother's personality. This was when the tug of love would begin. 'Shall we start with people to telephone?' she went on briskly.

They compiled a list. Edna turned out to be little more experienced in the business of death management than Lily, but they made a start. The point of the funeral ceremony quickly became obvious – a precise point of conclusion and also an elaborate piece of organization that absorbed much of their energy. The sad, reflective stuff would have to come later. How many would be asked, and who would contact them; the invitations back to the house afterwards and what to serve. All these needed thought and discussion. Then there were Alec's effects (more strange vocabulary). The clothes and shoes, the spectacles and cufflinks to be disposed of. Insurance companies and doctors to be contacted. They made decisions about all these things, which was easy enough in the abstract. Lily did not relish the actual moment of opening her father's wardrobe or sifting through his papers.

The phone began to interrupt them, and it became Lily's job too to field the calls. Again, she was happy to act as Edna's shield, and surprised that she could articulate the words and absorb the condolences that began to flow down the line. They punctuated their work with hot drinks and at some point a sandwich. When Lily looked at the clock, it was after two. Time to think about saying goodbye.

She was already dressed in black. Quite unconsciously she had picked out mourning as the only colour to travel in and take with her. Now her mother went to change and she was left alone for a few moments. She wandered into the sitting room and contemplated her father's armchair, part of a three-piece suite that was as much a fixture of Lily's existence as the mole on her left elbow. The Braithwaites had always owned these chairs, this sofa. Reupholstered more than once, they were always covered in wine-red velour, with polished wooden arms. Our first married purchase, Alec had said proudly. Every previous stick of furniture had either been home-made or a hand-me-down from well-wishers. But the suite had been a landmark, the product of an expedition to Birmingham, with Edna in her best costume and Alec in a double-breasted suit. Lily had had the clothes pointed out to her from other photographs. It had become a point of pride never to replace this furniture, only to get it re-covered or its arms French-polished. Lily sat in her father's chair, broad in seat, generous in cushions. She waited for the tears. Where were they?

Edna came downstairs in a navy sweater and bottle-green skirt. 'I've nothing in black,' she said. 'Alec always said it made me look pasty.'

They were both confounded by this. It was true. Alec had ruled Edna's wardrobe as he had most of the other details of her life. No black, no bright blue, nothing floral. No make-up other than lipstick. No flat shoes and no stilettos either. And definitely no tights. Edna must be the last woman in England still wearing suspenders, Lily used to think as a teenager, although now fashion had caught up with her.

'Had we better go shopping?' Lily asked. It seemed sacrilegious, absurd, but what else were they to do?

'After we've seen him,' Edna answered. 'We'll have to.'

At Jones's, they were met by Catherine, the large-framed daughter who had taken over the business after Stan had retired. These were family acquaintances – they had been customers in the shop – and Catherine had attended the same school as Lily, although in a younger class. There was something bizarre about a funeral home being run by a young woman, Lily felt, but she was glad of the informality. Catherine was doing her very best to minimize their pain.

In a mutedly decorated office, she offered them a folder on caskets and explained about the paraphernalia of the occasion. The cars, the ceremony, the flowers, the urn and what to do with it. It was like a multiple-choice exam, and Edna, after years of deference, seemed constantly to look to Lily for guidance and decision-making. So decisions were taken and plans laid. Monday began to come into focus, and another list was formed, of outstanding details that were not part of Catherine's duties. Flowers were to be ordered from a florist, music tapes from a high street shop. Not much mystery there.

When it came to the ashes, Catherine ran through their options, including one which Lily had not expected – burial.

'Oh, yes,' Catherine explained, her pink, farmer's wife face flushed with her efforts on behalf of the late Alec Braithwaite who had sold her her engagement and wedding rings and teething rings for her two sons. 'Burial is quite common after a cremation. I can call the cemetery now, if that's what you'd like. We put the urn in a small casket, and you can have a private burial ceremony. Then, when you're ready, we can help you organize the stone.'

'What do you think, Mum?'

Edna looked unsure but said nothing.

Lily realized that she wanted there to be a place recording her father's passing, not just a rosebush or a garden shared with others. She turned to Catherine. 'Yes,' she said. 'We'll bury the ashes.'

When everything was done, including the sums on a calculator, a silence filled the room. Lily knew what was coming next and dread fell upon her. Death. A body. No matter that it was her father. One of life's mysteries and terrors was here, in the next room, and she was going to meet it. She became conscious of her heartbeat and the coldness in her fingers. Edna interrupted her train of thought.

'Lily, will you go in first? Tell me if it's alright.'

What could she do but agree? Catherine, who had discreetly left the room, was now back, beckoning her like some servant of another realm. Lily got up and followed. Beyond the corridor was a windowless room with diffused lighting. Thank heavens no taped organ music was playing, nor were there obvious tokens of religious belief. Tall vases in the corners contained sprays of flowers. There was no other furniture than the long box – was this a bier? – on which the coffin stood.

'We've given him only the finest quality,' Catherine said. 'I wanted him to look his best for you.'

Lily heard the words in some distant corner of her brain, heard the kindness behind them, but her eyes were magnetized to the coffin and she walked towards it, while Catherine quietly left the room.

There he lay, in his good suit, eyes closed, hands crossed. It was just like every scene you had ever seen in a film or on the television. He looked asleep. He looked benign. A smile seemed to hover at the corner of his lips. His plump fingers, capable of such delicate work repairing damaged jewellery, had the same relaxed curl as when he dozed in his chair. This was a joke he had played. He would wake up at any moment, smile at her and drive them home.

Up close, it was still no different, and she reached out her hand to his. It was cold. Another cliché tested for truth. He was marble, ice. Horror-struck, she snatched her hand back. Yet the expression on his face softened her fear. This *was* her father, and a huge love welled up from the lump of pain under her ribs. Now she could weep, pulling tissue after tissue from her pocket. Speech seemed quite natural and she harangued him for leaving, for abandoning her, for not saying a proper goodbye.

'How could you go? I need you, especially now after Frank and everything. What will I do, with no one to watch out for me? How will Mother manage? Why did you have to leave us?' The words poured out, and the tears poured down, until the frenzy had passed. Then she mopped her face dry and walked towards him once more. She would have to say goodbye. She would have to fetch her mother. She bent down and kissed him on his cold brow. Horrible though it was, it was also perfectly right. He was not alive. The kiss had proved it. She did not want to tear herself away, but she must fetch her mother.

Edna was waiting outside, clutching her handbag with both hands. Catherine was with her, but silent. Edna rushed towards Lily.

'It's fine, Mum. He looks wonderful,' and she glanced towards Catherine with a smile of gratitude.

Holding her mother's hand, Lily went back into her father's presence, but standing back, allowing Edna to go forward. Hearing her mother's laboured breathing as she too wept, Lily knew that her time of concentration, of dialogue with Alec was over. She left Edna alone and walked out into the fresh air.

Edna emerged quite soon, embroidered cotton handkerchief pressed to her face. Lily settled her in the car.

'What about shopping? Do you feel up to it?' she asked.

'Mm hm,' her mother affirmed, muffled behind her handkerchief. And so, like something out of an absurd comedy, they went into town and bought Edna a black raincoat, a black shirtdress with gold buttons, a black pillbox hat with a veil and a pair of black court shoes. It was a curious spree, and despite the solemnity, the women relaxed a little, Edna parading the clothes, Lily offering wise metropolitan advice. For a moment they contemplated tea in town, then reality returned and they drove home. Both were exhausted, and Lily acknowledged, as she helped transfer carrier bags into the house, that she was going to find herself doubly drained by this experience, with both bereavement to deal with and the role of surrogate parent to Edna. A deep, dark shaft of loneliness speared its way through her.

Neither woman was hungry, but common sense dictated a meal, so Lily put together an omelette and they sat at the kitchen table to eat it. What now? Was television permitted? Lily felt the need for some solitude and suggested her customary retreat, a bath. When she emerged, she found her mother was upstairs too, busy in her bedroom, sorting out piles of Alec's clothes.

'Do you have to do that now?' Lily asked, almost irritated that her mother couldn't rest after the day's labours.

'I wanted to make a start.' Edna turned to the dressing table, then came to Lily with her right hand cupped. 'Would you like these?'

She was offering Alec's best gold watch and his tie-pin. At the sight of them, Lily melted. Her knees buckled and she sat down quickly on the double bed. Now it was her mother's turn to comfort her, and Lily sat with Edna's arm round her shoulder, feeling like a child, letting the waves of tears ripple through her, scenting again her mother's familiar odour.

'I didn't mean to upset you,' Edna said.

'No. It's okay. I'm glad to have them. It's just, they're so inseparably a part of him. He always wore the tie-pin. If he's left them behind, then he's definitely gone.'

'But he has,' Edna said prosaically.

'I know. I wish I'd seen him, you know, before.'

'You mustn't say that. You two were always so close. He knew how much he mattered to you.'

'Do you think so?' Lily was not certain. Yes, of course, she and her father had always shared an obvious love, but now, more recently, had she made sure that he knew her feelings had not altered with adulthood?

'Of course. I was jealous sometimes. He thought so highly of you. And of course he worried, especially just now. Sometimes he seemed to talk of nothing else.'

Lily felt the need somehow to reassure her mother. 'But you always came first.'

'Probably.'

There seemed to be no rancour in Edna and Lily was relieved. Perhaps they would be able to refashion the geometry of the family without needing to explore the darker corners of the triangle they had once been.

Both women were silent, side by side on the bed, and the darkness outside deepened.

'I'll make us a drink,' Lily offered finally. Soon after, they went to bed.

Much was accomplished in the next few days. By Sunday, everything was in place for the funeral and Lily had also rung Clive again to establish that she could stay away until Tuesday or Wednesday. She had been into town and picked out recordings of Plácido Domingo singing 'Ave Maria' and Artur Rubinstein playing the Moonlight Sonata. She had sat in on innumerable visits from friends and neighbours, over cups of tea, and had been allowed out on her own a couple of times, to visit Tesco for supplies, including boiled ham and bottles of whisky for visitors after the funeral.

She and her mother had talked little and often. They had been kind to each other and the only jockeying for position had come at the cemetery office, where a mild dispute had arisen over where to bury the urn. Lily had favoured a quiet hillside, but her mother had fixed on the shade of a cedar tree and would not be budged. Lily felt that she knew best what her father would have preferred – the view and the open prospect – but her mother became petulant. A squabble was brewing but the cemetery officer had clearly handled such situations before and suggested a walk to both spots, as a cooling-off period. As they traversed the tidy paths, Lily realized how badly she was behaving and backed down. Edna was a little ungracious in her triumph.

Monday dawned hazy, blue and very beautiful. All the glorious waning of autumn was on display as the cortège wound away from the Braithwaite home, on to the dual carriageway and down to the crematorium. Lily and Edna sat in the deep upholstery of the black undertaker's limousine and Lily was distracted by the predictable urge to nod in queenly fashion at passers-by who stopped to gawk. In front, the coffin was scarcely visible under its tumulus of floral tributes, including Lily's own bearing a card inscribed: 'To my most beloved father'. Behind their glossily polished Daimler, a line of cars stretched back out of sight. Alec had been popular and a respected local trader.

The ceremony itself was brief, not especially personal, until Eric Perry the gents' outfitter got up and delivered a short eulogy to his fellow shopkeeper. Lily lost her composure at the picture he evoked of small-town life in the fifties and sixties, and wept in silence for the remainder of the occasion. As the coffin rolled away, to the sounds of Rubinstein's piano chords, the whole congregation seemed to shuffle and sob.

Outside, no one seemed too sure of the etiquette and the opposite of a wedding line formed, with Lily and Edna shaking everyone's hand and absorbing their quiet words of condolence, before finally the snake of slow-moving cars followed the route back to the house. Here jackets were shrugged off and ties loosened. Lily couldn't seem to fill the kettle often enough, and the sandwiches and fruit cake vanished from the serving plates with fairy-tale speed. In the sitting room, the noise level rose and a giddy excitement seemed to buoy everyone up, including Lily and Edna, who circulated and starred in the perverse joy of the hour. Outside, the sun was still shining and a gilded light fell upon the garden and spilled into the room.

But the energy slowly ebbed, people drifted away, and at the end of the afternoon Lily and her mother were left with the depressing detritus of crumbs, dirty china, glasses and crumpled paper serviettes. After Lily had closed the front door behind the last mourner, she joined her mother, slumped on the sofa. More work to do, she thought, exhausted now that the force that had compelled them forward was gone. For the first time, she felt an urge to be back in London, free of obligation to others, alone to lick her new wounds. But she was less free now than she had ever been. She was going to have to take care of Edna.

Her mother was sitting back with her eyes closed, shoes kicked off. Was she asleep? As Lily looked at her, she wondered what Edna's future would be. Financially, she was probably perfectly safe. Emotionally, she might be as fragile as a blown eggshell. What would Lily's own responsibilities be towards her? More frequent visits, to start with at least, and as much reassurance as it took. And where was she going to find the resources for all that?

Edna's eyes were open now, fixed on the ceiling.

'Shall we make a start?' Lily asked.

'In a minute,' her mother answered. She seemed to have something to say. 'Thank you for being here, Lily. I think we did him proud, don't you?'

'I think so,' she answered with difficulty.

'He wasn't always an easy man to love,' Edna went on, slowly. 'Because of his childhood, I suppose. At the beginning I used to find it very hard. He wanted his own way, and if he didn't get it, there would be those silences. Like a sulky child, I used to think. I can remember my own mother saying the same about your grandad. With Alec, I found the easiest way was to let him think he had won.'

But he had won, Lily thought.

'But then, although he seemed so sure of himself, at home I could see that he was often frightened. He would ask me what to do. He'd never admit it, but he needed me.'

Lily was not convinced. Her mother was rewriting history.

'When I said to you, when Frank left, about never knowing what couples have agreed between them, well that was because I made the choice not to leave your father. I can't say I've never regretted it, but it was the right thing.'

Mentally, Lily's jaw dropped. Now she was really confused. Alec loved and needed Edna more? Then why had she seemed so servile, so martyred?

'Was there someone else?' she asked.

'Yes,' her mother admitted. 'Don't worry, this was long before you were born. And it wasn't what you think. We were only ever friends. Do you remember Queenie Long-hurst?' Lily did, vaguely, a family acquaintance when she was very small. 'It was her brother, Harry. He was in the merchant navy. He wanted me to leave your father and go abroad. He died in a car crash, not that long ago, as it turns out. He'd had an easier life than your father, and it had made him more kindly. I was tempted. I'd be lying if I said otherwise. I think a marriage with him would have been more of a partnership. But I couldn't destroy your father – and my going would have done that to him.' There was a pause. 'And I did always find Alec a very manly man.'

Both women smiled at this. It was as close as Edna was ever going to come to acknowledging a sexual appetite.

But what was Lily to make of it all? Was it true? She was sure Harry had existed, her mother would never have invented him, or presumably his offer. But if she had had the upper hand then, when did she give it up? Had her father known about Harry? What would his account have been? Was there any objective truth at all? What would Margot say?

Her brain whirled. Mole wives taking command. Domineering fathers turning into needy little boys. She felt rather feverish. And just when she was girding up to take care of her mother, here Edna was, turning the tables and giving abundantly clear signals that she had a brain of her own.

'But why did you let Dad boss you around? You got so cross all the time.'

'Oh, he liked to think he was the man of the house. Where was the harm in that?'

'The harm was in you seeming so unhappy.'

Had Lily gone too far? Her mother looked angry. 'Every marriage has its ups and downs. We had an understanding, your father and I.' She stopped, looking a little tight around the jaw.

Some understanding; a dictator and an other. Lily did not want to argue, today of all days, but knew that her face and the accumulated, shared knowledge between mother and daughter contradicted at least in part what Edna was propounding.

There seemed to be nothing more to add. Both women knew what they thought. They were unlikely to agree. Their versions of history, and of their love for Alec, would have to coexist side by side for the moment. Perhaps in the years to come it might be possible to superimpose the memories more comfortably one upon the other. For now, both women thought they knew best, were loved best. Lily found that the harmony she and her mother had shared had somehow been shattered. They were back to their familiar conflict over Alec's affections, even now, with him reduced to a mound of cooling ash in Catherine Jones's parlour. Some things never changed.

Scratchy and not a little frustrated, she stood up and began to gather dirty glasses. She would leave her mother to her own authorized version. Truth, she felt, could not be divisible from behaviour. But then she remembered Frank. And Hugo. A strange kind of gulp bubbled up from her throat and left her mouth like a gasp. Tired, confounded and feeling very isolated, she went into the kitchen, turned on the hot tap in the sink and squirted in a vicious jet of washing-up liquid.

Chapter 13

Lily caught the last train to London on the Tuesday evening. She had spent the day helping her mother clean the house and then going through papers. There seemed to be no copy of the will at home; Edna would see the solicitor about that shortly. Meanwhile there were insurance policies and pension schemes to look at, as well as Alec's handful of investments. Being an old-fashioned man, he had acquired a small bundle of shares in companies he considered copper-bottomed, and had then left them to ripen. Several had lost value over the years, others had done better and issued more shares or been the subject of take-overs. Edna clearly felt sentimental about this legacy and, despite Lily's advice, insisted on keeping it, mouldering away, in her portfolio. But her other income looked safe and healthy, and with the mortgage paid and no major outgoings, she had every prospect of a calm financial future.

Lily felt she had accomplished as much as she could. Leaving Edna with a promise that she would be back the weekend after next for the burial ceremony, she climbed aboard the eight o'clock train with a profound sigh of relief. She had treated herself to a copy of *Marie Claire* and now lashed out on a Bloody Mary to go with it, and settled back for the journey home.

At the house, which was miserably empty without the cats, she found a small stack of mail, including condolence letters from Clive, Andy and Dorothy, on whose answerphone she had left a brief message. Also, there was a card from Hugo. Beneath the printed message of sympathy he had written: 'I know there is nothing I can say to make you feel better, but if there is anything I can do, you have only to ask.' Nice phrasing, she thought coolly. She had a momentary, skittish thought of testing it out, but dignity prevailed. Enough pain already.

On Wednesday morning she went back to work. Her desk was very tidy; clearly Monica had been keeping an eye, possibly also a hand on matters. Lily went to thank her.

'Don't give it a thought,' Monica said, examining her closely. 'Are you going to be okay?'

'Fine,' Lily reassured her. What else could she say? To avoid thinking about how unfine she really felt, she asked, 'How've things been here?'

'Not great. Thre's a rumour going round about redundancies.'

So jolly Hugo in the pub had not been hypothesizing after all.

'How many?' Lily asked.

Monica shrugged. 'Stories vary. Ten per cent maybe.'

'Has anybody asked Hugo outright?'

'No. He's been a bit moody. But –' Monica took her glasses off, always a sign of tension.

'What?' asked Lily.

'A couple of people did suggest you might. Although I said that wasn't fair, given the circumstances.' The words tumbled out in a rush.

Lily closed her eyes. She could imagine feeling flattered that some of the staff saw her as their spokesperson, but not today.

'I will,' she said. 'But give me some time.'

Back in her office, she put the notion of redundancy to one side and contemplated instead a teetering in-tray and a diary cross-hatched with rescheduled appointments. Leafing forward a few weeks, she realized that coming up fast was the Brighton trade fair. Like Glasgow, this was a key buying event, but the timing, within sight of Christmas, lent it a festive, often rather inebriated quality. It would mean another three days out of the office. She had better get on top of things before then.

Hugo appeared shortly after ten. His expression was grave, and he came round her desk and hugged her. She stood inert in his arms, her heart thumping as her senses sent urgent messages to her brain in response to his smell, his warmth, his strength. Her sexuality leapt awake as if cattle-prodded. But she knew that that was not Hugo's intention. She controlled herself very carefully. When he stepped away, she merely thanked him for his card.

He shrugged. 'My father died a few years ago. It was bloody hard. We weren't all that close, but his opinion always mattered. And then he wasn't there any more. I'm probably still trying to impress him.' At this, he looked oddly serious and more owlish than ever.

Lily had stopped her mental fluttering by now and sat down again, keen to get away from the swamps where personal revelations overlapped with personal relations. 'Is all quiet on the GBF front?' she asked, knowing better.

'Pretty much so,' he answered. 'Christmas looks like it will be a late start, but I think we're ready. You might want to just double-check on the top twenty.' This was an invention of Hugo's, a kind of stock bestseller list which helped not only Lily but the whole company to focus on the most lucrative and fastest-turning-over lines. It was turning out to be a surprisingly good idea. 'You'll find one or two notes from me about items that came up. Oh, and I think it's ultimatum-time for those Italian glass-bead suppliers of yours. It may be nice gear but if they can't deliver, it's not worth the aggro.'

Gear? Lily thought. My God, he's a sixties child. 'Have

they let us down again? Leave it with me.' Brisk Lily, efficient and professional Lily.

He was at the doorway now. Good. She wanted to get on. The redundancy conversation would have to wait.

'Oh, one other thing. I think I'll come to Brighton. Can you book me in and get me a pass?' And with that he was gone.

Lily forced herself not to think about a three-day, two-night trip to Brighton in Hugo's company. She must focus on work. She must focus, period. She picked up the first document in her tray and gazed at it like a newly landed Martian. She felt as if she were deep underwater, as if a thick clotted atmosphere held her suspended, deaf and uncoordinated. She tried again, and managed to decipher the letterhead, the gist of the words. It was a change-of-terms offer from one of the larger suppliers – more discount for bigger bulk orders. She would have to look at their sales profile and calculate the benefit versus cash flow. She put the piece of paper down, jittery at the thought of how much effort just that one sheet of A4 would require. Below it lay another piece of paper, and another. What on earth was she supposed to do?

She went and fetched a hot drink, and decided on her return simply to read all the pieces of paper and sort them into priority piles. That seemed manageable. In amongst the layers of business correspondence, she found one or two sealed envelopes marked 'Personal'. More condolence cards, from professional acquaintances. People were astonishing. One card in particular, from Jimmy Khan, seemed, in its careful phraseology – respectful yet oddly tender – to deliver a soft punch to the aching place in her diaphragm. She sat back in her chair and covered her face with her hands, willing herself to get a grip. When she looked up, Hugo was in her doorway again. He said two words.

'Go home.'

Lily could not agree, but finally they compromised on her working at home for the day, and she packed up all the correspondence, informed Monica and Pat, and slipped back out on to the street. At least, she consoled herself, she could pick the cats up now, and then settle down to work on the sofa.

Somehow home did seem a more congenial place in which to engage her brain, its comfortable hush broken only by familiar noises – the sighing of the gas boiler, the clang of Ron closing his front gate. She and the cats made a nest amongst the cushions, and there she worked through the papers, planned her tasks for the following day, and felt at the end of it some small sense of achievement. Then she lay, eyes closed, semi-conscious, allowing her psyche to explore her battered emotions.

She decided that she had touched bottom. There could be no lower place to go. No particle of herself seemed free of pain. She felt herself to be a failure, a naïve optimist who had set up her life in various cocky ways, only to have them serially flattened all around her. What was she good at, apart from her job (which she might be about to lose)? What had she achieved? She felt as if she stood on the friable edge of a cliff, with pebbles and small clods of earth already disappearing down into the void. She was that close to the limit. Only the gentlest of abrasions would send her over.

She must have fallen asleep, because when the phone rang, it was dark. She reached out for the receiver while slowly uncurling her cramped limbs.

'Lily, it's Andy.'

'Oh, hi,' she said. 'Thanks for the card.'

'Please, don't thank me. I wondered how you were.'

'Surviving.'

'Do you want company?' Funnily enough, she thought she might.

'I'll be there in half an hour.'

She was just about to get up and turn the lights on when there was another call, this time Dorothy.

'I'm doing okay. Honestly,' Lily told her friend.

'I don't think so,' said Dot. 'Your voice has the weight of the world in it.'

'All right, I'm at rock bottom, is that what you want to hear?' Lily felt provoked by her friend's perception.

'I'm sorry, I'm sorry. I only wanted to know if there was anything I can do. Do you want to be visited? Or to come here?'

Lily explained that Andy was on his way. Also, that with Peter in residence, she didn't want to interrupt her friend's idyll.

'It isn't like that,' Dot assured her. 'We're too old for the moonstruck phase. And he's very good at taking the hint and going out for a walk.'

'Are you happy?' Lily wanted to know.

'I'm embarrassed to tell you this, with your plateful, but yes. There are problems, of course, but if it's of any comfort, we're none of us too old for a fairy-tale romance.'

'Will you come over soon? Tomorrow, or the weekend.'

'Whenever you like.'

They finalized their arrangements just in time for Lily to get herself and the room sorted out before Andy arrived. In his rollneck sweater and tweed jacket, he looked tidy, possibly a little bachelorish. Lily noted that her infatuation for Hugo had cleansed her of sexual feelings towards Andy. Just as well.

He had brought a bottle of brandy and a sheaf of takeaway menus, and insisted that they order some food in.

'You're worse than my mother,' Lily laughed, enjoying his domestic solicitude.

He was gentle with her, not discussing the death until they had eaten, drunk some wine and then moved on to the brandy. Even then, he asked little, just let her ramble through whatever seemed significant.

'It's like an onslaught,' she mused aloud, 'all of it from left field, from the direction I'm never looking in. Just one damn thing after another. I had this terrible thought, when Mum rang the second time, to say Dad had actually died. I thought, oh no, here we go again, just when I reckoned I might be getting over Frank, here I am back in the misery. Not a very worthy thought at your parent's death.'

'What do you think you are, some kind of saint?' Andy replied. 'Don't be so hard on yourself. After all your knocks, aren't you allowed to have the occasional black thought? You'd be less than honest if all you could admit was to thinking about others, just at the moment. Personally, I think getting through your MLC, sorry, mid-life crisis entitles you to any thought, any action, just to survive. I know that's how I looked on mine.' He leaned over to top up their glasses.

'Mid-life crisis? Is that what this is?'

'Isn't it?' he queried.

'I've no idea,' Lily answered. 'I don't know the dictionary definition.'

'Nor me, but I gather you know it when it happens. I certainly did. I just felt out of control, some kind of punch-bag with all the certainties of life being ripped from under me. It wasn't the same sequence as yours, although relationships came into it. There was a death, though, and a professional failure.' He stopped, seemingly disinclined to offer the details on a plate. Lily thought he would probably answer questions if she asked, but she was too tired.

'I don't feel old enough to be having a mid-life crisis,' she said.

'You don't have to be middle-aged. It can come at any

time from mid-thirties to early fifties. It's about your life exploding from within.'

'That sounds like it. Thanks for the diagnosis. So what's the treatment?'

Andy sat back. 'Like I said, whatever you need to do to get through. It takes as long as it takes, and all you can do is hold on tight till it's all over and then see where you come to rest. I did all kinds of things – started working out, went to some counselling sessions, treated myself to CDs and concert tickets as often as I wanted, explored bits of myself I hadn't really faced up to, had a couple of affairs. I'm not sure I recommend that last part.' There was a pause. 'I felt I had nothing left to lose, so why not open up, go a bit wild.' Another pause. He looked at her, as if considering something, then seemed to change his mind. 'One wacky thing I did was to go to an astrologer.'

Lily laughed at his joke, then saw from his face that it was the truth. 'You went to an astrologer?' she gawked. 'But you're an accountant.'

'Is there a law against it?'

'No, but you know what I mean. A cool head for figures and all that, and now you're telling me you went to visit Gipsy Rose Lee.' She took a long sip from her glass.

'It wasn't like that. No crystal balls or pieces of silver.' He smiled. 'I only went because a hard-headed friend of mine recommended her. My reaction was the same as yours to begin with. But it was brilliant. Maybe you should go too.'

Lily made a scoffing sound.

'Well, why not?'

'Because I don't need to hear rubbish about tall dark strangers.'

'No, it really isn't like that. In fact, it's amazing, like psychotherapy mixed with magic. All you give her is your time and place of birth, and then she gives you this complete run-down of your personality. No holds barred. She doesn't really predict the future, anyway. Just describes who you are and suggests how you're going to respond to things. Well, I found it helpful, anyway,' he finished, a little shamefacedly.

Lily forced herself to be less dismissive. Why should she make Andy feel embarrassed when he was trying to help her, and being pretty open in the process? She was intrigued by the idea of someone telling her about herself and frankly she didn't want to know anything about the future if it was going to be as crammed with horrible landmines as the recent past had been.

'Do you still have her address?' she asked, not least as a gesture of reconciliation.

'Never go anywhere without it,' he said, reaching for his wallet. Sifting through various pieces of card, he eventually passed over an oblong of pasteboard decorated with an Egyptian symbol – an ankh? Lily wondered. She read only a name – Julie Bell – and a phone number. 'You have to book in advance,' Andy went on. 'At least a couple of weeks. She's very busy. That's when you have to give her the details. Do you know exactly when you were born?'

'No,' said Lily. 'But I know someone who does.'

Lily was phoning her mother on a daily basis and when she called the following evening, she found Edna somewhat depressed.

'Has anything happened?' she enquired.

'Not really,' her mother answered. 'I did go and see about the will, though.'

'And?' Lily asked. Surely no surprises there. Hadn't Alec simply left her everything?

'No, nothing to worry about. Your father was very good. He left nothing to chance. I'm to inherit the house and everything else, apart from a bequest to you.'

Was that the problem? 'What kind of bequest?'

'Five thousand pounds, and that platinum chain you liked. Remember?' Her mother still sounded sour. What was the matter? Surely not the money. The chain then. Could it be the one that sprang to Lily's mind? It was a beautiful piece of engineering that Alec had bought from a sales rep one Christmas, more to indulge himself than anyone else. His shop had catered to the lower-middle bracket, shopgirls and women workers in the local factories, and there had been no place in it for modern or designer items. He had not been able to resist the flat perfection of this ribbon of metal, though, and Lily too had adored it, cleaned it, dressed the shop window around it. All this had happened something like twenty years ago.

Of course, the chain had not sold and eventually Alec had had to admit defeat and remove it from display. Lily had assumed he had returned it to the firm who had supplied it, but apparently not. He had put it away for her. She was rocked by the rush of memories even a mention of the chain had engendered. As if with a crumb of the madeleine on her tongue, she was invaded by pictures of the poky little shop, of the games she had invented as a child with the box of discarded and broken items, of Saturday afternoons spent in the backroom while her parents served customers, the smell of Silver Dip, and of the rancid municipal lavatory, complete with VD poster, across the road which they had had to use.

The chain represented Alec's and Lily's special bond. Lily supposed that was what Edna minded, that even beyond the grave her husband was able to remind her that their daughter and he had a better understanding than the one she had referred to after the funeral.

Lily, weary from a day back in the office, where she had behaved much more normally, but needed to paddle furiously below the surface to achieve that impression, and now weary again from enforced solicitude towards her mother, and a sense that she might be punished by silence and sulks from Edna in exchange for a legacy from her father that actually meant something, almost felt like hanging up the phone. But she battled on.

'Do you mind that he left me those things?'

'No. Why should I?' Tight-lipped.

This was hopeless. Lily decided to move the conversation on. 'Good. That's okay then. Can I ask you something completely different?'

'Yes.' Edna sounded wary.

'Do you know the exact moment when I was born?'

It was obviously the perfect distraction. Edna began a long reminiscence of the night she had spent in the cottage hospital, in labour, alone with just a nurse, husbands not, in those days, normally expected to be at the birth. Between the pains, the two women had gazed out of the window at a remarkably clear summer sky, in which the stars had twinkled like in a Walt Disney cartoon. An auspicious night for a birth, they had agreed, and Lily had arrived just as the stars left the sky the following morning, soon after four a.m.

Almost breathless after this long description, Edna ground to a halt with the question, 'Why?'

'Oh, just something someone asked me,' Lily answered. But she had noted the time on her pad.

The next day, in a quiet moment before lunch, Lily called Julie Bell. A deep, rather sexy voice answered.

'Er, you don't know me,' Lily began awkwardly, 'but a friend recommended you and I wondered if you could give me a consultation.'

'Reading,' Julie Bell substituted. She audibly consulted a diary. 'I could fit you in at the end of November,' she said eventually, and suggested a date and time which Lily accepted. 'Do you know the time and place of your birth?'

Lily volunteered this information.

'The fee is seventy-five pounds, half now, the rest after the reading. Please bring a ninety-minute cassette tape with you. Do you have my address?'

Lily did not, but wrote it down quickly in response to Julie's instructions. Putting the handset back on its cradle, Lily felt rather surprised at what she had done, but also vaguely amused. Had she finally gone barmy? Well, why not? Crazy times, crazy remedies. She mused again on the label of mid-life crisis. Her image, such as it was, was of men, not women, going off the rails, chucking over well-paid but impossibly demanding jobs and moving to the country to become self-sufficient. Or leaving safe wives of twenty years' standing, for flighty juniors with riper ovaries.

Could it happen to her and those like her? Why had nobody warned her that, however inoffensive the sand-castle you made of your life, fate was going to come along and stamp it flat anyway? She had a mental picture of a Monty Python foot descending on her from the heavens. Lily thought it was about time her luck turned. In the mean-time, she would take a leaf out of Andy's book and devote this weekend to being very kind to herself.

Did that heading include having lunch with Hugo?

She met him in the lift. 'I'm just nipping out for a sandwich,' she explained.

'So am I. Let's go to that Jewish place.' He was standing rather close.

Lily, her senses prickling, fell in with the assumption, justifying it to herself with a silent promise that she would ask him about the redundancy rumours.

They walked down to a café near the Farringdon Road, where elderly waiters with expressions of timeless world-weariness patiently explained latkes and kreplach to the ignorant.

Lily had some chicken soup. It seemed fitting. Hugo

140

devoured a salt beef sandwich and a piece of cheesecake without seeming to taste either. His interest appeared more in satisfying his appetite as quickly as possible.

She hoped he wasn't going to ask about her father. Thankfully, he enquired instead about a flap that had blown up about some strings of faulty beads, rather beautiful things, golden and speckled like tigers' eyes. They had sold in well, but a trickle of complaints from several shops had turned, within the last twenty-four hours, into a flash-flood.

'Don't worry,' she told him. 'I've had it out with the suppliers. They were very apologetic – as they should be. They'd specified nylon thread and single knotting, but what they delivered was neither. We'll get a refund on the whole consignment.'

He nodded. She hoped that he had registered she had taken care of it and limited the damage. That, bereavements notwithstanding, she was back on the case.

So would this be a good moment? She drew breath. 'Hugo, can I ask you something, scotch a rumour that's been going round?'

'What rumour?'

'That there's going to be a staff cut-back. I know when you talked about it in the pub, you said it was only hypothetical. But apparently people are worried.'

Hugo took his time lighting a cigarette. Lily wondered if she had overstepped the mark. Too late now.

'Do you really want me to answer that?' he asked coolly.

'Of course, or I wouldn't have asked.'

'No,' he told her, like a parent. 'You don't. You don't want to be the bearer of bad tidings – just supposing there were any, that is. And you're certainly not the kind to lie to your friends.'

Lily wondered if that was a compliment.

'So what do I say to the others?' she answered.

'Whatever you think they'd like to hear.'

Was that Hugo's policy? Was that why he'd promised her a rosy future together that night in bed? She realized that if she wanted a straight answer, she had come to the wrong place. Perhaps she could tell her colleagues that.

There was a pause while they ordered coffee. When it arrived, Hugo said idly, 'I nearly rang you last night.'

Lily blinked.

'I was staying in town,' he went on, playing with the sugar bowl, heaping the grains into a cone and patting its sides with the back of a spoon. 'Jay's taken the girls to see her mother.'

'So why didn't you?' Did Lily say that or did the words just stream out of her ears, in illuminated script?

'I wasn't sure you'd feel like visitors. It seemed a bit soon after . . . you know.'

Did people in mourning not have sex? Lily supposed she had to respect Hugo's consideration, but cursed the man's rare and misplaced sensitivity. 'I wish you had,' she said, in a quiet voice.

'Do you?' He looked at her now, and as before, on the night of the party, she felt herself dissolve. 'So do I, now. It was bloody uncomfortable on my brother's sofa. Well, there'll be other times.'

Lily had time to dwell on these words, all the time in the world after they had returned to the office and the watched clock on her wall crept at snail's pace towards five thirty.

The good news, she supposed, was that he had thought about her when an opportunity had presented itself, that he wanted her, that 'other times' meant the door of a future with Hugo was ajar. And in answer to his semi-expressed question, she had answered clearly, yes, she was available.

The bad news – and this was a lesson he had already taught her – was that this on–off romance was going to be defined solely by Hugo's impulses and availability, not hers. Forget equal partners. He would lead. She would follow. Take it or leave it.

A bit like a mephisto waltz. The only thing she could do was wait for him to return and whirl her away. Well, unsatisfactory or not, she would take it. The only question was, when would he be back to claim her?

Lily was still pondering this when Dorothy came to supper the following evening. The knowledge of Hugo's desire had restored something in her, lifted her spirits a little. Unfortunately she had also had the 'Blue Danube' playing in her brain all day.

Peter had gone out, taking his eldest daughter bowling and then for a meal as a birthday treat. Lily had decided that she and Dot deserved something special too, and had spent the afternoon preparing a meal of great splendour.

'Blimey,' was Dorothy's first response to the wild mushroom ragout in puff pastry and chilled champagne which awaited her at the table.

Lily blushed. Both women knew what this kind of food and drink cost, and veered away from mentioning it. 'It's for both of us,' she said in a hurry. 'I wanted to celebrate you and Peter, and also give myself a treat in the process. I haven't cooked for ages. I wanted to do this for us,' she ended lamely.

'Stop apologizing,' Dorothy said, giving her a hug. 'It's brilliant. Thank you.'

They ate, savouring mouthfuls, smiling gleefully at each other over their feast which somehow had an illicit flavour. Lily had decided not to mention her most recent conversation with Hugo – what was there to say? – but she did tell Dot about Andy and Julie Bell.

'But I've heard of her,' her friend said, rather impressed. 'Somebody else I know went to see her. Now who was it? Oh, I know. Do you remember Bernard Wilson, the Oxford don who wrote that book about maths and music? Looked like a bank manager. Incredibly conventional. Well, he swore by her. I think he'd had several – '

'Readings,' Lily interposed.

'Is that what they're called?'

'Apparently.'

'Well, he said she'd changed his life. And he was the last person you'd think of as flaky. When are you going to see her?'

'Not for a few weeks. There's Brighton to be got through first. Hugo's coming.'

'Uh-oh,' Dot commented. 'And how are you going to play that one?'

'Very cool,' Lily answered. 'Well, that's the plan. Have you finished?' She cleared the plates away and came back with a tray of stuffed aubergines, courgettes and peppers, and a dish of pilau rice studded with pine nuts and raisins, flecked green with parsley and tarragon.

Dot's eyes rolled.

'Just in case you need to save a little space, there's baked figs and ginger ice cream to follow.'

'Thanks for the warning. I'll confine myself merely to three helpings.'

'And now I want to hear all about your blissful new life,' Lily said, settling down in her chair and picking up the serving spoons.

Dot smiled. 'Do you really?'

'Well, if I can't stand it, I'll go outside and vomit,' Lily reassured her. 'No, honestly. Of course I want to hear. Yes, I'm green with envy, but I'm really happy for you. Thank God something good is happening for someone.'

Dot paused from her meal and looked at Lily with compassion. 'Dear friend. Wouldn't you rather talk about your dad?'

'No. Not just now. I know you'll listen, but I'm all talked

out on that just now. So tell me. What's it like, sharing your life and your tooth mug?'

'Oxymoronic, in a word, I suppose,' Dorothy answered. 'Wonderful and frightening. Glorious and irritating. A voyage of discovery.' They both laughed. 'I'm having to bite my lip at various unsavoury little habits that I won't share with you over the table, but you know what I mean.' Lily smiled and managed not to remember the details of some of Frank's less fastidious ways.

'Instead of the two romantic peaks each week, life's more of a high plateau. It's great to go shopping, share meals and have sex in the morning or during the day. But I find it difficult to cope with his guilt about Carol and the children. There's quite a lot of that. She phones fairly often, and although she's being civilized, she's pretty tough too. I can't criticize her for that. I don't think she's a bitch. But she does play the children card. And that breaks him up every time.

'They're not babies.' Peter's children were eight and twelve, Lily knew. 'But they're taking it hard. The younger one, Amy, in particular. He doesn't know what to do. He goes over regularly, but that seems to upset everyone as much as it does good. He's not sleeping too well either. So he's tense. So that makes me tense, except I'm supposed to be loving and soothing and am not allowed to show it.'

Dorothy had stopped eating and the expression on her face suggested these problems were not just passing clouds.

'Does he think he's done the right thing?' Lily asked. She did not know Peter very well. He was rather cerebral, a little tortured-looking. Was he one of those people who could never really find happiness in his choices? What did Frank call them, life's inconsolables? Not that Frank had any room to talk.

'He would say that there is no right thing, just a series of choices. He is being sincere to himself, and them, and even me. But I don't think he realized how painful it would be. Difficult to imagine, isn't it? That he hadn't thought what this would feel like before he started. But that's chaps for you.'

Impulsively, Lily reached over and held her friend's hand. This didn't sound much like bliss. Getting what you wanted was a messy business, it seemed. Everything seemed to come with strings attached, as if fate were some nanny-like creature who couldn't resist the opportunity to deliver the cloud along with the silver lining.

'The other night,' Dot went on, 'he went out for a walk and I could tell when he came back he'd been crying. It was terrible. It's *his* mid-life crisis, but I can feel it infecting me too. I've started to feel guilty about the children now, and I've never even met them.'

Lily's ears pricked up as that MLC phrase came round again. She explained to Dot about Andy's diagnosis of her current history.

'Well, why not?' Dorothy commented, picking a final almond out of the now cold pilau dish and licking her fingertips. 'All we need now is for mine to start, and then we can all three of us go down together.'

'Do you think women had mid-life crises before they knew about feminism? Or was it just a guy-thing till then, along with jock-straps and hernias?'

'Good question. Things *Cosmopolitan* never warned us about, part forty-three, the mid-life crisis, or how to cope with a cosmic boot up your backside. Not at all the same as the menopause. Well, it will be interesting to hear Julie Bell's take on it. Meanwhile, are you going to take the rest of Andy's advice and be kind to yourself?'

'I never thought I wasn't,' Lily said.

'Even if it means saying no to Hugo in Brighton?'

Or if he rang sooner? There was no easy answer to that

one. In fact Lily didn't even want to think about it, so she confined herself to a cynical twist of the lips and went off to fetch pudding.

Chapter 14

The following Saturday, Lily got up early and dressed carefully in the clothes she had laid out the night before: a John Smedley fine wool polo-neck, a pair of black wool crêpe trousers and a matching jacket cut long like a riding habit. She pulled her hair back in a chignon. A pair of earrings she had bought on holiday with Frank a couple of years ago – hammered silver squares inset with green lacquer fish – lent just a touch of levity to the severe ensemble.

Once again she journeyed to the mainline station and bought a ticket for the north. Once again she shared the train compartment with football fans in strange synthetic shirts, bingeing on lager and salted snacks even at this hour of nine o'clock, raucous and self-conscious in their peculiar rituals. One particular boy caught her eye, a thin, blond lad whose wish to be a part of the foul-mouthed pack was compromised by an elderly woman in an adjoining seat whose repeated dozing tended to tip her knitting on to the aisle's mucky carpet. Some engrained piece of behaviour kept forcing him to bend down, pick it up and return it gently to her lap. The war between peer pressure and parent power was an amazing struggle to behold.

It led Lily to muse on her own parents' power and what strange rebounds might occur now that one half of it had been extinguished. Was she going to continue to be quite such a Daddy's girl now that he wasn't there to shower her with approval? Was it too deeply etched into her to be shrugged off? And what counterbalancing forces would come from her mother? Who was going to take care of or hold control over whom? Godzilla or King Kong?

*

There was no power struggle during the morning's formal proceedings. Lily and her mother stood side by side at the grave, while a short ceremony was read and the alarmingly small casket, no bigger than a sewing chest, was lowered into the regular-sized space. Lily had to stifle an hysterical urge to giggle at her first sight of the pint-sized box which a dark-suited Jones employee carried to the graveside balanced on both hands, although he could as easily have tucked it under one arm. Had it come in the same funeral car, sitting foolishly on the plinth in the back, or quietly on the back seat of an ordinary saloon? She forced herself to focus on the moment and fortunately sobered up as her mother dropped a handful of claggy soil into the hole. Now it was her turn, and as she scattered her damp handful, and said another farewell to her father, the emotion of the moment descended on her with lightning speed and she wept.

Then the cemetery employees took over, two men in dungarees and wellingtons who had been waiting, leaning on their shovels, in the background. The gravediggers. Were they wise philosophers, angels of transit for newly liberated souls? They looked more like a couple of labourers, keen to get home for their dinners and an afternoon's televised sport.

Catherine Jones accompanied the women back to the house and saw them to the door. She said nothing, respectful to the last, simply shook both their hands and then drove away. Lily was moved at her ex-school acquaintance's composure.

Her mother seemed to be fumbling a little with the lock and Lily offered to help.

'No, I've got to get the hang of it,' Edna answered, and finally, with some combination of pulling and turning, got the door open. Then she ran to the alcove which contained the coat-rack and tapped on a pad that was emitting a high-pitched electronic whine. The noise stopped and Edna turned to Lily, perspiring lightly but with a look of some triumph. 'There,' she said. 'All clear.'

Lily had been looking at the lock, which was a heavy new one with brass plates on either side of the door. Now she examined the alarm keypad and recognized it for the expensive variety she had not had fitted in her own home. She was impressed. Her mother had been being practical.

Edna disappeared into the kitchen and returned with a key. 'Here, this is the new front-door key. And I'll explain the alarm to you. It's taken me a while to get used to it.'

'Well, it's a very good idea. Does it help you feel safer?'

'Not especially. I've never felt unsafe in this house. But everyone said I should take steps. Apparently thieves make it their business to read the "In Memoriam" columns. New widows are easy targets.' Edna used the word widow with a glimmer of inflection that surprised Lily. Was it pride? Lily was left to wonder as her mother turned away and took off her hat.

Over soup and a sandwich, the two women caught up with each other. Edna had been busy these last couple of weeks, but even the phone contact had not conveyed to Lily the degree of activity. Leaflets about driving lessons were stacked in one pile, information sheets from the library about adult education in another. Lily was a little confused by all this industry, even a little put out by it. Was Edna over her bereavement so soon? Lily wanted her mother to start a new life, but not necessarily to abandon Alec quite so abruptly.

She said nothing, though, knowing that the business of the chain had still to be resolved. And indeed, after lunch, her mother produced it from a drawer, boxed in a red leatherette case, within which it nestled on ruched ivory satin, now rather yellowed with age. At the sight of it, a quarter of an inch wide, as flat and pliable as a snake, Lily breathed in sharply. She tried not to cry but a single wayward tear trailed down her cheek. Lifting the necklace from its box, she was struck by its lightness. It was platinum, cold and gleaming. She fastened it round her neck and tucked the loop it formed beneath the neck of her sweater.

Edna sat across from her, silent, an unreadable expression on her face.

'Do you mind me having this?' Lily asked finally, wanting to clear the air.

'How could I?' her mother answered. Indeed, how could she?

'You look as if you do,' Lily persisted.

'Oh, Lily, you and your father . . .' Edna said no more, the weariness of her voice speaking volumes, decades of patient and not-so-patient absorption of a continuous source of simultaneous pride and rejection.

Lily realized that her wish to wipe away the jealousy was an infantile thing. She couldn't make it better, any more than her mother could say she minded. Perhaps the grown-up thing to do would be to accept things as they were.

'So how do you think you're going to cope?' she asked her mother instead, gesturing with her eyes towards the leaflets. 'You look as if you've made a good start.'

'You have to keep going. Everyone's told me that,' Edna answered, and Lily glimpsed the sizeable support network that had swung into action behind her mother. The Braithwaites had, after all, lived in this town all their married life. Her mother was surrounded by people she had known practically since adolescence, men and women who, as couples, widows or widowers, would buoy her up in the continuum of their Midlands generation, possibly the last to have stayed put, not left home in teenage years and gone to seek their fortune in London or further afield. Here, unlike in London, Edna would not have to lose her place in the social pack, indeed it would embrace her more warmly in her needy hour. For this resource, Lily was grateful.

The afternoon drifted by. The power struggle that was forever Lily's and her mother's relationship switched sides between them as they chatted, first the one taking the upper hand, then the other. Edna reminisced self-indulgently, Lily cajoled a little. Edna touched on a few of her plans – a gardener perhaps, maybe a game of bridge one evening a week; Lily made a few suggestions – getting in touch with Saga, taking up bowls. At some point, Edna asked if Lily had communicated her father's death to Frank.

'It's funny you should ask,' her daughter answered. 'I rang him a few days ago. I don't know why really. They didn't get on, did they? But I did want him to know. He said he would come round one night next week.'

'How's he getting on, did he say?' Edna enquired mildly, as if after a wayward son.

'We didn't talk for long, but he sounded okay. It was all rather dispassionate. Losing Dad seems to have pretty much displaced my feelings for Frank. I didn't have any pangs when we spoke, but I'll see what it's like to meet up again. Maybe that will be different.'

'So there's no one else just yet, then?'

'No, Mum,' Lily answered, not wanting to give her mother the opportunity of pointing out the shortcomings of her involvement with Hugo. 'No one else just yet.'

Early the following week, Lily was just coming back from showing a visiting sales rep out of the office when she bumped into Clive.

'Ah, Lily,' he said, smiling down from his lanky six feet five inches. 'Just the person I was looking for.'

'Really?'

'Yes. How are you?' His pale blue eyes looked at her with some avuncular concern.

'Er, fine, thank you.'

'You seem to be coping admirably in your dark days. I was very sorry about your loss.'

Lily knew this. He had already communicated it in his letter as well as when she had used him as a conduit to Hugo.

'Look, I was chatting to Andy. We're having him and a few friends for a meal on Friday night. Would you like to come along?'

Lily blinked. An accountants' Friday night out. Well, that would be one for the social studies surveys. Could she say no? Should she? She heard her mother's voice. 'Of course you must go. Get out and about, Lily. You'll never meet anyone staying at home.'

All the more convinced she should decline the invitation, however kindly meant, she then found herself going for the double bluff. Don't do it if Mother says so, don't not do it, just to spite her. 'Thank you,' she said, after only a split-second pause. 'That would be great.'

'Good,' Clive answered. 'Perhaps Andy can give you a lift. Save me drawing a map of darkest Surrey.'

It could be worse, Lily thought to herself as she returned to her desk. At least if she were to partner Andy, she knew the social engineering of the situation. And it would be interesting to glimpse the interior of chez Clive. Monica and Pat would want to know all the details.

The next evening, a chilly, clear one after a day of startling autumnal sunlight, Lily responded to the knock at her door to find Frank, posed awkwardly on the step, clad in an unfamiliar belted raincoat.

'That's new,' she commented as he came in. It suited him, but she wasn't going to admit it out loud.

'It's one of those American military surplus ones,' he answered with a familiar note of vanity. He hung it on the coat-rack and followed her into the sitting room where she had lit the fake coal fire. Huntley and Palmer were doing their floor arabesques in front of it, on the half-moon mat. Frank ruffled both their stomachs. They took no notice.

He sat on the sofa and she sat opposite, observing the new haircut too, but recognizing the pullover from a craft shop they'd visited one long-distant weekend in the Yorkshire Dales. Not everything swept away then. She wondered whether he was noting changes and continuities in her. She had embarked on a phase of pale lipstick. Would he notice? Her long overshirt had originally been his, but he had never liked the pattern and she had thought of it as hers for an age.

He did seem to be watching her carefully as he lit a cigarette, but then he had always been thoughtful about emotional stress, that was the one area in which he had been a true partner. 'I was really sorry about your dad,' he said finally, and she believed him. 'He was quite a guy. I bet you're taking it hard.'

She was robbed of speech. It was true, of course. Despite the be-kind-to-yourself treatment, which seemed mainly to consist of spending money on items of food and clothes, the days were grey and tasted of ash, appropriately enough. Apart from her hunger for Hugo, its flame rekindled by what he had told her at lunch, all else was tedium.

'Have you thought about a bereavement counsellor?' Frank broke in, ever the professional.

'No, but you clearly have. Am I coping so very badly, do you perceive?' she snapped back.

'I just thought, knowing how deeply you and your father were involved, that you might need a bit of extra support.'

'I'll be fine,' she said, wanting very much to seem strong

even in her loss, for him not to find her wounded over and above what was customary.

'How's your mother managing?' he asked.

'Disconcertingly well,' Lily answered wryly, glad of the switch of focus. 'I thought she would disintegrate without him to hold things together, and without the full-time job of taking care of him. But it's not like that at all. She's developing all kinds of new interests. Somebody else seems to be emerging.'

'Yes, I'm not surprised,' Frank commented, insufferably. 'She was always a very thwarted personality. That abdication of responsibility never fitted. That's why there was so much passive aggression. Enforced child status. It's never sustainable.'

Lily had forgotten Frank's fixation with Transactional Analysis, which seemed to boil everyone down to parent, adult or child. Her own lack of belief in therapies of all kinds followed closely from having lived with someone who had tried many on for size during the length of their relationship. This last seemed hugely oversimplified, but it clearly suited Frank, who had much of the overdeveloped child in him.

She began to lose patience. Perhaps his visit was kindly meant, but the truth was that Frank had been consistently horrible to her parents when they had been together. (To be fair, he had been the same to his own parents, too.) What was the point of this small talk? To show that he still cared for her? She began to feel that this no longer mattered. They had been apart for some four months now. They weren't 'staying friends'. They were becoming strangers. Why not just draw a line under things?

After Frank had stubbed out his fourth cigarette, Lily leaned forward on an impulse and said, 'While you're here, why don't we discuss the furniture?'

His expression switched. The self-satisfaction gave way

to something more suspicious. 'You didn't mention this on the phone. Is there a problem?'

'No problem. I just think it's time you took your things away, don't you?'

There was a pause, but eventually he was forced to make the obvious reply. 'I suppose so.'

Lily enumerated the items they had bought jointly – the bird's-eye maple dining table, chairs and matching sideboard; the art deco three-piece suite they had found in a junk shop and had re-covered in pastiche patterned velvet. The pine Welsh dresser in the kitchen. A tiled washstand in the bathroom. Various framed prints. 'And then there's china and cutlery and pans, as well as all the things you had before we moved in here.' A pretty ugly group of plates and second-hand cookware, she remembered.

She hadn't thought about any of this until now. At the beginning of the split they had discussed money and the house, but somehow never got on to the furniture, the goods and chattels. Perhaps it was something to do with her father's death, but suddenly she had an overwhelming urge to be free of Frank's stuff, which seemed to weigh round her neck like an albatross.

'I don't want any of the kitchen stuff,' she said, 'and if it's a toss-up between the three-piece suite and the dining table, I'd rather have the former.'

The wind seemed to have been knocked out of Frank's sails. 'Okay,' he said lamely. 'I suppose I'd better arrange for a van. Can you manage for a couple more weeks? I'll need to fix up storage too.'

Magnanimously, Lily agreed to two more weeks, but then she wanted shut of it all. Mentally, she dusted off her fingertips and felt at some level well rid.

On Friday evening, Lily took a bath and then stood at her wardrobe door in her dressing gown, trying to imagine how she should look for supper in Surrey. Should she dress up to dazzle the country mice, or undercut everyone with understated elegance? Why was she feeling so combative anyway? Ever since her evening with Frank she had acknowledged a mild fury fizzing away inside her. Cool it, she told herself, opting for an English Eccentrics silk shirt patterned with classical architecture symbols and a superbly cut pair of black wool trousers, a trophy from a long-distant designer warehouse sale. Female lounge lizard, she declared to herself, clasping her father's chain around her neck. Perfect for the note of lofty disengagement she felt towards the evening ahead.

Andy, punctual as she might have predicted, was in a good mood as they made their slow way through the Friday night traffic. His job was going well and the chain was expanding.

'Your fiefdom will be growing, then?' Lily asked.

'Yes, I'm going to have to add probably two more members to the department. In fact, just between you and me, one of the reasons for this evening is that Clive wanted me to meet some neighbour's offspring who's working as a trainee in the City. He thought she might do for the junior slot.'

'Oh great. You're going to be talking work all evening and conducting an interview over the prawn cocktail.'

'Probably. It'll give you an opportunity to get to know Judy, Clive's wife.'

'What's she like?'

'You'll find out,' was all he would say.

They drove into the green belt and eventually left the motorway. Although it was dark, Lily could see pine trees and scrubby patches of heath between the suburban developments. Houses round here seemed to come detached, with double garages and encircling gardens of considerable acreage. Veering down a lane planted with matched rows of silver birches, Andy finally turned off into a driveway and pulled up before a neo-Tudor, half-timbered house outside which two carriage lamps illumined the front porch.

Clive was quick to answer their knock and swung the door open to admit them. Lily noted his carefully folded cravat and matching embroidered waistcoat, before he swooped down to administer a polite peck to her cheek. 'Come in, come in,' he urged.

Andy was ahead of her, hugging a stocky woman in a Laura Ashley three-quarter-length patterned dress complete with broad sash and a toning velvet headband. He turned. 'Judy, this is Lily.'

Lily shook the outstretched hand.

'Hello, Lily. Come on in. We've lit the fire. Come and meet everyone.'

They seemed to be the last to arrive, and in the vast living room discovered four strangers sitting on plump sofas either side of a fireplace wide enough to roast an ox. Lily had time to glimpse cabbage rose wallpaper and horse-brasses before being urged to join the right-hand sofa where a young couple smiled up at her. She knew they were a couple because they were holding hands.

'This is Annabel and Robin,' Judy explained. 'Newly-weds. That explains their good humour and the fact that they are utterly inseparable.' She smiled at the pair who seemed oblivious to her note of irony. 'They'll learn,' she said to Lily. 'Now what will you have to drink?'

Lily opted for a glass of wine and embarked on a conversation about weddings and honeymoons with the bright-faced couple. When in doubt, ask questions, was her old social recipe, but she hardly needed to exert herself here. Once Annabel had begun on the details of her dress, the marquee and the honeymoon suite in St Lucia, she was unstoppable. Robin confined himself to stroking her hand in a meaningful way and fielding the frequent eye-contact she flashed in his direction.

Keeping half an ear and eye on all this, and assuming that Annabel was the trainee accountant, Lily allowed herself the occasional glance at the other group, standing round the facing sofa. Judy and Clive were entertaining three men, Andy and two other accountants, she guessed. One late-middle-aged man wore cavalry twills and a blazer, the other and younger was in a dark navy suit and what she thought was probably called a Friday shirt, one of those explosions of colour magnanimously permitted to office workers, in the pretence that they could blossom a little with the weekend in view. This shirt was a strong shade of violet.

Half an hour ticked by, with Annabel going into the minutiae of covered buttons and her wedding breakfast menu, Lily draining her glass and completing an inventory of the room. Vast though it was, with French windows at the far end, she was able to note in the low lighting that it was full of clutter. There was a piano with piles of music, untidy bookshelves, several low tables strewn with maga-zines, embroidery, open books, drooping flower arrange-ments. Next to the music centre, itself a sea of CDs and tapes, sat piles of newspapers. Photos of two retrievers, one golden, one black, sat on the mantelpiece, and their smell and toys were on the air and underfoot. Lily knew there were children too, but the evidence of their presence was less immediate, just the occasional acid-bright splash of colour – some Lego bricks, an action toy, a plastic ruck-sack. Presumably they had a room to clutter all of their own.

Judy seemed to be happy to stay with the other group and Lily began to wonder about food. Shouldn't Clive's wife be in the kitchen, bringing to perfection some Delia Smith three-course masterwork? Instead, she was happily standing about with a bottle of Australian Chardonnay in one hand, topping up her own glass and anyone else's within reach. Some hostess, Lily thought, thirstily. But she had to admit, Judy did look remarkably comfortable, not at all like a wife in mid-dinner-party frenzy.

At last Judy seemed to wake up to her other guests and announced to all, 'Well, shall we eat?'

The consensus was yes, and with very little delay the group made its way through a side door into another messy room, smaller, but also graced with fake oak beams, in which a long oak refectory table was laid for eight. Clive placed Lily between the two accountants – they had to be – whom she had not yet met, and Andy opposite, next to the garrulous Annabel who had not however been separated on her other side from Robin.

Clive sat down in the carver at the head of the table and Judy appeared within seconds with a tureen of soup which she placed in front of him. Clive ladled a pale green, steaming liquid into bowls while Judy topped up wine glasses. As she passed Lily, she introduced Mr Cavalry Twills as Anthony and Mr Friday Shirt as Paolo.

'Are your parents Italian?' she asked Paolo, who did indeed have Latin colouring and blue-black hair.

'No, they're from Tenby,' he answered. 'Wales.'

'Yes, I've been there,' Lily remarked. 'So you're a Celt, then.' That would explain the colouring. 'But why the foreign name?'

'It's something of a family mystery,' Paolo answered, without any trace of inflection. 'My father died when I was just a baby. I don't think he wanted the name. But my mother was adamant. There's talk of a prisoner-of-war in a camp near to where they lived,' he finished darkly.

Lily looked at Paolo with some surprise. The brief story, with its glimpse of wartime taboos possibly broken, was a wonderful one. He seemed neither embarrassed nor amused by it.

'And is your surname Jones?' she enquired, half-joking, wondering what wonderful juxtaposition might have been formed by this Italo–Welsh conjunction.

'It is, as a matter of fact,' he answered, with a suggestion of Welsh lilt.

Lily contained herself and drank some soup. Paolo's expression was bland.

'How did you come by Lily?' he asked after a minute.

'An aunt, deceased,' she told him. 'My father's much-loved sister. She died of meningitis in an orphanage.'

'Gosh, that's very sad. But it's a lovely name,' Paolo said, looking at her rather directly.

'I think it's rather gloomy. Makes me think of Victorian funerals and drooping Pre-Raphaelite women.'

'Oh, no,' he persisted. 'It's willowy and serious. Like you,' he ended, turning back to his bread roll.

Lily gulped down some more soup and turned to Anthony, who was placed between herself and Judy. They seemed to be having a conversation about payroll computation and Judy, a little wild-eyed, seemed pleased that Lily had inclined their way so that she could branch into a conversation about GBF.

'Lily's their chief buyer,' she explained to Anthony.

'Only buyer,' Lily corrected.

Anthony seemed to have no comment on this. Presumably he knew about the company, being a friend of Clive's.

'How are you finding the new boss?' Judy asked Lily. Lily's heart did a somersault but she doubted there was any hidden agenda here. As far as she knew, Hugo's and her involvement was a secret from everyone in the company.

'He's quite an individualist,' she said, judiciously. 'Have you met him yet?'

'Only briefly,' Judy answered. 'Clive and I were going to the theatre and I picked him up from the pub where they were having one of their after-hours management meetings, so-called. How can you bear that, Lily, the way the men have the really serious conversations about work over a drink when the women have gone home?'

It was a rhetorical question, but having sampled the pub meetings, Lily reckoned she wasn't missing much.

'Anyway,' Judy went on, 'I thought Hugo was a real handful, in all senses.'

Lily became aware that Clive was listening from the other end of the table and possibly indicating that Judy should not be indiscreet. Andy had glanced up too.

'Oh, Clive thinks the same but he won't admit it, will you, dear? Hugo seems to be taking a very close interest in the accounts. Not above a little sleight of hand, is my feeling. And then there's his Don Juan complex. Not to mention the way he wanders around looking like he needs a mother to comb his hair and tuck his shirt-tails in. Quite a liability, I'd say.'

Lily flushed at the mention of the Don Juan complex and hoped Andy had turned back to his interviewee. 'Well, the company seems to be doing reasonable business. And I've found one or two of his ideas beneficial,' she responded, possibly a little defensively.

'Glad to hear it,' Judy answered. 'But he's one to watch. Short attention span, that's my feeling. I don't think anyone should relax while Hugo's in charge.'

Lily was struck by the acuteness of Judy's character analysis and looked at her with new respect.

'What do you do?' she asked her hostess.

'Oh, this and that,' Judy answered easily. 'I keep the show on the road. Allow Clive to run like a well-oiled machine.' She smiled at him down the table. 'My real love is philosophy, but there's precious little time for thinking, what with the house, the brood and the dogs, on top of the responsibilities of Surrey wifedom. My plan is to get back to teaching in about five years' time. Until then, I keep the home fires burning.'

Teaching? Nobody taught philosophy at school, did they? This must be Judy's way of saying that she lectured. Lily was impressed. Clive's wife was an academic. Interesting camouflage, then, the big-girl's-party-dress look, complete with coloured tights and flat shoes, well-brushed hair and no make-up. Was that because Clive liked her to resemble an overgrown teenager, or because she could operate more easily looking like a cross between Miss Piggy and your favourite sister? Certainly all the men round this table seemed at ease in Judy's company, while she, with a shrewd twinkle in her eye, seemed utterly mistress of the scene.

When the soup was finished and the bowls cleared, Judy was back, again within minutes, with a big casserole – 'Chicken stew,' she announced baldly. 'Free range if anyone has qualms' – and a platter heaped with baked potatoes. Again, Clive did the serving.

'You've gone to a lot of trouble,' Lily said to Judy as she sat down again. 'And on a Friday night, too. Aren't you exhausted?'

'No more than usual,' was the frank reply. 'There are never enough hours in the day, don't you find?'

'No proper delegation,' was Anthony's comment. Judy lifted an eyebrow at him.

'And I haven't gone to much trouble at all. I've never seen the mystique in cooking. Why peel potatoes when you can cook them in their skins? The soup was out of cartons and I think I cooked the chicken last May. Where were we all before freezers and microwaves? I don't have much in common with Shirley Conran,' she went on with a self-deprecating smile, 'but when it comes to the "Life being too short to stuff a mushroom" point of view, she and I are as one.'

Lily expected Anthony to comment that he liked stuffed mushrooms, but instead he complimented Judy on the chicken. 'Mandy cooks a fine beef stew, but loses her flair with chicken – quite hopeless, always dry.'

Lily gathered that Mandy must be Mrs Anthony.

'How is Mandy's mother?' Judy asked solicitously.

'Not too bright,' came the calm reply. 'We're steeling ourselves for the worst. Funny how there's been so much death this autumn, don't you think? First Brian, then Marjorie. And now, well soon probably, Mrs Leverhulme. Sombre times.'

Lily noticed Judy flashing her a look, before she quickly averted her face towards her plate. She had managed to put her father out of her mind for the evening, but this sudden reminder acted as if to stop up her throat. She stared at the archipelago on her plate, the island of baked potato and the hillock of chicken breast in their lake of gravy, and watched them blur through her filling eyes. She cleared her throat and drank some more wine and forced herself to think of something else.

'And what do you do?' she said, bright and brittle, turning back to Paolo.

'I'm an accountant,' he answered, quick as a flash.

'Where?' she prompted.

He named a large accountancy firm that she had vaguely heard of. Their offices were in a monolithic building near Liverpool Street Station.

'Do you commute from Surrey?' she persisted. 'That must be a long journey.'

'No, I live in Southwark. It's not so far.'

'Oh. I'm confused. I thought you must be a neighbour.'

'No, I'm a cousin of Judy's. She takes pity on me

periodically, a lonely divorcé in the big city. Gives me my one square meal of the week.'

Lily softened towards Paolo a little, giving him the benefit of the doubt on the question of a possible sense of humour. She had a passing thought that perhaps this was a set-up, a touch of match-making. After all, if Clive and Judy were using the occasion to feed a lonely neighbour and set up a job interview, why not throw in a couple of lonely hearts too? Lily bristled for an instant, then decided to sit back and relax. Despite Judy's dismissiveness, the food was good, the wine plentiful and the company on her side of the table tolerable. Andy, on the other hand, seemed to be having a struggle with Annabel. His plate was empty whereas she had scarcely had time for a mouthful. Her job prospects looked in jeopardy.

Lily turned back to Paolo and permitted him to quiz her, extremely gently, on her life, her work and her single status.

After a pudding of blackberry and apple crumble accompanied by a tub of Marks & Spencer clotted cream, they returned to the living room for coffee. Anthony declined, saying that he still had the dogs to walk. Robin and Annabel took this as their cue and left too. None of the remaining group actually used the term 'early night' but everyone was thinking it.

After the mass departure, Andy, Judy and Clive were left facing Lily and Paolo on the squashy sofas in the warm light of the fire. The three old friends seemed thick in some conversation about another acquaintance who appeared to be in deep financial trouble. This left Lily to the tender mercies of Paolo. He was clearly making a play, and she wondered coolly to herself whether this was because Judy and Clive had engineered him into the situation and he was behaving like a good guest, or whether he was really interested.

More to the point, how interested was she? From her detached point of view, the answer was a firm maybe. He was attractive enough, physically speaking. On the conversational level, she was much more sceptical. But so what? Couldn't she just amuse herself for once, be flattered a little? This would be being kind to herself, wouldn't it?

'What kind of music do you enjoy?' Paolo asked imaginatively.

'I'm not sure I know any more,' she answered him. 'I think my taste for pop music stopped in the eighties, but I haven't replaced it with anything else. How about you? I'm trying not to think clichéd thoughts, you being Welsh and all. But are you musical?'

'Well, I don't sing, if that's what you mean. But I'm passionate about the opera.'

'Really?' Lily asked, with a mental yawn. 'I've never seen any. I tend to bracket it with ballet. Great in theory but kind of foolish in practice.'

'Ah, well, you've clearly never been,' he rebuked her. 'If you had – well, that's if you liked it – you'd know it's the most thrilling thing in the world.'

Lily opened her eyes wide, partly as a joke with a sexual subtext, partly at his genuine and childlike enthusiasm.

Paolo did have the grace to realize his possible over-statement. 'No, well, you know what I mean – the most fun you can have with your clothes on. But how can I describe it to you? At its best, and it often isn't, opera is incomparable. Cathartic music, heart-stoppingly beautiful singing, and great passion. And then there's the risk. Will the singer achieve all the notes and manage not to fall over or bump into the scenery? There's so much going on, but when it works, it boils down to a kind of simplicity, well, a perfection, really.' He stopped, his eyes alight. There was a pause.

'Well, I'd better take a look,' Lily said, mainly to help

him out. Privately, she remained suspicious that this was her kind of entertainment.

'Maybe I could take you,' he offered loyally.

'Maybe you could,' she answered.

Andy drove Lily home just after midnight. Paolo was staying the night with Clive and Judy, but she had given him her phone number. Now, as the night air whistled past the car and they sailed the empty dual carriageway back into London, she felt mildly pleased with her evening. A new adventure to be embarked on, another step along the road away from her recent multiple tragedy pile-up. Could a pale ray of light be piercing the thunderclouds overhead?

'What did you make of Annabel?' she enquired sweetly.

'What was the name of that famous archaeologist, the one who excavated Troy? Schliemann, was it? I felt a bit like him, hacking away through the layers, finally after years of dedication coming across a glimpse of possible treasure. No, I overstate my case, but there is, probably, underneath the organza – what is that, by the way? – and the three-layer wedding cake, a brain of some middle-sized potential there. I'll give her a proper interview next week, if she can be surgically parted from Robin, that is.' He paused for a moment to overtake a dented Volvo whose driver was manoeuvring rather erratically. 'And how did you got on with Paolo?' he asked in turn, possibly a little archly.

'Well enough,' she fielded. 'He's an opera fan. He's invited me to go along.'

'Good for you,' Andy answered noncommittally.

'Do you know him?'

'Not really. I'd heard about him at second hand. His divorce happened soon after the two of them arrived in London – a few years ago now. I think he leaned quite heavily on Judy for a bit.'

'She's quite something, isn't she?' Lily commented.

'Judy? Wonderful woman. The cleverest and most able person at that table, I would say.'

'So comfortable with herself,' Lily mused aloud. 'I think I'd like to be like that. She looks as if she's made all her bargains with her eyes wide open.'

'And you don't?'

'I seem to make mine in a coma,' she answered, perfectly seriously.

Chapter 15

Paolo telephoned the following day. At nine o'clock in the morning. A bit too keen, Lily thought to herself as she answered his polite enquiries about her journey home and her night's sleep. He appeared to be phoning from the railway station where Judy had just dropped him.

'I've got some tickets for *Don Giovanni* next Saturday,' he said enthusiastically. 'Will you come?'

Why not? Lily thought, but her heart was sinking slightly. 'Okay. Yes, thank you. But you know I'm an absolute philistine, don't you? Wouldn't you rather take someone who would be more certain to appreciate it? Isn't it horribly expensive?'

'I want to take you,' he said firmly. 'And they're not the best seats.'

'Do I have to wear evening dress?' she asked.

'You can if you like. I tend to go in jeans.'

The weather grew chillier as Lily worked through the week and so did her mild excitement about her date. By Saturday, she was decidedly tepid about three or more hours of Mozart in the company of an earnest backwoodsman.

'Is he an utter deadbeat?' asked Dot, who knew of old Lily's tendency to cool and cancel and had phoned to deliver a pep talk.

'No, that would be unfair. But boredom does not fly out of the window when he walks in the door.'

'You can't know him well enough to be sure of that,' said Dorothy.

'True. But I have this gut feeling,' Lily answered thoughtfully.

'Do you fancy him?'

'A bit.'

'Then I don't see the problem. Check out the sex, soak up the culture and if it's all hopeless, promise yourself you'll never see him again.'

They met at a Middle Eastern place near the Aldwych and shared pitta bread, hummus and stuffed vine leaves. Rather intimate for a first date, thought Lily, dipping her bread into the same beige pool as Paolo, who seemed oblivious.

'Do you want me to tell you anything about what we're going to see?' he asked between mouthfuls.

'Is it difficult to understand?' she countered.

'No. Not at all. It's very modern in a way. All about relationships and attraction.'

'Oh.' She paused.

'Would you like anything else?'

They ordered Turkish coffees and then Lily asked Paolo about his divorce. There was a silence that lasted some moments.

'It's still not something I find it easy to talk about,' he said finally. 'We hadn't been married that long although I'd known her for years. Chris, her name is. We grew up in the same town.'

'Was anyone else involved?' Lily enquired, wondering if she was being too intrusive.

'No. She just said she'd made a mistake. That was all.' He sipped at the recently boiled coffee.

'And since then?' Lily delved again.

Paolo looked a little less uncomfortable now. 'Various encounters,' he answered cryptically. 'You can't win the lottery if you don't buy a ticket.'

*

They walked up to the opera house and joined a swelling crowd of sleek folk. But Paolo moved Lily through this group and round the corner of the building. There, climbing an endless flight of stairs, was a homelier crowd, all seemingly in high good humour at the prospect of the entertainment ahead.

At the top, they found their seats, steeply raked towards the distant stage, and decidedly cramped.

Punctually, the conductor appeared, the safety curtain rose and dramatic music ascended from the pit. Lily thought she might have heard this bit – presumably the overture – before, and relaxed. Shortly thereafter the curtain went up and scenes of attempted rape and vicious murder unfolded on the stage. She found herself enthralled. There was a lot to take in – the words to read, projected above the action, the music to listen to, the singing and the drama to absorb. But she found herself beginning to agree with Paolo. It *was* thrilling. And then she realized it was all about Hugo.

Seduced, abandoned but still wanting more, one of a long list, Donna Elvira on the stage was Lily, and Don Giovanni, plausible and eternally predatory, was Hugo. She felt herself grow hot as the peasant girl Zerlina was seduced by a silky aria. Yet she could not deny her own response to this heartless man whose velvety voice hinted at ecstasies to come. How sexy and masculine the Don's singing was. She began to feel vaguely aroused, and more conscious of Paolo who was sitting, rapt, close by her side. His profile, illumined by the stage lights, was really rather classical.

During the interval, Lily told him how much she was enjoying herself and he smiled with gratification. They drank wine and Paolo's arm strayed round her shoulder as they leaned against the wall in the bar.

Then they went back to their seats. The second part was

more violent and cruel, Lily thought, but just as magnetic. The final scene, with Don Giovanni dragged down to hell, unrepentant to the last, filled her with a strange sense of admiration. What a towering figure he remained, compared with the feebly crowing survivors.

Outside, in the drizzling street, Lily felt energized. When Paolo suggested a drink, she agreed.

'I don't suppose you'd like to come to Southwark, would you?' he suggested tentatively.

'Isn't it rather a long way?' she answered, indecisively.

'My car's just round the corner.'

So Lily went home with Paolo, to a little Georgian house in the lee of a tower block. Inside, a huge pair of speakers dominated the none-too-clean living room. Paolo put his CD of *Don Giovanni* into the player and went off to find drinks. He returned with two full glasses and sat down by Lily on the sofa. She took the proffered wine and sipped it, while leaning back, eyes closed, letting the music wash over her. When a sound caused her to open her eyes again, she was just in time to see Paolo's face descending for a kiss.

She snapped her eyes shut again and felt his lips meet hers. The kiss was dry and careful, a sort of labial push with a vague circular grinding motion. It went on for a while, with Lily experiencing very little but Paolo, judging from his breathing at least, becoming quite excited.

'Come to the bedroom,' he urged, breaking off.

Should she? The music in the background, reminiscent of the passion of a few weeks ago, seemed to encourage her, although the kissing had rendered her as aroused as a collapsed lung. Could she say no? Probably. In fact it would be the wiser course. But Paolo's lips were back on hers again, and as his hand shaped itself to her breast, she heard again the seduction aria and her groin responded. So when he stood up and reached for her hand, she offered it and he led her out and up the stairs.

What on earth possessed you? she berated herself the following morning, lying in her own bath, a flannel across her eyes. All your instincts said no, and still you went to bed with him. What sort of behaviour was that? Not only was it bad sex, but he could have been any kind of nutter. No one knew where you were. Take some responsibility.

Just chalk it up to experience, counselled another inner voice. And next time, go with what your gut tells you.

Paolo's sexual technique had proved little more enlivening than his kissing. For a start, his bedclothes were grubby, and such vestiges of passion Lily had been clinging to as they entered the room dissolved at the sight of a wrinkled sheet dotted with crumbs, fluff, pubic hair and nameless matter. But he was already unbuttoning her shirt and now she felt it really was too late to change her mind. So he undressed her, and then, after her half-hearted attempt at his shirt buttons and fly, himself. Guiding her to the bed, he encouraged her to lie back, stroking her breasts and stomach rather aimlessly the while.

Lily made herself respond by running her hands the length of Paolo's flanks, his back and shoulders, all of which were long and lightly muscled. This helped her a little. Moving round to his stomach, she encountered a longish penis, less erect than she had expected, although it braced itself a little more as she stroked, then gripped it.

Paolo's fingers descended to her groin and explored it, sufficient at least for him to know where to fit the head of his cock. Her clitoris remained undisturbed by his foraging.

After another tongue-free kiss, he turned away and fiddled in the beside-table drawer, soon producing a condom which he applied to himself with some dexterity. Lily experienced her first suspicion that Paolo, for all his unsophistication, might have been investing regular and quite substantial sums in the lottery.

Turning back, he checked first breasts, then vagina and discovering all was still in place, climbed on top of her. Lily's only wish by now was for this to be over and she opened her legs, willing herself to moistness by remembering her night with Hugo. Paolo's penis duly slid home and he began to breathe loudly into the pillow, his face averted from hers.

She expected him to come quickly, but the intercourse was a protracted business, necessitating considerable effort and silent labour on Paolo's part. Lily tried to assist, but nothing she did elicited a different tempo or response, so eventually she just waited, trying not to let the dismay she felt invade her completely. Not only was she a reluctant partner, but she didn't seem to be that attractive to him either. What on earth were they both doing?

Eventually, with much groaning, as if the effort pained him, Paolo reached his climax. His sweat had a faintly acrid smell to it. Lily had already decided, while he had been thrusting, that as soon as was decently possible, she would summon a minicab and escape. She allowed an interval of what she guessed to be five minutes, then enquired after the bathroom.

Emerging from a cold-water wash and fleeting contact with the towel she found hanging on the doorknob, Lily began to dress. Paolo, who had been silent after his ejaculation, seemed surprised.

'Oh, I never sleep well in a strange bed,' she told him smoothly, hinting at yards of sexual experience.

'Well, if it's what you want,' he commented, with minimal regret in his voice.

She phoned a reliable cab firm whose number she had carried for years. Informed of a twenty-minute wait, she went downstairs and sat dumbly on the sofa, hating herself.

Paolo appeared in a green towelling bathrobe that ended mid-thigh.

'Can I get you a cup of coffee?' he asked, bland as ever in his mini-robe.

Lily felt a little hysterical. 'No, thanks,' she managed.

He pottered off to make himself one, sparing both of them an unendurable silence. And at last the cab arrived and transported Lily to the glorious peace and fastidiousness of her own home.

For the early part of the following week, Lily had to struggle hard to shake off the taint of shame and disgust she felt towards herself, not Paolo, for the weekend's proceedings. Her depression deepened at the sense that whichever door she opened in her search for respite, she found herself running into a brick wall or distorting mirror. She seemed all the more confounded by the imprecation to be kind to herself. Perhaps the kindest thing at the moment would be to retire to a convent, rather like Donna Elvira in the opera, the music from which continued to whirl in her head.

But a retreat would not be possible for at least a week or two, because the Brighton trade fair was coming up in the fast lane. In fact, she would need to be there the following Sunday, with the main business of the event taking place on the Monday, running into the Tuesday morning.

'So what's the drill?' Hugo asked, descending on her unannounced as usual, first thing Tuesday morning. He was carrying a Styrofoam cup of cappuccino which he plonked wetly on her desk, patting his pockets in search of cigarettes. Lily's stomach flipped uncomfortably, as it had now got in the habit of doing each time the phone rang at home. Of course it was never Hugo.

'I tend to get there late afternoon,' she told him. 'Maybe have a drink with a couple of people, but basically work towards an early start on Monday and get most of the buying and viewing done by close of play that day. Monday night isn't exactly formal but people do eat together. Then Tuesday I mop up and leave slightly ahead of the herd. The trains are pretty good.'

'Trains? No, we'll drive,' he asserted. 'I'll pick you up. It's the right side of London, after all.'

So he did remember where she lived.

'Oh. Okay. What time?'

'About two?'

'Fine,' she agreed, with as much breeziness as she could muster.

Lily had been trying not to dwell on the prospect of this trip, but as she packed her bag on Saturday afternoon, she found herself laying out newer underwear and a luxurious black silk kimono printed with gold chrysanthemums which she had owned for years but rarely worn. She had also invested in a packet of condoms, telling herself that these were for generic needs, not specific ones. But after unprotected – though unforgettable – sex with Hugo and then a mildly late period, she had decided not to burden herself in that particular way again. However she had opted not to go back on the pill. Her current bonk rate scarcely merited it.

So admit it, she told herself, you're up for grabs, so to speak. If he asks, you're not going to say no. Which would be more painful, she argued back, denying yourself another night with Hugo or being frozen out again afterwards? That was an easy one – devil or deep blue sea.

Hugo was as impossible to read as ever, standing on her doorstep early on the Sunday afternoon wearing a corduroy jacket over a faded brushed cotton shirt and chinos. No acknowledgement was made of any previous visits. He refused a cup of coffee and seemed keen to hit the road. So Lily closed the door on Huntley and Palmer who would be fed by her neighbour Ron for this short separation. Hugo's car turned out to be a maroon Jaguar, as wide and unwieldy as a small barge. He drove fast and swore a good deal, clearly at ease in the messy interior with its mute reminders of domestic life – open packets of boiled sweets, items of sports clothing, parking tags from supermarkets, a Gameboy and a chiffon scarf.

Lily, in black denims and a suede shirt, settled back in the well-padded front seat, her heart pounding arhythmically despite her best efforts at self-control.

'Do you need me to map-read?' she asked.

'Nope. But you could put some music on.' He gestured towards the glove compartment, inside which was a clutter of CD boxes, all containing classical music. There was some opera too and an unwelcome flash of Paolo burst upon Lily's inner eye. She could not think of many things her two lovers might have in common, except perhaps this taste in music. Two lovers. Just think of it. A few months earlier she had been monogamous, the landscape of romance extending before her as full of surprises as Norfolk. Now she had slept with two men in as many months. Was she in danger of becoming a loose woman? Hardly, but her extended experience did not feel a happy thing either. Perhaps being a bit more selective might help. Should she select Hugo tonight? Should she select Beethoven's Seventh now, which she and her father had hummed along to many times? Probably not, if it would make her cry. Choices, choices.

'Mahler Two,' Hugo instructed, and she was glad to be guided. She slipped the disc into the player.

Muscular, apocalyptic music filled the car as they sped south, leaving behind the south London suburbs, the Sunday supermarket queues and lunchtime boozers. Once on the motorway, Hugo moved into the fast lane and stayed there, clocking a cool ninety miles per hour.

'What's that you've got round your neck?' he asked. 'A sample of one of next year's bestsellers?'

Lily was wearing the chain again. She did so quite often, feeling comfortable with its cool embrace, its simple beauty that adapted easily both to casual and dressier occasions. As Hugo asked, her fingers moved unconsciously to touch it and she realized this gesture had become a new part of her repertoire.

'My father left it to me,' she explained quietly.

'Oh.' Hugo's voice softened. 'I meant to ask you how you were doing. That's a family heirloom, then, is it?'

'I'm okay.' Was she? 'And no, this isn't really an heirloom. There's not much in the way of Braithwaite heritage – my father was put in an orphanage, along with his sister. Their mother couldn't cope. He never got back in touch with her, never really forgave her. So there aren't any roots on that side of the family. No, this is something he bought for the shop, and then kept for me, after it didn't sell.'

'He didn't have your flair for buying then.'

Lily smiled faintly. 'I think in a way he was never able to indulge himself like I can. He always wanted to stock beautiful things – expensive watches, designer pieces – but that wasn't what sold.' She mentioned the town where she had grown up. 'It's not a particularly wealthy place and there was already one jeweller who catered to the upmarket trade. So Dad pitched towards the workers, and they wanted gold but cheap. He majored on production-line stuff. It worked very well.' She fell back to thinking of Christmas holidays in her teenage years, when she had worked alongside her father, selling charms, dress rings, children's bangles, to be packed in tiny scarlet boxes lined with cotton wool.

'So you grew up in the business,' Hugo observed.

'Yep, man and boy. Hopelessly unqualified for anything else.' She broke out of her reverie. 'That doesn't apply to you though.'

'No, I don't suppose so,' he answered coolly. 'I like to keep moving.'

Lily let that one pass.

'What did your father do?' she asked after a beat.

'Sold insurance, door to door. A bloody awful life. He used to come in looking like a whipped cur. My brother and I would shrivel at the sight of him. We didn't need any encouragement to do something different.'

'Does your brother have his own business too?'

'Yeah. He sells holidays, would you believe. Specializes in flash private villas and yachts. He's done pretty well.'

Lily couldn't quite interpret the expression in Hugo's voice. Admiration? Disparagement? 'Are you close, you two?'

'Not really. I've always been a bit of a loner.'

Again, an opportunity for comment. But Lily had sworn to herself that she was going to make no reference whatsoever to past intimacies. She wanted to do more than just survive Brighton; she wanted to emerge from it with her professionalism burnished. To do this, she had realized, she must devote all her resources to the job. With job losses rumoured, nothing was more important than convincing Hugo of her skills and talents, her crucial value to GBF. The private stuff, well, he would have to make his own choices about that. But she would offer him no opportunity for criticism. She would emerge the invaluable, irreplaceable member of staff.

The music boiled through the car and obviated the need for much conversation, although Hugo asked a few questions about the fair, making it clear that he would use Lily's presence to familiarize himself and make introductions, but also planned to be independent and work his own connections. Lily laid out her own buying procedure. This was a pattern she had established of old, combining refreshment of existing stock lines from established suppliers and presentations of their new product, with a detailed trawl of new traders or those with whom she had few regular dealings. In this way, she felt reasonably sure that she had covered the waterfront in terms of viewing goods, as well as having a chance to ask what was selling well to competitors and the trade at large.

'Sounds pretty encyclopaedic to me,' Hugo commented, blaring his horn and cursing at a baby Fiat which was daring to enter the fast lane in front of him.

'It's essential with our customers,' Lily explained. 'They may not be conscious of it, but they have long fashion memories, and there's a big difference between dated and retro. Do you have much sense of our customer profile?'

'Yes and no,' he answered, ambiguous as ever. 'But then I don't find it easy to see women as types.' He turned towards her. 'Do you see men that way?'

Good question. 'Depends on the categories,' she answered blandly, suppressing the urge to giggle.

'Talking of which,' he went on, 'keep your eyes open for men's ranges while we're there. Nothing definite, yet, but I'm thinking about a bit of expansion.'

Lily looked at him questioningly. 'You mean broadening the range within the shops, or new outlets?' She frowned at either thought.

'Dunno yet.'

He was obviously giving nothing away. Yet Lily's antennae quivered.

'Is that such a good idea?' she asked. 'Isn't our USP that we're unashamedly and exclusively female? Should we be diluting our image?'

'If Next and Jigsaw can do it, why not us?'

It was a good point, although the argument did not subdue Lily's misgivings. Margot, she wondered, are you listening? She sent out an early warning on the ether, hoping that, like Batman, her ex-boss was tuned to the receiving of SOSs.

She knew better than to argue with Hugo. On top of everything else, he paid her wages. And redundancy was in the air. No, she would be the professional she prided herself in being and research the men's range. But that didn't mean she had to like it.

They entered the outskirts of Brighton, which looked bleached and flat in the white autumn light. Their hotel, which again was doubling as the fair site, was big and modern and faced directly on to the seafront. Lily checked in while Hugo parked the car. They had arranged to meet for a drink in the bar at seven, which left plenty of time for unpacking and a walk along the beach. Lily, a Cancerian, had always been magnetized by oceans and rivers. Now, alone and wrapped up warmly, crunching over shingle, battered by strong sea breezes and the roaring waves, she felt herself purified.

Back in her room, she changed her heavy shirt for a jersey one with a zipped front and entered the bar punctually, to find Hugo ensconced in an armchair, with Sammy Morris and the two owners of Mitchells around him, all of whom he had met at the summer party. Lily joined them, and sipping a gin and tonic, entered the boisterous conversation. During Margot's reign, she had never noticed the rarity of women players in this particular game, but tonight, glancing round the busy bar, she realized she was heavily outnumbered, and that many of the women there were wives, possibly doubling as business partners, but clearly a minority.

One drink turned into several, and then dinner, during

which the group of four joined forces with the Posner team, who specialized in clock and watch imports. Nine people sat down to eat and Lily found herself seated across from Hugo, happy to chat with young Martin Posner, third generation in the business and a nice enough lad. Mid-twenties, she estimated, reminded as she was increasingly these days that she must seem almost maternal to such youth, although to be fair he was flirting gallantly. Lily had drunk a little more than was customary for her and was enjoying the spice of sexual badinage over the stringy roast chicken.

Decaffeinated coffee seemed not yet to have been invented in Brighton, so at the After Eights stage of the meal, which turned out to be after ten, Lily decided to call it a night. She stood up a little unsteadily and took her leave of the table. Hugo scarcely looked up. Walking up to her room on the second floor, she forced herself to screen out all thoughts other than setting the alarm clock and getting to bed. She locked her bedroom door, turned on lights, opened her window, flicked through the hotel's brochures and eventually wandered into the bathroom to clean her teeth. It was while she was leaning over the basin, frothing at the mouth, that the telephone rang. Her stomach plunged like a high-speed lift and yet she felt calm and took her time to answer it.

'Hello.'

'Hello, Lily.'

She waited.

'I was wondering whether you'd like to come up for a nightcap.'

Up? 'I don't know your room number.'

'410,' came the answer.

She put the phone down. Remembering her handbag, the condoms and her key, she went back into the closely carpeted corridor and climbed two more flights of stairs.

Hugo was waiting for her, his door ajar, his top three shirt buttons undone. No sooner had she entered the room – a big one with a bay window open to the sea – than he swept her up in his arms. She melted. Their kiss was as wonderful as she had remembered, and oh she had remembered, times without number, since the magical night of the party. Comparisons were odious, but so was any thought of Paolo's mechanical intimacies, next to this raw, electrifying sensuality.

Breaking off, Hugo reached for the zip on Lily's shirt and drew it down to her waist.

'I've been wanting to do that all evening,' he said, pulling her close again.

Was that true? If it was, he had masterly powers of concealment. That was the trouble with Hugo – he was impossible to read. She, on the other hand, must seem like an open book. Avid for skin contact, she undid the last of Hugo's shirt buttons and pulled the soft cotton away from his chest and shoulders, the better to hold herself against his heat. Meanwhile they kissed and kissed, twisting and urgent.

Hugo broke away again. 'Bed,' he said, removing her shirt entirely, unfastening her bra. She attended to her jeans herself, while he quickly shed his own clothes and pulled back the bedclothes. Then he turned back to her and she stood before him, naked too, only the gleaming white metal of the snake-like chain round her neck catching the low light from the bedside table. 'You look a picture,' he said and, like a magician, ran his hands over her body, setting her on fire wherever he touched.

They knelt on the bed, face to face, Hugo's hard penis trapped between them as he wrapped his arms around her whole torso and pulled her to him. She wanted him to envelop her utterly. She wanted these powerful arms to shield and shelter her. Tears pricked her closed eyes. If only she could dwell here. It felt as safe as her father's love had been, she realized, in a curious flash of detachment.

Awkwardly, without breaking away from each other, they lay down and Hugo pulled Lily on top of him. This was not a position with which she was much familiar, yet instinctively she bent her knees, and by doing so found herself perfectly poised over him.

'Wait,' she said, forcing herself to break out of her delirium.

'What is it?' he asked, a little sharply.

She tossed her hair out of her eyes and reached for her bag, to pull out the Cellophane-wrapped box. He groaned.

'Come on, Hugo. Join the twentieth century,' she said firmly. He was in no position to argue, literally or figuratively. As speedily as she could, she ripped open the foil packet and applied the condom, thanking Venus or whichever deity it was who had delivered the thing into her hand the right way up.

Hugo had settled himself on the pillows like a pasha while she performed her task. Now, majestic in flesh pink, he looked like the best kind of Christmas present. She knelt over him and he reached for her breasts. This was a powerful distraction and she allowed herself a moment of pure selfishness. A delicious network of gold wires seemed to make complicated, honeyed connections with her groin. Lowering her hips, she centred herself over him and amazingly, with no guidance from anyone's fingers, the arrowhead of him joined her. She froze, as much to effect a physical snapshot of the sensation as anything. The effect on Hugo was like a mild electric shock, a reflexive spasm, and within a millisecond he was deep inside her. It was Lily's turn to groan.

If she bent her torso forward, she discovered, her breasts moved against his chest as she rocked herself on him. He seemed to like this. The forward pressure of his ever stiffening penis against her vaginal wall set up a great heat within her, which was stoked by the brushing of her nipples against his skin. Hugo placed his hands on her hips, the better to indicate his preferred tempo, and she obliged with an easy, effortless movement, just teasing him occasionally with a break in the regular rhythm. She marvelled at her own adaptability, and the control she had assumed, physically at least. She was mistress of the situation, of the heavy fullness inside her.

Hugo was going to come. She could tell it both from the engorgement within and the change in his breathing which she remembered from last time. It seemed that she was not. Ah well, such was life. She was still happy to grant him the pleasure, and rested, feeling bountiful, after he had arched beneath her and then gradually subsided.

She lay on top of him, nerve-ends tingling, the sound of surf outside matching the slowing of her heartbeat. As he dwindled, she wondered what to do with her own arousal. Would Hugo offer to caress her, devote himself solely to *her* pleasure for a few moments? She lay still, waiting. When he moved, it was to twist and stretch out a hand to the cigarette packet on the bedside table. In the same action, she slid off him. So much for equal strokes.

'Ahh,' he sighed, lighting up and inhaling deeply. 'You know, Lily, you're quite something.'

'I bet you say that to all the girls.' She seemed unable to resist a touch of the sardonic.

'What do you take me for? No, don't answer that.'

She paused for a moment, then spoke her thoughts. 'We do generate some kind of electricity.'

'Mmm, true,' he commented and she wondered if they might segue into a conversation about doing it again, in the future, more often. But he reached over to tousle her hair, then tweak her nearest nipple, which had the effect of jump-starting her sexual hunger. However, for Hugo, the evening's exertions seemed over, at least for the present. There was no follow-up. Instead, after a few more drags, he stubbed out his cigarette, commanding, 'We should get some sleep,' before disappearing into the bathroom for a moment.

When he returned, it was her turn, and as she sat on the loo she examined the toiletries laid out round the sink. Electric razor, splay-bristled old toothbrush, expensive toothpaste, comb and flannel peeking out from a Liberty's peacock-feather-printed toiletry bag. Rather effeminate for Hugo – must be the wife's, she realized with a mild pang. She went back to bed.

Hugo was lying on his back, breathing heavily.

'Goodnight,' she said, leaning over to kiss him.

He patted her on the shoulder like a pet, but it was obvious he was already semi-comatose and within seconds he was snoring at her side.

Lily lay, wide awake, listening to Hugo, to the sea surging outside in the blackness. Should she masturbate? Could she just let her desire go, and enjoy lying here, next to her lover? She tried that, willing the soft pulse in her vagina finally to stop beating. It wasn't easy, and the more she tried, the more awake she felt. Dozing seemed impossible, with Hugo rattling gutturally in her left ear. She tried rearranging the bedclothes over him, urging him to turn over, but there was no budging him.

She looked at the luminous hands of her watch. It was after midnight. She must get some sleep. She forced herself to close her eyes and relax her breathing, to think of sheep, to focus on the rhythm of the waves. She lay there for twenty minutes. Nothing worked. But it was worse than that, she had begun to think. Now her brain was trudging round the circuit of work, sex, Hugo, father, Paolo, Frank. Like the ball-bearing in a pinball machine, she ricocheted from one problem to another. Was Hugo going to sack her?

Or hole the ship that was GBF? If he admitted their sexual chemistry, was he going to bed her more often? What did the future hold, without Frank or her father, with the only truly available men being the walking wounded, like Paolo? Where, oh where was sleep?

There was no remedy for it. She was going to have to go back to her own room and read for a while or watch television. Anything to stop her mind shoving her over these interminable hurdles. She could vaguely remember where her clothing had fallen, and got up, half hoping Hugo would awake and pay her some attention.

No such luck. He was lost to consciousness, all his hungers sated. She could not help feeling just a shade of disappointment – or perhaps irritation – at her own remaining frustration. Zipping up her shirt, she remembered her bag and key and groped for the door. The corridor was deserted as she pulled it firmly shut behind her. Thank God. The last thing she wanted at this moment was a farce-like encounter with one of the patriarchs of the jewellery world. Still, at least she had her trousers on.

Her own room was cool. She lit a couple more lamps and put the television on softly. There was a kettle and a dusty selection of sachets on a table by the bed. Perhaps a cup of cocoa was in order, she felt. Best to draw a line under the unfulfilled passion of the evening and go back to the beverages of the celibate. She was trying not to think about Hugo's selfishness, now made flesh. She could grant herself sexual release, but she was no longer in the mood. Her eyes felt gritty, her body and brain weary. She sipped synthetic hot chocolate, watched a dreary made-for-TV movie and fell asleep with the lights on.

The radio alarm woke her with all the gentleness of a dog barking. She leapt alert, managing to snatch the cold cocoa mug in mid-air as it sailed off the bed towards the floor. Breathing quickly, she looked at her watch. Seven o'clock.

Time for a shower. She had arranged to meet Jack and Frieda Millen, an elderly couple who had devoted their lives to watchstraps, for a working breakfast at eight.

With her hair washed and make-up applied, she checked her watch again. Seven forty-five. She picked up the telephone and punched in 410. Hugo answered after a couple of rings.

'It's me. Lily.'

'Yes.'

'I hope you don't mind that I left. I just couldn't sleep.'

'Not a bit,' he answered magnanimously.

'I had a lovely time, though. Maybe we could resume tonight,' she went on, hating herself yet unable to fight the need to try and pin Hugo down.

'We'll see,' he said. He could have been her mother, doling out sweets according to some self-determined sense of what was fair. Lily recognized a brick wall when she bashed her head against it. She put down the telephone with a sick sensation in her gut.

Chapter 16

Hugo dropped Lily off at her front door just after four o'clock on the Tuesday afternoon. Once again he refused her suggestion of tea or coffee – had he taken an oath never to enter her house again? – and drove off with a cheery wave. She closed the door behind her with enormous relief, dropped her bags and knelt down to rub noses with the cats. Nature was a wonderful thing. Though they probably saw her merely as a tin-opener on legs, you'd be hard pressed to believe, from their combined purring, that they were not actually happy to have her home for her own sake.

She picked up the mail and wandered into the living room, where she noticed the answerphone light blinking rapidly. She punched the replay button and collapsed on the sofa, shortly to be buried under an avalanche of black fur.

There were messages from Paolo – suggesting another trip to the opera, God save her – her mother and a company which wanted to replace all her front windows for nothing. And then three from Dorothy. The first of these, undated, was a recording of her friend crying loudly, in the gaps between asking, 'Lily, are you there?' The second, left on Monday evening, was calmer and took the form of an apology for disturbing her. The last one, which had been recorded a few hours earlier, was longer and gave some background. As Lily had already guessed, the problem was Peter. He had not come back on Saturday night. The slough of despond over his children had deepened, sucking in not only him but Dot too. They had argued fiercely and he had slammed out, leaving her to imagine that he had gone back to Carol. But no, he had spent the night driving about,

189

exhausting himself and punishing them both. He had come back on Sunday and they had patched things up, but the joins were visible. Dot sounded very rattled. Lily picked up the phone immediately.

'Dot, it's me. I'm sorry. I was in Brighton.'

'Oh shit, of course you were,' her friend answered. 'I knew that, but I was in a state. Beyond logical thought.'

'Do you want to come round?'

She arrived with all the speed London Transport could muster.

'Tea, coffee, wine, whisky?' Lily offered to the haggard figure who followed her into the kitchen.

'How about coffee with whisky?'

'Sounds good to me,' Lily replied, filling the glass pot of her filter machine. 'It might also be the time to break open the ginger shortbread I've been hoarding since last Christmas,' she went on, groping around in her store cupboard for the tartan box.

They shared the burden of bottles, plates, mugs, jugs and so on and finally settled in the living room which was now toasty warm, Lily having turned the central heating to high.

'Tell me all,' she instructed and Dot went back to the beginning of her miserable weekend.

'The atmosphere's like cold porridge,' she finished, 'so thick you could sculpt it. It's not that we're not friends. We just seem to have lost the art of communication. There's no joy, just this omnipresent guilt. Every time I hear anything on the radio about kids – illness, abuse, birthdays, anything – I feel dreadful. We both know it's irrational, that children do cope if a marriage breaks up, but it's getting to the stage where I almost want him to go, just to be free of the burden. Of course I don't, not really. I do love him.' Her mouth went square and she began to weep. 'Although I don't see how we're ever going to be happy.'

Lily went over to her friend and held her tightly. Dot's

crying increased and Lily waited for the jag to peak, then soothed and patted her till she was in control of her breathing again. After much sniffing, Dorothy finally released her, grimacing at the wet patch she had left on Lily's shoulder.

'God, what a mess. I meant your sweater. But we are too, Peter and me. Is this the curse of getting what you wanted, like the Monkey's Paw?' Lily remembered the short story Dorothy was referring to – heartbroken parents pleading to the gods for their dead son to be restored to them, only to hear a blood-freezing hammering on their door, the sound of a body risen from the grave. Was there no such thing as innocent happiness, except for the under-fives? And how could you compute the real cost of the price tags attached to the objects you desired?

'A bit like me and Hugo,' Lily volunteered, wondering if her friend was ready for – would even welcome – a change of subject.

'Omigod, yes.' Dorothy brightened visibly. 'What happened? Two nights with Hugo. Tell me, was it bliss followed by paradise?'

'More like chalk and cheese.'

Dot raised an eyebrow, a gesture of which Lily had always been jealous.

'It was history repeating itself. The first night we spent together, the second, well, it was as if I didn't exist. He didn't want to know me.'

'There's a word for that,' Dot commented.

'Yes, I know – bastard.'

'No, seriously. Disassociation.'

'Don't tell me, you edited a book about it.'

'Well, I did as a matter of fact. You do something you want to do but don't approve of, and then you act as if you didn't, so you didn't.'

'That made a whole book?'

'I'm simplifying a little, for the less sophisticated reader.'

Lily threw the empty shortbread box at her.

'So give me the grisly details,' demanded Dorothy, and her friend told her the story of Sunday night. 'And on the Monday?'

'It never happened. We were the perfect team, me doing the rounds, him chatting up all the bosses. I dazzled him with my expertise – actually I was on very good form, and there were some great goods.' Lily saw Dot's eyes glaze over. She was reminded that her friend's interest in jewellery matched her own in Restoration playwrights. 'Not only that,' she went on quickly, 'but he'd asked me to work on this new idea he'd had, and again, I found what he was looking for, so full marks to me.' Here Lily paused. She'd put on a very good show in her trawl for male consumer goods, but in the pit of her stomach she now knew she hated Hugo's idea of introducing a men's line, that it flew in the face of everything that was special – and successful – about Margot's vision of the company. But now was not the time to discuss the problem with Dot.

'Then, in the evening, we had dinner with various people, and I left the table first, like the night before, and – well, the call never came.'

'Did you call him?' Dorothy asked.

'Eventually, yes.' Lily had tried twice, once after mid-night, once half an hour later. 'There was no reply.'

'And what did that mean?'

'Take your pick. He knew it was me and chose not to answer, or he wasn't there, in which case, where was he and with whom? Do you get the impression I might have thought this through already once or twice?'

'No comment in the morning?'

'Butter wouldn't melt.'

'Aren't you furious?' Dot wondered.

'Distantly. Infatuation's a funny thing. Anyway, isn't this what being on the rebound is supposed to be all about?'

They sat in silence, contemplating perfidious masculinity.

'So you're back where you started,' Dorothy stated.

'I would say that's a fair assessment of the situation. Dangling on a string, which is tweaked every now and then, to make sure I'm still attached. And when I've shown I am, off he sods again.' She shook her head. 'It's like having an affair with the Scarlet Pimpernel.' They both sniggered. 'What about you? What's the way forward with Peter?'

'I honestly don't know. I've wondered about suggesting the kids live with us.'

Lily was sobered by this evidence of the depth of Dot's attachment. Dorothy was the first to admit she must have been standing behind the door when maternal instincts were being handed out. 'That's never going to happen, is it?'

'No,' Dorothy admitted. 'It would be a pretty untypical judge who took the children away from a capable mother, even though Peter and I could play happy families quite convincingly. What really needs to happen is for him to let go. Accept the decision he's made and the feelings that go with it. Take on board the fact that some situations don't have tidy conclusions. But he doesn't seem to be able to live with himself, and maybe soon not with me either.'

There was not much more to be said, and eventually Dot went back to her uneasy flat, leaving Lily to return the call to her mother. Paolo she had consigned to the outer darkness.

Early the following week, Lily was summoned to a strategy meeting with Hugo, Clive and Mark to discuss the plans for a men's range at GBF.

'Well, we'll have to change the name of the business, for a start,' said Clive, unenthusiastically.

Hugo acted as if he hadn't heard.

'No, we've thought about that,' said Lily, more smoothly than her conscience dictated. She sent out another silent prayer: Please, Margot, rescue me. 'Men – or boys, to be exact – could also be seen as girls' best friends, if adorned with our sexy-but-masculine ornaments.'

'Do you have samples?' Mark asked, a salesman to his toenails.

Lily produced the file she had put together illustrating signet, wedding and other rings, identity bracelets and copper bangles, earrings, cigarette cases and lighters, tie-pins and studs, cufflinks and brandy flasks. First Mark, then Clive pored over the photos in their glossy Cellophane sheaths.

'Wow,' was Mark's comment. Clive confined himself to a noisy inhalation and exhalation of breath. Then both of them spoke at the same instant.

'It'll cost a fortune.'

'When do we start?'

'Yes and next spring,' answered Hugo complacently, getting up from the conference table to fetch an ashtray from the windowsill. Coming back, he passed Clive a piece of paper with numbers on. 'Here's my rough costing for the stock, the launch and the extra display materials. And here,' another piece of paper, 'is my projected turnover chart.'

'I don't see anything to cover diminished revenue on existing lines,' Clive said, eyes moving rapidly over the information in front of him.

'Not significant,' said Hugo airily.

'But we'll have to reduce some of the female range, just to make space,' chipped in Mark.

'Only the bottom end. The slow movers. Not worth factoring in.'

'Where's the money coming from?' enquired Clive.

'The bank, of course. Plus some good housekeeping.'

'For this *and* the mail order start-up?' This last was another of Hugo's new ideas. Lily had had to admit it was another stroke of some brilliance.

'Sure.'

Lily was watching this two-hander like a Wimbledon rally. Despite her reservations, she had done her bit, produced the goods, and Mark seemed happy. But the stand-off between Clive and Hugo deepened her worries. Clive might be conservative and dull, but his stewardship of GBF's finances had always been impeccable. He was not negative by nature, just cautious. His resistance both in principle and practice to Hugo's ideas suggested a more deep-seated reluctance to support their new boss. Did Clive share her sense of protectiveness towards GBF's identity, for financial reasons, or was something else going on below the surface?

But Clive's truculence and awkward questions were not going to divert Hugo's plans. He had an answer for everything and a hide thick enough to repel any unstated criticism. Eventually, Clive ran out of steam.

'Right, then. Any more discussion?' No one spoke. 'Okay, Lily, over to you. Time to place those orders. We want the best deals you can get. And remember, these are stock orders. Go for premium discounts and lock them into follow-ups wherever you can. Everything is top secret for the moment. Mark, you, me, David and Colin need another meeting to cover marketing and design. And Clive,' he added drily, 'well, thanks for your support. I'll handle the bank myself.'

Hugo stood up, collected his papers and left them to it.

Lily continued to hold her peace while Clive slammed his folder down on the table. Mark drummed his fingers on the arm of his chair. 'I don't really have a problem with this, from a sales point of view,' he commented calmly.

'I'm sure you don't. More turnover, more security. All fine and bloody dandy.' Clive's voice was low, almost private. 'But you need a pair of dark glasses to read these projections, they're so sunny. It's just not realistic, and the borrowing will be crippling. And for what? To dilute our profile and take us into markets in which we have no track record. Don't misunderstand me. I'm as keen on growth as the next man – sorry, Lily. But we can't behave like kids. We're looking at major investment here. Hugo had better be telling himself the truth, because he certainly isn't telling us.'

Clive's dark declaration weighed heavily on Lily for the rest of the week. Was the good ship GBF really in peril? Strolling through Covent Garden on Saturday with her mother, they both stopped in front of the flagship GBF store, Edna to look at the window display, Lily to consider the rate of business inside. The shop was nicely filled, with quite a lot of attention being paid to a new range she had introduced for Christmas: organic forms based on flowers, leaves, feathers, made of fine mesh and thin, beaten plate, highly polished and interchangeable in yellow and white metal, in a range of designs for fingers, wrists and throats. There were few men to be seen. Indeed the GBF shops, Lily now realized, had always been temples to powerfully female instincts of affordable but distinctive style. What would happen when their sanctity was breached? Or forcibly violated?

'Your father wouldn't have given houseroom to those earrings,' Mrs Braithwaite remarked, nodding towards some particularly delicate chain streamers hanging like wind-chimes in the window. 'Tissue-paper thin. I can hear him saying it.'

Since when were you any authority, Lily was tempted to ask, but bit it back.

'Do you get many complaints?' her mother pursued, as graceful as a heffalump.

'No more than average,' her daughter answered stiffly, wondering again, time beyond number, why conversational exchanges between herself and her mother had to be conducted with so much veiled aggression.

They eventually moved on from the black-and-gold shopfront and continued their stroll down towards the old fruit-and-vegetable terraces. Lily was conscious of slowing down her normal rate of progress to match her mother's more leisurely pace. Edna was looking around her as brightly as a sparrow. It had been her own idea to visit London instead of Lily journeying north again. 'I could make a start on my Christmas shopping,' she had suggested, raising a topic that Lily knew would eventually require discussion but which filled her boots with lead.

'Did you say you wanted to go to the Body Shop?' she asked Edna.

'Yes. I've made a list. I thought I could get some little things there, you know, smellies, but not such old-fashioned ones as at home. I think I'm going to need quite a few little presents. Joyce was telling me that both the bridge crowd and the bowling group go in for gift-giving. But nothing too ostentatious.' Edna foraged in her handbag and came up with a piece of pale blue notepaper. 'Here we are.' There were two columns of names on it. Incredible, Lily thought. Her mother had already plugged herself into a circuit board of social activity. Bridge, bowling, and she was talking about joining a local archaeology group after Christmas. Each evening, she seemed to have the choice of staying in or going out, with kindly folk offering to give her lifts to every venue, since she had not yet taken her driving test.

'I don't want you to think I'm rushing to forget your father,' she had said to Lily over a cup of coffee, shortly after arriving at Euston. 'But I can spend too many nights sitting at home, missing him and feeling lonely. It's not good for me. And I've always liked a bit of company.'

Lily had nodded her agreement, both to the philosophy and the character description. Another sacrifice Edna had made to her marriage was her own gregariousness. She enjoyed people, 'having a bit of a natter', as she called it. Alec had not, and apart from the annual Chamber of Commerce dinner dance, would not be lured out after dark any night of the week. And if he did not go out, then Edna could not go either. Lily really did approve of her mother striking out for her own kind of life, even if she herself inclined more to her father's way of things.

'What about your Christmas shopping?' Edna asked now. 'Have you got much to do?'

'Not a huge amount,' was the honest answer. 'Which reminds me,' Lily went on, 'what would *you* like for Christmas?'

'Now that's a good question.' Her mother fell silent for a minute. 'I'll have to let you know.' Another pause. 'And shall you be coming home for the holiday?'

At last. There was no avoiding it. 'Well, yes. Yes,' Lily answered, forcing herself to sound brighter than she felt. 'Is that what you'd like?'

'Oh I think so.' They had reached the Body Shop, through the assault course of shoppers, tourists and mime artists. Edna paused on the threshold. 'We should have Christmas just like we always did. This year at least. It's what your father would have wanted.'

Lily nodded and smiled wanly. The shop door opened and a sweet fug drew them inside.

Chapter 17

Flicking through her diary the following Monday morning, in search of an appointment she thought she had made, Lily noticed the name of Julie Bell written firmly against the time of 2.00 on Thursday afternoon. She had forgotten all about it. She was going to have her fortune told.

She jotted down a reminder to herself to nip out at lunchtime and buy a cassette tape. Then she sat back in her chair and allowed herself a brief fantasy of what she would like the stars to reveal. Well, a partner, of course. A partner, today. Or if not today, then bright and early tomorrow. A Hugo-shaped partner? Probably, although Dot's unhappiness was fresh-minted in her mind. She couldn't deny it, one aspect of Lily's sense of self would have been immensely boosted if Hugo had declared himself unable to live without her, if he tore himself from his family to be with her for ever and always. But her more pragmatic self knew that even if this dream scenario unfolded, there would still be the ever-after to contend with. And if Peter's and Carol's push-me/pull-you state was anything to go by, this was a permanent quicksand. Anyway, did she really want to live with Hugo? No, his ideal role was as lover, kept in a box under the bed, like a sex toy, to be summoned whenever the fancy took her.

Thinking of Hugo, she had better mention to him that she would be taking Thursday afternoon off, and she walked along to his office, still musing on the best that Julie Bell could detect in her stars. Fame? Fortune? Perhaps an immediate redistribution of her body mass – two inches off her hips and one added to her bust, plus nips and tucks in various places? A magic carpet?

Approaching Hugo's room with her head in such clouds, she was surprised to hear raised voices, but before she could turn and slink away again, the door was flung open and Clive appeared.

'Fine,' he threw over his shoulder. 'It'll be on your desk before lunch.' He strode away down the corridor, his long legs giving him tremendous acceleration.

Lily, flattened against the corridor wall by the blast of animosity released from Hugo's office, blinked as Hugo himself appeared to watch Clive's departure.

'What are you doing here?' he asked her. 'Problems?'

'No. I just wanted to ask if I could have Thursday afternoon off,' she answered defensively. She felt bold enough to risk Hugo's wrath. 'What's up between you and Clive?'

'Nothing's "up", as you put it in your delightful Midlands way,' he said rather cruelly. 'Clive has simply decided that he would be more appreciated elsewhere, and I agreed with him.' The expression in his eyes brooked no discussion. 'And yes, you can have Thursday afternoon off provided Project Brainchild has been safely put to bed.' This was Hugo's code for the new men's line.

Lily was shocked by this glimpse of Hugo with the gloves off. She limited herself to a nod and walked smartly away.

The westbound tube train on Thursday lunchtime was populated more by tourists than workers, gaggles of French teenagers with fancy backpacks, glamorous Italians in furs, soft leather and gold. Lily watched them twittering like starlings over maps, while marking the stops to her own destination. She alighted in a quite unfamiliar corner of London and had to consult her *A to Z* to find Julie Bell's street. Her flat was located in an unremarkable sixties block overlooking an elevated section of the dual carriageway heading out to the airport. Lily found herself confused

– she had expected something more gothic, she supposed – and a little daunted, as she rang the bell for number 47. She announced herself when the intercom clicked on and was invited to take the lift to the fourth floor. The door hummed open and she was in.

Julie Bell was standing in the doorway of her flat as the lift doors opened. Lily shook the warm, strong hand of a tall, self-possessed woman aged somewhere between fifty and seventy. Her grey hair was held in a loose chignon by a pair of chopsticks, and as she leaned comfortably against the doorjamb, her fine grey wool dress flowed in easy, expensive drapes to mid-calf. Lily being Lily, she was magnetized by the astrologer's jewellery, which was neither foreign nor runic, but very unusual designer pieces which Lily thought she recognized from the craft shop at the Victoria and Albert Museum. Around both wrists were wide, asymmetrical bands of pewterish metal, and the woman also wore a ring and a matching brooch, all of them twisted, beaten and tortured into unnatural shapes suggesting an elemental battle for domination.

'Come in,' Julie Bell invited and led Lily, via a stark white hall, into another white room, heavily scented with cigarette smoke, overlooking the busy traffic. Obviously double-glazed, it admitted no sound from outside, so the tiny urgencies of the cars seemed dreamlike and ridiculous. Power was concentrated instead in this blinding space, which contained two ergonomically shaped chairs in pillar-box red and a low white table formed like an artist's palette. On this sat the tape recorder, an ashtray, cigarettes, lighter and a small cactus flowering to match the chairs.

Lily took the seat indicated, settling herself and shedding coat and bag untidily on the floor, as there was nowhere else to put them.

Julie sat down elegantly and cleared her throat before turning on the tape recorder and inserting the cassette Lily had handed over. She lit a cigarette and Lily wondered why so many people in her life seemed addicted to the weed and whether passive smoking was another failing she could add to her list of shortcomings.

'Okay,' Julie began, tapping her cigarette into the lava bowl of the ashtray. 'Can we first of all establish that you understand I don't predict the future.'

Lily nodded. 'Yes, I know that. Although I don't really know what you do do.'

'Then let me explain. With the information you gave me I drew up your chart and that for me maps out your psychological dynamics, the pattern of your development.'

Lily nodded, although she could see no chart.

'Each of us, I believe, is composed of a cast of characters, and our charts reveal bits we can identify and bits that are unconscious. The unconscious bits we may not own, although often we find ways of mirroring them back to ourselves. So there can be a coincidence between events and character. I'm more interested in character, and if we focus on the hidden bits of the chart, you have a chance to get in touch with all of yourself and make better decisions. I can't give you a new self, but I can show you how you might have more choices.'

'Great,' Lily said, following it so far and warming to a notion of upgrading her life's pick-and-mix.

'I'm going to talk about transits and progressions – these are the so-called "predictive" aspects. Transits are the recent or current movements of planets. If a transit crosses something on your birth chart, it serves to summon some part of your character. So to that extent I can predict patterns in you. No further.'

She broke off to extinguish one cigarette and light another. She had no notes, but apparently needed no prompts, the words seeming to surge like a source within her.

'If we look at your chart now, I would say something quite critical is happening, by which I mean a big push for change is taking place. If you are receptive to that, you can open up voluntarily. But if you try to reject or deny it, to nail things down as they are, the change will be forced out more explosively.

'I would say that you, at present, are in the middle of a very powerful movement which in popular psychological language is referred to as the mid-life crisis.'

Lily's jaw was going to drop, but she managed to keep the hinge closed. Were Julie Bell's real skills investigative – finding her friends and making discreet enquiries of them? Surely so much accuracy was not available from a date and an obscure geographical location. Perhaps it was a lucky guess.

'Astrology has a cycle that reflects this crisis – the opposition of Uranus to its own place in the birth chart, a process which takes roughly forty years, say between thirty-eight and forty-two. What the opposition does is clarify what has not been developed. So people go along thinking they are one thing and suddenly they are brought up short. Their sense of identity falters. They need to change but they don't know what they are supposed to do.'

Two lucky guesses in the space of as many minutes? Lily was beginning to feel a little uncomfortable, skewered as she was to her chair by Julie Bell's scalpel-sharp résumé.

'What we can do is to look at what is hit in the birth chart, to give us an idea of the areas to work in.' The focus of the astrologer's eyes shifted from the middle distance to Lily's face. Lily felt almost mesmerized by the green gaze. 'So in yours, Uranus is connected with the sun, which falls in the eighth house. This has to do with what is invisible, the unconscious, the world of motives. People with the sun in the eighth, they spend a long time trying to be normal, but then something happens that feels like a blow of fate –

say a marriage breakdown, or depression, or illness or an accident. It erupts from below. Suddenly life seems a lot more complicated.' The woman paused to swallow. 'With the sun in the eighth, this is almost inevitable. And it requires you to change your way of seeing life, to look at what is underneath, even if this is not what you would choose.'

Another nail rapped smartly on the head. With smooth articulacy, Julie Bell was pulling together the exact feelings, bewilderments and seismic shifts Lily felt had coloured her life since Frank had walked out, or possibly earlier.

'The change you are in the midst of is a lot to do with letting go, most importantly of the person you thought you were. My advice is, be willing to be confused for a while. If you feel you are in a fog, that's good. Your task at the moment is to find out what really supports you below the level of the conscious.' She paused. 'So, what has been happening to you?'

Lily had settled into the role of listener. She was almost too stunned, both by the novelty of being asked a question and the sequence of mirrorlike reflection, to answer. It was as if Julie Bell were reading her like a teleprompter. 'Well, my relationship ended a few months ago. And my father died. There've been some changes at work too. So quite a lot really.' She felt herself becoming emotional.

If Julie had noticed the quaver in Lily's voice, she did not comment. Instead, she was silent for a moment. 'I think we should focus on the relationship, and also on your parents, your family patterns. Everyone carries baggage from their families, patterns that go back to childhood, that go underground but force you to respond in certain ways. I'm not blaming the parents, by the way.' Lily nodded. 'They inherited baggage from their parents too. It goes back to Adam.' The oracle smiled at her little joke.

'Now, if we look at your mother, we see two people. An

unresolved conflict. On the one hand you have Neptune in the house of the mother, and that gives you a martyr, someone who sacrificed, gave everything, suffered, was a victim. But on the other hand, you have Mars and Saturn there, which indicates something very different – a highly intelligent woman, lots of spirit and energy, someone who could have made so much of herself if she had had the courage to be alone and separate.'

Lily's eyes widened as Edna sprang to life, fully formed, in the white room.

'So you, I believe, have a double message, a model of the feminine as victim, along with the knowledge that there is something better. Your mother told you that love means selflessness – although actually she was very needy – and you have modelled yourself on both those messages. Whenever I see Neptune as the mother, I think of her as a baby. I think you colluded with your mother – you're a Cancerian and naturally sympathetic. So you picked up her misery, her need to put someone else first, her fear of asserting herself, her fear of aggression. And you've taken this into your own relationships, taught yourself not to listen to your needs, pushed your own desires under, become the victim while constantly hoping for a reward.'

Now Lily's response was to blush, or was she burning with shame?

'That's your parents, your mother always hoping your father would pay her back, but he never did. He escaped her, and he escaped you too.'

Lily looked up at this, puzzled but also ahead of Julie, understanding her portrait of Alec's eternal ambivalence. She opened her mouth to interrupt, but there was no stopping the flow.

'Transits mark separations from family patterns. Your pattern makes you both want commitment but also fear it, like your mother, so you choose people like your father who don't want it, which is acting out the conflict.' Yes, yes, Lily thought. Frank. Hugo. Commitment to both was like garlic to Dracula. 'You have to find a better way to resolve it,' Julie advised with considerable understatement.

Another pause for breath and a nicotine boost. 'You had a very idealized relationship with your father, too, didn't you?'

Lily nodded, gobsmacked.

'He seems to have been a very tricky man. Very charming and fun to be with, but not capable of sharing himself wholly, neglectful of others' emotional needs. Someone who seemed to offer protection and strength, but who wasn't necessarily there when called upon. Someone who had poor parenting and never really grew up. If you adored him, you might choose men like him and then wonder why they want to be mothered. Perhaps you need to pick up on your mother's strength, not her martyrdom, and your father's emotional immaturity and instinct for self-preservation, not his charm. The pattern is trying to break up now, anyway. You have an opportunity. Grasp it – give yourself a chance to emerge as a separate individual.'

Julie stopped, as if to compose her thoughts or mentally shuffle her prompt cards. Lily was glad of an instant's respite. She felt as if she were drowning and her life flashing before her eyes. Her parents, her lovers, herself, all paraded like the newborn, stripped to their essences, against a backdrop of sun, moon and stars.

But now Julie was off and running again. 'Transits to the sun are concerned with a sense of individual reality emerging. This can only happen if we are on our own for a while.' The woman's eyes seemed to narrow a little. 'You are being reshaped – it's exciting and powerful, but lonely, frightening, confusing and painful too. That's because of Neptune. The bad news is that you have more of it in the coming months.' Lily winced. 'Also Saturn will go retrograde over the next year and this denotes a time to accept reality. No knight on a white charger is about to appear.'

Lily shrank further into herself. Julie Bell gave her the most fleeting of sympathetic smiles. 'But Uranus's transit also goes on for another year, which means more changes, yet a freeing of energy. Nothing leaves your life under Uranus which you are not better off without. You have outgrown the old patterns. Allow the movement to take place. Travel lightly. Accept what comes along – lovers, friends – if you want to, but don't look for permanence. Trust your instincts, accept this as unavoidable. And if you can't handle the emotions, pull into yourself for a while. It is better to stay depressed or be alone than to be in hurtful or bad company. Get into the spirit of it. Learn how to amuse yourself. You're not as helpless or as chaotic, certainly not as defenceless as you think.'

Helpless? Chaotic? Defenceless? Is that what I think? Lily was finding it hard to keep up, so fast was Julie's flow, and so damnably accurate. Thank heavens for the tape. There were so many things she wanted to go back and examine. Well, there would be time. Meanwhile, she pinned back her ears again.

'The instability may not only be in life but in work too. But if your job rocks, or even folds, try to remember that you will end up in a better place. Cancerians are very security-conscious. I understand – you must be hating this upheaval. But it's for your own good.' Not that old chestnut. 'You need to stretch and expand yourself. I don't know where you will end up, but with a Uranus transit, trust it, it never destroys without a good reason.'

Now Lily was feeling angry. Who had determined that she had to change? God? The stars? Why couldn't she carry on as the person she was? And yet before the question even formed itself, she had rejected the petulance of that response. If forced – and she *was* being forced – she could see the possibilities of a better self.

'This is a time to look after yourself,' Julie pronounced.

That again, Lily thought.

'Think about what you eat, how you sleep. Focus on how to nurture yourself, what makes you feel good, what gives you pleasure. A heavy transit to the eighth house sun is a big thing. Don't underestimate how much peace and quiet you need. And good boundaries, effective defences. Say no to people who ask too much. Put yourself first. Stop neglecting yourself. You're a late developer and you have lots to discover – how to amuse yourself when you are alone, what matters to *you*, what do *you* like.'

Was that a question? Lily sat facing Julie, swamped in truth and unable to speak. Julie seemed to understand. She carried on talking for a while, mopping up areas she seemed to have overlooked, going back to underscore a point. But it was clear the session was coming to an end. Eventually she leaned forward and clicked off the tape. Lily wrote her a cheque. There didn't seem to be any small talk. Lily paid this strange woman who had just performed some amazing act of intimacy on her, received the tape, put on her coat, expressed her thanks and walked out of the flat like a somnambulist.

It was four o'clock on a windy November afternoon and Lily turned herself in the broad direction of central London and walked. She did not know the local geography or bother to look at the map. She just wanted to absorb the deluge that had descended on her. It was like a miracle. Did Julie have Kryptonite vision, that she could read her psyche like an X-ray? How could she know so much about her mother and father? And Lily didn't just mean facts. Julie knew their dynamics, their secret souls. And hers too. She seemed to have had voiced to her the precise sensation of being Lily, here and now. How was that possible?

She smarted at the accuracy of it all. As she walked blindly along, she admitted to herself her split personality, her simultaneous rejection and embracing of her mother's martyrdom and self-abnegation. This, in a way, must have been what Margot was talking about. She acknowledged her father's idealization, and how he had excluded the bits of her he didn't want to know. She could see where she had played Edna to Frank and Hugo both, and how she had sought the Alec in them. How indeed the pair of them had offered her just that – the mercurial side of Alec, shelter from the storm underneath an umbrella which blew inside out.

She accepted her own neediness and fear of being alone. And for the first time she wondered whether she could rein herself in for a while, not look so hard for a substitute partner, learn to be herself. Julie's words were so true. What did she like? What truly gave her pleasure? She had to admit, she didn't have a clue. Well, it was about bloody time she found out.

It was dark by now and a miserable light rain was falling. Lily awoke to her surroundings – an unexceptional high street in which electric lights shone warm, golden and deceptive. They were not offering comfort, just fast food and overpriced convenience groceries. Consistent with the themes of the afternoon, she acknowledged, acidly. Distantly she could see the navy blue and red tube logo and stepped more purposefully towards it.

At home, she made herself some lemon and ginger tea, and then sat down and phoned Andy at his office.

'Oh, Lily. Good. I wanted to hear the details. I haven't spoken to Clive yet, only Judy, who sounded pretty pragmatic.'

About what? Oh God, Clive's resignation. Or had he been given the push? Office politics had gone right out of her head, although in fact Clive's dismissal had been a source of anxiety, both to her and her colleagues. 'Er, yes, well, I'm not sure I know that much.' She was finding it hard to re-enter GBF's disrupted atmosphere, after her interplanetary voyage. She forced herself. 'Things seemed to come to a head over Operation Brainchild – don't laugh, I can't tell you what it is, one of Hugo's new schemes. I don't know if that was the problem itself – probably just the catalyst.' She was musing out loud. 'Clive didn't think Hugo was behaving as scrupulously as was proper.'

'Hugo to the life,' Andy opined. 'It was always going to be a style confrontation, Clive's belt and braces versus Hugo's now you see me, now you don't. I feared this would happen. I warned Clive too. The Padmore method has always been to try and move faster than the eye can see, and unfortunately he's tended to succeed, take his profits before the consequences catch up with him. Clive was never going to be able to stomach it. He's probably better off out of it. Knowing Hugo, this is probably just the tip of the iceberg.'

Lily had a glimpse of herself leaning on the rails of the *Titanic*, calmly watching the scenery float by.

Hugo's preference was quite clearly to live dangerously and also only for himself. Lily felt a frisson down her spine, but then remembered Julie's words of advice. In essence, her message had been not to fear change. Well, perhaps if change showed her a friendlier face, this would not seem so impossibly difficult.

'Sorry,' she apologized to Andy. 'I was just digesting all that against the backdrop of what Julie Bell just told me.'

'Oh, God. Was your reading today? How did you get on?' he asked, animatedly.

'I'm still reeling,' Lily answered. 'But thank you for suggesting her. It was one of the most extraordinary things I've ever experienced. She was so accurate, so utterly on the button, not just about me, but everyone else too, especially my parents. It was almost embarrassing, like sitting there with no clothes on.'

'I know. Unbelievable. It's like being with a seer, isn't it, although I gather from talking to other people that it's all perfectly scientific, if you call astrology a science, that is.'

'And did it all come true, like she said? I mean, her predictions of how long it would take for things to shift, and the nature of the changes?' Lily was half hoping that Andy would say no, that she would not have to soldier on alone for many more months.

''Fraid so. Couldn't fault the woman.'

'I see.'

Andy was clearly being discreet and not enquiring the details of her reading, so in gratitude she told him the bit about work. 'So I suppose I should try not to feel anxious about revolving doors at GBF. Even if the place comes crashing down about our ears, apparently I'll end up better off. Maybe Margot will come back and snatch me away, offer me a partnership in a Mexican tin mine.'

'Well, there is life beyond GBF,' Andy commented. 'I'm proof of that.'

'But what happens to the Hugos of this world?' Lily asked rhetorically. 'Do they ever get their comeuppances? He's so cavalier, so selfish about getting his own way, whatever the cost to others.' She had to remember not to blow the gaff about sleeping with Hugo, but was actually meaning something else, something she hadn't quite put into words before, her sense that Hugo was rending the fabric that was GBF.

'Life ain't fair,' was Andy's dispassionate maxim. 'There will always be another woman for Hugo to seduce, another bit of business for him to do where his quick wits and lack of scruples will give him the edge. But you have to take the long view. What's happened to his soul, you have to ask yourself. And when he's on his own, and really looks at himself in the mirror, what does he see?'

Couldn't you ask that about all of us? Lily thought. Herself included?

Chapter 18

Although Lily had delivered a two-week ultimatum to Frank to arrange the removal of his goods and chattels, it had taken him until now to book a van and arrange storage. Duly, on the following Saturday morning, she made sure she was up and about early, breakfasted and presentable before nine o'clock, which was when he had told her to expect him. When the doorbell rang just after nine, she opened the door to a set-faced Frank, who was followed into the house by a couple of impassive lads, one shaven-headed and skinny, the other with terrifying musculature bulging beneath his Iron Maiden T-shirt. With few additional pleasantries, the three of them set about manhandling on to the pavement the various items that Lily had marked with red stickers.

She and Frank had had another phone conversation about the final splitting of their common possessions, and in some cases, where they could not agree, sets of plates or glasses had been divided in two, generally leaving three items for each, a solution that worked as a compromise but left both of them with small, unusable trophy groups of crockery and glassware. Lily had spent quiet moments over the preceding weeks bagging and boxing the smaller things up, expecting the move itself to be a disturbing experience and not wanting to prolong it in any way.

Her expectations were now borne out. Watching the tangible proof of ten years' cohabitation being carelessly shifted out of her home and piled in the van, she felt a great emptiness. For some of the time, she went and huddled with the cats whom she had shut in her bedroom, for fear they would inadvertently get packed up and shipped off too. The three of them curled up on the bed, and Lily listened to the thumps and instructions from below, finding each moment excruciating, feeling, even though she herself was not leaving, like a screaming root being pulled up from the earth.

Why was this part so hard, compared to everything that had preceded it? She realized that she was experiencing a great sense of violation, that although part of the hurt was Frank finally purging all trace of himself (at her instigation, she reminded herself), the rest of the pain was the invasion of her home. Forced both by Julie Bell and the thugs downstairs to focus, she realized that this pile of bricks and mortar in fact meant a great deal to her. Initially she had thought of the house as a burden, and then, after the break-in, as a besieged island. But it was far more, she now saw. Not only a haven and a place within which to withdraw, this was a space in which she was wholly self-determining. Perhaps the choices were trivial – where to put the kitchen table, what colour to paint the bathroom – but she made them, no one else. Here was a place where she was free from bullying or coercion. Here was at least a partial answer to Julie Bell's question about what she liked. Well, she liked this house and being the mistress of it.

Did that mean she should give it a makeover, a face-lift to celebrate the completion of her sole occupancy? She felt in no hurry. The point was less that it should be an interior designer's dream than that she should be comfortable here, messy or tidy, painted or scuffed – although looking round the bedroom, maybe it was time for a change. Big though the room was, the dark, veneered wardrobe, tallboy and dressing table she had bought from a local junk shop – another thirties discovery – did nothing to lend light or air. And the wallpaper, pansies on a cream ground, was mimsier than her current temperament dictated. What about painting it over? What about turning the spare room into a dressing room? What about plain walls, possibly lemon-coloured, and floating muslin curtains? What about painting the floorboards white and moving out every stick of furniture except the wooden bed and the cream bedside tables? She was beginning to elaborate with thoughts of Japanese-style lighting and what, if anything, to hang on the walls when she heard Frank calling her from down-stairs.

He was standing in the hall, hands in jeans pockets, sweater flecked with fluff.

'We've taken all the bags and boxes – thanks for packing my books, by the way – and my desk, and the dresser and washstand. That just leaves the dining-room furniture, if you're sure you want the three-piece suite.'

'I thought that was what we'd agreed.'

'Well, we did,' he said shiftily, 'but to be honest, I could use a sofa and chairs just now.'

Did he mean Anna of Bromley was under-represented in the upholstery department?

They both went into the living room, the back half of which had been devoted to the formal dining furniture. Lily and Frank had rarely held dinner parties, but they had eaten in here themselves, just the two of them, on high days and holidays, birthdays and anniversaries. The table's wood veneer was the colour of golden syrup, a marvellous lustrous yellow in which the commas – the 'bird's eyes' in the maple – curled like miniature bass clefs at irregular intervals. The top was square, under which slid two further leaves, allowing it to be extended to seat six. The chairs had curved, tulip-shaped backs which Lily had polished lov-ingly, eliminating scratches and lending the wood a further luminous glow.

As they contemplated the set, Lily thought of their expedition to buy it – a response to a small ad in the local paper, which had sent them racketing off into the Friday night traffic to Richmond, where a batty old dear in a mansion flat had given them stiff gins and an account of pre-war Rangoon before they loaded their great, thrillingly cheap find into Frank's car. It had been a squeeze, but with the hood down and the boot held closed with washing-line, they had driven their treasure home in one freezing trip.

She looked at Frank. He was probably remembering too. She ran her fingertips over the smooth dip of a chair-back. 'They're so beautiful,' she said quietly, contemplating the group of chairs which stood attentively round like obedient children. Sadness came over her again, a strange kind of grief, she knew, for inanimate objects of little commercial value. But this old furniture possibly represented the best of what was gone, moments of fusion and shared delight, the points when she and Frank had come closest to togetherness. And that in itself was a condemnation. If what they were best at had been shopping, not caring and cherishing, then no wonder it had come to this – two impatient lads, a dented Ford Transit van and a pile of cardboard boxes.

'No,' she said. 'We had a deal. You did agree.'

'I know,' he said lugubriously and picked up one of the chairs to stack it upside down on another.

Mind out, she wanted to shout. Be careful with them. But she wouldn't allow herself. Frank, when in sulking mode, was inclined to be destructive, and all the more so if cautioned against it. She had made her decision. The table and chairs were his. She went back upstairs, eyes closed, hands over ears, determined to screen out any noises that denoted scraping or splintering.

Fifteen minutes later it was over. She went out to the pavement to observe the big lad close the van doors and the skinhead rev the engine. Neither was being particularly friendly, probably because, in her wish to speed things along, she had not offered them tea. Tough, she thought.

They can stop at a greasy spoon if they're thirsty. I've just taken my name formally off the treaty that says all visiting workmen are entitled to unlimited free hot beverages and biscuits, in exchange for barely adequate workmanship and a generous spray of pee in the vicinity of the toilet.

Frank was heading for his car. 'Bye, then,' he called.

'Bye,' she called back, refraining from, 'Keep in touch,' or, 'Take care.' She didn't want him to do either.

His turquoise 2CV pulled out into the street and the van followed, deafening music pulsing from its vibrating shell. She leaned against the front garden wall, watching both vehicles negotiate a right-hand turn at the bottom of the road and disappear from view. As she stood there, an elderly woman walked past, pulling a wicker shopping trolley on wheels. Lily knew her by sight – she was one of the street's older residents, not yet displaced by swag curtains and a four-wheel-drive roadster.

'Oh, you've not moved, then,' the older woman commented, approvingly. 'When I saw the van and the furniture outside, I thought you might be leaving us. We'd be sorry to see you go.'

Presumably 'we' meant the other pensioners in the street, like Ron next door, who preferred continuity.

Lily smiled. 'No,' she declared. 'Not me. I'm staying put.'

Dot had invited Lily over for supper that evening, as an antidote to the expected glums of the day. Lily was happy to be going out, though her mood was less black than she and her friend had feared. Indeed, if she were feeling trepidatious, it was more to do with the unpredictable emotional temperature she was likely to meet chez Dorothy and Peter.

She turned up at the flat promptly at seven thirty, holding a plastic bag containing a bottle of decent South African red, and rang the bell. Standing on the step, she listened out for raised voices. But the Dot who opened the door was wreathed in smiles. The two women hugged, then drew back and examined each other closely.

'How are you?' they chorused at each other. 'No, you first.'

'No, you,' insisted Lily.

'I'm fine. Really. Things have stayed calmed.' Dot was speaking at half-volume, filling in the gaps since their last phone conversation of a couple of days ago. 'We had a very long talk, several in fact. Well, I'll tell you more another time.' By now they were nearing the top of the stairs, close to the open front door to the flat where Peter was waiting, also smiling.

'Hello, Lily. Come in and be cherished,' he invited, clearly possessed of affection in abundance and spilling over.

'Was it awful?' Dot asked. 'You poor thing. Come and sit here, by the radiator.'

Lily felt like a child in this blizzard of loving attention. She was stripped of her coat, seated in an armchair and helped to a large glass of wine and her own dish of rice crackers, while the other two bustled around like fussy relatives. When they bumped into each other in the doorway, they smiled and hugged each other.

'Sorry,' Dot apologized. 'You must find this revolting.'

'Absolutely disgusting,' Lily agreed, with a broad smile. 'Domestic harmony? I wouldn't give it houseroom.'

'How did Frank look?' her friend wanted to know.

'Well, not penitent, unfortunately. But I think the term hangdog could fairly be applied.'

'Any regrets?'

'Do you mean him or me?' Lily asked.

'Either of you.'

'I can't speak for him, although there's a strong streak of sentimentality in the man. He could be weeping over the

Bakelite eggcups even as we speak. Me, well, I'm no Edith Piaf. Or Norman Lamont. Ha, ha. But according to my latest wise woman, emptying out the garbage is written in the stars.'

Peter had joined them now, sitting next to Dorothy on the sofa with a possessive arm round her shoulder. Lily watched them as she gave a potted account of her visit to the astrologer. Dorothy's eyes grew round, hearing of such accuracy and mystery combined.

'I'm jealous,' she said, like an eight-year-old. 'I want to go.'

Peter looked patronizing and parental, for which Lily loathed him. 'Shall I buy you a reading for a Christmas present?'

Dorothy turned towards him. 'You're a sweetheart, but we can't afford it.'

This seemed to deflate him somewhat. 'I'll go and check on the dinner,' he said.

'Don't mention the C-word,' Lily pleaded. 'I don't want to think about it until 24 December at the earliest.'

'I agree,' said Dot as Peter left the room. 'Joking apart, it's a very sore subject.' This was the only reference to potential disharmony and Lily took the message. Tonight was for good companionship and steering a safe course. Fine by her.

Soon Peter summoned them to the kitchen, where many candles were burning, their flickering light doing a reasonable job of disguising the mayhem of pots and used utensils on most surfaces. 'He's done all the cooking,' Dorothy explained, indicating Lily's chair, at the far side of the carefully laid table.

'A treat for both of you,' Peter said, 'or at least I hope it will be,' producing a huge salad bowl heaped with avocado, chicory leaves and what looked like crumbled Stilton.

'Definitely,' said Lily, allowing him to deposit a sizeable helping on her plate.

Even better humour spread round the table with the pleasurable effects of the food and wine. Peter took care to keep plates and glasses filled, as attentive as a Michelin-starred *maître d'*. Lily felt she owed it to both of them to give good value as a guest, and found this easy to achieve.

'So he cooks, does he? Washes his own socks too? Puts the loo seat down every time?' she asked as Peter cleared the salad plates and set out clean ones.

'Perfectly house-trained,' her friend answered. 'Has even been known to transfer the contents of the dirty-linen basket to the washing-machine. Hasn't yet mastered the art of putting the duvet back inside a clean cover, but nobody's perfect.'

'Oh, yes, they are,' Peter said, planting a kiss on Dot's head after depositing a large square dish on the table. 'Roast vegetable lasagne, with no burnt bits. And I'm going to do the washing-up. There's just no faulting me.'

It was true, there was nothing to criticize either in the meal or his attentiveness, although his vaguely lordly presence – the master and his harem? – and the 'don't-mention-the-war' areas of conversation lent the vaguest of constraints to the overall mood. Lily yearned for the open acreage of a one-to-one, anything-to-be-discussed conversation with her friend, but told herself to stop complaining. As partners went, Peter was being more than accommodating. Frank had been known to be a lot less hospitable when friends of hers had called, sitting silently and unbudgeably with her and them, or radiating 'go away' vibes from another room in the house.

There was a complicated pudding of chocolate, encased in chocolate, with chocolate sauce on top, followed by coffee and port. 'A weakness of mine,' Peter told Lily.

'Preferable to cigars,' she replied, tasting the rich sweetness. Christmas thoughts came unbidden to her mind – her father accumulating handfuls of cigars in torpedo-shaped dull metal canisters, along with packets of stockings for Edna, boxes of chocolates, calendars and diaries, all gifts from jewellery suppliers, which were then stacked up under the tree, inappropriately Lily always thought, since they weren't proper presents.

And now the rituals of Christmas were to be pickled and preserved by Edna as a tribute to Alec's memory. That was something else she didn't want to mar her evening by dwelling on. Instead, she drifted back into the conversation Peter and Dot were having about a review of one of Peter's authors' books in the previous day's paper.

'He's got an axe to grind,' Dot was saying of the reviewer, 'of course he has. He thinks it's his subject, that no one else should dare write about the man. And that was a particularly weaselly trick, to start off with a paragraph of praise before a flurry of body-blows.'

The reviewer seemed to have wrapped a devastating critique of this biography in a loose fold of congratulation, taking advantage of some errors in the illustrations to pull the whole work apart.

'Well, at least the first paragraph is quotable,' Peter said, surprisingly sunnily. 'But to complain that the book was a rush job, when Malcolm took an extra two years to write it –' He turned to Lily. 'It's always the same. Reviewers usually build their whole case around an opinion which is mistaken, as often as not, or else just plain unfair. And there's no right of reply. We can't write in and put the record straight. That doesn't make good copy. And no one wants to read us bleating. But it's bloody exasperating and meanwhile the author's gone to pieces.' Peter was warming to his subject.

'No more shop talk,' Dorothy announced. 'It's unfair to Lily.'

'Well, I could tell you all about the latest trends in the jewellery market,' Lily suggested.

'No, anything but that,' the other two cried.

She smiled. 'Okay, I'll spare you. But in exchange, I might need some advice about rearranging things at home, now there's space.'

'Oh, yes,' Dot commented enthusiastically. 'I love giving advice,' and they launched into a ground-zero reassessment of Lily's house and how to use it. Peter was at a disadvantage, never having visited it, but he claimed this gave him the freedom to be more inventive.

'No, I don't want a loft conversion. Or a glass wall down the back of the house,' Lily scolded them, fending off some of Peter's and Dorothy's increasingly wild suggestions. But an alcoholic hysteria had set in and the pair were trying to outstrip each other in absurdity. It was contagious and led to insane giggling. The three of them finally relocated to the sofa, to watch some half-baked movie and get their breath back before Lily took a minicab home.

The image of the happy pair, entwined on the doorstep, waving her off, remained frozen on Lily's retina as she travelled back from east to west. Sobering up in various ways, she wondered about the new, emptier home she was about to enter. It truly and at last was the dwelling of a single woman.

She realized she felt no fear, just a touch of sadness at her oneness. Yet the contrast with Dot's and Peter's slightly hectic twosome was interesting. She was not sorry to be leaving them to it. She found herself dwelling on the title of a book glimpsed on Dorothy's bookshelf, *Loneliness and Solitude*. She thought she was beginning to see the difference.

Back home, having closed her own front door and disconnected the alarm, Lily stood still in the hall, while the cats wiped their whiskers against her legs, and focused on her perception of the newly vacated rooms. She did not need to visit them or see the dints in the carpet where pieces of furniture had left their ghostly imprints. This was not about mourning but expansion. She wanted to move her imagination into the voids. On the one hand it was absurd, almost indecent, that a single person should own so much space. But then why should she not be permitted this small luxury? She could afford it, just.

With this self-awarded permission she could feel her heart lifting a little. This was hers. She could do exactly as she pleased here, use the rooms or not use them, keep them in pristine order or treat them as rubbish dumps. She was not going to rush into anything, or possibly even think too hard, for once in her life. She was going to try and drift comfortably into the airier environment and see what ensued. Thank you, Julie, she acknowledged to herself as she brushed her teeth. You have granted me a little heart's ease.

Chapter 19

It was that time of the year when somebody seemed to be tinkering with the calendar's timing mechanism and the days began to whirl by ever faster. A seasonal ringmaster was whipping the population along towards the Gadarene precipice of Christmas. Looking back or stepping aside was not permitted. The movement was forward only, and faster. Shop, spend, celebrate. The rules were very insistent on these matters.

At GBF, a 'good' Christmas was crucial, and there was pressure on everyone to throw in every last ounce of effort to keep the shops immaculate, fully stocked and as appealing as a box of crystallized fruits, right up to the last available moment on Christmas Eve.

This whirlwind of stock-checking and chasing, which had been picking up speed for some weeks now, helped distract Lily and her colleagues from Clive's departure and the fear of redundancy, both of which had generated a cloud of unease. 'Whatever we said about Margot,' Monica commented to Lily one morning, 'she never treated anyone like that. There was never any unpleasantness.'

'There were never any sackings, either,' contributed Pat, around whose switchboard they were standing.

'Was Clive sacked?' Lily asked.

'Depends who you talk to,' said Monica.

'That's not the point,' Pat went on. 'The feel of the place has changed. It just isn't as happy now. Or as straightforward. I don't trust Hugo. Do you?'

Lily didn't want to answer this. She knew the man had feet of clay, but if she admitted it, she'd be condemning herself out of her own mouth. Monica saved her the need.

'I didn't trust him from day one,' she stated, with sibylline conviction.

'Why not?' Lily asked, curious and sceptical.

'I'd never trust anyone who sweet-talks people on the phone and then rubbishes them when he's put the receiver down. It's slippery behaviour. Oh, he's too clever to be caught out by you or me, and he knows it. It's like the three-card trick. But I wouldn't trust him with my life-savings.'

'But you have. Well, your pension, anyway,' said Lily.

'There's not much I can do about that, is there?'

'There's nothing any of us can do. Except quit.' This was Pat.

None of them could afford that.

'Anyway, we should be in for a decent end-of-year bonus, if things keep on the way they're going,' Lily pointed out.

'How do we know Hugo is going to pay bonuses?' Monica asked darkly. 'It's not in our contracts. Margot did it because she wanted to.'

This left them all temporarily silent. The Christmas bonus had been a Pink tradition, usually announced on the day of the Christmas party, an event arranged for the final Friday before the holiday, by which time the year's end calculation could be established with reasonable accuracy and a slice of the profit shared out equally between all members of staff. As yet no mention had been made of either party or pay-out. Lily thought she might ask Hugo about both, and reassure herself that if any member of staff were going to get bad news, it would be after the holidays. But he was often out of the office these days, presumably interviewing replacement accountants, and she failed to pin him down.

Meanwhile the countdown to Christmas proceeded. Lily had had a long phone conversation with her mother, and they agreed that she would not visit again until Christmas Eve, when she would stay until the day after Boxing Day. They discussed presents and food, and Lily did her best to inject a little variety into the traditional menu. With no Alec present, might they miss out on a first course and go straight to the turkey? No, they may not, but melon could be substituted for prawn cocktail if Lily bought and brought it. Presumably Brussels sprouts could be jettisoned since both Lily and Edna hated them? Grudgingly, this was accepted, but again it fell to Lily to buy the replacement; some interesting salad leaves, she decided. What about the custard for the plum pudding? Could they finally have cream instead? Not on your life, was Edna's adamant reply. Lily had a momentary vision of her mother reverently placing a small steaming jug of solid custard on Alec's grave as a seasonal memorial. Well, two out of three was not so bad.

Hugo finally shattered the silent suspense three weeks before Christmas with a note to all staff announcing a party in the upstairs room at the Jupiter on the Friday preceding the holiday. A collective sigh of relief went up from the GBF offices. Proprieties seemed to be being observed.

Glimpsing him in residence one morning, Lily decided to grasp the rare opportunity and beard the lion in his den.

'I hope you've got fat little festive stockings prepared for all of us. And no P45s,' she said brightly, hoping he would take the hint.

'Oh, yes. Nuts in the toes and tangerines in the heels,' he answered, leaning back like an unfrocked Santa Claus, 'isn't that the tradition?'

'You're not going to tell me, are you?' Lily knew that

Margot would have explained to Hugo about her end-of-year practice.

'Tell you what?' he asked, feigning innocence. As usual, he was playing a cool poker hand, while keeping all his options open.

Lily couldn't help wondering whether the Christmas party might be an occasion for them to spend another night together. For she still wanted to have sex with him, despite his behaviour, both personal and professional. What would you rather have, a cash bonus or Hugo's body for the evening? she asked herself as she went back to her desk. She pretended to debate this, but knew she was fooling no one. After all, money wasn't everything.

By the time the party arrived, everyone at GBF was close to exhaustion, especially Alice and Sanjay who were struggling to keep the accounts department going without a third member of staff to lead them. Lily had practically shouted herself hoarse trying to bully a last-minute resupply of snake bracelets out of an agent acting on behalf of a manufacturer in Kuala Lumpur, of all places.

'I don't care who else you disappoint,' she had thundered at the woman in Southampton who was sitting on ten gross, saying they were promised to Fenwicks. 'I'll halve our payment period – fifteen, not thirty days – if you'll Securicor them up overnight.'

The woman in Southampton finally agreed to split the delivery between both customers and Lily first telephoned Dispatch so that they could lay on distribution to the shops and then went along to Accounts to make sure her promise was kept when the invoice came in.

Alice, slight and serious, her freckles faded now it was winter, looked up wearily from her screen which was lapped by a sea of papers. She pinched the bridge of her nose between finger and thumb. 'Malaysian Imports?

They're in Portsmouth, aren't they? No, Southampton. Yes, I know who you mean.'

'Will you tell Sanjay too? I don't want to break my word. We may need them again.'

'Maybe you could leave him a note?' Alice suggested. 'I'd hate to forget, and I've got to get through these before the party.'

Lily glanced down at the papers and recognized some of her orders for the new men's range. Her heart sank.

'Hugo dumped them on me this morning. He wants a set of spreadsheets urgently. I don't know why I said I could do them in time.' Alice looked a little tearful.

'He can be very persuasive,' Lily said drily.

'Mm,' said her colleague, looking into the middle distance.

In the toilets, sober shirts and sweaters were being swapped for lurex and satin. Women jostled for space at the mirror, applying dramatic make-up, and the air held invisible pockets of spray from competing perfume atomizers. Lily, ambiguous about office parties at the best of times, changed into nothing more glamorous than chocolate-brown velvet jeans and a lace shirt, her only adornment the now permanently worn chain, which glittered satisfactorily at her throat. As she emerged, she bumped into Colin who was sporting a gold lamé bow-tie. 'You're missing the spray of mistletoe behind your left ear,' she remarked.

'Catch me later,' he called back as she disappeared down the corridor.

'You'll be lucky,' came her parting shot.

The Jupiter had decorated its function room with its perennial taste and restraint. Crowd-control barriers of streamers and a blizzard of tinsel hung from the ceiling, while a venerable fake Christmas tree, witness to several previous years' festive debauchery, dominated one corner,

228

partly concealing the disco equipment. Along the right-hand wall stretched the buffet table, imaginatively laden with sausage rolls, chicken drumsticks, French bread and mince pies. The paper plates were stacked, awaiting their calorific burdens. All arriving guests turned left immediately on entering, making a beeline for the bar.

Lily decided she was in the mood to become a little inebriated. Why not? she asked herself. You've just about made it to the end of the year. And what a year. You've survived everything fate and the planets have hurled at you, even if you've got the scars to prove it. Let your hair down for once. You're among friends. And the evening holds distant promise.

Standing at the bar, she surveyed her colleagues. By no means bosom pals with all of them, she nevertheless acknowledged the group as a surrogate family. Hugo might have shaken them up, cut one or two sheep out of the flock and spooked the rest, but they were still a unit and she was part of it. She had not dwelt on the significance of the relationship until this moment, and smiling across the room at Colin, who now did indeed seem to be sporting a twist of mistletoe in his buttonhole, she acknowledged to herself its subtle value.

The cheap booze flowed, the music bellowed, the faces of her workmates grew pink and moist. Speech became difficult in the din, and there was a slow drift to the food and the clear patch of lino at the far end of the room which constituted the dance floor. Hugo had put in a relatively late appearance and was working his way down the room like a seasoned host. He popped up beside Lily, who was standing with David and the other marketing people, causing her heart to thump in competition with the disco beat.

'Are the troops having a good time?' he asked patronizingly, brimming glass in hand.

'Thank'ee very kindly, guv'nor,' Archie replied, tugging an imaginary forelock with the fearlessness of youth.

'We're not used to such lavishness,' Lily said wide-eyed. 'Crisps *and* Twiglets.'

'Nothing's too good for my staff – ' started Hugo.

'Don't say it,' warned David. 'There'll be mutiny if nothing's what we get.'

'Patience, my children,' Hugo said with a papal gesture, before moving away smoothly to the next group.

'What's he up to?' wondered Phyllis, Mark's assistant.

'I think we may soon find out,' said Lily slowly, watching Hugo progressing in leisurely fashion towards the disco, which doubled as a PA system.

Indeed, moments later he was standing at the mike and a hush fell upon most of the assembly.

'Well,' he said, taking a gulp from his glass, 'if I was more of a sadist than I am, I'd keep you waiting for the information you all want.' He paused, playing to the gallery. 'But I'm not, so I'll tell you straight away, a bonus *will* be paid. And, as custom has it, it will be lumped with your salaries and deposited in your bank accounts this side of the Christmas break.'

A ragged cheer went up.

'But' – a collective groan – 'I have also decided to introduce a small Padmore innovation.' Eyes rolled. 'You can all choose between the bonus,' and here he named the figure, 'and an extra week's holiday. All answers to be conveyed to Monica by midday on Monday.

'So you can stop sticking pins in my effigy now, and concentrate on having a bloody good time. You deserve it. You've all bust a gut, and I thank you for it. Margot said you were a great crowd and she wasn't a bad judge. So, party on.'

Some clapped, some hurrahed, some patted each other sardonically on the back. All smiled, more or less happily.

Probably instinctively, Hugo had judged his audience's mood correctly, and offered pure carrot, no stick, and not a mention of Clive or change of any kind. And the choice between cash and time-off-in-lieu seemed to be catching people's imagination, if the buzz of conversation were anything to go by. Lily assumed that idea could be ascribed to pure self-interest on Hugo's part, although presented the way he had, it looked like a gesture of thoughtfulness towards the staff group. Two hundred bonuses added up to a sizeable tranche of cash. If only half the workforce took the holiday option, that would leave some £50,000 extra on the bottom line. Hugo's ability to line his own pocket while still coming up smelling like a rose was a lesson in advanced capitalism.

With the formal proceedings over, the evening now changed gear. Those only interested in hearing the news soon left, and the room thinned out dramatically. Committed dancers and drinkers took up their respective positions, and those who were happy to drift between the two settled in the middle, around sticky-topped tables filled with glasses and bottles. Lily by now was experiencing some numbness of the lips, a sure sign of mild intoxication. Yet her brain was not so relaxed as to forget its orders for the evening – keep an eye on Hugo and position Lily to take advantage of any signs of availability. Her lover was currently part of the sedentary group, across and to the right of where she was sitting, leaning back on two legs of his chair, alternately smoking and fiddling with the crumbs of a sausage roll. Lily turned back to those around her and tuned back into the conversation.

It was about three-quarters of an hour later that the urge to pee forced her out and up the stairs to the rank pub toilets. Another, smaller function room was to be found at this level, the door to which was ajar even though the room itself was in darkness. Lily would have thought nothing of it, had she not heard a muffled groan as she came past it a second time, on her way back downstairs. She smiled, intrigued, wondering if perhaps Colin had snared someone with his twig.

Rejoining the others, she declared to the group, 'Someone's at it in the upstairs room.' She looked round the tables. Her heart clutched. Hugo was no longer there.

'I know who that'll be,' said Mark.

'So do I,' replied Sanjay gravely.

Lily looked at them both but could not bring herself to ask. Pat could.

'It's Hugo, isn't it? Our own private Casanova.'

The other two nodded.

'With Alice. I thought as much.' Pat nodded in turn. 'I saw them kissing round the back of the building late the other night. It was like a scene out of *Beauty and the Beast*. I don't know what people see in him.'

Lily sat transfixed. More than anything, she hoped no one in the company had ever linked her name with Hugo's. Hearing her colleagues' contempt for their boss and bewilderment over lost Alice caused her to wish, with fists tightly clenched, that she had maintained their good opinion. She fought her rising gorge and her twin impulse to rush from the room without another word. She must stay a little longer, just a few minutes, enough to cover her tracks, even if she had to count the individual seconds. The last thing she wanted, though, was still to be sitting at the table when either Hugo or Alice reappeared.

Was there to be release? Could she bear to sit here like a flayed rabbit, sweat prickling her brow, eyes glued to the last half-inch of beer in a pint mug in front of her, for fear that if she lifted her gaze, her tear-ducts would unfreeze and dump their contents down her lacy front?

Enough, she said to herself. It's been long enough. At least four minutes. She groped for her handbag, which seemed to have got tangled up round the leg of her chair. That took another thirty seconds. Too soon? Better that than too late. She looked up, but took care to catch no one's eye.

'Well, you guys . . .' Such studied casualness. False, false. They must all notice. 'I think I'm going to call it a night.'

'No, Lily.'

'You can't, it's not even ten.'

'Party-pooper.'

'I know, I know, pathetic, isn't it.' Think of an excuse, quick. 'But I've got to get up early.' Yes, not bad, but why? 'I've got to help a friend. She's moving house.' In Christmas week? Well it would have to do. 'Don't let me break up the party.'

They assured her she wouldn't, and fondly, or so it seemed, bade her goodnight.

She moved as swiftly as she could towards the door, her brain clear of alcohol now and as sharp as a midnight frost. On the landing, the coat-rack was a hillock of assorted garments, and in her desperation to find her own, she began to wrench others off the hooks and pile them on the floor. Then she repented, and having found what looked like her long grey microfibre mac, she spent further uncomfortable seconds heaping them all back again. Her ears strained for the creak of floorboards above. She thought she heard movement, but knew that if she turned round, she would be transformed, if not into a pillar of salt, then a column of salt water. Free at last, she grabbed all her belongings and hurtled down the stairs.

Taking great gulps of night air, she ran up Holborn, blind to the lights, the other revellers, the traffic. But she could not flee her demons. They were in her mind, filling her imagination with thoughts of Hugo, and Alice in his arms. Her arms. Hugo was hers. He had chosen her.

233

No, merely you *first*.

She stopped at the kerb, heaving, fearing she would throw up in the gutter. But her stomach at least was under control. She realized she was both cold and sweating, and put on her coat.

Go home, her automatic pilot instructed. Find a taxi and get back to the safe place. She did not need to be told more than once. She looked up, and thanked the blessed Lord. Not one but two vacant taxis were cruising smoothly towards her, yellow 'For Hire' signs illuminated like stars in the east.

Chapter 20

As luck would have it, Christmas fell on a Saturday that year, which left a full working week to go. Lily had spent a sizeable part of the weekend after the party in bed, the pain in her heart having the effect of nailing her to the mattress. Humiliation seemed to have invaded every cell in her body. And yet looking at it coldly – was there any other temperature in the world? – what was the big deal? She had no more lost Hugo than she had ever owned him. Two fucks. That was all she had had. That was all perhaps Alice would get too, perhaps all anyone ever got, except the blessed Jay, Mrs Padmore, whose implicit or explicit marital arrangements with Hugo were beyond imagining.

What had Julie Bell said – better no company than bad company? She was beginning to see the wisdom of that. Solitude and safety. These, increasingly, were her preferred options. Being alone in her own dear home, relaxed and free, without lovers, was perhaps the best she could have for the present.

The obligations of Christmas shopping forced her outdoors late on Saturday afternoon, but this, Lily soon realized, was a mistake, since by four thirty the shops looked like the Normandy beaches on the evening of the D-Day landings, with only debris and flotsam remaining. She shopped with all the enthusiasm of a recluse. Forcing herself, she bought the slippers her mother had requested, a bag of assorted expensive French make-up for Dorothy who now denied herself such extravagances, and some charity wrapping paper. The rest would have to wait. She crept back home again and chose not to reply to her answerphone messages from Paolo – would he never take the hint? and how come he always managed to time his calls to miss actually speaking to her? – and Andy. He was the last person on earth she wanted to talk to at the moment, desperate though she was to tell someone of her ludicrous pain. It would have to be Dot, but Lily contained herself till Sunday afternoon, so as not to cloud her friend's weekend too early.

'Oh, honey, what can I say?' was Dot's sympathetic yet pragmatic comment, once the sorry story had been related. 'You can't be surprised, surely. It was only a matter of time.'

'I know, I know. There's nothing anyone can say. I should get mad or get even. It was just one of those things. The man's a bastard. He's sick. It's a compulsion. We should pity him. I know all of that, but sod it, it hurts. It really hurts.'

Dorothy soothed and tutted, fulminated and nurtured in all the right proportions. It did no good, but it was all part of the horrible process and Lily had to go through it, to hear back from someone everything she knew, down to the minutest observation, for herself. The whole experience felt like *déjà vu*. Nothing came as a surprise. She certainly didn't blame Alice, whom she liked and whose seduction, she expected, had been as economical as her own. So why was she behaving like a felled tree? Get up, get on, she urged herself. She applied spurs and whips to her weary flanks and by the end of the weekend she was just about back on her feet.

By Monday morning, hollow-eyed but in control, she could breeze into the office with the best of them. She did not want to hear any gossip about the party and threw herself into work the minute she arrived. It was almost eleven thirty before she came up for air, wondering whether it was safe to venture into the corridor, at which point Monica appeared, office telephone list in hand.

'So what did you decide?' she asked. 'Take the money or open the box?'

'What?'

'Hugo's choice. You haven't forgotten.'

Oh, heavens, the bonus. Lily had not given it a thought. Nor did she now. Her brain did it all for her. It made the synaptic connection, opened her mouth and triggered her vocal cords to speak. She heard herself say, 'The extra week.'

'Not the money?' asked Monica.

'No,' said Lily. 'Not the money. I'd pay that much, no, I'd pay more, for another five days of freedom from this place.'

Monica looked at her with some surprise. 'You're sounding very jaundiced this morning. Alcohol, hormones or just Christmas?'

Lily smiled tiredly at her. 'Would you settle for life?'

She caught the train on Friday with all the joy of a condemned woman. Ferrying the cats to their prison, locking up the house and leaving London for a first Christmas without her father seemed like enough of an ordeal without Hugo's slap in the face. Still, one small mercy, at least she had not had a Christmas card from Frank.

Her suitcase bulged with wrapped presents and brown paper bags of fruit and vegetables from Berwick Street market. She rammed it behind two seats on the train, heedless of the consequences, and squeezed into her reserved place by the window. With some relief, she noted that the adjacent seat was occupied by a serious-looking woman with two books and no personal stereo, who was giving few obvious signs of the need to make conversation.

The train was, of course, packed, and the passengers' alcohol consumption and decibel level high, yet oddly Lily seemed able to sleep for much of the journey. Feverish and assailed by sudden noises, she dreamed of tall buildings, vertiginous danger and hostile crowds. In her waking moments she dwelt on Hugo's final, pre-Christmas tour of the office, and the Judas kiss he had planted on her cheek.

'Don't worry, you'll survive,' he had said, meaning the family festivities. Or maybe even the round of redundancies. But Lily had taken it as a prediction about himself.

I'll do more than that, she promised, somewhat vaingloriously.

The train rolled into the station on time, and Lily hauled herself and her bag on to the platform and then down the steps to the tunnel beneath the tracks, to emerge on the street. There, to her amazement, stood her mother in a paisley-patterned car coat.

'Surprise,' said Edna, with only a passing resemblance to Cilla Black. She dangled a set of car keys in Lily's face.

'You passed!' cried her daughter, amazed and delighted, and embarrassed too that she had forgotten.

'First time,' her mother said proudly and led Lily to the car park across the road where sat a radioactive-purple Nissan Micra, as newborn as if it had just popped out of a mechanical womb. 'Nobody thought I would. They're very prejudiced against the elderly, those examiners.' She sounded highly knowledgeable. 'But I'd made my mind up.' She opened the mini-boot and Lily stowed her case.

Behind the wheel, Edna seemed a little less confident and Lily tried to conceal her tight grip on the seat as they swooped out of the car park and across the path of a bus to reach the left-hand side of the road. 'Whoops,' her mother said, breathlessly, but then settled down as they proceeded round the roundabout and up the main road.

'Well, that was a treat, being picked up from the train,' Lily said. 'I was imagining I'd have to wait ages for a taxi.'

Her mother smiled. An astonishing sight. 'I've not been looking forward to the holiday,' she admitted. 'I don't suppose you have, either. It won't be the easiest of times. I thought it might help us get off on the right foot.'

Lily looked at her mother's profile. Edna tore her eyes away from the road and they made contact. 'Thanks, Mum. I appreciate it.'

At home, the living room was crowded with cards, and familiar ornaments and picture frames had been stuck with sprigs of holly. A large framed photograph of her father now dominated the mantelpiece. The picture had been taken at a friend's sixty-fifth birthday party the previous year, and showed Alec sitting back with a comfortable smile on his face. Lily looked at it fondly. She realized how little time she had spent thinking about her father in London these past weeks. But here, in his shrine, she would be able to devote some space to communing with him. This felt like a good thing.

'I thought we'd have something to eat and then dress the tree,' Edna said, tying on her apron as she entered from the kitchen. 'I've saved it for you.' She nodded towards the medium-sized fir which was standing naked in the corner. 'Sidney helped me get it in the stand.' Next to it stood an ancient cardboard box, its provenance lost in the mists of family history. Lily had always known it as the Christmas decorations container, and at the sight of it a wash of seasonal memories invaded her senses. Although everything in the house and all its ghosts were tinged with sadness and the palpable absence of her father, she could not resist a feeling of warmth at being here. Scents of pine needles and gingerbread, reassuring glimpses within the box of favourite glass baubles and ropes of tinsel, a knowledge of order and process throughout the evening and the days ahead – this was all surprisingly reassuring, and the child in Lily hugged itself in the face of such continuity. She had moaned and whinged to her friends in London about wanting to stay put, to have Christmas in her own home and in her own metropolitan way. But here was actually the place to be. Observing the rituals was the right thing to do, and invoking Alec as they inevitably would was another, surprisingly appropriate means of saying a further gentle farewell to him.

She remembered Julie Bell's advice, to reverse her views of her parents, and she resolved to hold on to and work with this in the days ahead, but for a moment she allowed herself to think warmly of her father. He it was who had invented all their festive rules – the hidden eggs at Easter, the sequence of events on birthdays and at Christmas. She and Edna would follow the order of service as an act of memorial, and as a salve to their own loss. It would be perfectly proper.

'Yes,' she said, 'let's eat. What are we having?'

'You know as well as I do,' her mother answered with mock severity. 'Lamb chops, baked potatoes and peas.'

Her father had loved lamb. With turkey in prospect for a couple of days, his appetite had been indulged on Christmas Eve. And instead of pudding there would be chestnuts. Alec used to tip them on to a newspaper, unfold his penknife and carve a cross in the shell of each one, to make them easier to peel after they had been roasted. Who would do that now? Following her mother into the kitchen, Lily saw the materials awaiting her at the table. In loco parentis. The unmarried daughter's lot. She did not mind in the slightest.

The evening proceeded in orderly fashion. The food was consumed, the dishes washed and then the tree dressed in the correct sequence. First came the glass needle that sat at the top. Then the candles in their individual tin clips, to be clamped to the tips of each bough. Alec had hated artificial lights, and continuing the fire hazard was part of keeping to tradition. Next, the glass ornaments were hung randomly, intermixed with chocolates wrapped in silver and gold paper and attached with glittering cord. Last of all came the tinsel, twisted around and looped like the contours of a snowfall. Alec had always instructed the process from his armchair, with Edna and Lily his little helpers. This year no one instructed. There was no need. Silently, but in fellowship, the women performed their tasks and at last stood back to admire their gaudy achievement.

'Perfect,' said Edna.

'You don't think another silver ball, just down here?' asked Lily, pointing to a low patch of emptiness.

'Maybe,' her mother said, squinting.

The last pendant was hung satisfactorily in place, and they allowed themselves a hot drink and a mince pie as a reward. Lily nursed her mug of herb tea and observed her mother in the television's glow. There was an admirable energy at work and Lily felt some shame at her own recent and prolonged maunderings. Her expectations reversed once again, she settled back into the red velour armchair, feeling oddly yet contentedly at home.

Lily did not hear her mother enter her bedroom during the night. Nevertheless when she woke up at seven, there at the foot of the bed was a stocking, lumpy but strangely lifelike, a festive prosthetic. She sat up and rubbed her eyes, feeling about six years old. The stocking itself was a familiar thing, red-and-white-striped cotton; it had made its annual appearance from as far back as she could remember. Inside it, she found fruit soaps, tights, chocolate bears, a low-fat cookbook and a pair of Tom-and-Jerry-patterned ankle socks. Her mother had made – was even now making – a huge effort. Not to be outdone, although she already had been, Lily got up and went down to the kitchen. She prepared tea and toast, and took it up to her mother on a tray.

In the double bed, Edna's curled form occupied at most a third of the space. Alec's larger-than-life absence still dominated. She awoke as Lily entered, and sat up, her hair flattened on the left side of her head.

'Oh, breakfast in bed.' She sounded pleased.

'Just a small thank-you for the stocking,' her daughter said, kissing her lightly on the cheek. 'I wasn't expecting it. I should have got you one.'

'I thought you'd like it,' Edna said.

'What's the plan today?' Lily sat cross-legged on the empty half of the bed while her mother ate.

'The usual. Breakfast, presents, lunch, a walk. Nothing different.'

Nothing different. Was that a curse or a joy? And anyway, it *was* different, all of it. It was Alec who, after breakfast, would put the ancient record of 'Silent Night' on the turntable and light the candles on the tree before throwing open the living-room door to allow Lily and Edna to come in and see the array of presents. Today Lily lit the candles and Edna found the music. Today they took it in patient turns to open presents rather than falling on them like vultures. In addition to the slippers, Lily had found a lacy wool shawl for her mother, a brushed cotton nightie and a jaunty pink mohair beret. She hadn't realized until her mother had opened everything that all the gifts were intended to keep her warm. Lily marvelled at her own unconscious and wondered what Julie Bell would have said. Was she trying to take care of her mother? Did she want to be kept warm herself? Guilty on both counts. Her mother had responded with a crushed velvet scarf, a calendar and a novelty teapot in the shape of the Mad

Hatter. If there were hidden messages there, it was beyond Lily's powers to decode them.

Alec was absent again at lunch, for the carving of the turkey and the opening of the wine. He was not there to cross his arms and offer crackers to the two women in his life simultaneously. He was missing for the Queen's speech which was the traditional moment for him to produce a box of expensive chocolate truffles. Both Lily and Edna had seen this one coming and had bought supplies themselves. When the two boxes appeared, the women's good humour faltered.

'Let's go and see him,' Edna suggested, so instead of the old walk through the park, they turned right down the road, crossed over behind the golf links and came eventually to the cemetery. On the pavements they encountered children riding new bicycles and other post-prandial family groups, some of them acquaintances who wished Lily and Edna season's greetings. In the cold, dry air, Edna's face looked pinched and bloodless. Some of the cheer had gone out of her.

'Chin up, Mum. We're doing fine,' Lily said, in the new spirit of accord.

'That's easy for you to say. You'll be off again soon. You don't know what it's like, in that house every day.'

Lily bumped down to earth. 'I'm sorry. I thought you were doing well.'

'I'm putting a brave face on it.' Edna trudged on, head down.

'Do you mean it about the house? Are you thinking of moving?'

'Why would I want to move?'

'Because of Dad's presence,' Lily answered with inappropriate logic.

'I like his presence. I wouldn't want to be without it.'

Lily could see the dilemma, and there was no remedy.

Being surrounded by memories was both desirable and agonizing for her mother. It had been relatively easy and finally wholly welcome for Lily to expunge Frank from her house. But if Edna wiped out Alec, what would she have left? They walked on silently. Edna seemed to want something from her – what? Just the resumption of old feuds? Somehow Lily wasn't surprised. This was as much the essence of their relationship as the recent mutual efforts at kindness and consideration. Did she think the slate had been wiped completely clean or her mother's personality totally refashioned? They were in a state of transition, together and separately. Nothing could be relied upon at present except the prospect of further change.

At the grave, which Edna had planted with winter pansies, and which now bore a stone engraved simply with Alec's name and dates, they stood in their own pools of silence. Lily tried to summon up images of her father, fresh ones that still contained a spark of vitality. This was difficult and her mind constantly led her off down tangential paths, so that she would come back to the present and realize she was thinking of anything but him. She tried harder. Meanwhile Edna stared at the stone as if her glance would bore through it. Her expression was steely and closed.

'Enough?' she asked at last.

Lily nodded. She needed to be alone here for it to be of real benefit. Perhaps she would come back tomorrow.

The rest of the day was harder going. There were few rituals left to be observed, but rather a lot of time remaining before bed. Lily suggested a jigsaw and fetched one from the airing cupboard, in spite of Edna's proclaimed indifference. Lily began it anyway, a 1,000-piece English idyll of thatched cottage, towering horse chestnut tree and flawless blue sky. Losing herself in the hunt for border pieces, she was still aware of Edna's withdrawal into herself. Lily did not mind, indeed she was faintly reassured that her mother had reverted to the familiar.

The landscape of Boxing Day was less clearly defined by custom. Apart from another large meal in the middle of the day, little was expected. Both women had by now seriously depleted their funds of goodwill and were showing signs of impatience for the holiday to be over. Edna seemed to be missing some of her bridge friends and rang a couple of them up for chats. Lily took the opportunity of the jigsaw to sink into a reverie. Thoughts of Hugo still circled like hyenas; chase them away as she might, back they would slink, making sniggering noises. How long had he been seeing Alice? Had he told her about Lily? Had he told anyone else? Instinctively she thought not. He was too habitually veiled to share his conquests.

Hugo seemed to see women as a kind of perpetual smorgasbord. His casual sampling of her, when the mood took him, suffused her with shame, as did the foolishness of her unextinguished hopes. She had still been waiting for him to crook his finger, while all the time he had already moved on and was snacking elsewhere. She shuddered, and at the same moment her mother walked into the room.

'Are you cold?' Edna asked, like a mother should.

'No, someone walked over my grave, that's all.'

They were back to their usual, more abrupt style. Later, side by side in the kitchen, they put together coronation turkey and rice, which they ate in semi-silence in the dining room.

'Have you got plans for New Year's Eve?' Lily asked her mother, to fill one of the pauses.

'There's a do at the community centre,' Edna answered. 'I've bought a ticket. I'll see how I feel.'

Lily expressed her approval, although her mother seemed not to need it. Sulky though she was today, she was showing many small signs of the strength that Julie Bell had identified. Maybe they had been there all along and Lily hadn't noticed. Whichever, Lily wanted to congratulate Edna, but wondered if it would be patronizing.

'If I said I thought you were doing brilliantly,' she ventured, 'would you be offended?'

To her surprise, her mother simpered. 'Thank you, dear,' she answered, seeming to take it as a compliment.

They moved on to traditional Christmas dessert number two, trifle. Lily could feel her waistband tightening.

'After we've done the dishes, would you mind if I went to the grave on my own?' she enquired cautiously.

'No, of course not. It'll give me a chance to tidy up.' This was Edna's code for getting out the Hoover and dusters. In her book, there was no bank holiday from cleaning.

Duly, an hour later, Lily set off for the cemetery once more, walking briskly in a belated attempt to burn off a few calories. Today the cloud cover hung at almost fingertip height, pressing down on the thinly scattered trees of the golf links and the low hills behind the graveyard. Was it going to snow? She pulled the collar of her coat higher round her ears.

The cemetery was as cool and refreshing as a drink of water. Squirrels stop-started between the trees and bold black crows hopped about with a confrontational air. Lily wished she had brought some flowers, but there were no shops open today in this part of the world. If she had had free choice, she would have hung a Christmas wreath on the gravestone, but her mother had shuddered at this idea. She must have had a bad experience with one as a child.

Taking up her station again at the foot of the grave, Lily found herself addressing her father, silently she hoped.

'Well, here I am again. Not such a bad Christmas, even without you. She's doing very well, you know. And I'm doing my best to take care of her.

'It's been pretty tough, without you. But I've tried to cope. That's what you would have expected, isn't it?' She could picture Alec nodding his silent approval. Good girl. Kick or be kicked. 'You know about Hugo, of course. And I know you don't approve. But then you never liked any man I got involved with. Okay, he's worse than most, but there's also a bit of you in him, isn't there?

'Julie says you didn't really love me, not all of me. It's true, isn't it? I'm not blaming you – well, I am and I'm not. I suppose what I want to say is that I still love you, in spite of also wanting to lay some responsibility for everything at your door.

'It's not that I wish you hadn't loved me like you did. As far as I remember, I had a happy childhood. But I can also see now that it was too much, too controlling. You should have given more to Mum. She could have done with a bit more cherishing. It would have been better if I'd been a daughter to you both, not a semi-partner to you and a rival to her.'

Something dark flashed across Lily's mind. If her father had treated her almost as an equal, could she possibly have repressed memories of more and worse involvement – like sexual abuse? She thought about this very hard. No, she felt utterly sure. There was not a trace of doubt within her of Alec's absolute rectitude on such matters.

This realization came as a relief, but there was more. Having offered a medium-weight rebuke to her father's shade, she felt mildly purged. What would he have said if she had criticized him to his face? She could not imagine having the impetus, or the words, until now, when of course it was too late. Pondering the curious order of things, she bade farewell to Alec until the next time, and walked home in the fading light, ears, nose and fingertips now complaining at the cold.

Boxing Night passed relatively smoothly. Neither woman

247

wanted another meal, so instead, while watching an Arnold Schwarzenegger movie, they opened a box of dates, cracked walnuts from their shells and sipped at the thick egg-nog which Lily found in the drinks cupboard. The jigsaw lay abandoned.

'Will you finish this, Mum, or shall I put it away?' Lily offered, knowing her mother's preference for empty, dust-free surfaces wherever possible.

'Leave it, dear,' Edna answered. 'I might have a look at it tomorrow.'

Lily smiled to herself. This was a notable first, although she was not going to comment on it. Previously, her mother had been as phobic about loose ends as she was about hairs in the plughole. Now she wanted something left open. Only a jigsaw, admittedly, but today a toy, tomorrow . . . Lily felt herself to be the spectator of something fascinating.

And then it was all over, and time to return to routine. Edna and Lily shared the *Daily Mail* at breakfast and tidied up the Christmas presents, after which Lily packed her bag. Edna reversed the car out of the garage, undulating a little in her route, but making it safely on to the carriageway and coming to a halt not too far from the kerb.

'I'll see you in a few weeks, shall I?' Lily suggested, as they drove to the station.

'Yes, I hope so,' Edna answered. Then, after a pause, 'It hasn't been too bad, has it?'

'Not too bad at all,' Lily reassured her. 'We never wanted to manage without him, but we can do it.' And maybe even quite like each other for much of the time, Lily continued silently. Perhaps one day they would even voluntarily re-enter together the minefield territory of Alec's unbalanced affections, but sufficient unto the day. What seemed to be more important for the moment was learning to communicate in their new language. Had they become equals? If not sisters, then cousins? Lily and Edna might have had to wait for the best part of forty years to discover friendship, but there was nothing to stop them enjoying it now. What had Julie Bell called Lily, a late starter? Understatement was hardly the appropriate word. Call her antediluvian.

There was no big leave-taking at the station. Just a kiss on the other's cheek and a confirmation of continuity in January. Lily retrieved her bag and watched as the cute purple car zipped off down the road and then braked fiercely at the lights. She had dreaded the holiday, she acknowledged to herself, and here she was returning home with a mild sense of achievement. Sod's law was a sod.

Some hours later, suitcase in one hand, cat basket in the other, she staggered through her own front door, noticing as she did so that she had stepped on an envelope with only her Christian name scribbled on it. Her overriding duty was to Huntley and Palmer, who were trampling each other in their frenzy to be free. That obligation discharged, she picked up the white square, now dustily imprinted with her DM sole, and recognized Dorothy's writing. What was this, a belated Christmas card?

She ripped it open and found a postcard of Picasso's weeping woman. It was dated Boxing Day and bore the words, 'P's gone. He won't be coming back. Ring me when you return. Dot.'

Chapter 21

Lily spent many of the ensuing hours with Dorothy, offering her friend the same support she had shown when Frank left. They haunted each other's homes and communicated ceaselessly by telephone. Roles reversed, Lily was now the more capable of the two.

'I despair of myself,' Dot said at some point, shaking her head like a maddened animal. 'Gullible, naïve, infantile. There aren't enough good words in the thesaurus. Talk about tipping your head back and offering your throat to the knife. I could have written the script. We're old enough to know better, both of us, all of us. Yet we fly these stupid bloody kites. I always knew that it was a kind of hiccup in time. It was obvious – Peter's guilt about the children was always going to defeat us in the end. Like I said, I even wanted it to. We were tempting fate. Waving at it, to attract its attention. And if I'd thought really hard, I would have known Christmas would be the final straw.'

Peter had not gone straight back to Carol and the children. His mounting distress at being an absent father over the holiday had succeeded in uncoupling him from Dorothy but had not yet reunited him with his sceptical wife. Instead, he had moved back in with his parents. But everyone knew it was only a matter of time. All sides except Dot were pushing for some kind of reconciliation. A return to the fold, after appropriate punishment, was inevitable.

If Dorothy cried, it was when she was alone. With Lily she was glassily calm, fearfully controlled. But her wattage was dimmed. She was functioning on emergency power. Lily was worried about her, but had to leave her midweek to go into the office. GBF never closed down for the whole ten-day period because the shops reopened immediately after Boxing Day, to scoop up some of the post-Christmas spending surge, and back-up was needed from head office. Lily had always liked working on these days, with office London a ghost town and the roads traffic-free. At GBF she found the usual skeleton staff, which, to her relief, excluded Hugo and Alice. Pleased at her undiminished professionalism, she set about powering cleanly through the tasks she had reserved for this period.

New Year's Eve they spent first of all in a local wine bar and then at Lily's where Dorothy was to spend the night. Neither of them could countenance passing midnight in the company of strangers. They were not even sure they would stay up after twelve. All they wanted was peace, warmth, liquor and the balm of friendship. Some kind of retrospective, however, could not be avoided.

'A bastard of a year,' Lily said, as the hour crept towards eleven and she opened a second bottle of Merlot. 'Here's to it.' She raised her glass. 'Let's hope we don't see its bloody like again.'

'I'll drink to that.'

Lily swallowed a rich, fruit-flavoured mouthful and leaned back, head spinning. 'Talk about a gamut of experience. Robbery and danger. Love and death. Pain and parting. Loss and – well, more loss. It feels like a Greek tragedy, although I suppose we've avoided murder, incest and the furies.'

'Speak for yourself.'

'Okay. It's New Year's Eve. You've got three wishes for the year ahead. What are they?'

'Not resolutions?' Dorothy asked, being fussy, by profession, about the difference between words.

'Nope. Imagine – I know it's hard – a good fairy

listening. She takes pity on these two suffering women. That's enough, she says. I'll wave my magic wand, show 'em a good time. What would you ask for?'

'You're expecting me to say Peter, aren't you?'

'Not necessarily,' Lily answered.

'There's no way to have him, unless I used the other wishes to simply pluck Carol and the kids out of existence. Not kill them off, just remove them, so they had never been.'

'Well, you could wish for that then.'

'No,' said Dot, 'I couldn't. Even as a fantasy. It breaks some kind of moral taboo. I can't joke about this stuff. It's too real. I feel as if I've come very close to something. Serious issues, the bones of life, what makes people who they are, their souls even.'

Lily glimpsed the depth of her friend's mental anguish. 'You're not a bad person,' she said.

Dorothy smiled wanly. 'It feels almost biblical at times. I'm not bad in today's terms. But at some other level, I do feel as if I've sinned, or at least that those children have been sinned against.'

Lily had a moment's thought for Hugo's children. Should she be feeling the same? She couldn't help it if she didn't. She felt more sinned against herself, then realized how supine that was.

'What about the wishes?'

Dorothy pursed up her mouth while she thought. 'Okay, not a lottery win, too predictable, but some other kind of financial windfall. An income, an annuity, a pension. I don't know. But the end of working out of necessity. That's number one. Number two? A perfect metabolism. The body of a sylph and the digestion of an ox. And no spots, no matter how much chocolate you ate.'

'That's three.'

'No it isn't.'

'Skin *and* metabolism.'

'Oh, alright. What are yours then?'

Lily had not set Dorothy up. She hadn't thought about this at all. Now she closed her eyes and said, 'Peace. I don't mean the world kind. Just for me. Calmness, tranquillity, the answer to all the questions. Serenity, even. And then – '

'Don't tell me, plenty.'

'No, I've had that. I was thinking more of pleasure.'

'Well, that's a good catch-all heading.'

'Yes, but I don't just mean sex. In fact, I don't mean sex at all. Just enjoyment. Getting savour out of things.'

'This is all very abstract,' was Dot's observation.

'Alright then, what I really fancy, right now, is a bloody good holiday.'

Lily had begun this fantasy earlier in the week, snared by the adverts which were budding in the newspapers and on television, picturing crystal seas and medieval hill villages. Warmth, relaxation, the gentle salve of air on skin. Just thinking about it made her purr.

'That's not such a bad idea,' Dot said, swirling the wine in her glass contemplatively.

'Well, we don't have to wait for a magic wand, do we? After all, I've got an extra week and surely, with a bit of notice, you could take off for a while?'

'It would take a few weeks to organize, but yes, I suppose I could.'

Lily's eyes grew bright. 'Well, where shall we go? Not skiing. Somewhere hot.' Then she remembered Dorothy's reduced income. 'Although maybe that would cost too much, this time of the year.'

'I suppose it would,' agreed Dot, who seemed to be following Lily's lead. 'But warm would do. That might even be better than hot.'

'What about borrowing somebody's holiday home,' her friend went on.

'I don't know anyone who's got a holiday home.'

Lily had to confess she didn't either. 'Well, do we know anyone who lives somewhere warm, whom we could stay with?'

Dot shook her head again.

Lily felt a twinge of exasperation. Dorothy wasn't trying very hard. Then she remembered how winded she herself had felt so soon after Frank had gone. Be kind, she admonished. She's suffering.

She cast her mind over her own possible candidates. Being the last of the Braithwaites meant there was no one to turn to in her family. What about friends? Hadn't there been someone from college who had fallen in love with the Far East when doing VSO, and had gone back to live there? Lily couldn't even remember her name.

Perhaps she should just offer to pay for the two of them. She had her father's legacy, after all. She'd earmarked it for something bigger, a change of direction up ahead in her life. But maybe she should break into it now. Except that Dot wouldn't accept charity. The subject had come up often enough since she'd gone freelance – over much smaller items, like meals and cinema tickets. Dot was fierce about being self-supporting. She'd never agree to the gift of a holiday.

So what was the solution? Somewhere cheap and chilly? That would surely defeat the point. And then it came to her. It was a daring plan. Would they be welcome? Was she brave enough even to phone and ask? Lily looked at her watch. Eleven thirty-seven. An auspicious moment, even if it was five hours earlier in North America.

She glanced over at Dot whose face was flushed and eyes glazed. Thinking of Peter, poor thing. The sight of her friend's lingering misery, the flavour of which she could still sharply recall, strengthened her resolve.

'Hey,' she said, to attract Dorothy's attention. 'How do you feel about New Mexico?'

Dot persuaded Lily to strike when the iron was cool. New Year's Eve was not a great time to invite yourself to stay, she maintained. Besides, the woman could easily be out, or hosting a party. Anyway, they were too pissed.

In the morning, over a late breakfast, they reconsidered Lily's idea, or stroke of genius as she would have it.

'People always say, "Come and visit," but they don't usually mean it,' Dorothy objected.

'Margot isn't people,' replied Lily, still unsure of her friend's commitment. 'She never says anything she doesn't mean.'

'So did she say just ring and volunteer yourself and a stranger to stay with me for a couple of weeks whenever you feel like it?'

'Not exactly. But she did say we were all welcome. And maybe she'd know somewhere nearby we could stay cheaply.' Lily was beginning to feel infected with Dot's doubts, then gave herself a shake. This was defeatism. 'Look,' she began again, 'it's our best hope so far, and with Margot, there's one easy way to find out. We should just ask. She'll have no qualms about saying no.'

'Sounds like the perfect holiday host.'

As morning became afternoon they got out Lily's atlas, since neither woman knew exactly where New Mexico was. Poring over it, remarking on half-familiar names like Santa Fe and Albuquerque, Dot suddenly said, 'Of course. New Mexico. It's where Georgia O'Keeffe lived.'

Lily looked blank.

'You know, the painter. Skulls in the desert. Luscious flowers.' It still meant nothing to Lily. Dot was incredulous. 'You must know her. She's an icon. You'd recognize her work if you saw it. It's all about colour and heat. Oh, and sex, of course. She loved the desert and the hills. Decamped to New Mexico from New York. God, I'd love to go there.'

That settled it. Now that Dot's enthusiasm was breathing on its own, without a life-support system, Lily felt prepared to phone. But where the hell was the number? She found it in what was now last year's diary. She must have scribbled it there when Margot circulated it, just prior to her departure. The digits shared a page with the legend 'Hugo's party'. Uninvited memories flew up from the paper like bats. Get back, she told them. Bugger off.

Clearing her mind, she sat down by the phone. It was half past three, half past ten in America. Should she wait till later? Would Margot be having a lie-in after her New Year celebrations? Unlikely. When running GBF, the woman had given every indication of being a lark, always at her desk by seven thirty. Surely she hadn't changed.

Lily picked up the handset and dialled.

The connection was quickly made and she heard the distant purr of an American ringing tone. After four rings, she began to get worried, then the phone was answered.

'Yes?' Margot, unmistakably. She sounded even shorter than usual.

'Margot, it's Lily – Braithwaite,' she added, having met no sign of recognition. 'Er, Happy New Year.'

Dot giggled in the background.

'Lily? You didn't wake me up at seven thirty on New Year's Day just to say that, did you?'

Seven thirty? Oh Christ, New Mexico must be far enough west to be in a different time zone.

'I'm really sorry, Margot. I thought it was later.'

'Well' – a yawn – 'I'm awake now. So, tell me why you rang. And how you are.'

'I'm fine. GBF's thriving.' A conscious fib, but now was not the moment to mention Operation Brainchild. 'All's well. How are you?' Surely Margot would expect her to ask this, before proceeding to the matter in hand.

'Extremely well.'

Lily was beginning to repent of the whole idea. Why on earth had she thought a holiday with Margot would be a good notion? The woman was as gregarious as Greta Garbo.

Nevertheless, metaphorically pinching her nose and leaping from the diving board, Lily plunged in. 'Margot, a friend and I were thinking of heading somewhere warm but cheap for a holiday in the next month or two. Maybe to your part of the world. Would you know of anywhere we could stay?'

A silence. Quite a long silence. Dot raised an eyebrow. Lily began to feel sick.

'What kind of holiday did you have in mind?'

'Well, relaxing, primarily. Maybe somewhere to swim, lie in the sun.'

'Lily, if you want a sunbathing holiday, this part of New Mexico isn't the place to come in February. It may be called the high desert but it's not desperately hot. People come here in winter for the skiing.'

'Oh.'

'If you did still want to come, I do, as it happens, know someone who has a cabin down south, in the hotter area, near Bottomless Lakes – that's a park where you can sail. Or walk in the forests. But it wouldn't be like Florida.'

'Oh.'

'It might be cheap, though. Probably free in fact, as it's just standing empty till the spring.'

'Ah.'

'Do you want to think about it?'

'I think we should.'

A few further pleasantries and Lily put the phone down, feeling pretty small. She had not exactly been at her most impressive. She told Dot what Margot had said.

'Sounds okay to me,' her friend commented.

'It does? I thought we'd been talking beaches, suntans, that kind of thing.'

'I don't like beaches. I told you, I'd prefer warm to hot.'

It was true. The women had never holidayed together, but Lily remembered now that, despite her dark hair, Dot was made miserable by very high temperatures.

'So you think we should go?'

Dot did. She wanted to see this O'Keeffe woman's desert. She wanted to breathe clean air, walk in the forests, fly far away from her sad flat in south-east London. The spark of the holiday idea had clearly caught the wind of her imagination and ignited.

'We'd have to come back, you know,' Lily reminded her gently.

The way forward, Lily decided, was to plug the information gap that her conversation with Margot had exposed. Even if Dot liked the idea of a winter holiday in New Mexico, she wanted to be sure that she did too, that she wasn't going along with it just for the sake of her friend's shallow pocket. Julie Bell was at her elbow again, insisting that she make the choice for herself.

So on 3 January, as normal life resumed in the city, she spent her lunch hour at Stanford's in Covent Garden, scanning books on New Mexico, coming away with the one that seemed to have the most to say about the south-east quadrant of the state, where Bottomless Lakes could be found.

'It's near Roswell,' she told Dot that night on the phone.

'You're kidding.'

'I'm not. It's loony tunes country. There's a big UFO research centre there. But there's also,' she conceded, reading from the book, '"an eclectic museum with a collection that includes paintings by Georgia O'Keeffe".'

'What did I tell you?'

'So you think we should go.'

'Lily,' Dot answered, as gravely as if she were taking vows, 'I do.'

That clinched it. The more Lily thought about the idea, the better she liked it. Travelling light, exploring herself, wasn't that what her wise woman had recommended? Well, this would be some fantastic voyage. Lily had never been to the USA, never mind a remote state in the south-west. It would be an adventure. Not exactly the lotus land she had first thought of. But fresh, different, something else to try on her taste buds, in her search for what she really liked. A prickly pear, perhaps, instead of a mango.

Was she persuading herself? Tell the truth now.

No. She thought hard, then thought again. In all honesty, this was what she wanted. A trip into the unknown, with her best friend.

She rang Margot again, this time with the book at her elbow.

'We'd like to come.'

'Good. I hoped you would.'

She did? Lily wondered for a moment if Margot might be missing something of what she had left behind.

They discussed the cabin, which belonged to Douglas, a friend of Margot's who wintered in the Caribbean. It came with a car, an 'all-terrain vehicle' – in other words a four-wheel drive. There would be no charge for either, although they'd have to arrange their own insurance, pay for petrol, food, firewood and so on. It could apparently get quite cool at night.

'You'll spend a few days with me, too, won't you?' suggested Margot, irresistibly. She lived outside Taos, a village on a high plateau not far from Santa Fe. They could loop back that way before catching their flight home from

259

Albuquerque and leave Douglas's car with her. 'I've converted a barn for guests. It's quite cosy.'

That was the end of that.

The flight cost £300 in February, which was the earliest either of them could get away. It obliged them to change planes at the 'gateway' entry point of Newark, just outside New York.

'Can you afford it?' Lily asked Dot.

'Yes. Somehow.'

'You know I'll lend you the money.' Lily felt obliged to make the offer.

'Yes, I know. And you know I can't take it. Don't worry, I'll manage. What about you? Is February a good time for you to be away?'

'As good as any.' Lily thought a little harder, but there was no impediment she could think of, provided she gave Hugo enough notice. 'You?'

'Freelances don't have holidays,' Dorothy answered. 'I'm as free as a bird. Or a roadrunner.' The New Mexico state bird. Dot had been doing her homework too.

'So shall I get my diary, then? If we decide the exact dates, I can book the flights.'

There was a pause. The women looked at each other, smiles creeping on to both their faces at the stupendousness of the whole business.

'Okay. Let's do it.'

Yessss.

Chapter 22

Lily decided the best approach was full frontal.

'Hugo, can I take some time off?'

She had strolled into her boss's office shortly after nine the next day. He had only just arrived, had not yet taken up his station in his swivel chair, in fact had his back to her as she spoke.

'God, Lily, don't do that,' he said, turning round, clutching his chest.

'Guilty conscience?'

He ignored this. 'When do you want to go?'

'In February. For a fortnight.'

He looked at her without expression.

'Is there a problem? I did opt for the extra week.'

'I know,' he said. 'No, no problem. Being the diligent worker you are, I don't need to ask that you'll leave everything shipshape before you take off, especially Operation You-know-what. Do I?'

So he had noticed. 'No, no need at all.'

'Okay then. Have your holiday. Just make sure Monica knows.'

Of course. What did he take her for?

'Going somewhere nice?' he asked casually, leaning against his desk, legs outstretched, arms folded.

'The States,' she answered, deciding for once in her life not to bare all.

He lifted his eyebrows and turned down the corners of his mouth. 'I must be paying you too much.'

You couldn't win with Hugo. Lily knew that now. Some part of her still pricked up at the passing indications that he was watching her – her choice of holiday not pay, the quality of her work – and the degree of sexual flirtation in his words and body language. He might want to fuck her again, she realized. Just because he had moved in on Alice did not mean she was displaced. She had been enrolled in his harem.

No, she thought, later, as she walked to the travel agent. You volunteered. And now you can quit.

Yes, but if the situation arose, would she?

She did it. She booked two return tickets to Albuquerque via Newark. They were locked in. In less than a month's time, they would be there. As she walked back to the office, she kept fingering the receipt for the tickets, running her fingertips along it for reassurance. The countdown had begun.

The first couple of weeks passed quickly enough. But Lily's intention of making charts of what she needed to achieve and setting up a timetable to work through them was eclipsed by Hugo's general memo announcing that fifteen members of staff had been 'let go'. Mark's department had, after all, taken the brunt, with ten of the victims among shop staff, and five at head office.

'What a way to see in the New Year,' Colin commented to Lily in the kitchen on the day of the announcement. 'I hope they all opted for the bonus.'

Lily nodded. She felt pained at the news, as well as an inevitable sense of relief that she had been spared. Andy had been right about Hugo, in every respect. A womanizer. A cost-cutter. A Janus, with one delightfully entertaining face and another that was ruthlessness incarnate. Moreover, his actions mystified her. Why cut the workforce if the company were stable and poised for expansion? Lily understood GBF. She could practically manage it herself and in Margot's day used to fantasize about doing so. But these moves left her perplexed.

Dark though the company's mood had become, the holiday still illumined Lily's path like a beacon. Settling down again, she compiled notes about work-in-hand and up-coming, to cover any eventuality during her absence. The cabin had a phone, and so of course did Margot. She would give all these details to Monica, who she knew would only contact her in an emergency.

Again, surprised at her own reticence, she had not mentioned to anyone at work that she was going to see their old boss. She wondered why. Did she feel embarrassed, the head girl vacationing with the retired headmistress? Maybe. Or perhaps it was to do with her private friendship with the woman, a fleeting thing, but still somehow enormously significant on the graph of Lily's progress through her mid-life crisis. Margot sat alongside Julie Bell on the newly configured altar of her household gods. Not exactly to be worshipped. But the occasional genuflection might be made.

She read every scrap of literature that arrived from the Roswell Chamber of Commerce, some of it absurdly hearty, and then went on a shopping expedition for walking boots and an all-weather parka. There were shops just off the Strand which seemed to specialize in such things. They were full of Australians. Lily hadn't realized it was all such an industry. She contemplated compasses and clear plastic map cases you could hang round your neck. Would it rain? Might they get lost? The literature spoke about well-signposted trails. Lily suspected she could leave it all safely to the Americans. They appeared to take their leisure very seriously.

Edna was a little wary, when told of her daughter's expedition during Lily's next visit. 'You will be careful, won't you?' she cautioned. 'It's such a violent country. They've all got guns, haven't they?'

'I don't think New Mexico's the same as New York, Mother,' Lily said, stoical in the face of Edna's predictably negative first response. 'Where we're going is a resort area.'

'What about Miami? People are always getting shot there.'

'True. But that's another big city. This is the countryside.' Lily was keeping her fingers crossed that her mother hadn't seen *Deliverance*.

Edna was unmoved. 'Just play safe. Don't get into any trouble. And take out plenty of insurance coverage. You don't want to get ill in America without it.'

Lily had noticed health care starting to figure quite prominently in Edna's conversation. She supposed this was another feature of the combination of her age and recent bereavement – a stronger sense of physical vulnerability. She also realized that her departure must be making her mother feel nervous and isolated. She tried to reassure her with phone numbers and promises to keep in regular contact, but clearly nothing was going to assuage Edna's separation anxiety except Lily's safe return. So they left the point moot and spent the afternoon at an antiques fair where Edna picked up a rather handsome card table on barley-sugar legs. With a new piece of green baize, it would come in very handy for her Tuesday evening bridge school.

The tail end of January operated at a different pace. A cold mist had descended over London and the short days never seemed to become properly light. At work, the mood was suspicious. The loss of colleagues was a slow wound to heal. On top of that, January, a sluggish month for sales, also brought with it the annual tedium of stocktaking.

Lily, wary but full of suppressed excitement, found it hard to concentrate. Her impulse was to avoid Hugo, but with perverse instinct he repeatedly sought her out, oddly unrelaxed about the details of the men's range, although as far as Lily could see, everything was progressing smoothly, with a launch date fixed for early May, when they would both present the new range and publish the first mail order catalogue. A designer had been brought in exclusively to work on these two items and he spent a lot of time with Hugo and Mark, the three of them poring over transparencies on a light box and squinting at layouts on a computer screen. She wondered what it was all costing.

She tried to keep a weather eye on Alice, but a new chief accountant named Bob had started work and the department was operating very correctly, allowing few opportunities for chat.

There had been the usual frequency of phone contact with Dot, but not too many meetings, although they had had a walk and then tea together one weekend, spending some of the time composing lists of what to pack, allocating who was to bring mosquito repellent, DiaCalm, tea bags and all the other essentials. Dorothy had lost some weight, and the skin beneath her eyes still had a smudged look. Lily recognized symptoms of her own appearance, a few months earlier.

'Heard anything from Peter?' she asked.

'Not in the way you mean. I saw him when I called in at the office.' Dot still edited manuscripts for her ex-employers. 'It was bound to happen one day. We were very polite. He was wearing his wedding ring again, so I guess that means he's been allowed back into the marital home.'

'How did you feel?'

'Very, very sad,' came the answer, with a piercing look from Dorothy that drained every drop of holiday excitement out of Lily for the rest of the afternoon.

With less than a fortnight to go, she met Andy for Sunday brunch at a local brasserie.

'So where exactly in the States are you going?'

'Can you keep a secret?' He nodded. 'I'm not sure why I don't want people to know, but we're going to see Margot.'

Andy laughed. 'What a brilliant idea. Give my love to the old dear. You're not staying with her, are you?'

'Only for a couple of days at the end. No, that would be too much. But she's fixed us up with a friend's cabin on the edge of the desert. Near some lakes. I can't imagine what it's going to be like, even though I've practically memorized the literature.'

'It'll be brilliant,' Andy assured her.

'You haven't been, have you?'

He shook his head. 'Not to that part of the world. But I've toured the West Coast. Americans are wonderful.'

Lily pulled a face.

'No, I know what you mean. But they're genuinely friendly and most people are tremendously hospitable. Plus they're amazingly organized – air conditioning, sights, everything. As for the food, well, you'll see for yourself. You'll have a ball.' He stopped for a mouthful of his onion soup, wrestling with the melted cheese on top. 'I hope you come back.'

She looked at him but he had his head down.

'How's Clive doing?' she asked, after a moment.

'Just fine. He got a couple of job offers, nothing to die for, but he took the one with the John Lewis Partnership. Started last week. A sane boss and a non-Mickey-Mouse outfit. He's a happier man.'

'I'm glad.'

'I hear Hugo's hired Bob Carney to fill his shoes.'

'Do you know him?' Lily had been introduced but had formed no significant opinion beyond disliking the man's pronounced Yorkshire accent. There was something phoney about it.

'Sort of,' Andy replied. 'He's a crony. Helped out with Hugo's business dealings before. A graduate of the Pad-

266

more school of legerdemain. Don't be fooled by that regional stuff. He's no provincial slouch.'

'Do you think they're up to something? You heard about the redundancies, presumably?'

Andy nodded. 'Hugo's always up to something. I hear he's cutting a swathe through your female colleagues, too. *Plus ça change.*'

Lily felt her colour rising. Did Andy know? She bent her head to her plate of scrambled eggs and smoked salmon. 'Really?'

He was either being discreet or remained genuinely ignorant. 'Well, Alice has succumbed. Sanjay says she's utterly smitten. It's always the serious ones who fall the hardest.'

Lily busied herself with the cafetière.

'I gather it didn't work out with you and Paolo,' Andy breezed on. 'Judy told me,' he explained, forestalling her inevitable question. 'Opera's not your thing, then.'

'Funnily enough, I was wondering if it might be. At least, I was thinking about going again. That was the high point of the evening.'

'That bad? Poor Paolo. Judy tries her best to find him suitable women, but there's obviously something you're all not telling us. By the way, I'll come with you if you need a partner. To the opera.'

'Yes, I do,' Lily said. 'But what do you mean, "all"? I know Paolo's playing the field, but how much cannon fodder has Judy supplied?'

He grinned. 'Don't look so agitated. We're not talking epidemic proportions.'

'You might have warned me.' Lily felt exasperated, but once again realized she was forgetting, in her rush for the role of wronged woman, her own freely chosen role in the proceedings. It really was time to draw that line under her passive, undiscriminating behaviour when it came to men.

Fishy imagery came to mind – bottom feeders, trawler nets. Even whales sifted their plankton. She stabbed at the last fragments of Day-Glo-pink salmon on her plate and resolved that it was time to start swimming against the tide.

And then there were only a few days to go. Lily began to separate out a range of clothes and lay them in piles on the spare bed: shorts, T-shirts, a couple of sweaters, cotton jeans and cords, a long linen dress that could double for formal wear. Then there were sandals, sneakers and the walking shoes. The weight was mounting up. She had bought a couple of books, to read on those cosy nights by the log fire. There was also a bulging pale green carrier bag, a response to Margot's request that she bring her some tea from Fortnum's. It was the least Lily could do.

The cats sniffed sceptically at the growing heaps and the empty suitcase. They knew what was coming next. Nevertheless, Lily was able to fool them on the Thursday evening, catching them unawares at supper and bundling them off to prison while they were still licking cat food off their whiskers. She and Dorothy were catching the nine thirty Newark flight on Saturday morning, but she wanted to be free to work late on the Friday if necessary.

Then she only had to suffer one last, interminable working day.

'I'll be here till at least six,' she told Hugo when he dropped in late that morning, 'if there's anything that suddenly comes to you.' She handed him a copy of the eight-page dossier she was leaving with Monica. 'I think this covers most things. Feel free to rummage through my files if you need to. I've no secrets. Monica knows where most things are.' She was hardly focusing on him, her mind running through final errands. In her imagination she was already halfway to the airport.

He flicked through her closely typed pages, seemingly without much interest. 'Where is it you're going again?'

'The south-west of the States.'

'Sounds alright.' Why didn't he just wish her *bon voyage* and let her get on with it? 'Well, have a good time. And make sure you take care of yourself.'

Lily looked up from her screen. His words were oddly flat. What was the matter with the man? They stared at each other like strangers. Then he turned and walked away.

Chapter 23

It was less a resolution, more a state of mind, but from the moment the women arrived in New Mexico, they elected to make as few references to London, or the people who characterized it, as possible.

'No Hugo,' Dot specified.

'Or Peter,' Lily counter-commanded.

'It's a deal. Although . . .'

Lily looked at her suspiciously.

'What on earth will we talk about?'

What had Julie Bell said, better no company than bad company? Well, here were two phantom companions who could be safely stowed, along with the empty suitcases, at the back of the wardrobe.

The women decided instead to devote themselves single-mindedly to their holiday, to the ten blank days in front of them, after which they would set off to Margot's for their last few nights.

'We'd better phone her,' Lily said on their first evening. 'Let her know we got here safely.'

'And thank her.'

'Without a doubt.'

Margot greeted Lily with what sounded like genuine warmth. 'Did you have a good journey? Any problems getting to Douglas's?' she asked. 'Anything you don't understand or can't make work?'

They had found copious instructions both in the car at Albuquerque airport and in the cabin, which turned out to be a lovely wooden bungalow, tastefully decorated and immaculately clean, on a vast private development,

SaddleCreek Estate, that resembled a park.

'The journey was a doddle. And everything here's been great so far,' Lily assured her. 'You must have made preparations like a military campaign. We can't thank you enough.'

'Nonsense. I'm glad you're happy with what you've found.'

'We insist on taking you out to dinner one night, when we get to Taos. As a tiny gesture of thanks.'

'We'll see,' said Margot. Lily thought she sounded pleased. 'Have you made any plans about what to do with your time?'

'That's the next thing on the agenda. We don't want to be too strenuous, but we do want to explore, wander about. Dot wants to retread the footsteps of Georgia O'Keeffe, but that's more your part of the world than here, isn't it?'

'Yes,' Margot confirmed. 'We could visit Ghost Ranch when you come, or there's a brand-new gallery devoted to her in Santa Fe.'

'I think she'd like one of those.'

'Well, enjoy yourself. And ring me if you need any-thing.'

Friends are quite some blessing, Lily thought, replacing the phone, finding herself moved by Margot's kindness.

Jet lag dispelled, they plotted out a few excursions for the days ahead. Roswell was irresistible, as was Ruidoso in the mountains. Neither of them was too fussed about the Carlsbad caves, but Dot insisted they visit Lake Arthur, a few miles south, to see the miraculous tortilla. She read out to Lily the story of how the face of Jesus had appeared to Maria Rubio one day in 1977, when she was preparing her husband's lunch. The sacred tortilla now occupied a shrine in the Rubio household. Lily wasn't sure a visit to the holy pancake was such a good idea if they couldn't guarantee their comportment.

Most of all they wanted to visit Bottomless Lakes, wander the trails, picnic and relax. So that was where they went the next day, following the signs to New Mexico's oldest park, which turned out to be a huge, well-maintained sequence of lakes, woods and wilderness that clearly catered for thousands in the high season but was now gloriously empty. There was no fishing or boating at this time of the year, the camp sites were deserted, even the car-parking charges had been waived.

Picking up trail routes from the visitors' centre, they selected a five-mile path that wound in a loop up through some low hills and came back along the water's edge. It was flagged with diamonds of yellow paint on low posts, so there was no danger of getting lost. Instead, they could saunter along, listening to birds calling and the breeze soughing in the pines. Lily felt rinsed by the air, the soft blue of the sky, the freedom from any requirement to think or talk. Dot too seemed lost in a trance. When they reached the furthest point, and descended the hillside to the rim of the lake, they stopped to rest at a bench and watched groups of migrating snow geese and heron swimming and fishing.

'How are you doing?' Lily asked her friend, who she knew to be shielding her grieving heart with a brave face.

'Pretty well,' came the answer. 'And yourself?'

'Just fine.'

So the compact was held, at least for the time being, although the women knew each other well enough to understand that even if certain names had not been uttered, that didn't mean they were not in their thoughts.

They settled into an easy, salubrious rhythm of simple food, gentle excursions, some reading, not too much alcohol and plenty of sleep. Most days in the first week they went back to Bottomless Lakes, selecting different routes among the hills and wetlands, extending their range, becoming familiar with the vistas. The weather held and a gentle sun laid a fine bronze on their features. Neither woman had any trouble adjusting to the American clock. Instead, over-stretched nerves took the opportunity to regain their elasticity and both of them began to feel astonishingly healthy.

'You look terrific,' Dot said to Lily one night over a dinner of roast squash risotto.

'It's the Californian Zinfandel,' her friend answered, topping up their glasses.

'No, seriously. You look as if you've been eating that dogfood – clear, tanned skin, glossy hair. It must be the marrow-bone jelly.'

'I do feel well. Not working clearly suits me. You're looking pretty rested too.' A pause. 'Not dwelling too much on you-know-who?'

Dorothy put down her fork. 'I'd be lying if I said I never thought about him. Or dreamed about him. But I think I'm coping.'

'Do you think you'll go back to the old arrangement?'

Dot shook her head. 'Bad idea. Anyway, Carol will keep him on a tight rein. No, it's pastures new for me. If I ever fancy anyone else again, that is.'

'I said that, remember?'

'Oh no,' Dorothy said. 'Does that mean it's my turn to sleep with Hugo?'

Lily had to laugh. 'It's every woman's duty.'

'That's what he thinks.' Dorothy looked over at Lily. 'So are you dwelling on him?'

'No more than usual.' She paused. 'Perhaps a bit less, in fact. But a few thousand miles and an oasis of peace will do that.'

273

'Still fancy the bastard?'

'Probably,' said Lily philosophically. 'Funny, isn't it, that whole business of whom you fancy and for how long. If Frank hadn't started getting the hots for other people – '

'We wouldn't be here now, for one thing.'

'True,' answered Lily, contemplating all the distance she had put between herself and the end of that relationship. For the very first time she realized she felt glad and free to be beyond her life with Frank.

They sat contemplatively at the table for a while. Lily felt they could be modelling for a piece of sculpture entitled 'A Pause Along Life's Road' – two women approaching their forties, wiser and more single, one looking backwards more than forwards, the other beginning to feel bolder about turning to face the future.

The days slipped by, low-key and low-maintenance. Twice they made excursions into the foothills of the Sacramento Mountains where the air was cooler, the vegetation taller and four-wheel drives overtook them with skis on their roof-racks. One night they bought a bottle of tequila and made margaritas which they sipped on the porch, listening to a selection from Douglas's extensive country-and-western CD collection. (One of the holiday games had been to formulate various identities for their absent benefactor. Most recently, Dot had decided he was a gay crime novelist, while Lily speculated that he was a mafia hit man turned state's evidence and given a lavish new identity, courtesy of the FBI.)

Dorothy seemed even quieter on this night and Lily worried that the music's syrupy sentiments had tipped her into a maudlin mood, but it turned out that her friend was identifying instead with the survivalist spirit. ' "Scarred by life's wounds," ' she began to sing along with Connie somebody. 'That's me, honey. You too.' She raised her glass at Lily.

'And healing nicely, thank you.'

'You are, aren't you?' Dot confirmed, weaving slightly.

'You will, as well.'

'Well, I just might.' She nodded, eyes closed. 'I very well might.'

Lily smiled, licking lazily at the salty rim of her glass. And once the two of them were properly back on their feet, what wouldn't they be capable of then?

The last two days wound down with a final visit to their favourite trail – the Winsor, an eight-miler that crested Crane Hill before dipping down to the waters of a small, clear sink-hole – and a meal in Roswell. It had been a tough choice between the Cattle Baron's Steak and Seafood House and El Burrito Loco, but they had finally settled on the Hungry American where they were served giant platters of broiled chicken and shrimp flavoured with lime and a variety of chillies. Around them sat families and couples, many of them as fat as well-stuffed sausages. Lily registered again how restorative their lack of company had been. Apart from occasional friendly exchanges with shop assist-ants and the SaddleCreek Estate dwellers, they had spoken to no one for the whole time. She felt ready now to move on, to visit Margot, even eventually to return to London and a more garrulous way of life, but these ten gentle days had marked a kind of barrier, a sundering from the old existence, its preoccupations and anxieties.

Perhaps it was too easy to sit here, miles from home, feeling you would never return to bad old ways, but she genuinely did sense some kind of shift, a loosening of her moorings. She rather liked the feeling.

And then it was time to pack their bags and clean the house.

Both were concerned to return Douglas's home to the pristine order in which they had found it, as a means of conveying an atom of their gratitude. Dot took the rugs outside and beat them, Lily brushed sand from the floors and shook out cushions. They stripped the beds early on the last morning and ran the linen through the washer and drier before they left. As a last gesture, Dot arranged on the dining table a thank-you card, a bottle of champagne and a magnificent jay's feather they had picked up at Bottomless Lakes, its sapphire blue glowing against the polished wood.

Then they closed all the internal doors and loaded the car, taking a moment to bid the house farewell as they locked up.

'A good house,' Lily said, patting the satiny paint of the front door.

'Douglas is a lucky man, whoever he is,' Dot observed. It was her turn to drive, and she turned away first, leaving Lily to look one last time at the white bungalow. Neither of them had brought a camera. It didn't seem to be that kind of a holiday. So instead she did her best to fix the image in her mind's eye, to serve as a mantra on sleepless nights ahead. Would there be any? These days she was sleeping like a top/baby/log.

Instead of driving directly north, they swung east on their route to Taos, to take brief advantage of the chance to see another corner of New Mexico. The road to Las Vegas – 'Not that one,' Dorothy had told her when Lily had first seen it on the map – passed through a bowl of scrubby desert with jagged mountains at its rim. This was a parched land, where only low cacti and squat bushes grew. But once they had crossed the interstate at Santa Rosa, the geography began to alter into something more craggy and European. The air temperature changed too, although the sun continued to be their steadfast companion.

Soon they hit the busy dual carriageway that would lead them to Santa Fe, and then they were passing the town itself, with its adobe buildings, wooden, old-style store frontages and dangling strings of dried red chillies. This was a tourist centre, and if Lily wanted to buy jewellery and pots, maybe here was the place to come. Every other shop seemed to be a gallery of some kind. But they didn't stop, because it was mid-afternoon already and the High Road still lay in front of them.

It turned out to be a spectacular route, first of all through eroded sandstone cliffs, then rolling hills dotted with aspens and junipers. The air grew ever colder as they climbed. Close at hand were orchards and cultivated fields, but beyond rose less tamed hills and behind them a series of stunning snowy peaks that Dot identified from the map as the Sangre de Cristos. Again they drove slowly, alert to the rugged beauty, the rich colours and crystalline light. Once more they had one of Margot's expert maps to guide them, and as they emerged from a heavily wooded valley alongside a river, Lily was advised to keep watch for signs to Ranchos de Taos, the hamlet south of the town where Margot had fallen to earth.

This was not the corner of the world Lily had imagined when first hearing that her ex-boss's retirement destination was New Mexico. She had envisaged cowboy-style cacti, *mesas* like Monument Valley and a baking heat, rather like the temperature of the desert they had crossed that morning. But this was high country, with mountains, tall pines and horseback trails. Trees shed their leaves here, snow and rain fell. The seasons had not abandoned it. So much for no more winters.

Still, Margot knew what she was doing. And as they rounded a bend in the road and found first her mailbox, then the turning to her ranch and finally the building itself, Lily was all the surer of Margot's unfailing judgement.

They pulled up on a red clay hard standing below the house, whose smooth pink walls ran in curves, occasionally pierced by lengths of square wooden beams. It seemed to be composed of two or three terraces, one on top of the next, each irregularly punctuated with deep blue painted wooden window-frames and balconies, the whole edifice harmonious and organic, radiating a timeless light. Around, on all sides, stretched bushes and meadowland, bound by a thick outer brake of trees. It was a haven. Who wouldn't want to retire here?

And as the throaty rattle of their engine died away, there on the lowest terrace appeared Margot Pink herself, in a fringed poncho woven in stripes of vibrant fuchsia, green and purple. Tanned she might be, and ethnically robed, but it was the same Margot, strong of profile, white of hair. She walked solidly down to greet them. Lily opened her door and jumped to the ground.

'Lily,' said Margot. 'And Dot. Good. Your timing's spot on. Come in. Bring your bags. We need to talk.'

Dot looked at Lily, an unspoken question in her expression.

'I've no idea,' Lily answered. 'But it sounds serious.'

Chapter 24

Inside the house, they were swept into a long, cream, beamed room from which glass doors opened on to a balcony. Margot had swapped St John's Wood chrome and mirrors for indigenous bad art and Native Indian artefacts. A candelabra made out of antlers hung from the ceiling. Acid paintings shrieked from the walls. On various shelves stood large pieces of hand-painted pottery and carved chieftains. A pair of sofas covered in black-and-red-striped rugs faced each other in front of a deep fireplace. Sandwiched between them was a massive square stone coffee table, on which stood wine glasses, a dish of salted nuts and a bottle of German wine in a cooler.

'Do either of you need a bathroom?' Margot asked. So she was not immune to American euphemisms, Lily noted. 'There's one at the end of the corridor.'

Dot headed off as instructed, while Lily took a seat on the right-hand sofa. 'What's up?' she asked. 'Is there a problem about us staying?'

'Oh no.' Margot dismissed the notion with a wave of her hand. There was a clash of silver bangles. 'I didn't want to burden you while you were at Douglas's, but the phone line's been red hot since soon after you landed. I've had Monica on twice, and Clive, as well as your friend Jimmy Khan and a broker I know.'

'Why? What's going on?'

'Apparently Hugo Padmore's gearing up to sell GBF.'

'What?' Lily shook her head. 'He can't be. We're getting ready for the launch – ' She stopped, realizing that this would be a perfect time to divest, with considerably enhanced profits theoretically in prospect. This made sense of the redundancies too. She remembered Andy's warning about Hugo's habit of moving faster than the eye could see. 'But why involve you?'

'What's going on?' asked Dot, coming back into the room.

'Good question,' Margot said. 'Both of them. Dot, I'm sorry, this may bore you. It's GBF business. There's a move ahead to sell the business to Concord.'

It took Lily a split second to absorb this. 'The franchise people,' she put in, for Dot's benefit.

'Exactly,' said Margot.

'Now I see why they've been contacting you.'

'Well, I don't,' commented Dot.

Lily was thinking quickly. 'Concord is a kind of holding company,' she explained, 'a net which pulls together disparate high street stores and sites. They buy up named businesses, then turn them into chains, and franchise them out to all comers, up and down the high street, in shopping centres. They're not interested in the businesses themselves, all they want to do is increase frontage, grow their turnover through an endless proliferation of outlets. That's why every town centre's got a sock shop and a tie business. If Concord gets hold of GBF, it will become the jewellery equivalent of W. H. Smith's. There'll be one in every airport lounge. Forget the unique nature of the concept. It would end up just a logo.'

'I see,' said Dot, 'I think. But what's to stop the essence of the shops remaining the same, even if there were major expansion?'

'Contradiction in terms,' Margot answered succinctly.

'You can't buy like we do for a big chain,' Lily explained. 'We use small suppliers, we can be quick on our feet when it comes to shifts in style. With an operation many times bigger, there'd be central buying and supply. The whole thing would slow down and flatten out. No more quirky, amusing, quick-off-the-mark orders. Suppliers would have to guarantee large-scale production. There'd have to be cemented buying cycles, pre-established scale-outs, long request patterns.'

'Okay, okay.' Dot held up her hands to stop the words. 'I get the picture. It's a bad thing. So what can you do about it?'

'That's the $64,000 question,' commented Margot.

'Are you planning to come back, get involved?' Lily asked her.

Margot shook her head. 'Out of the question. But I'll do what I can to put a spanner in the works.'

'Which means what exactly?'

Margot paused. 'I'm being a terrible host. Would either of you like a drink?'

Opening and pouring the wine took a few moments, during which the older woman didn't speak.

'This is a spectacular house,' commented Dot, partly to fill the silence.

'Thank you,' Margot answered. 'Would you like to see your rooms?'

'I'd rather hear what you're planning,' answered Lily. She turned to Dot.

'Me too,' her friend said, loyally.

Margot ran her tongue over her lower lip. 'I do have one idea. It doesn't, unfortunately, salvage dear old GBF, but it would have a similar effect.'

'Really?' asked Lily. 'What does it involve?'

'In a word,' replied Margot, looking her squarely in the eye, 'it involves you.'

The laying out of Margot's plan did not take long, but it left all three women silent and Dot looking from her friend to her host and back again.

Finally, Lily sat up and reached for the glass of wine that had stood untouched on the table while Margot had delivered her speech. 'That's quite some act of faith,' she said, her expression very serious.

'I wouldn't propose it if I didn't believe it could work,' the older woman replied.

'You'd be prepared to sink a large slice of your capital into a new venture, just at the point when you've settled into retirement?'

Margot nodded.

Lily fell quiet again. 'I'm very flattered,' she said eventually. 'It would be a huge responsibility.'

'I'd keep a little in reserve,' Margot assured her with a smile.

What she had proposed was that Lily leave GBF and take as many key members of personnel as she could with her, to start up a new, initially smaller business, keeping to the original company's essential principles. By stripping out the creative and managerial talent within the old organization, Margot and Lily would be devaluing Hugo's asset at a stroke. Whatever price he was in the process of agreeing with Concord – and the Pink spies weren't wholly clear about how far negotiations had progressed – it would be substantially dented if the core of the business got up and walked out, extracting a fat slice of goodwill and setting itself up in competiton.

Margot had proposed six shops to start with – London, Birmingham, Edinburgh, Manchester, Bristol and Dublin. As before, the mission statement would be affordable fashion, but the opportunity would be taken to update the business, both in terms of presentation and range. 'GBF was long overdue a face-lift,' she commented, unsparingly.

'Speed would be of the essence,' she went on. 'Not so much in terms of start-up, but in putting your team together. We have to assume that Hugo could finalize his deal any day. If the breakaway isn't announced before-hand, it won't achieve the purpose. Although you would still have succeeded in jumping ship.'

Lily was wondering whether she could live up to Margot's expectations. She knew she was good at buying. She hoped she had the trust of her colleagues. But, fantasies aside, could she really lead a team? Could she manage a business?

'Yes,' Margot said, even though Lily hadn't opened her mouth. 'You can do it. If I didn't think so, I wouldn't have suggested it.'

'You really wouldn't come back? You'd do it much better. People wouldn't think twice.'

Margot shook her head. 'I don't want to. But nor would it be right. You're the same age, give or take, as I was when I started up. That's what it needs – vigour, freshness. Don't worry, I'll be at the end of the phone if you need me. But this would be your show.'

Lily turned to Dot. Her poor friend. She deserved serious compensation for her patience. 'I know you hate jewellery. But what do you think?'

'I think, go for it. It's the chance of a lifetime.'

'Bravo,' said Margot.

Lily sat twisting the chain at her throat. 'It's a great notion.'

'What have you got to lose?' Dorothy asked.

'Margot's money,' she answered. 'I feel very uncomfort-able that she's taking all the risk.'

'Well then, put some of your own in.'

This suggestion was a stroke of genius. Lily had known her father's £5,000 had been given to her for a reason. This was it. Alec was giving her a leg-up. With her own cash invested, the business wouldn't feel like charity or an idle woman's plaything – not that either was a fair assessment of Margot's proposition – but something in which she had a personal stake. She'd be working, at least in part, for herself. Self-employed. Now there was an idea.

The room had grown dim and Margot got up and lit some lamps. Dot's words had faded away some moments ago and Lily was still lost in contemplation.

'I declare a moratorium,' Margot announced. 'You're right not to give me an answer straight away, Lily, and rather than sitting here watching you think, how about settling into your rooms while I make supper? You must both be at the ends of your tethers.

'Tomorrow we could go to Ghost Ranch, although I should warn you, Dorothy, that even though she lived there, there's nothing of Georgia's in the museum. It's a study centre for natural history. There's an anthropology museum too. You might prefer Santa Fe, where they've just opened a whole gallery to her.'

Lily was relieved that the spotlight had been turned off her. 'I think Dot should choose. She's been a saint.'

'I vote Santa Fe,' her friend said, standing up.

'Santa Fe it is, then. And not another word about – what shall we call this? What's the opposite of a Trojan Horse? – until this time tomorrow.'

'How about Operation Adam's Rib?' suggested Dot.

'Perfect,' said Margot, rising to her feet. 'Now come with me.'

Their rooms were cell-like, roughly plastered spaces above what had been some kind of barn. Furnished with heavy, Spanish-style wooden chairs and beds, they were hung with less violent, more representational art. Bright striped rugs covered the floorboards. The mood was kitsch but comfortable.

Margot offered them a supper of guacamole and grilled trout, locally caught, she claimed. She asked them about their holiday, after which the conversation drifted in various directions. Dot explained to Margot what she did for a living. Margot described her new life, which included sitting on the board of a local arts centre, dabbling in the stock market, lessons in New Age healing, developing the network of friends that was growing from the seed of a cousin and her husband who had moved here ten years previously, exploring the Internet and reading as many mysteries as British and American book clubs could supply. The important thing, she explained, was to stop working and start the fifth age when you still had enough marbles. She said she was very happy. Lily thought she sounded just slightly bored.

She had rather left it to Dorothy and Margot to keep the conversation going, her own mind dipping in and out of what was being said over the table, then returning to Margot's extraordinary proposition.

What should she do? It was the chance of a lifetime, and yet she felt afraid – of failing, of Hugo's wrath, of jeopardizing other people's money and livelihoods. She wished she could ask advice – of Alec, of Julie Bell. Should she ring Andy? No, she must think it out for herself, although remembering Julie reminded her of the woman's advice that, whatever upheaval came her way, she would end up in a better place, that nothing was being destroyed without a purpose.

Had all of what had preceded this moment been, then, for the purpose of setting her up for this decision? The disappearance of Frank, her involvement with Hugo, even the death of her father? If all the negative aspects of the MLC had been about a late conversion to adulthood, well, what could be more grown-up than saying yes to Margot's invitation and going into business herself?

Was that the right reason to do it? Was there a right reason? She was too tired to decide. She could see, across the table, Dot's eyes crossing with fatigue too. Nor had this escaped Margot's attention. Ignoring their polite suggestions to help with the dishes, she packed the two of them off to bed.

They spent the next day in Santa Fe, Dot at the O'Keeffe Museum, Margot at the bank, Lily looking at the silver and turquoise jewellery that seemed to be on sale in every shop. Yet little of it caught her fancy. Instead, she fell in love with the Pueblo pottery, with its simple shapes and black, white and ochre decorations. Would she manage to get any of it home safely? She decided to take the risk, buying a geometrically painted vase for her mother and a small dish decorated with snakes for Monica. For herself she bought a flattish bowl with a narrow neck, its black organic shapes painted on a strong yellow ground. It fitted perfectly in her hand.

She also picked up a present for Dot, a necklace of Zuni Indian animal fetishes, its beads alternating with tiny polished stone effigies of foxes, eagles, beaver and buffalo, each connoting a virtue – gentleness, leadership, perseverance. Lily intended to give it to her on the plane. This was in keeping with her feeling that she was Alice in a wonderland of future possibilities and that everyone deserved presents. For Margot she had selected a single fetish, a large, stylized white crystal bear with a turquoise zigzag heartline, denoting strength. Whatever was decided by the end of this brief final sojourn, Lily wanted the woman to have a token of her esteem.

They returned home in the late afternoon, having shopped at a supermarket for the meal that lay ahead. Margot had accepted the joint invitation to dinner that had been mooted at the beginning of the holiday, but that was scheduled for the next day – their last – in Taos.

Back at the ranch, Lily and Dot were urged to go for a walk. 'There's a trail round the back of the trees that leads up into the hills further than you'll want to go,' said Margot, brushing aside offers of help with dinner, which was to be a casserole featuring beans, rice, beef and green chillies. Lily suspected she wanted some time to herself.

So the two women wandered off, wrapped in borrowed scarves and gloves against the cooling high-altitude air.

'Well done,' Dot said as they climbed the path.

'For what?'

'Not talking about the one subject on your mind all day.'

'When Margot makes a suggestion, I'm conditioned to obey.'

'I can see why,' Dorothy commented with a laugh. 'I'm not sure whether she's the irresistible force or the immovable object. But have you reached a decision? I've been dying to ask you.'

Lily filled her lungs. What would it sound like when she said the words? 'Yes,' she answered. 'I'm going to say yes.'

Dot turned to her, grinning hugely. 'You are? That's brilliant.'

'Is it? Tell me I'm not being the biggest idiot this side of the millennium.'

'Of course not, you nitwit. I'm half tempted to offer my services. No, don't worry, I'm not going to. But it's abso-bloody-lutely unmissable. You couldn't have decided anything else and still lived with yourself.'

'I know. That's what decided it in the end.'

'Christ, what do you think Hugo will do?'

'Don't. That's the last thing I'm going to think about.' Lily felt sick at the idea of being on the receiving end of the anger she had seen directed at Clive.

'You're right. Sticks and stones. Besides, you've got one or two other things to sort out first.'

'The number-one task, as I've said, is assembling your team.' Margot had given an approving smile on hearing

Lily's answer, lit a cigarette and called for a toast to Operation Adam's Rib. Then she'd got on with it. 'Have you identified who you'll want?'

'I've started to, but I wouldn't mind hearing your thoughts.'

'Ideally, Monica, Mark, Colin, Sanjay and Alice. Clive, if he'll come. Oh, and Tom, of course.'

'Not David?'

'Can you justify a full-time marketing specialist?'

'Not necessarily, although he'd be valuable. But wouldn't the blow to Hugo be all the more of a knock-out if we eliminated sales, design, marketing, administration and supply, all at the same time?' A pause. 'Maybe we could make a saving by not including Alice.'

Dot gave Lily a sideways look. 'Would they all come?' she asked. 'And don't you all have service contracts?'

Lily looked blank.

'Restraining clauses,' she explained, 'precisely to stop you setting up in competition.'

'You mean like golden handcuffs?' asked Lily.

'Well, sort of. But cheaper. It's common in publishing. To prevent star editors going off with all their bestselling authors.'

Margot waved away the irrelevance. 'It doesn't apply in our business. And there's an excellent chance they would all come, given the circumstances.'

'Perhaps we're not nailed down because we're not deemed creative,' Lily said to her friend, to cushion Margot's brusqueness. 'Although it's something to think about for the future, given that goodwill resides in the team as well as the business.' She turned back to their host. 'Presumably I should try to cherry-pick some shop managers too,' Lily went on. 'But that feels like the second stage, once I've got the head-office people on board.'

Margot nodded. She handed Lily some sheets of paper.

'Here are the cash projections. The money will be available by next week. Bank details are on the second page. I suggest you have a preliminary meeting as quickly as you can, and give people a deadline by which to make up their minds. It's a rush, I know, but they'll understand when you explain the reason.'

'I'm surprised that damaging Hugo matters to you,' Dorothy said to Margot.

'Are you?' The older woman's expression was cool. 'To be fair, I'm less motivated by a sentimental attachment to GBF than by my distaste for liars. I never thought Hugo was in it for the long haul, but I did believe him when he said he'd defend GBF's independence and integrity. Principles matter to me. So does keeping faith. Teaching Padmore a lesson isn't as important as starting up GBF mark two. But it offers its satisfactions.'

'I dare say Lily would agree,' Dot commented blandly.

Lily agreed more than she hoped Margot could imagine, but didn't want the woman to know all the reasons why. Over the last couple of months, in the scales that were her relationship with Hugo, the balance had tipped furthest away from indulgence, closest to a powerful distaste for the man. Either physically or in some other way, he fucked people over, Lily now saw, and then he walked away. Because of the role he had played in restoring her desire after Frank's departure, perhaps she would always harbour some crumb of lust for him, but the rest of her had moved on. 'Yes,' she said to Margot with a warning glance at Dorothy. 'I'm assuming your reference to integrity means you've heard about the male range Hugo's introducing. I have to confess I'm a party to it.'

'Monica told me. Don't feel guilty. You couldn't have done differently.'

'I could have argued harder.'

The older woman shook her head. 'If this was his long-

289

term strategy, nothing you could have said would have stopped him.'

Dot interrupted the ensuing silence, airing something that had briefly occurred to Lily. 'You'll have to think of something better than GBF mark two.'

'You're right,' said Margot, draining her glass. 'Dinner's ready, by the way. Come and eat.'

As she ladled out the food, she came back to Dorothy's last remark. 'We do need a new name. Any ideas?'

They chewed in silence. 'How about "Beyond Rubies",' suggested Lily.

'Who's Ruby?' asked Margot.

'It's "above rubies", I'm afraid,' Dot commented, pedantically.

More thought. Lily asked, 'Is there anything else in the song?'

Dorothy, who had never seen *Gentlemen Prefer Blondes* and was to be pitied, was unfamiliar with 'Diamonds are a Girl's Best Friend'. Margot and Lily attempted to sing it to her, although neither was word-perfect.

' "But square-cut or pear-shaped, those rocks don't lose their shape," ' they chorused in contralto and soprano, ' "Diamonds are a girl's best friend." '

'Great lyrics,' agreed Dot. 'Pear-shaped's nice, but wrong. Are there other diamond shapes? Or names for individual gems?'

'Solitaire, baguette,' they brainstormed. 'Lapiz, coral, jade.'

' "Jades"? No,' Dorothy answered her own question. 'Too much like jezebels. And they're synonyms for whores.'

'What do you think about "Brilliants"?' This was Lily.

'Brilliance?'

'No, Brilliants. With "t" and "s" on the end. It's another name for diamonds.'

'Not bad,' commented Margot.

They could think of nothing better. The subject exhausted, the casserole eaten, they spent the rest of the evening watching *Dallas* and *Bonanza* repeats on cable television. The words brilliance and brilliants kept fizzing and popping in Lily's brain, like fireworks. Only when she finally got to bed did they ebb away, leaving a faint shower of stardust on her inner eye.

It rained on their last day. Grey-bellied clouds drooped over the mountains and deposited relentless quantities of water, hour after hour. Margot lit a fire and they sat about, Dorothy reading, Margot and Lily taking their plans further.

'I'd feel better if you had some defined role,' Lily said, not for the first time.

'Do you need a security blanket?'

'To start with, yes.'

'An honest answer,' Margot acknowledged, stubbing out a cigarette. 'The best I'll offer is non-executive director.'

'Done,' said Lily.

Critical paths were drawn up, stock profiles considered. They discussed turnover and return on capital. Lily's £5,000 was a drop in Margot's ocean, but she still liked the idea of having a share and wondered if the notion should be extended to all members of staff.

'Why not?' was Margot's reply. 'You can stage a management buy-out when you're profitable enough.'

Was that a joke? Lily began to feel less confident. This whole notion seemed half-baked and unreal. She should back out, while there was still time. But she kept the thought to herself, through a snack lunch and Margot's siesta. Dot had gone to start packing. Lily stayed by the fire, listening to some of Margot's Native Indian CDs, watching the rain become a light drizzle. Perhaps it would stop by the time they went to Taos for some final shopping and an early dinner.

Probably the best time to withdraw would be when they were back in London. A cowardly phone call. But where would that leave her? If Hugo went ahead with his Concord deal, who knew what would happen to her job? It could as easily be eliminated as enhanced.

It seemed to be a choice between passive and active. Margot's route required her to lead from the front. Hugo's obliged her to bob like a cork on someone else's ocean. How could she opt for that?

Kick or be kicked, advised Alec. Trust in the planets, contributed Julie Bell. Restore those temples to female taste and instinct, was her own admonition. So what was holding her back? Only common sense, fear of the unknown, self-doubt, all the responses any normal human being would have in the circumstances. She couldn't expect to feel sure of herself. It would be foolish if she did. This was stage fright. The only way to dispel it was to get out there and give the performance of her life.

Taos, whose streets all seemed to lead to the central plaza, was cute enough, even when wet. It was far less self-consciously arty than Santa Fe, although gift shops still abounded. They were to dine at Doc Martin's – Margot was a fan of their pheasant ravioli – but first, there was jewellery to be bought. A friend had a shop on Kit Carson Road that Lily must see. Dot told them to pick her up from the Taos Bookshop when they were done.

Margot's friend Josie was of Navajo descent, and the quality of her stock reflected her close contact with the Native Indian community in the local pueblo. Her shop was tiny, its goods displayed in wood-framed vitrines hung on the plaster walls. Lily, who had found much of the turquoise and silver she had seen up till now resistible, was magnetized by the skill and sympathy on sale here. The stones were only semi-worked, retaining their natural shapes, pitted and unpolished. They sat in asymmetrical settings on brooches and bracelets, chased and delicately incised, subtly ornamented to flatter the rough-hewn stones.

'Are you thinking Brilliants should run a sideline in ethnic goods?' Margot asked her, after Lily had bought a pair of droppers long enough to brush her neck and a wide bracelet to match.

'Not really. I think we should leave the bazaar to Liberty's. But we could try some of these less expensive items for Christmas – the turquoise beads, say. Maybe some of the earrings.'

She turned to Margot in alarm, realizing she had stated what might well be a contradictory opinion. 'Why? Do you think that's the way we should go?'

Her expression made the older woman smile. 'No. Your answer seemed to me absolutely right. You know, Lily, for this to work, you're going to have to develop the courage of your convictions. It's very likely that we will disagree about something in the future. You'll have to learn to stand up for yourself, for what you want.'

This echoed the Pink maxim of old – 'Next time, make sure you get what *you* want' – the one that Lily had flouted with Hugo, and Paolo. But not, latterly at least, with Frank, or Dorothy. She thought she might already be learning.

'So would you like to ask Josie whether she'd be interested in supplying Brilliants with a few gross of beads and earrings, later in the year?'

'I'd be happy to,' Margot told her as they walked back to the bookshop.

'No special discounts for friends, I'm afraid.'

'That's more like it.'

They dined in a room painted pink, purple, yellow and turquoise. The menu was fusion food, European crossed with New Mexican, its flavours spicy but balanced. The portions were humungous. The table's mood became progressively more celebratory and the women acknowledged it by ordering a bottle of Napa Valley fizz. This led to more toasts and a promise by Margot to be in the UK for the official launch of the new business, which was pencilled in for September.

'Purely as a mascot,' she had commented. 'You'll have to let me know the colours of the new livery, so that I'm suitably dressed. Not black and gold this time, I presume.'

'I haven't decided,' answered Lily, feeling the mantle of responsibility settle more comfortably on her shoulders.

At Albuquerque airport the next day, where tom-toms echoed auspiciously from the loudspeakers, Lily handed Margot her present. 'I bought this before I decided to say yes,' she explained. 'It's a gesture of friendship, one woman to another. And of course of thanks for the holiday.'

Dot held out a gift-wrapped copy of *The Moonstone* which Margot had apparently never read. 'The world's best mystery. A fitting thank-you for such a superlative holiday. Oh, and please thank Douglas for us.'

'Yes,' Lily echoed. 'Do thank Douglas. Can we ask – it's been killing us – who is he?'

'Douglas? He's my accountant.'

And then, to Lily's amazement, Margot kissed them both and walked out of the airport, the dazzling mustard of her boiled wool jacket long visible among the crowds.

'An accountant?' said Lily, looking crestfallen.

'She's covering up for him,' Dot reassured her. 'He's really Lord Lucan.'

Chapter 25

They landed at six o'clock on Sunday morning. London, as seen from the tube, seemed imperturbable. They had not been missed.

The weary women separated at Green Park, with promises to phone that evening, and then Lily was on her own again, as she had not been for two whole weeks. She felt incomplete. But perhaps only for today. Tomorrow, and here her stomach revolved like a spin dryer, she was going to have to get to work on Adam's Rib.

Who would she speak to first? Better a conversation than anything in writing. Then she realized that in the case of Clive she didn't have to wait till tomorrow. She could ring him today.

The house smelt musty. Lily's first act was to let in some fresh air, then turn on the heating. There was a dune of mail and a dozen phone messages. She would attend to all that when she had fetched the cats and bought some food. And had a bath and filled the washing-machine.

In fact it was late afternoon by the time she had properly caught up with herself, emptied her suitcase, shopped, spoken to her mother and abased herself before Huntley and Palmer, who stalked the house, sniffing and calling, outrage in matching fur coats.

When Lily finally sat down to ring Clive, she closed her eyes for a moment as if to meditate. This was it, her first chance to speak the words that might bring about the fall of the house of Padmore. How savage could it all get? Did she hate Hugo enough to destroy him?

It's only business, she remembered. Stop turning it into a Greek tragedy. What she was really doing was playing Hugo at his own game. Risky? Possibly. Terminal? No.

She picked up the phone and dialled.

Clive answered. 'Hello, Lily.' Polite. 'How are you?'

'Very well, though a bit weary. I've just come back from holiday.'

'Oh really.' He sounded less than fascinated. Fair enough. She'd probably interrupted tea and the *Antiques Roadshow*.

'Clive, forgive me for ringing out of the blue. I saw Margot while I was away. I know you've been in touch with her.'

'Oh, do you?' Now he sounded wary.

'It's okay. Everything she told me was in confidence, as indeed is this conversation with you.' She felt she had his attention. 'Clive, Margot wants to finance a breakaway movement from GBF, to set up a new jewellery business. I'm to spearhead it. I need to get a team together very quickly. I'd like you to be in it.'

There was silence. Lily could imagine Clive ingesting her words in that focused way of his, and processing them.

'I'd need to know a lot more, of course,' he said carefully.

'Of course. I'm proposing to hold a meeting here on either Tuesday or Wednesday night, depending on the others, whom I haven't approached yet. Will you come and hear what's on offer?'

Another silence, but shorter. 'Absolutely without commitment, and in the strictest of confidence, yes, I'll come.'

Lily hugged to herself the tiny fact that Clive had not said no to the whole idea as she made her way to work, half an hour late the next morning. She had found it hard to wake up and was fighting disorientation as her time clock attempted to adjust back. Knowing she needed to be as sharp as a tack, she decided to flood her system with caffeine, to shock it into alertness.

Double cappuccino in hand, she entered GBF's premises as nervously as if it were her first day at a new school. All seemed in order. Pat hailed her from the switchboard.

'Welcome back. Had a good time?'

And so it went all along the corridor, greetings and conventional expressions of pleasure at her return, which did something to relax her nerves. On her desk were four piles of papers, each labelled in Monica's script: two weeks' work sorted into urgent, high priority, low priority and WPB. An empty WPB was standing closest to this last heap, so that she could drop the pages straight in, once she'd read them.

Lily shed her coat, sat down and drank the coffee. As she did so, Hugo materialized.

'You decided to come back, then.' He lodged himself against the doorjamb. 'Had a good time?'

Mouth full of milky coffee, she could only nod. She was wearing the turquoise earrings, which tickled her sun-tanned neck.

'You look terrific.' He was appraising her as if doing a valuation for Sotheby's. She felt her traitorous pulse quicken.

'Thanks. How's it been going?' Sitting back, she realized she was finding it easier to pretend about work than she had thought. Maybe everyone could fib if they put their minds to it. Hugo hadn't, after all, been born a deceiver.

'Pretty well,' he answered easily. 'Staff's settled down again. Takings are reasonable. Those rings you picked up in Brighton – the ones with little square stones – have started to move. Various other items need reordering. You'll see when you log on.'

'And Brainchild? All well?'

'Yup.' Not a flicker. 'We've got proofs of the brochure

and ads. Come and have a look when you're next passing.' He straightened up. 'Oh, one casualty, though. Alice quit. I'll need to find a replacement.'

He drifted away, lighting up as he went. Same old Hugo, shambolic in style, thoughtless in deed and as busy as an anthill where he couldn't be observed. No, she'd have no regrets.

Monica was her next visitor, as hot on Hugo's heels as his shadow.

'We need to talk,' she said, a little melodramatically.

'Let's have an early lunch,' suggested Lily.

In the sandwich bar, where privacy was guaranteed by the raucousness of the Italian brothers who ran the place, Monica explained that in her agitation she had phoned Margot again the previous day and therefore knew what had been decided. When asked whether she had any clearer sense of Hugo's timetable with Concord, she shook her head. In fact her knowledge was limited to some misfiled documents she'd come across and a phone conversation reported to her by Pat, both of which were now more than a week old.

'It would be enormously useful to find out the timing, if we can,' Lily said, leaving it to Monica to persuade Pat to eavesdrop on Hugo if the two women wanted to take the risk.

Then she outlined her immediate plans. 'Could you make a meeting at my house tomorrow or Wednesday? I'll be filling in the background then. I'd really like you to be part of the new business. But I should warn you. You won't have very long to make up your mind.'

'I don't need very long,' Monica told her. 'I've already decided. I'm in.'

Lily grinned. 'Don't you think you should talk it over at home? There are financial implications. Like you'll lose your redundancy entitlement.'

'I'm ahead of you, Lily. I've done the talking, and the thinking. Hugo's going to sell us all down the river. I don't know who else you're planning to approach, but when they hear that the choice is between Concord and you, backed by Margot, they'll bite your hand off.'

Monica was not entirely right. As Lily made her stealthy way round the office, picking her moments to talk to the chosen colleagues, she did find some of them, like Tom and Sanjay, more than ready to meet her halfway. But David and Mark, with more substantial family commitments, were cagier, while obviously interested. However, they did agree to come to the meeting, which looked like being on Wednesday, and to respect the confidence. Colin practically self-combusted with glee at the idea of a conspiracy and the means of delivering a one-fingered gesture to their two-faced boss. She had to make him promise to say nothing and hoped to God he would manage to control himself.

'Sounds like it went pretty well,' commented Dot, who rang that evening to find out how the gunpowder plot, as she referred to it, was proceeding. 'Some barrels already in place. Fuse starting to be laid.'

'Stop all that,' Lily told her. 'Firstly, this is serious. And second, remember what happened to Guy Fawkes.'

'You mustn't be frightened,' Dorothy told her. 'What's he going to do, when it comes to it? Shout a bit? Say something spiteful?'

'Tell the others we were lovers?'

'Get real. Hugo won't do that. He's probably forgotten. Sorry, Lily, but what I mean is, it's irrelevant. It's got nothing to do with work. Sex is his hobby. This is about money. Light years apart.'

Lily knew Dot was right. It was a fantasy. Maybe even a useful one if that was the worst she could imagine. As for insults and spleen, well, she hoped she could weather whatever he flung her way. She tried to remember the angriest anyone had ever been with her. She could only think of her domestic science mistress at school, Miss Poole, when she had put four tablespoons of water into her pastry mix instead of four teaspoons, and her jam turnover had grown a blister as big as a fried egg. Compared to that, Hugo's disparagement would be as nothing.

The meeting was convened for eight thirty. What did you serve to a bunch of co-conspirators? Dutch courage? Lily opted for beer, wine and fruit juice. Would they have eaten? She couldn't pass round plates of sandwiches and folded napkins. It would be too much like the Mad Hatter's tea party. She settled instead for a supply of crisps and nuts.

Monica arrived first.

'Shall I take minutes?' she offered.

'That makes it sound very formal. I haven't typed up an agenda.' Lily panicked, then got a grip. 'Yes, thanks, Monica. Bullet points of what's been agreed and next steps would be very useful.'

The woman had brought a shorthand pad with her. Lily could have kissed her, just for being another female intelligence.

Sanjay and Colin arrived together, looking suspiciously as if they might have come via the pub. Mark and David made another pair, rather more grave of mien. Tom left his bike in the hall. Clive brought up the rear.

Lily hadn't told them individually who else was invited, so there was a certain amount of joshing as the group composed itself in the living room.

'Okay, we're all here,' she told them, when they'd each got a drink. She gave them a second to absorb that and make what they would of any absences.

'You've all got a reasonable idea of why we've assembled. I hope you've kept absolutely *stum* about what I said. It's imperative that when we act, whoever "we" are, it remains an absolute secret until that moment.' She looked at Colin. He looked straight back. So far so good.

'The other priority is speed. Not so much for the sake of the new business, but to deliver the blow to Hugo.'

No one had argued about the desirability of achieving this, once they had heard about his treachery towards the business as a whole and the individuals who worked within it.

'Monica has already agreed to be a part of the team.' She smiled at her. 'What we need to agree tonight is a deadline by which the rest of you can have made up your minds. I know that in order to do that, I have to answer all your questions – to the degree that I can, at this stage. So I propose to give a swift run-down of what Margot and I have established, and then leave it to you to ask me about anything I haven't covered. Okay so far?'

They expressed their agreement in nods and grunts. Lily paused for breath, surprised that the words, which she'd only half-rehearsed, had come out as well as they had. She pressed on, outlining the six-shop strategy, the adherence to essential principles, while simultaneously modernizing and refining the old GBF approach which had served them all well but was looking a little tired. She laid down the rough timetable and explained the steps on which it was based. She coloured in the financial background, both the overall investment and the smaller but equally crucial details, like salary levels and bonuses. Margot and she had agreed that as far as possible they should try to match current levels of pay. But anyone jumping ship would have to sacrifice years of service entitlements. There was nothing she could do about this. She had chosen to abandon them herself.

When she had finished, she turned the floor over to her

audience. 'Okay, your turn. Any questions?' She sat back and swallowed a mouthful of wine.

Tom wanted to know where she planned to locate the new premises. David asked about the promotion budget. Mark had several questions about staffing levels in the shops and sales targets. Sanjay and Monica asked nothing. Colin pulled three draft designs for a 'Brilliants' logo out of his briefcase.

'Christ, I hope no one saw those at work,' Lily said.

'Don't worry, I did them at a friend's studio, in my own time and alone. And I've got the disk.' He tapped the briefcase.

'Does this mean you're in?' she asked.

'If you use one of them, it does.'

So that made three. The others carried on asking whatever they could think of and Lily did her best to give straight answers. Sometimes she didn't know them, and said so. Eventually they ran out of questions.

'Is that it? Well, then can we agree on how much longer you'll need to make up your minds?'

She looked round the room.

'Twenty-four hours?' volunteered Clive. 'I'd like one final conversation with Judy.'

Lily looked at David and Mark. They looked uncertain. But Sanjay said, 'Yes. I think that's fair. We've already had a few days.'

'The shorter, the better,' contributed Tom sagely.

So the decision seemed to be taken. Lily asked them all to phone her at home the following evening.

'What happens after that?' asked Sanjay.

'Well,' said Lily, 'unless you want to do it individually, I could give Hugo all our resignation letters together on Friday morning. With the exception of Clive, that is.'

'You mean miss seeing his face?' Colin looked disappointed.

'I'm all for that,' said Monica.

'Some of us are on different notice periods, presumably,' observed Mark. A positive sign.

Lily nodded. 'But no one's is longer than three months. That's what I'm on. We'll have to negotiate that bit, although I wouldn't be surprised if Hugo wanted us to clear our desks pretty quickly. If you need to take any strategic information, it might be best to remove it tomorrow. On Friday, we'd all better come with a bin liner.'

After they'd gone, she tidied up and phoned Margot.

'Have you thought about a press release?' the older woman enquired.

'Not in great detail.'

'I suggest you formulate it tomorrow. Have it ready to roll on Friday morning. You don't want Hugo sitting on the information about your coup in order to stitch up his deal. Make sure Concord has it fairly early. And the financial desks of the newspapers too. It's probably too small fry, but you never know.'

Thank God for Margot's lateral vision. Approaching the endgame, as they were, Lily's focus was on her confrontation with Hugo. Dignity, she kept telling herself. Sang-froid. Keep the desk between you.

She kept distracting herself with this throughout Thursday, which was a slow day, the clock scarcely creeping from minute to minute. Was it the jet lag making it feel as if the top of her head were coming off, or the accumulating expectation of what tonight's phone calls would contain?

Late in the afternoon, Monica popped in, ostensibly to wish her good luck for that evening, and to hand over her letter of resignation. Lily already had Colin's. Should she give them to Hugo opened, unopened, in a file, fanned out in their envelopes like a hand of cards? Did it matter? Would he tear them up? Set fire to them? Chew them up and swallow them?

Calm yourself.

As she picked up the envelope, Monica cleared her throat.

'Is there something else?'

'Yes. Look, I've got a confession to make. I've told someone about your plans.'

Lily was aghast. 'Christ, Monica. Who?'

'It's okay,' her colleague assured her. 'Honestly. It's Pat. You can trust her. In fact, she wants to join us.'

Lily took this in. She had budgeted for someone rather younger and cheaper to double as receptionist, switchboard and assistant to Monica and Tom. Would Pat be prepared to do as much, even if Lily could find the extra salary somewhere?

'She'd need to roll up her sleeves, help you out with admin and so on. Do you think she'd be prepared to muck in?'

'No question,' Monica responded. 'She'll sweep the floor if she has to.'

'Tell her I'll have to take another look at the figures – '

'Great.' Monica was halfway down the hall when Lily called her back.

'But after that, keep it zipped, yes?' Monica nodded, penitent. 'And tell Pat the same. Not a word. This is war. Careless talk . . .'

The first phone call came just after seven. It was Sanjay. He was in. Tom rang on the dot of eight. Another yes.

Lily was beginning to feel sick from all the tension and thought she'd better eat something. Cooking was out of the question. She'd just poured herself a bowl of cereal when the phone rang again.

'Hello?'

'Lily, it's Clive.'

Clive. Good. She had been feeling pretty confident about him.

'Lily . . .'

Shit. He was backing out.

'You're not coming.'

'No,' he answered, sounding sheepish. 'It's not that I think the venture isn't sound. Judy and I both think it's a winner. It's just the financial uncertainty.' She made no comment. 'We have to think about the children, their school fees. I'm not in the same position as the rest of you. My existing job isn't going to fold up.'

She couldn't criticize him, although she wanted to.

'Okay, Clive,' she said, feeling rather tired. 'I understand.'

'I'm sorry, Lily. Really.' A pause. 'Have you thought of asking Andy?'

'We couldn't afford him.' She hadn't intended to insult Clive, but out it came.

'He might be prepared to offer some part-time input. He's no fan of Hugo's, as you know. Between him and Sanjay, you could probably manage.'

And save enough to pay for Pat.

'Thanks. I'll think about it.'

She replaced the receiver and sat down, her mood transformed from optimism to nihilism. It was going to fail. She was going to end up with a bunch of willing but junior staff, all the key posts still to fill, a killer punch that whistled past Hugo's jaw and a lot of egg on her own face.

She wished she'd never started this.

When Mark rang, she forced herself to pick up a bit, although she could hear the flatness in her 'Hello'.

'Hi, Lily. How's it going?' Was he fishing to find out

what the others had said? She snapped out of it. 'Just fine,' she told him. Could she bluff him into accepting?

'It's not an easy decision,' he began.

Spare me the truisms.

'No,' she answered, mustering a gram of sympathy.

'And I wanted to raise the question of commission.'

'Oh yes?' She had wondered if this would happen, a little arm-twisting by someone savvy enough to gauge his own strategic value.

'I know GBF doesn't operate on a commission basis, but I wondered if the new set-up could see its way to a retainer plus a percentage?'

Thank Christ she and Margot had already thought round this particular corner. Indeed, she had worked out a formula which would cost her the same amount of money if current sales performance were not exceeded. If it was, she'd be able to afford to pay him more anyway. She named her figures.

'Is that your best offer?' Meeting him halfway had taken the wind out of his sails.

''Fraid so, for the first year, at least.'

There was a silence.

'Do you want to ring me back in an hour?' she asked. She felt she had won a point, in outflanking him, but wondered if she was about to lose the game.

'No,' he said slowly. 'No. There's no need.' Another pause. Lily's fingers drummed the arm of the sofa. 'I'll take it.'

'Terrific.' She couldn't stop herself. It was terrific. Mark would have been hellish to replace.

That left David. And he left it until after eleven o'clock. Lily wondered whether to ring him, but every instinct told her not to. When the phone finally rang, she forced herself to let it trill three times, then picked it up slowly.

'Sorry to leave it so late.' Well, at least he'd apologized.

'Still talking it over?' she asked carefully.

'No,' he answered. 'Nothing like that. I fell asleep after *The X-Files*. I should have rung you earlier. Include me in.'

Chapter 26

Friday. A windy day with a hint of vernal warmth. There were primroses in the garden, Lily noticed, as she pulled up the blind in the bathroom. And a thrush was pecking at the lawn.

She had whiled away some of the previous evening pressing to perfection a white shirt with fake pearls for buttons, a favourite she had picked up in a Comme des Garçons sale. She would team it with a pair of dark brown pencil-cut trousers and her suede ankle boots. All of these were trusty items in her wardrobe. Presentation felt crucially significant on this, possibly her last day at GBF.

Her own letter of resignation had taken precisely four minutes to write and ran to a single sentence. Its long white envelope lay inside a clear plastic sleeve alongside the other two. She had arranged that Sanjay, Tom, Mark and David would all hand theirs over before nine that morning. Her plan was to deliver them to Hugo first thing, synchronous with the press release which Monica would be faxing to all parties.

She looked at her reflection once more in the hall mirror. 'It is a far, far better thing I do,' she intoned, 'than I have ever done . . .'

So get out there and do it.

On days like this – had there been any other days like this? – Lily wished she smoked. Anything to keep her fingers occupied and help her to sit still. The tube journey – always a magical mystery tour, courtesy of the Northern Line – was especially unendurable. The crowds of fellow workers seemed particularly determined to block her way. Walking down Holborn, it was as if she had the momentum of someone travelling down an up escalator. By the time she reached the office, she felt utterly spent.

But there was Monica, grinning like a Hallowe'en lantern, and Pat, who punched Lily's arm at being told she was on board. In her office, Tom and Sanjay were loitering guiltily, envelopes in hand. She ushered them out as quickly as she could. Mark seemed to be taking things a bit more soberly, but David couldn't resist an exaggerated wink as he handed over his letter. She accepted it without a word. It was still a few minutes to nine.

When Pat appeared, letter in hand, she looked grave. 'Hugo's just phoned. He's not coming in until later.'

'Did he say why? Is he at Concord?'

'No, he said he was still at home.'

Lily paused. 'Pat, I hesitate to ask this, but how crafty are you prepared to be, for the sake of Brilliants?'

'Do you mean, betray my position of trust, my privileged access to confidential phone conversations?'

'That's exactly what I mean.'

Pat had no scruples whatsoever in shielding from Hugo, when he appeared, any messages that might be left by Concord that morning. Or indeed newspapers, calling for a comment. Lily was determined to get her own statement in first, to deliver the blow cleanly. It seemed the right move, appropriately conclusive. She had an image of Hugo's head, tidily severed and dropping neatly into a basket, while Pat and Monica knitted steadily away in the background.

Pat promised to call her the minute Hugo crossed the threshold.

But Hugo didn't appear.

Lily did some work. She tidied her desk. She answered one or two phone calls. And still he did not appear.

Swivelling her chair, she turned to look out of the window, her hand going to her throat, to touch her father's chain.

It had gone.

She tried to remember the last time it had been there. Had it dropped off on holiday? On the plane? Now she came to think about it, she couldn't remember seeing or feeling it since the weekend.

Was its disappearance a blow, or a symbol of liberation? Perhaps it was simply an encouragement for her to spend a moment communing with Alec. Was he bidding her farewell? Or was she cutting free?

She touched the smooth, now-unadorned skin at the base of her throat and within the dips of her clavicles. She had a picture of Alec smiling down on her. She smiled back.

'It's a big day, Dad.'

'You can handle it,' he told her.

Could she? Yes, of course she could. These people – and she reached for the folder of letters in her handbag – they're depending on you.

She checked the clock for the umpteenth time. Just after eleven. Where on earth was Hugo?

He hadn't appeared by lunchtime. Members of the team kept drifting by her office, eyebrows raised, like Groucho Marx.

No, she would shake her head at Colin or David, nothing so far. And off they would go again, affecting nonchalance.

At twelve thirty, Monica offered to fetch her a sandwich.

'I'm not hungry,' Lily told her.

'You've got to keep your strength up. You're eating for seven.' Lily had told her about Clive and knew that she would have told the others, although no one had commented. She must speak to Sanjay later. She couldn't do it now.

Lily compromised on a Kit-Kat and a Diet Coke, but

even by the time Monica had reappeared with her order, Hugo still hadn't put in an appearance. They both scoured the *Evening Standard*'s business pages. Thank God, there was no mention of GBF.

Lily rang Pat. 'Any more news?'

'Nothing. But I'll tell him to see you the minute he appears.'

'Has he had any callers?'

'One or two,' Pat answered calmly. 'Now where did I put those message slips?'

By two thirty Lily was feeling frazzled. Her finely composed outfit was crumpled and when she went to the loo she saw that her nose was shiny and most of her eye pencil had come off. She repaired the damage, wondering how it would be if she opened the toilet window and screamed at the top of her voice, to release some of her pent-up anxiety.

Instead she walked back to her room. As she did so, she glimpsed Hugo in his overcoat, heading towards his office. Her heart started to flutter.

Pat phoned.

'I know, I saw him,' she told her.

'I gave him your message. He said he'd be along in a minute.'

'Did he ask about calls?'

'Calls? What calls?'

Lily released a bubble of madcap laughter. And Hugo walked in.

'Joke?' he asked, sitting down in her visitor's chair.

'Friday hysteria.'

'You wanted to see me?' He slumped further back against the padding, looking as if he were going to put his feet on her desk.

'About five hours ago.' She couldn't resist it. Was she stalling for time?

'Tell me about it. Crisis with Jay's mother. She's had to bugger off again. So the girls have gone to stay with her sister. In fact,' he said, his voice turning languorous, 'I shall be going home to an empty house.' From his semi-reclining position, he gave her an appraising glance. 'Got any plans for dinner tonight?'

Lily breathed as steadily as she could. She opened her desk drawer and reached for the Cellophane folder which she had transferred there from her handbag.

'It's an interesting question,' she said, eyes very wide. 'But before I give you an answer, perhaps you should read these.'